Immortalibus Bella

I0687485

SL Figuhr

www.slfiguhr.com
Email: info@slfiguhr.com

Follow SL Figuhr on Twitter:
https://twitter.com/SLFiguhr

Like SL Figuhr on Facebook
www.facebook.com/SLFiguhr.Author

ISBN-13: 978-0-9911498-0-3 (SL Figuhr Publishing)

ISBN-10: 0-9911498-0-7

Library of Congress Control Number: 2013919779

Book / E-book cover design:
www.celairen.com
https://www.facebook.com/celairen1

Manufactured in the United States of America

Acknowledgments

Edited by:
Lynda Dietz

Cover Art by Celairen, using designmethod/Shutterstock.com,
OlegZhevelev/Shutterstock.com, Dynamicfoto/Shutterstock.com
Nataliia Antonova/Shutterstock.com,
EkaterinaVBorisova/Shutterstock.com,
MPFphotography/Shutterstock.com

DEDICATION

Thank you to all my friends, both old and new, and my family, who supported and encouraged my endeavors through countless rewrites and rant sessions.

CONTENTS

CHAPTER ONE

"You know what I miss the most?" Colin mused. "Technology. Life was so much easier when one could book a flight online, call anywhere, and have a room ready and waiting at the end of a journey."

"I miss grocery stores, gas stoves, hot running water, instant heat and cold air." Eron played the game as they walked.

A derisive snort from Mica interrupted their remembrances.

The two friends lagged behind to escape the harangue of their self-appointed leader, continuing their conversation as they walked.

"I think he's tired of living." Colin made excuses.

"Out of the three of us, it should be me. He just needs to suck it up. Shit or get off the pot," Eron groused.

"Still, where have the remnants gone? The metal? The concrete?"

"Buried under the land, or hauled off to be reused." Eron scowled. *It wasn't supposed to be this way. Damn mortals and their wars.*

* * *

Mica crested the stony hill to find his friend Eron resting comfortably on a large gray boulder scored with an undecipherable glyph. Why this should irritate him, he didn't know, but like the steadily rising temperature, so did his anger. "Thanks for scouting ahead. Wouldn't want to be met by any bandits." The sarcasm slipped out.

His dark-haired friend merely drank from his canteen before shutting his eyes. "Blow it out your ass. Your forced march toward nothing, leaving us too tired to fight, is the problem."

The other man clenched his jaw. He refused to be drawn into an argument. He turned his head to see how his brother was getting along.

Colin walked up, dropping his pack with an audible sigh.

"This isn't nap time."

"I need a break, bro. This path isn't the easiest to navigate. Besides, I think I'm getting a hole in my boot sole." He sat down, inspecting the bottoms.

It was petty problems like this that prevented the men from catching up to Nicky and finding him. Mica walked a few more paces, the elevation giving him a clear sight line of their destination. The rocky gray mountains they were traversing curved around a valley. A middling-sized town sat below, surrounded by forests, a river cutting it in half before emptying into a harbor. He checked the hand-drawn map he had purchased from a merchant. The view seemed to match up with the map.

He recapped his canteen, turning to the resting men. "Break time's over. Let's go." He received no reply, his brother now scribbling in his journal, his friend trying to fake sleep.

"I said let's go! Now! Put that damn thing away; you can record your observations later." Mica barely kept from snatching his brother's pride and joy and tossing it over the precipice before them.

"You can always take over scouting duty, O Obsessed One," Eron remarked without opening his eyes.

"I've had all I can take of your bitching and whining. You made a promise to me. If you have any honor left, you'll keep your damn word, seeing this through to the end. The end which is down there." Mica turned away from his friend to stare blindly over the landscape.

Eron huffed to himself. "It's all the same: 'go here and all your questions will be answered.' But they never are."

Mica stared at him. "This is it, Eron. I know it is. I can feel it in my bones."

He snorted. "Your bones are liars. You've been feeling it for a while now. Dementia setting in? Alzheimer's, maybe? The man had his head up his ass. He saw a young man, not a little boy."

"Bickering isn't helping," Colin offhandedly remarked, now scanning the land through a spyglass. "It's just the fatigue and hunger speaking. We'll feel better once we eat and sleep."

"This. Is. It." Mica replied forcefully. "Our quest will end here. Finally, after countless years of trials and tribulations, we will be rewarded," he continued with enthusiasm.

Eron sneered. "And how do you explain the age problem?"

Mica gave a steely-eyed glare. "Tricks. The boy's up to his old games. Nicky hired someone older who faintly resembles him to pretend he's Nicky to throw us off his whereabouts."

"He's gone. If he wanted to be found, you'd be tripping over him," spat Eron, standing abruptly.

Mica went rigid, turning on his friend furiously. "The king of Gemica's women were adamant about the fact there was a little boy matching Nicky's description with the King of Macinas when he visited."

Eron's hands curled into fists, wanting to plow them into his friend's face for what he considered the man's stupidity and ignorance. "I don't need to figure anything out. You're the one wanting to twist the truth because you can't or won't accept it. Nicky is gone. He's been gone for decades. He'll surface when he wants."

Mica sneered. "Shut your filthy, lying mouth before I shut it for you."

"I think there's a castle hidden beyond the forest, by the far circle of the mountains, and it doesn't look like ruins," Colin casually remarked.

"What?" The quarreling men turned in irritation at the intrusion.

Eron's brow furrowed. "There are two rulers? The King of Gemica didn't mention that. Odd." He reached for the glass, more to piss his friend off than because he cared about the anomaly.

Colin handed the piece over and began flipping pages in his journal.

"We don't have time for you to write it down," his brother warned.

Colin ignored him while looking for something, stopping now and again to read bits and pieces.

"Let's go, brother. Now! Forget whatever it is," Mica repeated as he situated his canteen.

"No, I remember . . ." He flipped some more and read another section before crying out in triumph. "I knew this place sounded familiar! Remember when we met the old crone who said she could see the future?"

"Not this crap again!" Mica groused. "She's a fake; they all are."

"Nope, sorry. I don't recall, buddy. What did she say?"

Mica fumed at his friend's egging on of his brother's delusions as he began reading.

"She said we would have many towns yet, and miles to go, before it would end. She said we would know we had found the place we seek when 'from behind a thick forest rises the spires of a castle, hidden in the mist and embraced by mountains in a crescent moon. A town harboring evil lies before the forest, and the town holds that which you seek.'"

He looked up at them, smiling to see his brother scowling while Eron scanned the stone peaks. "Huh, what do you know? He's right."

Mica snatched the spyglass out of his friend's hands, almost ramming his own eye out as he took a look. After a moment, he found what the other two men talked about, but barely. A bead of sweat dripped in his eye, and he blinked, staring harder. The hidden building was now in plain view, a lighter gray than the mountains. It perched on its rock aerie, spires proudly stabbing the firmaments, pennants blowing in the breeze. Mist billowed out from twin waterfalls to either side of the castle on its perch, the sun bouncing off the cascading water and producing faint rainbows in the spume. A long causeway stretched from the rock base over the swirling maelstrom of water created by the cascades joining below. The stone road ended in pillars topped by carving. A wide dirt track led away and disappeared into the forest. Sweat obscured his vision again.

By the time he blinked it away, the castle was gone—only its towers peeked up over the forest. Mica lowered the glass a bit to rub his eyes—damn! He must be getting heat stroke or something. He set the glass back to his eye, but the scene was the same, lots of forest and the hint of something more. He handed the glass back to his brother.

"I think you're both crazy. I saw nothing." He paid no attention to the protests behind him as he descended the stony track, his thoughts keeping him company.

Mica recalled with startling clarity the fantastic tale the little boy who called himself Nicky had spun, like something out of a book or a really bad movie: an evil man forcing him to be an apprentice in some cult with strange, dark rites after killing the boy's family. Nicky didn't understand why the man had done it or how his parents drew the attention of such a figure. Mica had taken the boy in, trying to get him help, and justice for his murdered family.

The man scowled, anger at how he had been tricked making him speed up into a jog, unmindful of his brother and friend trailing behind, or of the path he followed. He had adopted the lying brat, was going to make him his heir, and the child tried to kill him. Mica's boots pounded the narrow, rutted track. The straps of his pack dug into his shoulders with each footfall, his sword slapping his leg. None of the discomfort mattered. He blocked it out, running down the twisting path. He stumbled, almost turning his ankle, and decided to slow down.

His heart pounded, sweat dripping, breath coming in gasps, as he stopped. Mica drained his canteen before realizing he was alone. He looked back the way he had come, but his traveling partners remained hidden from view. The big man slumped to his knees, head hanging down.

If I can just finish this quest, I can rest. Letting the kid escape and believing any of his bullshit was a mistake. I will not be duped by him again. If he had just been content with taking his wrath out on me, and not those I cared for, it would never have come to this.

He sat back on his haunches, realizing he needed to find a source of water. What was taking those two so long? He had just refilled his canteen from a rushing brook when Colin and Eron appeared. Now he had to wait for them to take a rest break. He paced back and forth, inhaling the crisp air.

"Done yet? Let's go." Mica gave them no chance to reply as he turned to continue.

"What about bandits?" came from behind him.

"I think infested was Gemica's idea of a joke," Eron replied.

Mica faced them. "The forest is possibly another hour's walk away. The town is on the other side of the forest. We can be there by tonight."

"Are you mad?" his brother demanded. "Look at the light. I don't think we should walk through an unfamiliar forest after dark."

"Don't be such a wuss," Mica said. "The damn track goes right into it."

"I'm being cautious. You do know what the word means, don't you? It'll be pitch black in there, perfect conditions for an ambush," Colin worried.

"When have I ever not taken care of you, little brother?" Mica asked.

"Just because it's near-impossible to kill us doesn't mean we need rumors preceding us about men who won't or can't die," Colin retorted. "I would rather not be met by peasants with pitchforks and torches."

"Ah, the good old days," Eron sighed.

"Great!" Mica enthused. "On we go." He started off.

Colin swore at his brother's back. The three men walked steadily onward across the Downs, last rays of the sun sinking as they came to the forest edge. The trees blocked most of the moonlight, making it difficult to see inside the forest and the road they followed. They had to slow their pace as their eyes adjusted. Eron heard a strange whistling sound.

"Down!" he yelled just as an arrow whizzed past the space he had been standing in and thunked into a tree behind him. "Damn it, Colin!"

He had made the safety of a tree, trying to peer around it. He saw Mica nip behind another one across the path while his friend dragged a leg behind him, arrow shaft protruding from his thigh.

Wild yells erupted from all around. Their attackers burst forth from the nearby trees and bushes, surrounding them. Colin was still out in the open. Eron knew the archers had to be readying another round. He slipped out of his pack, and tackled his friend. The man let out a scream of pain, drowned out in the thunking of arrows, as they landed behind a tree. Colin hissed. It would take his leg a while to heal even after yanking the arrow out. Eron drew his sword, not sure where Mica was. The bandits laughed and jeered.

"Come on out, and maybe we won't kill you!"

"Yoo hoo! Here piggy pig, pig!"

"Oh, there are no bandits in here; it's too close to town, he said," Colin grumbled, sweating and grimacing. "Where's Mica?"

"Bastard's hiding across the road," Eron whispered back.

Colin nodded. "Go flank the archers. I'll draw them out so you can get rid of them."

"Thanks, bud. First round's on me." Eron checked the trees, keeping crouched down and moving into position.

"There you are," he heard a man call as he saw one of the archers close by. "Where are your friends? Get 'em out here."

Eron struck, killing two out of four archers before gaining the safety of the trees on the other side of the road. From there, it took a further ten minutes to thin the band down. The remaining handful gave up, fleeing toward the mountains. The two men walked over to Colin's 'corpse,' guarding it while they waited for him to reanimate. He sat up with a groan as his friend reached a hand down to help him up.

"Nice look." Eron squeezed his friend's shoulder, saying to Mica, "No bandits, huh?"

"You're still alive."

"And your brother's the one they saw die," Eron shot back.

Colin was leaning against a tree, resembling a porcupine. Besides the arrow sticking out of his leg, there were four in his back, another in his side, one in his upper arm, and half a dozen in his chest. "A little help here? I don't fancy going into town like this." He was trying to inspect his clothes. "Damn, I don't think I can repair this much damage," he muttered to himself.

Mica walked over to tend to Colin, snapping the fletching off and pushing the rest of the barbs and shafts through and out of his body so final healing could begin, unmindful of his brother's muffled screams of pain.

"We should have gone after them."

Eron seethed inside. *I told the smug bastard to wait but no, it's hurry, hurry, hurry. We may be impossible to kill, but it doesn't mean you act like an idiot.*

Mica ignored Eron's mumbling, waiting for his brother to wrap his cloak tightly about himself to hide the blood stains and holes in his clothing. "Come on, brother, let's get you into town."

Eron and Mica supported Colin's weight as soon as he felt able to continue on. It was slow going before Colin was able to walk unassisted. They emerged from the forest to find a big bright-yellow moon illuminating the way. The road widened, though still rutted, passing through a long open grassy meadow. The men were close enough to the town they could see the outlines of buildings making up the outermost edges of the town. The dark hid a lot of detail. What the men could see of the town was not cheerful; it looked and smelled like many a squalid backwater teeming with poverty and disease.

"Oh, joy. Another shit hole," Eron muttered under his breath.

The men guessed it was close to midnight as they trudged into the area. An overpowering stench of putrefaction saturated the air, singed their noses. Dour images seen through a haze of wood smoke did not give them much hope for decent lodgings. Most of the buildings were shuttered tight. Their fears were confirmed at the first inn they came across. A good strong wind could blow it over, but the decrepitude of the place didn't stop it from being full. The proprietor told them of a tavern where they would be guaranteed lodgings. Colin didn't like the lack of guards as they made their way through the town. Flaring torches outside the tavern showed a creaking wooden sign—a fist with bloodied knuckles—hanging overhead, proclaiming, "The Bloody Knuckles." The three men shared a glance, but shrugged and entered. The ill-lit, filthy, smoky interior gave the tavern a sinister look. Men, along with a handful of women, bristling with weapons, cast looks of suspicion, hate, greed, and murderous intent toward the newcomers. The three men let their hands drop to their sword hilts, missing a small group of people turn their backs hastily away. As the travelers worked their way farther inside, one of the members of the group who had noticed them went up to a big man at the bar to whisper in his ear.

The three men gave a collective sigh of resignation, sitting down at a wobbly table, preparing to order what dubious fare the place provided. The sounds going on above led them to believe the tavern doubled as a brothel. They returned the curious patrons' looks with blank, empty stares. After a ten-minute wait, a malnourished girl of about fourteen made her reluctant way to their table.

She had new and old bruises covering her exposed skin. Her tremulous voice was hard to hear over the noise. "May I get you something to eat or drink?"

"Both for the three of us, please. Ale will be fine, the best you have."

The girl nodded, scurrying away. They watched her try to avoid the grasping hands of the men, while flinching at each crude remark flung her way from the patrons.

"Wonderful. Nicky never disappoints," Eron observed.

Mica snorted. "Oh, I have no worries he's found someone to sucker into caring for him. It's so much like all the other places we've been; I just know he's here."

The girl came back with the ale, temporarily stopping the conversation. Each man reached for his mug, cautiously sampled the brew, and shuddered at the sour taste. They tried to take the smallest sips possible.

"Shall I call the girl back over and ask for wine or spirits?"

"Don't bother, Colin; they're not likely to be much better."

He nodded glumly, thinking back to the times when it was possible to get a decent brew even with the cheapest of spirits. After the initial sip, Colin set the mug aside, drawing out his journal and ink to record the day's travel. He was proud of it, keeping the leather cover supple by rubbing animal fat into it and wrapping it in a bit of silk tied with a silken cord. The journal was as long as his forearm and about a foot thick.

Eron assessed the tavern. A raised platform with a large stone fireplace dominated one wall; before it, men, drunkenly carousing with scantily clad women, filled benches around a long table. The serving slaves could hardly keep their mugs filled. Directly in front, patrons rolled dice and bet. A few played with cards made from wood or tree bark. The bar itself was crowded with a boisterous group contentedly harassing the serving girls. At the far back, barely seen in the flickering light, a set of stairs led up into gloomy darkness. Thick layers of dirt and grime covered the whole scarred wooden tavern floor. Very few of the patrons appeared as well-dressed or half as clean as they were. Filthy, coarse fabrics woven of wool or cotton were paired with leather and fur. It was a contrast to the three men whose clothes had a tight weave, showing not a patch or repair from skillful mending, including their dusty fur-lined cloaks. All the men seemed to carry a weapon, be it a bow, sword, club or short knife, and sometimes more than one. Eron noticed some had made attempts at armor; there were a few pieces of cured leather, some wooden shields, and a very few scraps of metal. He noticed the bartender eyeing them fiercely between yelling at the girls.

Turning back to his companions, Eron remarked, low-toned, "A flask of this swill says we get robbed the moment we step outside."

The two brothers looked up, giving rueful smiles. "I say it comes in the dead of night while trying to sleep."

The girl came back, sliding bread trenchers of food in front of them. Colin hurriedly dumped his journal in his lap before she set his meal on top of it. She moved a step away, naming the price. Mica fished out coins, which the girl scooped up before running off.

Mica pulled a face as he brought out his dagger and fork to cut into the meat. The first bite all but made him gag. The other two, seeing his reaction, did their best to choke down what they were able.

"I think we would have been better off on the outskirts and hunting. It would surely be more palatable than this . . . this mess," Colin voiced the idea in Eron's mind.

Colin shoved the remains of his meal to one side to finish writing his observations of the day's walk and subsequent events.

Eron washed what little he had eaten down with another sip of foul brew.

"No more of this, Mica," Eron spat, once he could talk again. "I'm sick of eating putrid meals and bad ale, of sleeping on lumpy flea-filled beds. I'm a human being, not a dog."

"This is it! This is the town." Mica was adamant. "What's a little bad food and poor lodgings compared to finishing our quest?"

"You've said that about the last forty-some towns."

"And I shall continue to say so, as it's true," Mica retorted. "Nothing matters but the quest." As if to prove his point, he attacked the food with more vigor and chewed heartily.

"Company coming," Colin murmured, lifting his mug to drink as the biggest person at the bar walked toward them. The immortals couldn't decide if he was mostly built of muscle, or fat. The floorboards trembled from his heavy tread.

His leather armor appeared new and unscratched, firelight gleaming off jewels and metal. His leather boots had hobnailed soles. Without asking, he spun a chair around, sitting down with them.

"Well, now, don't you three look pretty," he leered, with blackened teeth and foul breath. "What ya here for?"

"Just passing through," Mica replied.

The man raised a brow. "Oh? Some kinda wanderin' mercenary, are ya?"

Mica replied softly, "Or something. May we know who you are, stranger, and buy you a drink?"

"Ah, a drink would be welcome now, and right nice of ya. I'm the sheriff of this town, those are me men." He jerked a thumb over his shoulder to the group at the bar. Turning his head, he bellowed, "Hey, Mary Elana, youse slut! Can't you see we's need refills."

Luckily for the sheriff, he missed the poisoned look all three men gave at his hailing of the girl. Their faces had the same bored expression as before when he turned back.

"So who the hell are ya?"

"Mica, Colin and Eron," replied Mica.

"Call me Jake." The girl approached with fresh tankards. The sheriff hawked, spitting on the floor in front of her. She set down the new mugs, snatching up the old. Mary Elana was not quick enough to escape Jake's hand snaking out to catch her around the wrist, forcing her to his side.

"Now, ya be good to these here men, ya hear me? I don't wanna be tellin' the lord about ya misbehavin' to anyone here." He leered at her in a meaningful way as a shudder went through her thin frame.

I hope you drop dead soon, you drunken sot, and leave me be, she thought, hoping he did not try fondling her.

The sheriff turned to his new acquaintances, booming, "Youse can have 'bout any most girl in the place 'ceptin' this one. This lazy slut here is our Little Lord's property an' ain't no man 'ceptin' him and her father allowed to touch her. Just warning youse before ya do somethin' stupid-like."

Mica had to remember to keep his temper in check. "I'm sure we'll keep it in mind. Thank you. Perhaps the girl would like to finish going about her job now?"

The sheriff stared at him for a minute or two, as if trying to decide whether or not Mica was being sincere, before he let go of the girl's wrist, smacking her hard on the ass. She let out a strangled scream, fleeing back behind the bar. His eyes hardened, voice no longer friendly.

"Ya better watch who ya try to give orders to around here. Could be kinda unhealthy-like to piss off the wrong person; ya might not make youse trip outta here in one piece if ya catch me drift."

Mica didn't trust himself to reply, remaining silent as his brother apologized for any misunderstanding.

"Are ya a pansy? One of 'em limp-wrist ones?" Jake sneered, grabbing at Colin's journal.

Colin moved it out of reach, but the sheriff's sleeve dragged across an ink stone. He cursed at the large black spot staining the fabric.

"Damn pansy ass," he roared. A slap of his large hand sent the offending item spinning onto the floor.

Colin swallowed his anger. Men like the sheriff did not need an excuse to try and kill him. He was about to offer to pay for cleaning as the sheriff grabbed his shirt to yank him closer.

The table wobbled, food and drinks falling off. The sheriff's other hand hauled back in a fist. Colin braced for the punch as his hands kept his journal and remaining writing implements from crashing to the floor. Mica pressed his dagger into the man's side.

"I wouldn't do it, sheriff. If you hurt my brother, you'll have me to deal with."

Jake snarled, "We's don't like his kind here, and ya'd better let me go if ya knows what's good fer ya."

"What kind?" When the man didn't answer, Mica pressed harder, making the sheriff mutter something which he repeated louder at another prod.

"The kind what don't like women."

"I can assure you, my brother likes women. You will let him alone, won't you? I'd hate having to leave this place so quickly for killing you when we just got here."

"Ya wouldn't make it out the door a'fore me men got ya."

"Possible," Mica replied smoothly, and after a heartbeat or two, the sheriff let go of Colin.

Colin eased back, peeling the journal from his shirtfront. The page he had just written was an unreadable, smeared mess. He risked a quick glance down; the ink blended with the blood stains on his faded brown shirt.

The sheriff looked around to see who had noticed; those closest hurriedly went back to their pursuits.

"I don't suppose this tavern has any rooms for weary travelers?" Eron asked.

Colin took the chance to look for his stone. He didn't see it and guessed one of the patrons had already stolen it. He added it to the growing mental list of things he needed to replace. He was rather upset with the loss of it, it being the last one he had. The sheriff sat back to drink deeply before replying, "Not unless ya want to lodge wit' the sailors." His smirk said it all on the subject. "Lucky for youse there might be a room. Tom'd be able to tell ya for sure. He's owner and bartender."

Colin noticed Jake's intricately designed clasp and decided to risk the man's wrath. "That's an interesting piece you're wearing, not in keeping with the rest of your . . . outfit."

He committed it to memory—thorny vines surrounding a grimacing face with a circle, star, and flames—to sketch out later.

Jake's face bloomed red. "Ya sayin' I ain't good enough for it, or I took it from someone?"

"Not at all," Eron smoothed over, yet his tone implied otherwise.

"It's a gift from the king for doin' me work so well. He don't mind how's I's do it, only that it's done. A part of me job is to tell ya that ya gots to see His Majesty tomorrow if ya wants to stay here. Other side o' the bridge. Ya can't miss the palace, top of the hill." He lumbered up, making his way back to his friends at the bar.

Chapter Two

If the three companions hoped last night's run-in with Sheriff Jake would be the worst the town offered, they were badly mistaken the next day. Breakfast was comprised of a second putrid meal washed down with more ale. The three men stepped out into the weak morning light, which revealed the full dismalness of the town. An auctioneer's loud cry echoed nearby. Mica turned toward the sound, his brother and friend trailing after. Within moments, they stood gazing upon a slave market. A wooden platform held rows of naked men and women, some with babies or small children clinging to them. All had iron collars around their necks.

"What'll you fine men give me for this next one? Sixteen years of age with plenty of work left in him. Captured in Tyronalese, good for farming or mining. Starting bid at one hundred."

"Vile!'' Mica spat, as a fast, furious bidding war broke out. "Let's move. I don't want to see any more."

He tromped off through the mud of the garbage-strewn street without waiting for a response. His friends hurried to catch up with him.

As they approached the bridge, the men saw richly uniformed guards, most likely from the palace, blocking access as one of them hailed the travelers.

"What business have you?"

"We wish to speak with your King. The sheriff has informed us . . ." That was all Mica had to say.

The guards stepped aside to allow the men to cross. The major street leading to the palace appeared paved with a mixture of rock and old concrete. Unlike the lower town, crude sidewalks existed, and no trash or animal droppings marred the way. The air even smelled better and was quieter. The men passed large houses made of stone or stacked concrete pieces. Some had personal guards in uniforms, and massive crested banners, hanging from the eaves, which nearly brushed the ground.

"Figures the little blighter would like a place like this. He's suckered some rich noble into caring for him," Colin muttered as they climbed the twisting street.

"Nothing warms the cockles of his heart more than seeing others ground down like he once was," Mica growled.

Eron remained silent, eyeing the big stone building that was their destination. It looked to have originally been a cathedral. The arrow slits and crude stone towers added to fortify the building for its new purpose clashed with intricate carvings and stained glass. A crude, manned wall with large iron-studded wooden gates signified the end of the street. The men joined the line slowly shuffling inside the compound.

Occasionally a guard bawled out, "All weapons must be surrendered. All visitors much be searched, all business must be stated."

Even with the queue, it didn't take long to reach the portal. Those in charge did their jobs efficiently. A pair of guards to either side relieved visitors of all visible weapons before waving them past. The second set did quick pat-downs, pulling people out of line for a more thorough search if they felt it was needed. The third station had two men at tables on each side of the pathway, taking down information.

"State your business."

"We've come to ask for an audience with your king. May we see him?" Mica asked, indicating his party.

"Who are you and what business have you?"

"We are a band of merchant men wanting information on a thief that is known to be in this area. And the sheriff said we had to present ourselves," he added as an afterthought.

The baleful glare said it all. "Thieves are the sheriff's concern. Next!"

Mica bared his teeth in a smile as he leaned a hand on the table, a silver coin showing between his fingers. "Sorry, I wasn't clear enough."

The plain yet rich dress of the man made him a clerk. "Is that so?" He cast a jaded eye at the offering.

Mica added a few more coins, still smiling. "The thief is no ordinary one. He preys on those with money and titles, then disposes of them."

The clerk's eyes narrowed as he took the bribe and signaled to a guard. They had a quick, low-voiced conversation before the man ran off, shortly coming back with yet another man.

"I am Mathias, the Captain of the Palace Guards. Come with me."

Colin noticed the palace badge had a different coat of arms than the sheriff's: three diagonal bars with a rearing horse and a crown to either side. His brother attempted to make conversation but was gruffly rebuffed. Mathias led them into a large whitewashed room. Plain, hard benches lined the walls. A middle-aged man clothed in bright, clashing colors and holding a staff stood before two tall doors.

"These are the men," the guard announced before being dismissed.

"Your—" was all that Mica got out before the man held a hand up for silence.

He studied them for a moment or two with his small, beady eyes. "I am Aranthus, His Majesty's most treasured and revered chamberlain. I must know your identity and your business in His Majesty's town before I decide if the King should be bothered with your petition. You may speak."

Eron raised a brow, Colin stared in disbelief. Mica kept his face expressionless, knowing they wouldn't be able to talk with His Majesty.

"No disrespect intended, sir, but our request is of a delicate nature—the fewer people who know about it, the better. While I'm sure you are a man of the utmost discretion, others may overhear who may not be as circumspect."

Aranthus narrowed his eyes slightly; he had no intention of letting anyone by him today, as the king was in a foul mood, and he didn't want it taken out on his hide. It was so hard to say nowadays what would set the man off. "Tell me what you can. I will do my best to impart to His Majesty the gravity of your situation." Aranthus motioned to a male slave behind him; the slave started taking out his writing implements. "There are some questions which must be answered first."

And here is where we waste precious hours which could be spent looking for the little boy, Mica growled to himself.

The Chamberlain was an exacting man, soon he knew all but what size of clothing the three before him wore. "Now, what is this delicate situation you cannot report to any but His Majesty?"

Mica glanced at the other two men, did some quick editing in his head. "We are looking for a young boy who was apprenticed to us. He ran off with a large portion of our wealth and a valuable family heirloom. During our inquiries, we came across information indicating the boy had settled down here."

Eron narrowed his eyes as the scribe's head came up sharply, but seeing he was noticed, lowered his head again and continued note-taking. Eron kept his eyes on the man, as he could tell by the slave's demeanor that he was avidly listening to every word.

"I'm surprised men such as you do not hire mercenaries to do what must be considered dirty work. Why do you stoop to conduct your own investigation? Perhaps you are not as successful business-wise as you would like us to believe. Mayhap you are even lying concerning the boy."

Mica gave a tight smile. "Truth be told, the last man we used came back with information on the little boy's whereabouts only after inadvertently alerting him and letting him escape. His incompetence lost us a year of searching. Since then, we haven't found many mercenaries who can handle the delicateness of the task of bringing the boy back to us for justice without losing him again."

"What makes you think the king will be able to help on such a mundane matter?" The contempt in the chamberlain's voice was scorching.

Mica bit back a hot retort, smoothly replying, "A leopard does not change its spots for long. The boy must be running out of funds and will no doubt pull a similar stunt on someone here. Whether he will pick another wealthy merchant or try higher, such as one of the nobility . . ."

Aranthus cocked a brow, laying a forefinger upon his lip. "Yes," he mused. "I do begin to see the problem. If the boy has set his sights higher, the nobles would be understandably upset. However, they are given leeway to dispense justice within their own households without going to His Majesty. It is possible this has already occurred, in which case we would have no record of it. You would do better to ask of them yourself."

Colin decided to speak up. "Forgive me, but if the boy hasn't tried it yet, who here would keep records of the merchants' complaints? Should we should try them first before disturbing the titled?"

Aranthus nodded in approval. "The sheriff handles all such

complaints, deciding if they are severe enough to warrant intervention by His Majesty's guards."

Mica ground his teeth as the other two men winced inwardly. After their run-in with the man last night, they doubted he would help them without some kind of massive bribe. *Why the hell must everything keep getting so damn complicated?*

"Ah, I see," Colin replied, a ghost of a smile playing about his mouth. "Where do we go to speak with him?"

* * *

Once outside the palace, the three started back down the steep incline.

Colin waited until the men were out of earshot. "I don't like this, brother. How are we going to convince a man who already doesn't like us to help? We are running out of coins for bribes. I don't think we have anything else someone like him would want."

Mica growled. "I don't know. Why don't we split up and see if we can seek out the places the little boy would most likely frequent. We'll meet back at the wretched tavern around dusk."

"You've really lost your mind over this, you know that?" Eron stopped in front of Mica, forcing his friend to quit walking.

Colin watched his brother's square jaw clench and unclench. "We can't sit around waiting for the boy to show himself. We're going to have to come up with a plan to get the sheriff's help until I can think of a better one."

"You may enjoy searching for a needle in a haystack, but I don't," Eron snapped back.

"It is what we've always done. It's worked in the past, and it'll work again. He doesn't change his habits, you know that. How many towns have we seen to which he's gone? They all had things in common. He always has favored hunting spots in the countryside, spots in town." Mica's eyes swept over his brother, patiently waiting for them to begin.

"Colin, you head out to the countryside, get the lay of the land. Eron —"

"Screw this!" Eron burst out. "I'm not wasting time on personal vendettas any more. Go grovel to the sheriff, kiss his ass some, do whatever is needed."

"What the hell is your problem?"

"My problem?! I'm looking at it! This is bullshit! You know why you can't get a handle on the kid? Because it's like he can smell your obsession, and runs off." Mica rolled his eyes in exasperation as Eron continued, "The expiration date on the kid's soul gem? Guess what? It's past. The sound of rushing wind you hear? That's The Guardian coming for the gem and your immortality; you're dead, he wins."

"Not if I find him first, and I'm not going to the sheriff until I can think of an angle that's going to get results and not more enmity on his part. You can take the docks."

Mica turned away from Eron, looking at his brother. "Colin, just scour the countryside. I trust you to come up with something to find Nicky's place out there without it getting back to him. I'll take the town."

"You . . ." Eron tossed his hands up in frustration. "Fine, go do whatever you want. Enjoy the taste of defeat while it all blows up in your face." He stalked off.

"We're meeting at sunset at the tavern," Mica called after his retreating back.

* * *

Eron strolled along the docks, trying to compose himself. Open sheds stinking of offal received newly arriving captives. His stomach roiled at the sight of human beings packed tightly into pens with barely enough room to stand, much less sit. A lot of the pens didn't have a roof, leaving the occupants to shiver in the raw drizzle. The misery around him illustrated it was past time to be done chasing phantoms, living in shit holes. *Fuck Mica's mad quest. I quit.* He turned around just in time to spot a handful of men do a poor job of looking elsewhere. *Oh, bloody hell! I don't need this. Time to teach a lesson about the dangers of spying.*

Eron zigged behind a pile of crates, threading his way through the stacks of goods and people, trying to find a secluded area. Rounding the next set of stacked cargo, he stopped, damning his luck for finding the only dead end. He turned to go back, cursing as a fist plowed into his face.

"I got 'im! Hey! Tell 'em I gots him!" the excited voice rang out.

Eron shook off the ringing in his head, repaying the favor by punching his assailant in the jaw. The man went down like a log. Eron nipped around him only to be met by a wicked dagger. *Of all the stupid moves, I had to go and not pay attention to my surroundings.*

"Bloody hell, how many are you?" Eron spat out in disgust as meaty arms wrapped around him from behind, lifting him a few inches off the ground,

"Not so smart now, are you?"

"Shut up, Jonas!" A fist plowed into Eron's gut, breath leaving in an explosive *whoosh.*

"Hold him still!" his attacker instructed, punching his victim twice in the face, once more in the gut, and four times in each kidney.

Eron had no time to brace himself; he hung in Jonas's arms, fighting to stay conscious, as the pain rolled through him. He felt his nose break, warm blood splashing down, making it harder to breathe. He couldn't remember the last time he had been jumped and beaten. Eron barely heard Jonas whine, "I wan' a turn too."

"Sheriff wants him alive to deliver a message." The speaker, noticing Eron was still awake, followed his words with a few more punches to the face and gut.

Eron's lip split with the last blow, blood trickling down his chin, left eye swelling closed as he wondered how much longer the beating would continue. He fought against unconsciousness as his attacker demanded, "Where's your friends?"

Incredulously, Eron replied, "You followed me just to ask that?" His body throbbed in pain. Stars floated across his vision, arms about him tightening and cutting off what little breath he had left.

"Quit squeezing him so damn hard, Jonas!" The dagger came up to menace his throat as the hold around him loosened a fraction, still not enough for him to suck in a good breath. "Keep it up, smart-ass; just give me a reason to cut your pretty-boy face."

The man pinning Eron's arms to his sides laughed. "We just wanna give 'em a warning."

"Which one? I do have more than one friend." Eron had a feeling he was the message.

The man cursed, the dagger slashing open the flaming, battered flesh. Blood flowed freely from the open wound.

"Don't do that," Eron warned in flat, emotionless tones, dark brown eyes going blank.

Jonas snickered behind him. "Ooohhhh. Or you're gonna do what? Hurt us?" The arms tightened their hold further.

"I said 'where's your friends?' The faggy one and the blockhead," the first man repeated, slicing the other cheek. "And we'll let you go."

"Last chance, stop cutting me."

"Tell us, or the next cut takes your balls."

Eron thought: *If it was just my face, I could deal with it, but my balls? Fuck them.* Even though he was in pain, gasping for air, he had time for one move to get free.

The men didn't have time to respond as their victim brought his legs up, kicking Jim in the groin. The man gurgled as he sank to the ground. Jonas staggered back at the sudden movement, his hold loosening. Eron grabbed Jonas's forearms with his hands, letting his weight drop, dragging his body toward the ground, breaking Jonas's hold. Eron's knees hit the wood; he twisted and overbalanced the other man. Pain ripped through his gut, causing him to writhe on the ground briefly, but he scrambled up as he saw the big man in his peripheral vision raising a club. Jim was down, breath wheezing in and out with a high-pitched whine. Eron kicked out, catching the man full in the gut. Jonas stumbled away, grunting, absorbing most of the blow.

Something the size of a small boulder slammed into his back, pitching Eron headfirst into the wooden dock as a sharp pain shot through his lungs. He rolled over to see an unknown third attacker holding a bronze sword, the blade bloody.

Crap on toast! The day just keeps getting better.

Bronze Sword and Jonas came toward him. The immortal did the only thing he could, rolling out of the way as the sword slammed down where he had been. He caught the club with both hands, almost losing his grip at the snapping sound his palms made. The pain sent long black streamers across his vision, and a greasy roiling through his belly. Eron knew he had to ignore it or they'd kill him, and he didn't fancy being reanimated under water. He shoved the club backward and rolled onto his knees.

Jonas wasn't expecting the move, so the butt-end caught him in the stomach. The third man stabbed him in his side. Eron gritted his teeth. While the sword was being withdrawn, Eron lashed out with a leg and dislocated the other's knee. The man went down with a scream, sword clattering a hand's breath away. Eron released the club, staggering to one side as Jonas plowed into him. They crashed down. Eron used the momentum to arm-chop Jonas' throat. The man gagged and spat, trying to suck in air. Eron turned at a scraping noise to see Jim, recovered enough to snatch his dagger back up, lunging toward him. The immortal caught the attacker's arm in a lock, bending it in such a way that the dagger was now pointing toward Jim's throat.

"Jonas!" the man bellowed as he struggled with Eron.

Using the man's arm as leverage, Eron spun him in a circle, scanning the tops of the crates but not seeing anyone. A quick jerk sent the dagger slicing deep across his assailant's throat, nearly decapitating him. Blood sprayed in an arc, the dagger clattering to the dock as Jonas crawled toward his fallen club.

"Ah, no, we can't have that now, can we? Not after what you just saw; you should have heeded my warning." Eron unsheathed his sword, striding over to the escaping man. He tapped Jonas on the back with it.

"Stop right there."

Jonas whimpered, "Don't. Don't kill me. We-we only wanted a bit of fun." He held a hand up, looking back at the man, the whites of his eyes showing in fear.

"What's the message from the sheriff?" Eron demanded.

"There ain't one," the man whined, his hand wrapped around the club.

Eron felt disgust, kicking the club out of the man's hand. "Get up! Now!"

Jonas screamed in pain, rolling over onto his back, clutching his injured member. "You bastard, you broke my hand!" he howled. "You ain't gonna get away with it!"

Eron cocked his head, studying the man before him. "Ask me if I care. Why did the sheriff tell you to follow us?"

Jonas glared at the man before spotting his club. "I ain't telling you nothing, cocksucker!" He spat at Eron's feet.

"Then you're useless to me. Get up and you can die like a man. If not," he shrugged, "die on your back like the dog you are."

"Fuck you!" Jonas shouted, dragging himself toward his weapon.

"As you wish," Eron replied, sword flicking out.

Jonas collapsed forward as Eron heard a scrabbling sound. He whipped his head around, scanning the tops of the crates, seeing nothing. It could be rats. He needed to get out of there. The third attacker was still hitching himself across the space, trying to escape. Briefly, he and Eron clashed swords before he was gutted. Eron wiped his blade off on a clean patch of the dead man's coat before jamming it back into his scabbard, wincing. It would take at least several hours for the damage to heal. He gazed at the bodies, wondering if they had anything useful on them. He was rewarded by two pouches full of coins and assorted jewels. That would help him get out of town. His new windfall contradicted the ratty clothing of the scum from whom he'd taken it. Eron secured the pouches to either side of his belt, beneath his cloak, using the inside of the cloak to clean the worst of the blood off his face before fastening it closed over stains and the wound in his side.

What's the best way out of here? It didn't take long to wend, limping, back to the main throng, making sure no one else was following him. He didn't want to use his new windfall right away, but keep it in reserve. That meant the few coins he had come with wouldn't stretch far —certainly not enough to buy a mount—but he didn't care to walk out, which left hiring out onto one of the ships, or finding a merchant train or group of travelers needing guards. Either option had its perils, but since he was here at the docks, he would try by sea first. The ships carrying human cargo he rejected as there was a chance he would become one of the slaves. A depressingly small handful remained; most of them could be classified as sea hags, the sails much patched, and only barnacles, seaweed, tar and pitch held rotting wood together. He noticed a beautiful sleek vessel out in the harbor. The two sails left unfurled had not a patch on them and from the top mizzen mast, a pennant flew, marking the ship's allegiance.

"Now there's a ship." He had not realized he'd spoken out loud until a rough voice at his elbow replied, "Aye. A beauty she be. *The Golden Hind.*"

Eron glanced over to see a tall, weather-beaten man in a blue coat, pants and hat.

"Are you part of the ship's crew?" he inquired politely.

"You could say so; are you looking to have business with the ship or just admirin' her?"

"Both, actually. I would be grateful if you could tell me with whom I must speak and where I can find him."

"That would be me. I'm the captain. I only think it's fair to tell you I'm not taking on new cargo right now," the man said.

"What about passengers?" Eron asked.

The man scrutinized the immortal, getting right to the heart of the matter. "I don't need crew."

Eron felt his heart sink but nodded politely. "I appreciate the honesty. I am a hard worker. I can only offer scant coin toward my passage, probably not enough for your ship."

"Hrmmm," was all the man said. "Try the *Kasper* or the *Queen Rose*. They'll take your coin and work you like a dog, but I haven't heard of them enslaving a man and selling him or any other type of monkey business. Can't say the same for the rest."

"Thanks," Eron replied, heaving a sigh and turning to seek out the two ships mentioned.

* * *

"You really are a sorry nag, you know?" Colin growled to his mount as it stopped of its own will for about the dozenth time.

An annoyed snort was his only response as the mare stretched down to crop at a juicy patch of grass. Colin wrestled with the hard-mouthed mount, managing to get her going in a slow amble. He hoped Eron and his brother were having better luck than he. He had stopped at the first farmhouse outside the town, using the story he had made up to find Nicky's country spot. The owners had been reluctant to say anything, so he was forced to continue on until he found some slaves who would talk. They gave vague directions to a lake townspeople used as a swimming hole. He turned onto a dusty track which wound off to his left, between fields in which slaves worked the harvest.

Colin hailed the overseer, and asked, "Sir, I'm trying to find the local swimming hole, only the directions I've been given are not the best. Am I on the right road?"

The man scratched his head, admitting he wasn't sure, directing him toward the farmhouse. A twenty-minute ride brought it into view. Carved lintel beams caught his eye. *That would be nice to sketch.* Colin introduced himself to the farmwife, asking permission to relax in the yard. He used his handkerchief to dust off a log before sitting and eating lunch while copying down the carvings as his hostess explained the significance of the carvings to him. She was one of the few women who didn't appear worn before her time, or so beaten down by her lot in life she moved like a zombie. He spent a pleasant visit before starting back off, Patty plodding down the road a bit more enthusiastically, having been given water, food, and a bit of rest.

"Ach, a body can't even start a revolution here. They'd probably end up being hauled off posthaste in chains to rot in a dungeon or provide entertainment for the king's rabble."

The mare ignored his babble, attempting to stop and swipe another mouthful of greens.

"Oh, no, you don't!" Colin warned her with a nudge to the ribs, slapping the reins against her neck to startle the mare into a trot.

In retaliation, the spotted mare did a jump-hop in a halfhearted attempt to unseat him. Colin chuckled in spite of himself, and with a short wrestle, had his mount going in a decent canter down the side of the rutted road. He spotted a thin winding path and tried to remember if it was the one he was told to look for. He decided to ride down it, and managed to tug the hard-mouthed mount onto the trail. The mare promptly dropped back into her ambling gait.

"I think you were misnamed," Colin grumbled. "You should be called Mule or Stubborn or Irritating, not Patty."

The mare flicked one ear back, shaking her mane as Colin moved branches out of his way or ducked. "I bet you've got a mule or two as an ancestor. Last mount available, my ass. If you stop one more time, I'll find a switch and beat the stubborn out of you," he threatened halfheartedly.

In the midst of another tug-of-war match with Patty over a patch of grass, a slight breeze stirred up, carrying a heavy stench. Colin forgot about the horse for a moment as he wrinkled his nose in distaste. "Strange, now I think about and smell it, I don't recall seeing any graveyards or burying grounds in town, or passing any. There has to be one someplace, though."

Colin hoped the breeze would blow again so he could try telling from which way the scent came. He sat for ten minutes by his reckoning, but the smell didn't come.

"Come on, you. This is the last, I promise, and then we can head back to the stable." Colin nudged the mare.

She started up reluctantly, and with much prodding and cursing, broke into a stiff-legged jog. Colin estimated they had gone about half a mile when the mare whinnied, rearing.

"Whoa, girl!" Colin tried to calm her, managing to stay in the saddle as she imitated a bucking bronco.

The mare, for her part, wanted no more of their ride. She tucked tail and head down, whirling to gallop toward the road.

"Steady, girl; whoa, there's a good girl. Calm now, yeah, that's good." With much coaxing and petting, Colin got the mare to stand still though she trembled like a leaf.

He nimbly jumped down from the saddle, taking the reins, stroking her neck until the trembling had stilled.

"What are you afraid of, huh? I don't see anything bad hanging out around here."

It was true, as far as he could see on the ground and in the trees; no predator lurked which would have caused her reaction. There wasn't even a deer or bunny or rustling leaves which could have startled her. Now he didn't have to pay so much attention to his mount, Colin noticed the stench was much, much stronger. He must be close to a burying ground, one not properly taken care of. Colin tied the reins to a low branch.

"There. Now you can eat as much as you like until I get back," he said with a final pat.

She snorted, uneasily shifting before warily reaching down to snatch a mouthful. Colin started up the path toward the smell, resettling his sword across his hips in case he needed use of it. Twenty minutes of walking went by before the trees thinned out as he topped a low rise. The stench was so overpowering he covered his mouth and nose with a square of embroidery-edged linen.

"By all that's holy!" The curse escaped him as he looked down at the mess in the ground. Flocks of carrion birds rose in a mass, revealing the source. They circled, cawing and cackling at the disturbance; when Colin didn't do anything else, they settled back down.

A broad, deep pit had been dug in a rough clearing with dirt ringing it. Most of the dead were barely covered, all the corpses in an advanced state of decay. Even though Colin had seen many bodies in all states during his lifetime, he still had to look away, fighting down the bile rising in his throat, before edging closer to the pit for a better look. Judging by the number of dead, the spot had been in use for a while.

"Where the hell are all these people from? Even with this place being a slave market, there shouldn't be this many bodies. We haven't even heard of any entertainment using humans which would produce this kind of death rate."

Colin shook his head, deciding to file the piece of the mystery away. He looked once more at the mess, unable to tell without going into it how they had died. He glanced up at the sky, noting the sun beginning its downward climb. If he wanted to be back by dusk on the nag, he would have to leave now. Colin figured he would try to find the lake tomorrow, hopefully with a better mount. Still, he lingered for a moment or two more, searching the area, rewarded by finding deep wagon wheel grooves on the far side of the pit. They disappeared into the dark forest. Wishing he had more time to find out where they went, Colin noted the direction they came from before hiking back to the mare. He hoped the other two had had better luck than he.

* * *

The more Mica saw of the town, the less he liked the narrow, crooked, filthy streets. The buildings were pieced together of wattle and daub, mud bricks, rotting wood and thatch, and mismatched stones. They all leaned at haphazard, bizarre angles. Mica was bumped and shoved continuously. He kept checking his coin purse to make sure it had not gotten stolen. Riders and wheeled conveyances splashed mud on those on foot; to his disgust, his cloak became coated. An understanding of how the town was laid out unfolded the more he explored. A tall wooden pole denoted the center of town; from there, the streets wound out. Craftspeople who didn't require a lot of water for their profession— weavers, coopers, and metal-smiths—huddled closest to the curve of the mountain and the path the three men had walked in on. Those needing water for their trade—the dyers and millers—had their homes and businesses along the river between the bridge and harbor mouth. The butcher shops huddled nearest to the forest. The traders and merchants whose wares depended on the ships lay before the docks. A sprinkling of other sundry homes and workplaces lay scattered throughout. Mica knew Nicky liked fine things, to make up for the fact he appeared an eternal boy. The first thing Mica did was search out the best-looking of the buildings, which belonged to the freeborn skilled laborers and craftsmen. As he walked, eavesdropping, he did not hear mention of Nicky by any of his aliases. Lots of craft and noble Masters complained about the ruler, King Maecenas, or made crude jokes about their ruler and his advisor, but nothing which would help his group find their quarry. As the afternoon waned, Mica had a mental list of over a dozen places that Nicky might provide with his custom, from a cobbler of fine leather shoes, a jeweler, and a tailor who only used brightly toned silks, velvets, and brocades, that fit what they were looking for. The immortal noted each purveyor's sign had a small, gold-leaf crown in the top right corner. He also kept his eyes out for other inns, but so far hadn't found one with empty rooms.

He stopped at a stall for a loaf of bread stuffed with meat, and a flagon of wine. A small section remained to be searched, but what would be the point? *What would the little boy do in whorehouses anyway? Watch? He's only twelve!*

Mica believed in being thorough; he wandered past the wooden houses of the whores anyway as he ate his bread. Women hung out of windows, calling out to him.

"Hey baby, you come in here and we'll treat you good."

"Mmmm, hello, muscles, is your cock as big as the rest of you? I can make it bigger."

"Hi, handsome, you want a virgin? I've got a nice young one, only three silver."

He ignored them, their enticements turning to heckling.

"What's the matter? You don't like women?"

"Faggot, you'll find no fudge packers here."

He passed a group of men walking out of a building, laughing and talking. Most of them staggered off down the street in the opposite direction from him while two men paused outside, as grooms came up with horses. Mica kept his head down, but his eyes rolled up as he finished off his bread and wine.

He heard one say, "Damn inconvenient to hold rites now. What the hell's the boy thinking? That damn fanatic priest is suspicious enough." The words set his heart pounding even though the rest of the conversation was lost in the sound of the horses' hooves as the men rode off.

Mica trailed the men. *It would've been smarter to keep watch on the other places, but there was something about the conversation!*

The men split up; he had to choose which to continue following. It was a long boring day trailing the man as he went about his daily business. Mica hoped his brother and Eron had had better luck.

* * *

The sun was slowly diffusing, making Mica aware he needed to leave soon to meet his friends. He lingered, hoping the man would come out of his house. Mica felt himself nodding off, when hoofbeats woke him in time to see a cloaked, hooded figure leave the house. Mica cursed softly as the sun sank; he had not anticipated this. The man didn't seem to be in a hurry, though, and by half-trotting, half-fast walking, he was able to keep the man in sight. His luck held as the man turned down the street past the Bloody Knuckles. Mica saw a few animals at nearby hitching posts, ripe for borrowing. Mica slipped the reins of the nearest horse free. The horse balked at the unfamiliar rider. Mica gentled him, cantering after the man. Mica began to breathe a bit easier once clearing the town limits, slowing the horse to a walk. He was getting too close to his quarry, who had slowed to a trot. Mica didn't want him to hear hoofbeats behind him and wonder who could be following him.

The two went deeper into the forest, along a rutted dirt track barely wide enough for a cart with branches poking out to snag an unwary rider. It was now full dark and the moon only gave a little light. Mica didn't know if the man was still in front of him. He needed to stop the horse periodically and listen, hoping the man hadn't turned off anywhere. Mica urged his mount to go as fast as he dared on the uneven surface. Just as he thought, *How lucky my quarry hasn't looked back!* his horse let out a loud whinny. Mica hissed in annoyance, bringing his mount to a sharp halt. He heard the rapid beat of a galloping animal. Mica swore, urging his own mount into a gallop, but after the beast stumbled and almost threw him, Mica reined in. He barely heard the hoofbeats now. It was no use; he had lost his quarry. He cursed and turned his horse back, but a shout broke the stillness, following the crack of a whip. It echoed eerily, making him unsure of its direction. Mica waited to see if it would repeat, rewarded when it did. This crack seemed closer, off to his left, with less of an echo. He nudged his mount toward the noise but the horse balked, refusing to go off the path. Mica nudged the horse into a walk, scanning for a break in the darkness which might signal another path. He thought he saw a darker patch, but the horse snorted, throwing his head up, muscles bunching to run. Mica dismounted, gently talking to the beast, trying to lead it.

"Whoa, there. Whoa, boy. That's a good horse. It's all right, just a few steps. Come on, just off the path a little. There you go, that's it. Good boy.'"

Still coaxing, Mica got the horse to enter the brush enough to hide them before the gelding balked. Mica gave up as the beast became edgy and panicky. He tied the reins to a low branch, letting the horse calm down and start grazing. He knew the gelding was a creature of habit, wanting his stall, food and water. If left untied, the horse would make his way back to what was familiar and comforting. Mica didn't fancy being left stranded with a very long walk back to the town.

Mica pushed through the thick forest toward the source of the shouts and whip cracking. The noise seemed to come from the other side of a thick tangle of trees and thorny brush obscuring the track. Mica dropped to his belly and slithered forward. It was a good thing he had done so: suddenly the branches thinned. He was able to see into a medium-sized clearing, illuminated by the rising moon. He wiggled back so his face wouldn't gleam, surreptitiously pulling his hood nearly over his eyes. He fisted the bottom part close over his mouth, so only a small oval remained. His free hand scrabbled in the dirt, bringing some up to smear on the exposed skin. Satisfied with his preparations, Mica settled down to spy.

The flickering torchlight revealed pens on the far side of the circle, which held raggedly clad figures huddled for warmth and comfort. Big bulky men in fur and leather stood guarding the pens. A slight breeze kicked up, rustling the leaves, bringing a faint unpalatable, familiar stench with it. He frowned a little, putting the smell out of his mind as he continued to scan for Nicky. Two torches illuminated yet another path out of the clearing. The breeze grew stronger. So did the stench. The indistinct muttering of the men cut off. Mica twisted his head, trying to see why. A line of heavily cloaked, masked figures filed into the grove, encircling a cluster of stones. He couldn't tell if the man he had been following was among them or not. The hood of one figure turned in Mica's direction as if looking right at him. A chill raced up and down his spine. A young male voice rang out, bringing everyone's attention his way. The participants intoned bastardized Latin phrases while holding fat, round black candles lit with a blue flame, similar to the one at which he and Colin had first met the little boy. But none of them were short enough to be a twelve year old, not even the leader. He wished the group would remove their masks, so he didn't have to watch the entire blasphemous ceremony. One of the cloaked figures detached from the group, the men guarding, scrambling to obey orders, to drag a prisoner to be chained to the altar. Each of the chanting men defiled the man with rods of some kind before moving on to other captives, while the prisoners still in the pens wailed and screamed. Mica's fingers dug into the ground, stomach cramping in rage. He was running battle scenes in his head, mapping out how to disable each of the chanting participants and the guards. One of the cloaked figures approached the altar, and the prisoner stretched out on it. The figure appeared to be inspecting the man, giving a nod of satisfaction as the chanting continued, and let fall its cloak. The screaming stopped for one horrified instant before commencing even louder, drowning out the sound of chanting from the group. Mica stuffed his fist in his mouth to prevent his own scream from bursting forth and clenched his eyes shut to blot out the sight of the figure, taking several deep breaths. He managed to pry his eyes open again.

The leader, who seemed to be growing shorter by the minute, beckoned to the guards and pointed out six more victims, who were delivered, struggling, one by one, to the altar. The group chanted again, anointing each one. The guards held the failing sacrifices up as the hooded figure slit throats, letting the blood splatter over the victim on the altar. Mica felt nausea well up and rested his head against the ground, closing his eyes.

Don't pass out; not now, not now. You've seen much, much worse.

Come on, Mica, don't pass out. You've got to see this through to the end and find out who each robed person is. They must not be allowed to go free any more than Nicky.

Mica got himself under control as the screaming reached a new crescendo. An unidentifiable, wisp-like substance was pouring out of the leprous body standing next to the altar with its victim. The leader appeared suddenly and markedly shorter; did he kneel down? He chanted again, marking the altar victim with what appeared to be thick paste from bowls presented by the other coven members. The captive on the altar began to scream in agony, writhing out of the guards' grasp before going still. The high priest spoke a few more phrases. The ritual appeared over when the participants stopped chanting, bowed deeply, and placed their candles on the ground around the altar before walking away.

Mica slithered a little closer to the front of the concealing mass of vegetation. His gut cramped, and he swallowed hard. *I swear every single one of these men will pay for what they've done this night.* He could see only a few people left in the pens. The high priest still knelt by the altar. All but two of the followers had filed out of the clearing, back the way they had come. Mica absentmindedly wiped sweat from his brow. The priest beckoned to the guards. An eerie silence filled the clearing. He lifted his head in time to see the high priest was no longer kneeling behind the altar, but was standing again.

"Get rid of this mess!" the high priest snapped out to the guards before striding away. Suddenly the captive rose from the altar.

"No! By all that's holy! You won't get away!" Mica didn't realize he'd shouted out loud. Branches gave way as he charged across the clearing. His sword sang free of its scabbard as he let loose a war cry.

The remaining hooded member supervising the cleanup had started to turn at the commotion. The guards moved to intercept Mica. His blade met flesh and sunk in. He was fighting the men until a voice rang out,

"Stop!" The command froze all in the clearing, including Mica, to his surprise and shock. Some trick of the light made the former captive's eyes glow red.

"Damn you!" Mica roared as the face split into an evil grin. The man's hand came up and pressed into his chest.

The man spoke an in an unfamiliar language, and Mica had the sensation of his body catching fire. He fell screaming to his knees, sword slipping from his nerveless fingers as the man bent over to keep his hand on Mica's chest.

"Tell me who you are and why you spy upon us?"

"Nnnnnoooooooo!" Mica screamed. His head felt like acid was being poured over it. Black spots danced in front of his eyes, on the verge of passing out, the pain intolerable. As his vision faded, he thought he heard the guttural voice laugh in wild amusement.

Chapter Three

After returning the mare at the stables, Colin went to the tavern, gloomy within, torches unlit. Passing by the bar, he noticed a band of carving under the edge, obscured by the patrons last night. He took a chance to kneel, knowing his pants would be soiled from contact with the filthy floor, inspecting it further. A coat of arms, vines twining around animals. Thorns piercing the animal and human figures. The same design the sheriff had on his clasp.

He was going to ask about both but Tom and some of the men stood, regarding him suspiciously. At this early evening hour, the place wasn't crowded as it had been the night before, thus enabling him to pick a table closer to the bar. He saw Mary Elana coming out of the kitchen.

"Do you have any ale better than last night's, lass?" She nodded wordlessly.

"I'd like a tankard, please."

She scurried off without a word. Colin wondered if something was wrong. When she came back to deposit it and collect coin, he tried to make small talk.

"I hope things go better for you tonight. You seemed a bit overwhelmed last night."

She dropped a coin or two in startlement, stooping to retrieve them. "I . . . I'm fine. It—it is always like that. I . . . I am used to it."

"Still, the barkeep shouldn't have you out among rough men."

Mary Elana stared at him with huge eyes as she placed his change on the table. *Mother of God! Please don't let him make a pass!* "I'm fine. I do what my father tells me," she replied curtly.

Colin scrambled to think of something else, remembering what he and his friends had seen from their journey. "May I ask another question or two of you?"

She was going to ignore him, but he continued, "Beyond the forest, up in the mountains, we noticed what looks like castle spires. Whose is it?"

Mary Elana blurted out, "You're stupid to go too deeply in that forest—those mountains—and no one has seen what you describe. You must be mistaken."

"No. It was shrouded by shifting clouds of mist, or fog. But we all three saw it. What is wrong with the surroundings?"

"It's just a trick by the clouds. There is no castle there anymore, and the forest is haunted."

"So one existed at some point."

She sighed, wishing for once her father would yell for her to get back to work so she wouldn't have to speak to this stranger. "Local tales say there used to be a castle there in times of yore, along with a city. It was said to have been destroyed by the ancestors of our current townspeople, but a monster roams what's left."

Colin chuckled. "I don't believe in ghosts or monsters."

"You should. People have gone into the forest and disappeared."

"Perhaps they ran off."

He raised an eyebrow but said no more as she scurried off. Her father gave her a suspicious eye as she headed into the kitchen to help her mother. Colin noticed he followed after the girl. He sipped cautiously. The stuff wasn't as bitter or chewy as last night's, both conditions he abhorred in ale. He hoped he would be able to say the same for dinner. And that he hadn't gotten the girl into trouble by talking with her.

He wondered if he dared bring out his journal to note his observations from his trip about the countryside and sketch out the carving around the room. Colin didn't want anything to happen to his journal, but he just had to record what he had seen. He reached into his pack sitting against the front of his legs, drawing out the book along with pen and ink. He saw the bartender reenter the room, noticing him. The man must have made a joke at his expense as the men leaning against the bar half-turned to him. They observed, laughing and cracking jokes. He wrote concisely about the countryside and the people he had met in his small, neat handwriting. He liked to include sketches of people or things that had stood out. He was lucky the farm woman had let him stay awhile, as he only had to record everything he'd observed after lunch. Colin began drawing the carvings around the bar. He noticed his light growing almost non-existent. The man looked up in alarm, but it was only the last of the sun going down. The bar was also filling up fast, the noise level rising. He sighed, carefully sanding the page he had been working on before putting everything away. He reached absentmindedly for his tankard, noticing it was empty. He looked for Mary Elana. Instead, he got the attention of another woman.

She flounced over, stopping with one hand on her hip. "Watcha' want, hon?"

"Some more ale; and what is there to eat tonight?" he asked politely, trying not to notice her fat jiggling.

"Stew and bread. Ya want any?"

"Yes, please. Thanks."

"Sure, hon." She smiled at him, revealing blackened and missing teeth while scooping his tankard up and flouncing off to get it refilled. She was back fast enough to have him wondering if Tom spit in his drink, though he'd watched the barkeep the entire time.

She set his mug down, leaning over so her top gaped open to give him a view of her watermelon-sized breasts with dish-sized areoles and cork-sized nipples. "Food ain't ready yet, hon. I'll bring it out when it is."

Colin thanked her. He paused in taking a sip, seeing Eron coming down the stairs with his full pack on his back, trying to avoid meeting anyone's eyes. Forced to go around a patron, he spotted Colin. Colin motioned him over, but his friend shook his head, moving on. He called out Eron's name while motioning more insistently, standing up to intercept. His friend finally came, scowling, clearly wishing he had left earlier. Colin sucked in a quick breath when he saw his friend's face: eyes ringed with fading rings of green and purple spreading down to his cheeks and jaw, scratches overlaying it all.

"With whom did you fight? Are you abandoning us?"

"Drop it."

"Why?"

"Colin, just leave it. I've had a long, painful day."

"You're not the only one and I'm not the one who's sneaking out.

Who did that?"

Eron refused to answer, looking toward the door. A wild-looking group pushed their way to the long table in front of the fireplace; they wore furs and leather, intricately braided long hair and beards, with only the lack of facial hair distinguishing women from men. He should've just grabbed his stuff and left out the back. Eron tried not to breathe deeply, his torso still aching from kicks, punches, and sword stabs. He noticed a heavily cloaked, hooded figure flitting from one pool of light to another before sitting at a recently vacated table in shadow. Eron could've sworn a brief flash or gleam came from under the hood. It reminded him of the eye shine of night animals' eyes, and he was unnerved enough to speak.

"What the hell? Who's got animal eyes?"

Colin snorted, taking another sip of brew as he looked at the newcomer. "I see someone trying to remain anonymous. Will you please just sit for one drink and wait for Mica before you leave? Or barring that, just tell me why now? I'm sorry you got the crap kicked out of you, but it's not like it hasn't happened to us before."

"What? I'm fucking tired of being a piñata for your brother. I know his time to find the little boy's running out, but I can't listen to him justify his mad quest anymore."

"I'm sorry you took a beating for him," Colin said. "Mica would at least wait and tell you straight if he was leaving his friends out to dry."

Eron scowled. "I've booked passage on a ship leaving with the tide. I can't wait and tell him in person." It came out defensive, as his eyes strayed to the shadows where the stranger sat.

Since he wasn't making a move to leave right away, Colin said, "I stumbled upon a massive burial pit in the middle of the woods."

"Really? I'm sure Mica will find a way to tie it to Nicky," he sniped dismissively as his eyes roved around the bar.

"This could be serious. It's about fifty feet around and looked pretty deep, judging from the pile of dirt around it. Plus, it's about half-full of corpses."

"This is a town, Colin. It requires a graveyard. So you stumbled upon it. Big deal."

"That's not what I said," Colin replied forcefully. "I said it's a pit. A mass burial. Not tidy little plots with wooden crosses or carved headstones. Even with a town this size, there still isn't enough to fill a hole that size. Most people seem to be in transit, being brought in to be sold and shipped out again."

"Why can't there be? Hell, the town and probably the farms use slaves. Who treats property gently? Work the slaves to death and dump them. I'm leaving, Colin. Tonight. Whether or not Mica gets his ass in here."

"My brother would look for you if you went missing," Colin chided him.

Eron gritted his teeth. "Mica isn't missing. Just really late. I'm sure he'll turn up. He probably heard another rumor about Nicky and went all delusional thinking it's fact and chasing after phantoms. Again."

Colin ignored his friend's sarcasm. "You're right. I may as well have a bite to eat." He signaled to Tom.

The man shoved the kitchen door open, bellowing for the girl. She scurried out, wiping her hands on an apron as the tavern keeper grabbed her roughly by her upper arm, berating her.

"Damn you! I told you to keep an eye out for the customers. You lazy cow! What the Little Lord sees in a disobedient slut like you, I'd like to know."

He gave her a shove in the direction of Eron and Colin, kicking her for good measure. Mary Elana staggered forward but managed to remain upright. She had angry tears in her eyes, and her face was red.

"What do you want?" she asked.

"We're sorry, lass, we didn't mean for you to get in trouble. Why do you put up with abuse? Why do you not leave and go somewhere else?" Colin inquired.

"Because women need their menfolks' permission, in this realm," she replied bitterly. "What do you care? If I am caught defying them, I will be punished. I have nowhere to go and no money. What do you want before you get me in more trouble?"

Colin sighed. "Food, since supper is ready."

She scurried back into the kitchen.

"Goodbye, Colin. I hope the search goes well. I bear you no ill will and only the best of luck." Eron backed up to leave.

"What if Nicky noticed him? Captured him?" Colin replied. "At least tell me which ship you'll be on so I can get word to you before it sails."

Eron hesitated. "It's his own damn fault if he did. I told him to let the little boy come to him."

"Fine, don't come and help me rescue my brother when he needs it. I want to know where to send the funeral notice," Colin snarled.

Eron gave a silent laugh. "Try my house. Oh, that's right, I don't have one. Why? Because I've spent the last ten years being dragged from one disease-infested hole to another. All courtesy of your asshole brother."

Mary Elana returned, thumped bowls down, and Colin fished out coin for the meal and more drinks and gently captured her wrist. She gasped, trying to pull back.

"Nay, listen a moment. I'm truly sorry you got in trouble. Take this; use it to help you get out of here and start a new life somewhere." He noticed his friend hefting his pack higher on his back while stepping away. "Eron, wait, come on."

"Let me go! I'll not take your coin and be in debt to you!"

She gave a wrenching sob at her father's bellow.

"Mary Elana! Don't dawdle! You know you're pledged for the Little Lord so don't try and be acting like the whores!"

"Please let me go!" she whispered fiercely, still tugging at his hand trapping her wrist. "I already told you, even if I had the money I have no way of escaping! They won't let me!"

Colin released her while tucking the coins away. Mary Elana turned, knocking into Eron in her haste to flee. Ignoring her father's shout, the girl avoided him and slipped into the kitchen. Eron angrily said, "Let it go, Colin. Can't you see you're making things worse?"

"You fancy, overdone excuse of a man had better listen up and listen good. No one interferes in me business, including me own git. So whatever vile plan you tries to trick her with won't do you no good. I'll see to it and so will the advisor and the sheriff."

The men had no opportunity to reply. Tom stomped behind the bar, pausing to have a few words with some men around it. They turned, glaring, clearly drafted into watching as the tavernkeep exited out a side door.

Eron swore. "I don't need this fucking bullshit on top of everything else. You're on your own with this one."

Colin glanced into the bowls before him. "You never used to be uncaring, Eron," he chastised his friend, getting an ugly laugh in return. Stringy vegetables and fatty chunks of meat in a watery broth comprised the stew. Colin tore a chunk off the burnt bread, slurping up some food.

"You have no idea of what I can really be," Eron quietly replied.

The men on watch set their tankards down. Colin saw Mary Elana back in the main room, conversing at length with the still-cloaked figure in the corner. It piqued his curiosity as she seemed to go out of her way to avoid talking overlong with the bar patrons. Eron was making his way to the door, but the group at the bar blocked his path. The entrance door slammed open, Jake stomping in, followed by a bunch of his men, the barkeep bringing up the rear.

"What the bloody hell?" Eron spat as he was shoved over to Colin's table.

"Youse don't take friendly warnings very well, I hear," the sheriff growled out.

A muttering came from his men in agreement.

"Oh?" Eron feigned surprise. "Sorry, I must have missed it amid all the other bullshit you've been spouting." Though antagonizing the man was foolish—he needed to leave, and Mica's quest depended on his cooperation—the recklessness bubbling in his veins all day wanted to break free.

The sheriff flipped stew into Colin's face, figuring the pansy would break first with intimidation. "There's a horse been stolen today. Mighty fine, mighty valuable animal. I've got his owner sayin' he saw a man soundin' like yer third friend ridin' off on his property. An' here we have only two of ya, and the bartender done telling me youse tryin' to steal his daughter away. Now what youse make of that?"

"What I think, Sheriff," Colin replied, calmly picking vegetables and meat off his sodden clothes, "is that you're trying to frame my brother and looking for any trumped-up charge to hassle us since we got here."

Jake's head whipped around as he snarled at Colin, face purpling in rage. Eron goggled. It wasn't like Mica's brother to bait someone.

"You're trying to set us up by kidnapping one and trying to extort money, or maybe kill and run the others out. I want to know what you think of that."

"Why youse—" Jake lunged for Colin.

His quarry shot backward as far as the men behind him would allow, drawing his sword.

The sheriff halted to prevent himself from being impaled. He signaled to his men, and they joined in. Eron tried fighting his way out of the mess, but he was quickly overpowered. With shouts and cheering, Jake's men dragged their victims into the night.

"Come on, men! We'll hang the fancy fops!" Coils of ropes looped the prisoners, letting the mob half-drag, half-kick their victims through the muck of the streets.

Under the cover of shouting and raucous laughter, Colin spat rancorously, "At least now you'll be free to leave once you climb out of the burial pit."

"Thanks for such a comforting thought. Here I was, thinking the unpleasantness of being hanged would be the worst. Now I also get to nap with corpses," Eron dryly shot back.

Colin grunted as a boot landed in his ribs. With a few more kicks, the friends lay panting on the ground as the sheriff held up a hand to bring the crowd to a halt. Booted feet obscured their view. The sheriff was giving a speech, bringing lots of laughs and calls for blood. Eron and Colin barely listened, frantically working to undo their bonds. But they were soon hauled up and more rope looped around their necks.

"I fucking hate you," Eron gasped before he was jerked up, choking.

"Aw, you've hurt my feelings, and I love you so much." Colin got the last word, right as he, too, was hefted up.

Chapter Four

I sat on my horse, surveying the town from beneath my hooded cloak, frowning. Ragged wooden huts interspersed with some of stone dominated one side of the riverbank, elaborate mansions on the other side. I realized some of the stone was really chunks of stacked concrete. Window sizes varied, reclaimed glass from an earlier world and time. The streets stank of offal, fish, horse droppings, and dead things offending my nose. The mud was riddled with refuse, homeless, corpses, and puddles. I didn't recognize one single building. It was as if everything I had ever known had been razed.

I turned the horse toward a tavern, according to the sign hanging from the side of the building. Judging from the outside, I would not like what would be found inside. I know, I know; appearances can be deceiving but believe me, after years of living, I knew. Okay, so being able to "hear" what went on inside also told me. The city had shrunk to a town not worth spit. It was a thief's paradise. River pirates, slave traders, murders for hire—and worse—called it their home. I considered it Elysium, but decent people, if any still existed, thought of it as hell.

At a nudge, my horse splashed into the two-story tavern's courtyard past a large group of men leaving. They dragged some women along. A young man uncoiled from a dirty patch of straw in front of the stable door, so begrimed and beaten that his actual age was indiscernible. He wore a metal collar; scanning his thoughts, my displeasure grew. Society had regressed; he was a slave. Windstorm threw his head up at the boy's approach, flicking his ears back. The stallion was temperamental, but before I could warn the boy, he was crooning to the horse, caressing the steed's velvety nose in admiration as I alighted.

Hrm . . . I needed a stable boy to care for the horse when I wasn't using him. "Keep him away from the mares, loosen his girth, but don't unsaddle him." He asked no questions, gathering the stallion's reins up as I pressed a coin into his free hand.

The boy looked up quickly in shock as I moved toward the tavern's door. *If only I knew you would be a kind mistress, I'd beg to be sold to you.* Light and sound spilled out the door. I should not have worried overmuch about concealing my identity; the flickering shadows hid much. Once inside, the foul stench of unwashed bodies, rotting food, spilled beer, and thick smoke assailed my nose. Ugh! One thing about industrialization was the lovely cleanliness of places. I've seen better pig sties! I took a moment to scan the room as I stepped through the doorway into a patch of shadow. Patrons stood at the bar or sat at a long table by the fireplace, with a few at scattered tables. Half-clothed slave women served food and drinks while being groped and pawed. Occasionally, high-pitched screams could be heard from rooms above, but no one seemed to pay the interruptions any mind. My nose wrinkling with disgust, I used my powers to influence four men into leaving their table near the door.

Other patrons are jealous of your winnings. If you don't leave, they will kill and rob you. The men gathered up their winnings, dispersing. Weighty stares from a group near the bar along with their loud and not-so-loud comments followed me as I sat upon a rickety chair. A pack of born fools, but even they could be dangerous in groups. Most of the patrons were filthy, and all bristled with weapons and bits of armor, including the few women who appeared to be warriors or mercenaries rather than prostitutes, whose skills afforded them respect from their cohorts.

Wish that person would remove the cloak. If it's a woman we could have ourselves some fun being as there's no other person with 'er. The idea came from one of the groups at the bar.

I seethed inside. So, we were back to "a real lady does not venture out after dark without her kinfolk in attendance, and not into a bar such as this," were we? We would see how long such things lasted now that I had awoken from my long sleep. I almost missed the low-voiced exclamation from another patron as I turned back toward the room. Drat! He noticed the strange gleam my eyes take under certain light levels. With luck, he'd consider it just a trick and forget about it. I was set to dismiss the man from my mind when I caught a scent—thin, hard to track amongst all the other smells in the room. I felt I should know it, though I couldn't understand why I found it unusual.

A young woman in her early teens, fully clothed, scurried over, causing crude remarks from both sexes.

"May I get you something, food or drink?" The painfully thin, trembling body. The haunted eyes, the fresh bruise on the cheek, the old ones decorating her exposed skin. *Please let this one be nice. Oh, please!*

"Yes, do you serve wine here?"

The girl's eyes widened in shock. *Oh, no! Pray the men do not find out you are like me.* "N-no. We-we have ale."

"Some ale, thank you."

"Would-would you like some-some food too?" she asked.

"No, thank you. The ale is enough."

The girl scurried off, soon back with a brimming tankard. I dropped some coins into her hand, and she slowly counted out change. *Do I dare to warn her if she doesn't know? But what if she does? No, it is not worth the beating if my father finds out.*

Hrm . . . interesting. I wondered if she would tell the truth. "Tell me child, is this place a tavern or a brothel?"

The girl hesitated. "It-it is whatever my-my father the bartender and the men here want it to be."

"What about what the owner wants?"

"My father is also owner."

"And what are those horrendous screams? Do you torture and murder people here?"

The girl finished counting out the change, wanting to ignore the question. I watched her take a breath before answering.

"No, my lady. Those are-are the rooms travelers use when they're not-not needed for new or disobedient female slaves. They are-are being broken in and taught their place before-before being put to work or sold again or-or . . ." She gulped, unable go on.

She placed the difference on the table, about to scurry off to answer the shouts of men for drink. Honesty deserves a reward. I pressed a coin into her hand.

The girl stared at it in shock. "Oh no, my lady! I can't accept it! It's too much!" *The last time I was given a tip, my father found it and took it and beat me for keeping it.*

"No, it is for you. Hide it well; make sure your father does not find it. Someday, you will need it to leave and start a better life somewhere.

Perhaps I may also be of assistance. I am Illyria." Giving my name was a gamble, but the girl's thoughts told me she wished to escape. With a quick mental nudge, she secreted the coin in her blouse.

What's that person want with her? The girl knows not to speak with the patrons. I caught the stray thought from one of the members of the group at the end of the bar. I didn't like the subtle nudging I was seeing between the men at the bar. "Thank you, child. That will be all for now," I was more curt than intended; confusion and hurt clouded her eyes for a moment before she scurried off.

I lifted the vessel to my lips as if to take a sip, continuing to view the group. I noticed a subtle relaxing of muscles, noted how most of them turned back to their drinks, but one of the men facing in my direction was talking to his companions, telling them what I was doing, I surmised. Now why would they take such an interest in the girl? Or maybe it was an interest in me since I had yet to remove my hood or cloak, though there were others similarly garbed. I tried to read their minds, but all I got was junk.

I sat, scanning the patrons, hoping for information I could use while pretending to drink ale.

"I knows he's cheating me. Come on, one more time and it'll be your last."

"Buncha slags in here. Can't he get any better-lookin' girls with his connections?"

"I just want outta here. I can't do this anymore!"

"No more, no more! Oh, God! I wish I was dead!"

I hit a blank spot. Two, in fact. I couldn't make out to whom the absence of thought belonged. Odd; another mystery. I surreptitiously poured half the ale out onto the damp, dirt-encrusted floor. I raised the mug again as if drinking.

A shout broke out near the center of the room. A man erupted from a table. "That's the last time you cheat me, you bastard!"

"I ain't got to cheat you of nothing! Sore loser, ain't my fault you can't play worth shit!" the accused yelled right back.

His accuser flung his ale in the cheater's face as the other two players began grabbing what coins and valuables off the table they were able. A second later, it was overturned by the cheat, scattering whatever was left over the floor as the two remaining men hurriedly backed up. The cheat charged his accuser, punches flying. Someone let out a whoop of joy, and one of the bar slaves screamed as men crashed into her, sending her tray of drinks flying to soak the men at another table.

I watched the brawl encompass the back half of the room. Even though the men had weapons, they used mainly fists. The nearest turned in their seats to egg the combatants on. Bets flew fast and thick as to who would win. Other tables nearer me ignored the commotion while carrying on with their drinking, gambling, and whoring. I surmised the behavior was the usual fare for the spot. I poured the remainder of the ale out on the other side of the table, raising the mug in the air, wiggling it as I had just seen another patron do. I got a different bar slave. She appeared to be about twenty, with stringy, greasy brown hair, on the hefty side, with the ubiquitous iron collar around her neck.

"Ya wanna 'nother one, hon'?" she asked.

I merely nodded, shooting the mug over to her, turning to watch the proceedings. I noted the dirty look from my peripheral vision along with the puff of air as she flounced off to the bar. The fight raged on, chairs being used as clubs on some of the men, others shoving heads into the tables and any other available hard surface. I glanced over at the bartender. He seemed unconcerned about the damage being done to his tavern, calling out only, "No weapons or out ya all go!"

The bar slave came back over, her top falling farther down. She leaned over, trying to see into the hood, giving me a look at her charms, along with a whiff of sweat, stale sex, and body odor so strong she must only bathe once a year if that.

"Here ya go, hon'. Ya want anything else?" she asked in what was supposed to be a sultry tone.

I shook my head, put down coin for the drink, gave her one as a tip. She propped a hand on her ample hip after collecting the coins. "Ya don't say much, do ya? That's okay, hon'. Ya don't have ta say anything, and I can take real good care of ya if ya want." *Ya gots ta say something, so's I can tell if'n you a man or another whore what don't belong here.* Her thoughts let me know if I did speak, she would rat me out in a heartbeat. I wanted to stay longer, unmolested. I held a hand up, palm out, then flicked my fingers in a "shoo" gesture. Her face went from tempting to peeved, her pout into a grimace.

"Asshole," she spat at me, flouncing off to serve a different customer, boards creaking under her heavy footfalls. *Probably dickless too.*

I watched her repeat the "bend over, top fall off" action on the next table, screaming with laughter as the man spilled her onto his lap and grabbed her breasts. *What is wrong with that person? That's some grade "A" ass they just passed up.*

Ah, charming: the group by the bar. I turned to the ending brawl. Two winners, staggering from blows, faces swelling, rapidly turning black and blue. Not the original starters of the fracas. Other patrons scuttled away from bodies, no doubt already having picked the pockets, or cut the money pouches. I saw men whose dress reminded me of Vikings walking over from the long table. They grabbed legs, dragging the fallen out, trailing through pools of blood. I could tell two of the six were dead. One was already missing his boots, another his fur-trimmed cloak. I had a feeling what weapons the men had left on them would soon be lifted.

A few slaves brought straw and spread it over the blood. Other men righted the remaining furniture. What couldn't be saved was tossed in the fireplace, making it flare brighter. Those who made bets finished collecting them or paying as everyone settled back into what they had been doing before the diversion.

Note to self: if I was forced to fight anyone, make it short and sweet. I casually gazed around. No one was paying attention to me. I poured the ale on the still-damp floor.

I held the mug up, wiggling it, keeping an eye out for who came over. I wanted the young girl from earlier. It took a few moments for the bartender to notice. I caught his mental signature, used my power to subtly suggest he send his daughter over. He bellowed for her, shoving her my way cruelly. I noticed how she ricocheted off a corner of the bar, tears spurting. She came over walking stiffly.

She slowly picked up my waiting mug, sniffing, trying to keep the tears of pain from spilling while sucking in a breath before quivering, "Would you like anything besides another drink?"

"No, thank you. Just the ale, please," I replied with a low voice.

She nodded, making her slow, painful way to the bar. A few at the bar shifted positions, but I noticed the quick scans they gave me. The man facing me glanced my way frequently. They could be protecting her from the patrons since she was the bartender's daughter and didn't wear a slave collar.

The coins waiting weren't an exact amount. She had to make change. Once again she protested at the tip, and once again I insisted she take it.

"Keep it, child. Someday I may be able to offer you work."

The girl drew in a breath as if deciding something, and took a gamble.

"Please, my lady, if-if I might not seem too rude. I-I'm not look-looking to-to be a-a . . ." She trailed off. I could imagine what she was thinking before she continued, "It would not do for the men here to find out you are a woman. They-they assume a female without a-a male companion in a bar at this hour is-is selling her services. They-they have no respect for us."

"I . . . see. It's kind of you to warn me. I agree, a woman who sells her charms would not last long in a town such as this. A poor father indeed who lets his daughter be abused, and who abuses her himself in turn. I am not talking about work in a whorehouse, child, but work in a respectable establishment, perhaps as a live-in housemaid. You appear to need . . . protection . . . from the men here."

My ploy was working: the nodding in my direction became more pronounced. I wondered what they would do, and how long before they took action.

The girl blushed. *Oh, sweet Goddess, if only it were possible.* Whatever response she was going to make was lost in an irritated bellow.

"Mary Elana! You lazy wench, get over here!"

Oh, dear God! "I . . . I'm sorry; forgive me, I must go now." She turned, and I reached out, gently catching her wrist.

She gasped. "No, no. Let me go! You don't know what the men'll do." She tugged frantically.

I let her go as her father bellowed. She flinched, scurrying to the bar, fighting off the hands, leers, and suggestive remarks of the patrons.

Her father intercepted, grabbing her arms, shaking the girl, berating her, before letting go to serve an obnoxious group. He spoke with them briefly, several of the men turning to stare at me. I waited for someone to come over and discover I was female. I really wasn't in the mood to kick ass. I shouldn't have pushed matters with the girl. I felt off-kilter. It was alarming how I had spent my first week awake in an unnatural haze, as if not in control of my own thoughts or body. I had never experienced such a thing after waking from a long sleep.

I watched a quick, heated argument among the group. After a few more moments, one of the men detached himself, starting over. His clothing and person were clean, undamaged. Their skin and clothes were dirty, showing signs of hard wear. Without a word, the man sat himself across from me at an angle, so his back wasn't fully to the room. His attractive face was thin, with dark brows and eyes, high cheekbones, a hawk's nose. His thick, dark hair, short cut with a sweep of bangs. His age, middle forties.

He tried peering into the depths of the hood hiding my face. "Hail King Maceanas and Lord Nicky, may they live forever. Might I have the privilege of knowing who you are, stranger, and buying you a drink?"

Interesting information he dropped. I dipped my head in acknowledgement, remaining silent, as the man's eyebrows briefly raised at my lack of response. Most towns did not include a noble's name in their greeting. Was it a way of identifying members of a secret sect? I raised a black, leather-gloved hand to signal to a slave girl, otherwise remaining quiet. I wasn't sure if I could trust him not to alert everyone in the bar of my gender.

"Perhaps you are newly arrived to our town, and not one of the king's vassals." He tried a different tack as a slave came to the table. He gave his drink order without looking at her. I shook my head in the negative, laying coin down on the table.

The slave snatched it up, running off.

Honestly, does no one believe in introducing themselves anymore or asking if it's all right to intrude upon a person's space? I pretended to take a sip of my ale. His frustration rose at my perceived rudeness. I wondered if it would occur to him I might be mute.

His eyes narrowed as the bar slave came back with a new mug. "To the king," he toasted. We raised mugs in salute.

He leaned his forearm on the table, trying to discern my face. "What is your name, stranger? I wonder why you persist in remaining silent, when the girl told us you can speak."

I knew she had said nothing of the sort. I had been able to make out every word she told her father, even with all the noise. I would have to say something, the gesture I knew to call him a liar a rude one.

I tilted my head to the side, jerked my still-covered chin in the direction the girl had gone, then brought a finger up in the shhhh gesture to draw it across the level of my neck. He gave a quick glance back at the men, who were all avidly watching us, though puzzled.

"I do not have time for gestures, or games," he spat. I shrugged my shoulders and did the gesture again.

The frown grew into a scowl. This was turning out to be fun. How long would it take him to either come up with the correct guess or get pissed off and flat-out try to hit me?

"I am only going to ask once more. What is your name, and what did you want with the girl? We observed how you detained her; no one will put up with it. Answer, or I shall let my men convince you of the need to speak."

And yet, I thought, *they would put up with the obvious signs of her abuse.* I dropped the act, the next few minutes letting me know if I could remain unmolested or if I would have to fight my way out.

"Who do I have the privilege of addressing?" I politely inquired.

The man leaned forward, his left fist smacking down, eyes and lips tightening in repressed anger, "As one of the king's enforcers, I demand you identify yourself as either vassal or stranger. An insolent woman alone, playing games, is not in a position to ask questions."

I cocked an eyebrow, smirking. "You have no identifiers to support your claim, nor are you in uniform. Why should I take you at your word that you are whom you profess to be? Furthermore, the men you have been making merry with do not appear to be clothed in anything resembling a king's livery or to comport themselves as a member of the active guard. If you are, therefore, off duty, I find your method presumptuous, and the excessive zeal for your work a trifle frightening. In either case, I think it remains in my best interest to ask you to provide proof of your claims. Barring that, kindly leave as I am not bothering anyone nor breaking any laws I am aware of. Enjoy your drink, and good night to you, sir." A flush infused his face, heightening anger pouring off him in waves. It's not my habit to tell nebshits or bullies what they needed.

He leaned forward to speak, interrupted by the slave flouncing back, leaning so he had a view of her breasts, and placing a fresh tankard down. The man curtly demanded, "Leave us!"

She gave a sniff. She didn't push the issue. She must be used to his manners as she left.

"Insolent woman! I could have you dragged out of here and whipped for your impertinence toward a king's guard!" I could tell from his mental signature he was aggrieved over something, at the end of his tether.

"Tell me, sir, what laws am I breaking? I could understand your opinion if I were a male intent on some dastardly deed. We have established I am neither, thus I must ask you to leave. I merely want to quaff my ale in peace."

To my amusement, he unconsciously squirmed a bit, hearing from my manner of speech I was not an uneducated slave. *She could still be a fancy whore plying her trade, thinking to ignore the king's laws, or an outsider. Or mayhap a daughter of the nobility, out on a lark, who is too scared to admit she is in over her head?*

I wondered why it did not occur to him I could be a warrior woman. His face grew concerned, forcing a tone of levity. "I see we have gotten off on the wrong foot. I am Saizar, one of the sheriff's men, as is the group I am with. If perhaps you are a noble's daughter out for a bit of fun, this is not the place for you, as I'm sure you have already seen. The men here are rough; should they discover you are female, they will not believe or care of your high birth. In fact, they will consider it a great bonus. You will be ruined and disgraced. Now, what noble house may I escort you to?" What would he do if I wasn't either whore or lady and a visitor? My rage rose at the implication that if I wasn't a highborn virgin, I deserved whatever vile fate the men visited upon me.

"Saizar, you said? Why, precisely, have you come to converse with me without knowing my gender or identity? I have noticed others entering the bar similarly cloaked, yet you make no move to question them. Is it because I choose not to remove my garment? Is there a law against keeping one's cloak on? Or maybe each new person subsequently coming in is known? Certainly it is within my rights to ask the reason why you feel the need to interrogate me and not the others?" What little he'd said had already provided me with information about the nature of the town. I pretended to take another sip of my ale as I watched him from beneath my hood. I could hear him grinding his teeth in vexation. *If she is highborn, everyone who touches her can be put to death. Damn!*

He forced his fists to relax on the table, leaning closer, hissing at me in menace. "It is my sworn duty to identify everyone in this town not a vassal of the king. I will only say, do not look to me or my men to protect you should your gender become known, since you refuse to cooperate. If you are a visitor, you are required by law to present yourself at the palace tomorrow and register your intents with the Royal Immigrations Office, if you haven't already done so. I will be informing them of your presence in town soon. If you are found to be breaking His Majesty's laws, it will be my responsibility to see you are duly punished for your transgressions. Enjoy your visit."

As he made to stand, I smelled the elusive scent again. Before I could sense where it was coming from, an influx of men covered it up. It would be wiser to let him go, but I couldn't help the laugh of derision slipping out. "Without the answers you seek? I can well imagine that conversation: 'Sire, some unknown woman was in the tavern last night. But I know not her name, nor her appearance, nor should she be a loyal vassal or visitor,'" I mocked.

He paused, one hand on the back of his seat, the other around his mug, face flushing red in rage. "I am sure the king will thank you for the tidbits you do drop." A tension-filled silence hung in the air between us.

Saizar swung back, trying to grab the wrist of the hand with which I was holding my mug. I let go of the mug, catching his between mine at a pressure point. "I would advise against it. I am not some weak maid you can bully." I pressed a tick harder.

I wondered why he would attempt such a move if he thought I was highborn. His thoughts told me such a move could get him punished if reported. It was a risky gamble; he must have been under high stress. I had a feeling he was not usually incautious.

His eyes popped wider with unexpected pain, his free hand clenching tighter around his sword hilt. He hesitated an instant. "You dare to assault a member of the king's guard? Shall I have my men drag you out?"

"Self-preservation. Shall I demonstrate just how painful this little point can be? Or will you leave quietly without any other ill-advised moves?" I replied calmly, watching as he gave another look around the room.

His back blocked his men from seeing what went on between us. The torch near us burned down, hardly throwing any light off.

I used more pressure. He began to crumple. "Bitch. Whore!" he squeezed out as his free hand left his sword handle, grabbing the back of the chair. "Yes, I promise."

"Very well, Sir Guard. Good night to you."

He snatched his hand back, inspecting it, rubbing the place I pinched. He stood, staring at me in puzzlement, "That move—," he began.

"I said good night, Sir Guard. Do not make me have to tell you again." My tone implied there were more moves where the first came from.

He gave a half-bow. "I would like to apologize, deeply, for my hasty actions. I beg another chance to make your acquaintance."

His men yelled out to him, he half-turned, telling them not to interrupt.

"I doubt we have much left to say to one another," I responded.

"Please." He gestured. I decided to see where a second round would take us. "I must have something to tell my men, the bartender, and His Majesty."

"You are the king's enforcer, you say? I thought a while ago you professed to be with the sheriff. Which is it?" As long as he was here, he would answer questions for me if I could cajole them out.

His jaw worked briefly, a quick flash of surprise in his eyes, not expecting me to pick up on the subtleties. "I guard where I am needed."

A smart enough answer, saying nothing and everything. "A multi-talented man, to be in the elite king's guard along with the sheriff's . . ." I almost said "trash" but changed it. My pause said it all for me, however. ". . . men. You must be familiar with everyone who lives here?"

He paused, thinking of how to reply. "Yes. There is not a townsperson I do not know."

"You must have a phenomenal memory." A bit of flattery never hurt; he inclined his head stiffly. "I shall remember, should I ever need your help. You may tell the bartender your warnings have been delivered. As to the king, I am just a lone woman passing through, not worth his time." I inclined my covered head regally before signaling for a barmaid to bring me another mug of ale.

He sneered. "You would do better leaving instead of sitting here drinking. Go home, before you are assaulted or sold for a slave."

"I thank you for your warning, Sir Guard. I shall take my chances."

He scowled, looking toward a distraction at the door. The bitter, angry look on Saizar's face changed to one of vicious satisfaction. I turned to see a beefy man with the sheriff's group yank another man, trying to leave, over to a table. A confrontation in progress immediately quieted the entire bar in anticipation of a second match. I found out the muscleman was the sheriff. That delightful temperament must be a requirement to joining. I found the byplay between the lawman and the accused illuminating. Bar patrons cheered the announcement of an imminent hanging. So that was what passed for entertainment around here. How quaint. A mad rush for the door ensued for those who did not want to miss the fun. I watched them go, feeling the air around me displace, Saizar leaning close.

"See what happens to lawbreakers? See what fate awaits you if you try to play a man's game and lose?" The satisfaction in his voice would have given anyone else fright. I barely managed to keep from rolling my eyes.

"I saw no laws being broken, only a man trying to leave. Do you always harass and torment those drinking here? It is a wonder the place does any business at all."

"We discover our criminals where we can," he replied.

"More like you make your criminals where and when you can, regardless of actual laws. Should you not be assisting the sheriff with such heinous men? Seems a frightful dereliction of your duties." The amusement was clear in my voice. His scowl grew.

Very few patrons remained. I watched the bartender pick up the dropped packs of the accused, passing them to his wife. She rifled them for whatever could be taken, while he mounted the stairs, I presumed, to loot the room which the man had rented from him. This was an unexpected bit of good luck. Casually I stood, taking mug in hand, walking toward the bar. Behind me, I heard Saizar snort in disgust before he slammed out the door.

Chapter Five

"The man is a menace! Standing outside for hours spewing his filth, scaring away what customers I have."

"Peter tried to hire men to shut him up, but the bastard advisor the priest saved sent his men to bring them back in pieces. Peter's wife still ain't right, I heard, after she opened the sack they came in."

"Disgusting is what it is, to let them women do those things while we wait here."

"Lucky fuck!" There was some crude laughter.

Aranthus stifled another jaw-cracking yawn as the harem attempted to play instruments and dance for the king's entertainment. He wished it was a night the king had chosen to attend or host a party. The chamberlain, at thirty-five, felt ennui settle in. It was his twelfth year of being His Majesty's chamberlain and slave. He could see the nights of sameness unfolding before him. *I almost want a revolt to happen. Or new gossip. Anything has to be better than this.*

The fat king dozed on his throne while the heavily carved doors opened to admit a guard leading someone in. Damn it, not another supplicant come to beg for favors. *For once I'd like to get to bed before the cock crows.*

As the two got closer, Aranthus could see the second person was a woman. Even he, who had seen many beautiful females pass through His Majesty's chambers, was stunned at the vision she presented despite her unconventional clothing. Tight pants, loose shirt, corset and knee-high boots, all in deepest black. She had two sheathed swords at her waist, of which the guard should have relieved her. Her skin seemed to have an icy sheen to it, making her green-and-honey-brown eyes appear on fire. Her wide, generous lips invited a man to kiss; rich dark brown hair was set in a high braided ponytail.

Instead of directing the woman to wait with the others, the guard brought her up the length of the hall. Their boots rang on the stone floor. Aranthus hurried down to meet them as the other supplicants began complaining in loud voices.

"Why's the bitch get to go ahead?"

"I've been here all damn night waiting to speak with the king!"

"Hell, if I let the king fuck me, can I speak with him too?"

"Chamberlain, the Duchess Illyria Sasha Nicolette Caladonea Maison du Corbeau wishes to speak with His Majesty."

At the whisper of her name, she turned from examining the entertainment, piercing Aranthus with a look. *A goddess enters the room. Bow before such power and glory or cease to exist.* His wits were befuddled by the sight of her. "She does?" was all he could think to say. "But I have never heard of her before." A thread of doubt in his tone.

The guard replied, ill at ease, "She says her ancestors were once from a country nearby. She is the last of her line and wished to return to a country close to the land of her birth."

The chamberlain replied peevishly, "Why does she not have anyone with her? And how dare a woman dressed as a mercenary claim to be a noble!"

"I—um, it is best if I let her explain."

Aranthus turned a petulant face to the woman, demanding, "Well, why are you dressed like . . . like . . ." He gestured with distaste to the outfit.

I gave a sweet, slightly naughty smile, saying in a voice velvety smooth, "Forgive the intrusion, Lord Chamberlain. I lost all my retainers but one guard to the bandits, trying to come here. He is grievously wounded; if he dies, I shall have no one. It was believed if I disguised myself, I would have a better chance of living to reach a town. I am hoping your Majesty will hear my case and grant me some help, no matter how limited it may be."

"Well . . ." Aranthus dithered.

The last thing the king needed at this hour was problems. His Majesty had woken in a bad mood. It had taken Aranthus most of the night to see the man provided with all he had demanded before his good mood returned. Then again, she was very beautiful, despite her clothes, and Maceanas enjoyed such women. On the other hand, the king had just stripped a noble of title and lands and was displeased with the titled nobles who remained.

"I would not interrupt His Majesty so late if I did not think the situation warranted it." I tried my hardest to look apologetic. "But I was," I hesitated deliberately, "informed I had to present myself to the king. I was led to believe it wasn't an option."

Aranthus blinked. I glided forward past the guard a bit, smiling. "I felt in light of my other problems, Chamberlain, my introduction couldn't wait. Please, what would it hurt? We would all enjoy my visit more than what is happening now." I quirked a perfectly arched brow in a knowing manner.

He felt everything move low down inside him as he blinked in befuddlement. The appeal reminded him of his earlier thoughts, making him forget his irritation at the interruption. He felt himself smiling back. "Who told you?"

I arranged my face into lines of distress. "One of the sheriff's men, as I was trying to find help for my guard. Please, I beg of you, will you ask His Majesty if he could spare me a moment of his valuable time?" I added a heartfelt expression along with gold coins, watching the emotions chase across his face.

"If you will wait where you are. I make no guarantees."

"Thank you, Chamberlain." I inclined my head graciously, turning the heat of my gaze onto the sleeping body of the king as Aranthus went to wake him. This was the tricky part: slipping quickly into the last remnants of his dream.

* * *

Garlands draped from building to building above the crowded street. Some were weeping with black armbands, but others jubilant. The king wondered what was going on. He couldn't understand why he was standing with the commoners. He should be at the palace. No sooner than he thought it, King Maecenas found himself in the throne room. All his nobles, with their wives and children—dressed in fine black silk, velvet and brocade mourning clothing—along with the palace slaves, ringed a coffin on a wooden bier. The throne was empty. Aranthus stood next to it, weeping. In front of the seat was Lord Nicky wearing the king's crown.

"Damn bastard! How did he get my crown? He knows he's not supposed to be up there. What's going on?" He pushed forward, meaning to shout out but found no one could hear him. King Maecenas looked toward the coffin, staggering back in shock. "That's me! What am I doing in there? I can't be dead!"

Nicky spoke, "Ding Dong, the king is dead! I am king! Long live the king! All hail King Nicky!"

"All hail King Nicky!" the mourners echoed cheerfully as they began to dance to music filling the hall.

"Noooooo!" King Maecenas screamed in horror, but he was ignored. Frantically he pushed through the dancers to get to Aranthus. He would tell Maecenas what happened. But his chamberlain chatted cheerfully with Nicky, now the king, on matters of state.

"How fortunate you discovered those men when you did, Majesty. Imagine what would have happened to the town if the late king had let them live," Aranthus was saying.

"I never thought my childhood friend could stab me in the back," King Nicky was replying.

"I never did anything! I've protected you since you were a boy! How was I to know those merchants were assassins in disguise?" the king cried to his tormentors, who ignored him. In a rage, he turned to look out the window. Below in the courtyard, three men hung, eyes and tongues bulging out.

The corpses spoke. "You should have given him over to us."

"You would be king still if you hadn't told the boy about us."

The king gave a scream of horror, stumbling back from the window, turning back to the two men at the throne. He tried unsuccessfully to get their attention.

"He can't hear you; none of them can," a cheerful feminine voice spoke by his ear.

Maecenas turned to see an unfamiliar, slim, beautiful woman smiling at him. She wore a tailored black silk gown. The front appeared to be on fire and a bird periodically rose from the flames.

"You see me, hear me! I'm not dead!"

She smiled. "Oh, but you most certainly are! Look at your nation," she invited.

Maecenas turned to see they were now on a balcony. Where the town had once stood, huge pits filled with corpses. Broken hulks of ships poked up from the water of the river port. One or two grimy figures rummaged amongst the ruins of the buildings. "What? No! Where did it go? Bring it back!"

"I'm afraid that's impossible. It's been this way for years and years." The cheerful tone had not abated one whit. "This is King Nicky's work. He didn't care for the town the way you did."

King Maecenas whirled on her in rage. "How do you know such things?"

She only smiled. "Open your eyes and look around you. Get rid of Nicky; see how things could be."

The king turned and saw his town. It was a marvel of stone buildings and streets interspersed with parks and greenery. Many ships lined the docks, with more moored in the river, waiting their turn. People in rich, bright clothing thronged the wide thoroughfares. Beyond the town, neat farms with patchwork fields stretched as far as the eye could see.

"I want to see myself," the young man commanded.

He was sitting at the foot of his council table. At its head appeared the lady in her black dress with the flaming bird. She was addressing his nobles, giving orders and they listened, obeying her.

"What? I am king! How dare you give orders to my nobles?" the man objected.

She turned to face him. The nobles mimicked her. "You would rather be dead? It can be arranged. Listen to me, take my advice and implement my plans. I will make this the greatest nation ever known."

His nobles spoke. "We are imitated the world over. Other kings and queens send their scholars here to learn."

"We are feared for the strength of our army."

"We control the most trade routes; the wealth of the nation overflows."

"I won't be a puppet!" the king yelled.

The room melted, the woman and the young man stood on a hill overlooking the darkened town. "You are one now, Majesty."

"No, I'm not! Begone, foul temptress!"

The woman merely cocked an eyebrow. "No?" Her gaze held pity and contempt.

The king stared at her. He didn't like the look she gave him, and he had a feeling she was right. Dark clouds raced overhead; a bright, silvery moon shone down, illuminating a patch of grass where Nicky and his slave appeared. The two danced around his throne, alternately sitting on it and shouting out orders. He screamed and rushed at them, trying to pull them off, but his hands passed right through men and throne.

The woman was standing behind the throne. She bent over until her crossed arms rested on the back of the chair and she laid her head atop them, giving a sad smile as the two figures continued to cavort. "Wouldn't you like to be free of them, Majesty?" she whispered.

Maecenas found himself nodding, even as he whined, "It's impossible. Not even the merchant men who want him will get him. His slave protects him."

"All things are possible if you know who to ask and how. Trust me, look for me, listen to me and the kingdom will grow and prosper into a nation. Glory, Majesty—it can be yours."

The room and everything in it was fading out. "No woman can make those promises!" the king protested.

"I am not other women. Take a chance and be great; ignore me and fall by the wayside." Her words echoed in the darkness, changing to the sound of the king's chamberlain calling him.

* * *

The king awoke with a snort, gazing around blearily. Aranthus had never had this much trouble waking His Majesty before. "Sire. Sire, there is a woman here to see you."

"You woke me." It was a flat statement with the beginnings of anger.

Aranthus hurried to placate the king. "Yes, Sire, there is a woman claiming to be a duchess who says she was attacked during her travels to our country."

The young man looked petulantly at his chamberlain as he fully awoke. "I will have this interloper thrown in the dungeons. You know I see supplicants when I want to, not on their whim. Fool!"

He looked to see who had the stupidity or obtuseness to disrupt his night. His breath caught in his throat. His eyes bugged out of their sockets. It was the woman he'd just dreamed about, only more exquisite, but what was she wearing?

* * *

Aranthus still babbled out apologies, but the king waved a hand irritably to shut the man up. The king beckoned his guard to bring me closer. They parted as one man led me up the steps almost to the top. His harem and officials began to notice how the king couldn't keep his eyes from me. I could feel the waves of resentment and jealousy flowing from them. It could've been because of how I looked; I had a sense His Majesty tried to sleep with every woman who crossed his path. Behind us, the waiting supplicants grew more strident, making the guards come to nervous attention.

"Your name? I know you not," he demanded.

I didn't curtsy, nor did I bow—a shocking lack of disrespect the king failed to notice but the court whispered about—as I repeated my name. The dip into his dreams had been edifying, along with two other pieces of information which, if true, could be useful. How to bring the subject up, though?

"Duchess? I have no duke," the king flatly stated, looking toward the back of the hall long enough to scream, "Shut them up or I'll have you all tossed in the dungeon!"

Aranthus cleared his throat nervously. "I believe, Your Majesty, she claims she was attacked while traveling here."

The anger on the young man's face grew. "Who told you to come in this manner and dressed that way? How dare you call yourself a duchess and make such wild claims? I'll have you tossed in—"

"In the dungeon," I sassed back, smirk crossing my face as the king's eyes popped wide. "My most humble apologies, but your sheriff accosted me not long after my arrival."

The king bristled, demanding, "You have not answered my questions!"

I bowed my head in acknowledgment of his rebuke. "Perhaps it would be best if I started my tale from the beginning?" I didn't give him a chance to reply, continuing, "I am the last living descendent of the Maison du Corbeau, who once held vast lands and wealth in the ancient city of Illthanthia. I do not know why they left, only that they did. I have wandered, living in many a land. Now I hope to settle into a permanent home. I do not know where my family's original country lies, but I have heard tales of your kingdom which intrigued me. I traveled here to see if it would be a place I would like to become a citizen of. Unfortunately, bandits attacked my escorts and me; almost everything I own was stolen. My people, except for one, were slaughtered; even now he lays dying from wounds received trying to save me."

He looked at me in disgust: how dare I come to him with petty problems? I could see Aranthus smirking. The lack of concern he showed for those entering his kingdom put joy in my heart.

"Why should I? And why should I believe your story?"

"I would be forever in your debt. I do not expect you to believe without evidence. I can show your guards the place I left my dying man. One of the sheriff's men told me you always want to know about such attacks."

"You should have left the matter with him; he would have told me himself," His Majesty snapped back.

"And chance his not telling you at all? No. I am sorry you do not seem to care what harm comes to your guests and travelers," I fired back.

The king's face turned purple as those within earshot gasped, falling silent, waiting for the answer. "You . . . how dare you! There is nothing wrong with my kingdom! Insolent! Aranthus! Escort her back out, and make sure we know where to find her."

Aranthus bowed, turning to me. In a deliberate insult, I turned my back to the king as I strode down the stairs. The slave clattered down after me to lead me back out.

"I do not advise angering His Majesty," he puffed as I exited the main doors, the waiting people hurling insults after us.

"I can only use my frustrations and sorrow for a poor excuse. I have lost all who are loyal to me just coming here, and I may yet lose the last of my faithful guards. Tell me, Lord Chamberlain, to whom should I turn? Who should I trust?" I spat out bitterly. He bought it.

"Well, I...I do not know, Your—" He stopped from calling me by my honorific, putting a hand out to stop my forward progress.

We halted at a cross-intersection of halls. He put a finger under his lip in thought. "I shall try my best to see His Majesty does not forget your situation. I must ask where you are staying, you understand. It has been commanded of me."

I made myself look down as if trying to control my anger before turning back to him, "I have not found a place. We are camped out in the open like a pair of beggars. If you know of an inn with an open room, I would be most grateful to hear of it."

He was shocked. "But, Your Grace! Do you mean to say you lost all your coin?"

"Coin is all I have. He could not make it any farther, so we are just outside of town. Please, Lord Chamberlain, do you know of a place with rooms to let?" I put a hand on his arm, giving a pleading look.

He rubbed the top of his staff. "It would not do for you to live outdoors. His Majesty must know you will not depart. Only, it's...forgive me, but most of the decent inns we have are spoken for by people coming for our Harvest Festival. There is one, but you may not wish to stay there if you have lost most of your wealth..." He delicately trailed off, also probing at the same time.

"Lord Chamberlain, at this point I would be most grateful for anything allowing me to sleep and consider my future." I played my part well.

"In that case, may I suggest the Silver Thorn? It is small, but should be adequate until you hear more. I shall even send a royal page with you so the proprietor will know you are not some commoner or, or, uncouth warrior." He dabbed delicately at his mouth and nose with a scented cloth, turning to snag a passing slave, barking orders which had the boy running off.

Aranthus turned back to me as footsteps, and hushed voices, came from a cross-hallway. I smelled the same elusive scent from the tavern, along with rotten eggs.

"What? There's nothing there, is there?" A man began to mutter something as I felt a subtle shift in the air.

All my instincts screamed it would be bad if he finished what he was muttering. Aranthus gasped in panic, trying to drag me back toward the throne room. I shook him off as I eavesdropped.

"No, nothing is there. If there was, I would tell you." The second voice deep, almost guttural, sent a frisson of panic down my spine for some reason, but his companion stopped whatever he had been saying.

His sneering tone traveled clearly to us. "Would you? I know you want freedom. I wouldn't put it past you to forget to tell me, hoping to be rid of me. Maybe I should remind you who is Master here."

For a moment, the air grew thick with menace, the kind only a supernatural being could produce. I didn't recognize the signature, so there was no way of knowing if and how dangerous he would be to me.

"You forget yourself, little boy, and what you are dealing with." The voice became deeper, clotted with things unmentionable. "One day your pride will be your downfall, and you will regret mistreating me."

The first voice answered with contempt, "Then why are you stopped here if it's nothing?"

"I felt a disturbance somewhere in your kingdom."

His kingdom? Had I not just meet the king? "What? Where? Who? Tell me!"

"I do not know yet. I shall tell you everything when I do."

"You'd better. I fed you well tonight."

"I needed it: being trapped on this plane without the proper sacrifice I am useless to you."

The voices got louder, while beside me, the chamberlain gulped, hissing frantically, "Quickly, bow! Keep your head down and don't move or make a sound. It is Lord Nicky and his slave. You don't want to meet him or let on we have overheard."

I did as he said, as I could hear his heart pounding in fear. I peeked up from beneath my long, thick lashes as the men came into view, abruptly stopping their conversation as they caught sight of us. I saw a young man of perhaps nineteen or twenty. He had short red-blond hair, about five foot ten. I tried to read his mind but could not. I knew instinctively I could never break through without his knowing it. It disturbed me; I could not recall ever having met a person whose mind I couldn't read. It made me think there might be only one other way, and I wasn't sure going that route would be warranted. His companion was covered head to toe in an enveloping black cloak with a deep hood. I straightened from my half-bow.

"Aranthus," the young man sneered, "why are you lurking in the hallway instead of attending the king?"

The other found me to be the more interesting. I got the impression he knew exactly what I was. It was a first for me; he didn't smell like kin. My instincts ratcheted up to fight mode. I forced myself to stay as I was, trying to use my power to figure out what he was. I felt amusement from the cloaked and hooded man as he easily rebuffed my attempt.

"Oh, but I am, Lord Nicky! I was asked to escort this woman out, as she displeased him."

Cruel gray eyes swung my way, slowly traveling down my body and back up in a manner meant to be insulting. "I must say, you are better looking than most of the whores trying to win the king's favor, even looking as you do."

"Please do not presume I am one," I replied.

Aranthus sucked in a breath as Nicky's face turned red. "How dare you speak to me thus! Do you not know who I am?" He took a menacing step forward.

"I see a young man who is making an ass of himself with his assumptions."

A nasty laugh issued from under the hood, and the chamberlain moaned in fear, hurrying to defuse the situation. "Your lordship, this is . . ." he hesitated, "Her Grace, The Duchess Illyria Caladonea Maison du Corbeau."

The young man stared at me speechless as the hooded figure made a strange humming noise. He turned to glare at the slave before turning back to me. I could see him fighting his rage down as he snarled, "You have proof of this?"

"My state of disrepair is not enough?" I asked insolently.

"You had better pray you speak the truth, or it will be my great pleasure to see you punished for your crime of lying." Lord Nicky glanced at the chamberlain. "You can get her out of my sight now."

"A pleasure speaking with you," I needled him.

Lord Nicky gave me a last glare, continuing down the hall with his hooded companion.

Aranthus let out a shaky breath, "I fear it was very unwise of you to confront him in that manner. He will not forget."

"Good, I am at least assured someone at court will be taking my claims seriously."

He startled at my words. "Your Grace, Lord Nicky and his slave are not to be disturbed lightly. The man has a terrible temper and can be worse than the king in punishing those who displease him." He shivered in fear, dropping his voice. "I've heard he sometimes lets his slave help."

"And what did he do to gain his title?"

"Lord Nicky is also the royal advisor to His Majesty," Aranthus explained as a page approached us. I had a feeling another visit to The Bloody Knuckles was in order, my instincts telling me it had a key role in this drama. I smiled gently at the chamberlain in reassurance. "Thank you, Aranthus, for being so helpful to one newly arrived. I shall not forget your generosity."

He glowed in pride, giving the page his orders before taking his leave of me. We strode out to where Domiano waited with Windstorm. The relief on the boy's face was plain as the stallion stomped, trumpeting and lashing out whenever anyone got too close. I saw the page pale with fright.

"Your Grace, I was not going to be able to hold him much longer."

I leaped into the saddle. "Vance will show us to an inn called the Silver Thorn. Step lively. My mount does not like to stand still long."

The boy bowed, taking the lead. Domiano gave me one long look before following on foot. It took less time than I thought. The inn sat at the bottom of the long, winding road leading up to the palace, before one crossed the bridge back into the town proper. The small stone building with stables only had ten rooms. One remained open, and even with the king's request I remain nearby, the proprietor was unwilling to bump another guest so I would have a better room.

"Pardon me, Your Grace, but from where do you hail? I do not recognize your accent," Nathan, the innkeeper, inquired as we climbed stairs.

"I travel much. My ancestors are from the old kingdom of Illthanthia, a name which will no doubt mean nothing to you as it no longer exists. Its exact location is lost although rumored to be near here. I was traveling, hoping to discover if those rumors were true and what, if anything, might remain when I was set upon by bandits."

"I am surprised you do not have a larger retinue with you."

"Unfortunately, the bandits infesting these hills killed them. I barely escaped with my groom and one guard who lies grievously wounded in the care of the healers."

He shook his head sadly. "No doubt you lost all your possessions, as well. I hope you did not lose your coin."

"What I am in dire need of is more servants to replace those I lost. Have you any suggestions?"

He wrinkled his brow in thought. "Surely you do not mean to stay here? I must advise you, His Majesty does not think highly of poor, expatriate nobles from any country showing up and wanting to settle here; his advisor, even less."

"So I have been given to understand. I do not know how long I will need to stay, or if I wish to. It depends on how fast I can replace what was lost and send for more funds."

We arrived at a small room, tucked under the eaves, as Nathan bowed nervously. "I know it is not large nor grand enough for a duchess, but it is all I have."

"Then I shall have to be content with it. I do not know how long I shall need the room," I warned him.

He never flinched at my words. "Of course, Your Grace. As long as you wish, it is yours." *Damn Aranthus! I better receive payment from the royal treasury for hosting her.*

"I keep odd hours, so I expect your staff to stay out of here. I will let you know when it can be cleaned. Furthermore, I have need of a guide who knows the town and all in it. I will pay well for the privilege of their knowledge as I will expect them to wait upon me, no matter the time of day or night."

He bowed. "Of course, Your Grace, I can find you such a person, but it won't be until tomorrow, I fear. Will that be acceptable?"

"Yes, it will." I paused then said, "My horse. He is not to be touched by any but my groom, Domiano. He is a temperamental beast, liking to kick and bite those unfamiliar to him. Also, Domiano will need a place to rest, and meals." I reached into the bag dangling from my waist, drawing out some gold coins.

Nathan's eyes widened at the sight. I placed a stack in his hand. "I trust this will be enough to cover my expenses for a while?"

He stared goggle-eyed at the wealth, then to me, his hand clenching over the coins, his manner now obsequious. "Your Grace, your every wish is my command. All will be as you say. I will have the guide here tomorrow. Your groom may stay over the stables, and eat with my wife and me. Thank you, thank you, Your Grace." He bowed low, backing out of the room, still babbling as I shut the door.

Chapter Six

The sun was painfully bright to Mica's eyes when he woke up. A loud groan escaped as he tried to move. His head felt as if his brain had been bathed in acid. Suddenly he had to throw up, and rolled over just in time. Bile came up, the pressure and pain leaving. What was wrong with him? As an immortal, he shouldn't have woken with aches. What the hell had happened last night? Mica shuddered, trying to remember, but couldn't. That lapse, that vacancy, scared and panicked him. He had to get back to town and warn his brother! But of what? Mica cast around for his sword, and found it lying a short distance away. He snatched it up and hacked through the vegetation to where he had left the horse, hoping the animal was still there. It wasn't. Whatever had happened last night must have been significant enough for the animal to sense, even at a distance.

Mica started the long walk back to the Bloody Knuckles. He staggered into the stable yard hours later, thirsty, hungry and bone-tired. Mica spotted his brother in the mud by the refuse pit. He yelled to him, not bothering with the incongruity. Mica staggered again, nearly falling, as Colin ran up, grabbed an arm, leading him to the tavern's side door. They banged through, ignoring the few patrons gaping at them. Colin was trying to tug him over to an empty table. He let himself be pushed into a chair as Colin called for wine and food.

"What happened? You're white as a ghost!" his brother exclaimed.

Mica stared at him uncomprehendingly, blinking. *Didn't they realize what danger they were all in?*

"Its face! My god! Its face, it . . . it . . ." He trailed off, staring around in puzzlement. Where had it come from? He only remembered seeing one face, hadn't he? But what was the lingering feeling of masks? *"You will not remember me. You never saw me."*

Colin wore a worried mien; this was the first time he had seen Mica in shock for over a dozen years. Mary Elana hesitantly approached their table with another tankard, cautiously slid it in front of Mica, then leapt out of his reach as she snatched up coin for the ale and scurried away.

"Here, have some ale first and then tell me what happened," Colin coaxed.

Mica just stared at him. "Are you insane?!" His voice came out in a screech. "It's not the time to be sitting around drinking, man! There-there's a horrible thing loose! An abomination to all mankind!" *Or was there? Why couldn't he remember?*

"Calm down and drink first! You've got the whole bar staring at us, and we're not very popular here," Colin commanded.

Mica snatched the tankard up, draining its contents in one gulp.

Colin signaled for Mary Elana as his brother hunched forward, trying to whisper.

"I saw them! I saw their foulness last night!" Mica paused, passing a hand over his brow, shuddering as another memory wanted to break free but couldn't. "I think it was . . . strange. Taller, before growing shorter," he muttered. "And something else . . ."

Mica waited until Mary Elana had taken the empty tankard to refill it before continuing.

"I was looking in town; a man told me." He furrowed his brow in concentration, trying to bring the now-hazy memories into clarity. "I heard his name mentioned and decided to follow him, around dusk I think it was. I . . . I borrowed someone's horse and followed him out of town. I don't know where I was; there . . . there was a clearing."

Mica jumped as Mary Elana placed the tankard and food in front of him. Quick as lightening, his hand snaked out, wrapping around her wrist, forcing her to bend over him.

"Get out of here now! It's not safe for a young girl like you! Do it if you value your life!"

His voice rose on the last words as Mary Elana whimpered, fighting to get free. Colin gently pried his brother's fingers free, smiling apologetically at the girl as he pressed some coins into her hand for her trouble.

"Sorry, he's had a bit of a shock. He didn't mean to grab you.'"

She flung the coins in his face, scurrying off behind the bar where her father intercepted her, demanding to know what was going on. Colin saw and grimaced. That's all they needed to cap off their day: another confrontation with the man. He hurriedly scooped up the flung coins before turning his efforts to calming Mica.

"Eyes. Red eyes. He—it—she—had red eyes. Why can't I remember? I know there was something there. I know it!" His fists pounded rhythmically on the side of his head.

"Mica? What eyes? Who has red eyes? Bloodshot? Whose name did you hear? Nicky's?"

Mica continued to stare, bug-eyed. "Don't they understand the danger they're in? Don't they care?"

"I don't think they do, frankly. How can they care when I don't even know what you are trying to say?"

Mica picked up the full tankard in a trembling hand, gulping down half the contents before setting it back. He took several deep breaths, trying to calm himself.

"Good, keep breathing deeply. Now start at the very beginning. What did you find in town?" Colin prompted him, slowly taking his brother through the events. Mica began shaking with the effort.

"In the forest somewhere is a clearing with pens and a-a double altar. I followed a man there, you understand, from his house on the nobles' street."

Little by little, the story came out. Mica slumped back in his chair, sweating, dazed, shock starting to leave his system. He ran a shaky hand through his hair, making it stick up in spikes, before taking another deep breath and looking at the face of his brother. Colin seemed to be struggling to absorb everything he had been told.

"I know it seems strange, but I know I saw something else! It protects them all! I . . . I think . . ." Mica trailed off in miserable puzzlement.

The two sat for a while in silence, mulling things over. Looking up from his reverie, Colin signaled to the bartender. He had to shove Mary Elana over to their table. She stood a good five feet away from their table, looking ready to flee at any unwanted movements.

"Please, another round. Thank you." Colin pressed the coins she'd flung down a moment ago back into her hand. "Please, take this as a token of our gratitude for putting up with us."

Mary Elana tried to give them back, "No, I . . . I can't. It wouldn't do any good; my father would only take it."

"Can you not hide it?"

She shook her head in the negative. "Thank you, anyway."

The sandy-haired man sighed; at least he had tried.

He turned to his brother as Mica registered someone was missing, "Where's Eron? He didn't run into those abominations too, did he?"

Colin looked at him wordlessly. How to explain? "No, he . . . he came back to the tavern . . ." He hesitated again, not sure how to phrase it kindly.

The pause made Mica instantly suspicious. In a terrible tone, he demanded, "Where is he?"

"He . . . he left. He came and got his stuff and . . ."

Red crept into Mica's face. "He what?"

"Eron thinks you're obsessed and going to get killed."

"Damn him! The ungrateful bastard!" Mica yelled, ignoring the looks the bar patrons gave him. He started on a low-voiced rant against the man until Colin interrupted.

"Brother, please. After what happened last night, I don't blame him."

It was too much for Mica. "So what? You're taking his side too? You're going to leave next?"

"No, bro, I'm not. But the sheriff has it out for us. We need to wrap our quest up quickly. We were almost hanged last night. Most of what we had on us was taken."

Now Mica looked even sicker. "You couldn't get anything back? Not even your swords?'"

"We got those back, and whatever was on us at the time,'' Colin said. "When we got here, Tom had our packs. A lot of stuff was already gone, which he claimed the patrons took before he intervened. I know he probably only grabbed them to steal our stuff himself."

Mica glared over at the bartender who pretended not to notice. "Our money? We have a brooch left—"

Colin cut him off. "No. Most of it is gone. Listen, brother: the brooch is the only thing we have to live on. We don't have enough coin. What I have in my pocket will only cover our food and room for tonight. We have to quit; otherwise we'll have to beg someone to hire us and start working."

"No! No!" Mica shouted, everyone in the bar looking again.

Colin tried to placate him, but his brother slapped his hands on the table top. "We'll camp in the woods, trap our food, take passage on a ship as sailors after our mission is complete. It'll be fine."

Colin rubbed his hands across his face, unsure how to say what he wanted. "Bro, I don't want to be a naysayer, but I'm beginning to think Eron is right. We've run into a lot of trouble since we got here. I think it will be for the better if we take his advice."

The grinding of Mica's teeth was audible. "You do side with that traitor!"

"Don't. We both know you haven't much time left. The brooch doesn't give us enough for food, lodgings, or horses. As things stand right now, we'll be lucky to get the soul gem back before your time is up, and The Guardian takes your life instead of Nicky's. Plus, Eron took his quarter of the trading rights. We can't in good conscience make a deal with anyone under these circumstances."

Mica would not be deterred. "No matter. We can make something up to replace his quarter. We'll be gone before they know."

A sinking feeling overcame Colin at his brother's uncharacteristic willingness to deliberately deceive, but he tried to put a brave face on it. "No." When Mica began to interrupt, he continued, "I'm trying to look out for you the way you do for me. We still have no solid leads on where Nicky is, or even if he is here."

"Yes, we do! I told you, the man I followed was involved in black arts, like the little boy so long ago."

His brother interrupted him right back. "It was a one-time bullshit deal! Face facts, Mica, everything depends on accuracy now more than ever. Did you hear him speak of the boy specifically? Did you see the boy at the ritual?"

"Yes!" Mica cried out triumphantly. "The man said, 'What's the boy thinking?'"

Colin paused, shaking his head; he had a feeling his brother was cracking under the strain. "Mica—"

"What?" The belligerent tone accompanied clenched fists.

"Our situation is perilous. The sheriff hates us. How are we going to ask him for information now? Eron said, before he left, that he was attacked earlier in the day by some of the lawmen. They were looking for us. He said they mentioned us specifically. Why would they do that unless somehow the little boy knows we're here? This is turning into— no, is—a total disaster."

"No, it's not!" Mica shouted, banging his fists on the table, causing it to wobble.

Colin could see the owner glaring at them as Mica continued to rant, his voice getting louder. "How the hell would the kid learn we're here so fast? Huh? What about what I saw? How do you explain it? We can't let those people get away with murder."

Colin sucked in air with a gulp of ale. He had forgotten how irritating Mica could be at times. "We don't have enough factual proof of who everyone involved is. It would take more time to find out than we have, and resources. If—no, I said if," he held a hand up as Mica opened his mouth to object, "we find out who they are while looking for Nicky, then we'll go to the king. Not before. You know how dangerous it is to make accusations without evidence to back it up."

Mica's face turned beet red and murderous. "Fuck you! A lack of support isn't like you at all! I have less than a month left to get rid of him!"

Colin sighed; he was beginning to feel tired of assuaging his brother's ego. "What the hell am I not supporting? Did you just hear what I said about Eron and me and the sheriff? Either the man we talked to at the palace or the scribe must have let leak for whom we're searching. Even murder by a cult doesn't supersede our problems. I'm not going to lie. After what happened last night, I'm tired too. We need to leave, take the soul gem back, let the little boy come to us. I don't want to abandon you, but after last night I can't take more."

He waited for the explosion he knew was coming. His brother didn't disappoint. Colin made a wiping motion with his hands; in one of the few times in his life, he stood up, leaving his brother at the table, and went upstairs to retrieve their stuff. Mica, for his part, stomped out of the bar. Once out in the chilly, windy day, he stopped to look up at the gray sky. He knew, as the one who had taken the soul gem, he faced death, and that sooner than he wanted. He prayed to whatever God might still exist that a miracle be delivered the companions to help defeat Nicky before The Guardian came.

As Mica fumed, he thought he saw Mary Elana crossing the yard out of the corner of his eye. A thought floated at the edges of his consciousness—something was necessary, something was part of a conversation—but he couldn't remember what either was. Mica wondered what she was up to. He had gotten the impression her father didn't let her out of his sight if he could help it. He found out a few moments later when the stable master finally stopped glaring at him and went back into the stables. Movement at the corner of his eye made him turn his head. The girl was standing there with a ragged, tattered shawl covering her head, holding a bucket full of water.

"Yes?"

Mary Elana blushed heavily, lowering her eyes, blurting out in a soft voice, "I . . . I wanted to apologize for the way I behaved toward you and your friends. I'm . . . I'm not used to men treating me kindly or-or wanting to help without expecting anything in return.'"

Mica nodded, saying in a friendly tone, "Don't worry about it. I'm sorry for grabbing you earlier and scaring you."'

She bit her lip, shifting uneasily, giving Mica the impression she wanted to ask something more of him but was too embarrassed to speak. He went on jovially, "You won't have to worry about my brother or me. We're leaving the tavern today so we won't be around much."

Mica could see she was shocked, although she tried to hide it. "Is-is it because of what . . . what the sheriff did to you-your friends yesterday?"

"Hm? Oh, no. Listen, Mary Elana." His fingers groped in his money belt, which was depressingly light, drawing out a few silver coins. "I know it isn't much, but I want you to have it as thanks for everything." Before she could protest, he rushed on, "I know you said your father would take any money from you but surely you can find a place to hide it? You shouldn't have to live a life being constantly abused and overworked."

Mica pressed the coins into Mary Elana's hand, closing her fingers over them tightly. "If you'll permit me to share some wisdom I've learned over the years?" At her hesitant nod, he continued, "Don't give up hope of getting out of here. There's more to this world, to this town even, than your father's tavern. The opportunity to change things for ourselves comes in many forms. It's not always obvious, or may frighten at first. If you ever get a chance to leave, take it. Don't ever hesitate to make things better for yourself. You have to look after yourself; no one else will. Believe me, it's something I've learned from experience."

Mary Elana looked down, taking a ragged breath. "Thank you," she whispered, peeping up at him through her lashes. "Please, may I . . . I?"

"Go on, ask your questions, I'll answer to the best of my ability," Mica encouraged her.

"How," she paused to wet her lips, "how do you know it's a chance for the better? That . . . that the people who offer it are good? That . . . that they don't mean you harm?"

He blew a breath out. "There's a saying: if it seems too good to be true, it probably is. What I mean is: if someone gives you something for free, or with little to no work, somewhere along the line there's a catch. It may not show right away; it may take years, or come at a bad time. If it's worth having, usually you have to work to get it. Tell me, in all your time at the tavern, have you not met men or women who made you think: there's something about them which seems off, or wrong?"

"I . . . I think so," Mary Elana said.

"Good. Sometimes it's hard to spot the bad from the good. Learn what you can from the experience and try and move on."

He hoped he wasn't confusing her. "Don't worry, we'll still be in the area and will probably be stopping at the tavern from time to time until we finish our business here. So if you ever need anything, just let one of us know, okay?"

Mary Elana nodded, glancing around her quickly; she was still safe from view. "Thank you. I . . . I . . ."

Mica shook his head, smiling. "No thanks needed." He paused to make sure they were not being observed. "Go hide those coins well and scoot. We don't want your father catching you and taking it from you.'"

Mary Elana blushed again and shyly agreed. She made her way across the stable yard again to disappear behind the tavern. Mica sighed to himself; he wished he could have done more for her but he didn't know what. There was no way for him or his brother to see she got somewhere else safe, not if they wanted to make sure their quest ended here.

After another twenty minutes or so, Colin came out with a disgusted look on his face.

"The ill-mannered lout was trying to make us pay again for our food and at least another two days' rent for the room! What, did he think we wouldn't remember what he charged us the first night?" Colin was highly indignant and Mica knew it took a lot to upset him.

"Well, at least we won't have to worry about it anymore." He reached out, taking his half of the load from Colin.

"So, any spot in particular for the forest or shall we just start walking?" Colin wanted to know.

Mica squinting up at the sun. "No, we've been going about everything all wrong. We must speak with the sheriff. We'll have to do whatever we can to get information from him, and check that he's not lying to us."

Colin raised his brows. "Are you forgetting he hates us? He tried to have Eron and me hanged. We were only saved because a contingent of palace guards came by and saw what was going on. Luckily, they hate the sheriff and put a stop to his fun."

Mica was shaking his head. "I can't believe I didn't think of it before. How stupid of me!" He clenched a hand, continuing, "I don't know what the hell is wrong. Ever since we got here, I've been unable to think straight. I'm in some sort of fog where all I can do is react to my emotions, and they're all horribly exaggerated!"

His brother tried to console him. "We've all been feeling it. It's because we're tired and worn out with looking. I know you don't have much time left. We should take the day off. Recuperate and get back at it bright and early."

"No. No," Mica replied hoarsely. "I see what we need to do now. Let's get it done and go from there." He started out of the stable yard after getting directions to the sheriff's headquarters.

* * *

The men spent a bit of time in the narrow, winding streets before stumbling across the building, a ramshackle wooden affair constructed of loosely joined boards intended for a scrap pile. Cautiously, the two men pushed the door open, blinking as their eyes adjusted to the gloom. They saw a shallow front room with a desk and chair, plain wooden benches, a second door, and torches. The floor was packed dirt. A cord, hanging by the desk, disappeared into the ceiling. With the door to the street closed, the room had a claustrophobic feel to it. Mica tugged the rope, hearing a bell ring behind the wall. The wait was long before the inner door cracked open, and a face peered out.

"What do you want?" the man demanded.

"We've come to make inquiries about a thief."

"Yeah, so?"

"This is the sheriff's office, is it not? We were informed by Aranthus that your office handles all complaints not related to the nobility. May we ask you some questions on the subject?" Mica used his politest tone. "We are merchants."

"All right, all right!" The man slammed the opening shut.

Colin and Mica looked at each other as the door opened and a different man stepped out with a slave. The slave sat at the desk, arranging a wet clay tablet and stylus. "Now, state your full name and what you do."

Mica breathed a small sigh. He complied, as did Colin. "Now, who do you think stole your money, and where and when did the theft take place?"

"It's a bit difficult, sir. The thief we tracked to your town, and lost him. The actual theft happened over a year ago."

"What are you wasting my time for? We do not handle thefts which haven't occurred in our town!" the man stated, turning to go.

Mica hurried to placate him. "I assure you sir, it is not a waste of time. The boy is a menace, and we believe if you would let us explain, you too would understand why it is important he is found. Please." Mica rested one hand on his coin wallet, tapping it.

The man of law stared at them a moment, his eyes straying to the coin bag, sneering faintly. "I have greater concerns besides a petty thief."

"We can contribute to the time it will take to hear our case and respond to it." Mica gave the man a few silver coins.

The man before him took the offering with a sour grimace. "Very well. Why should I be concerned with a boy thief?" He adopted a bored expression.

"The boy follows a pattern: a wealthy merchant takes him on, in a work capacity or sometimes as an apprentice. When he has gained the merchant's complete trust, he, along with his accomplice, robs him of everything he can. We came across two nobles in other towns, duped by this boy. My associate and I believe the boy may have already fleeced some merchants here. He may have wormed his way into the nobles' circle. Unfortunately, we cannot be sure, and we do not want to go to the king without proof."

"And you want me to do what for you?" the man asked.

"We are trying to discover if any merchants have made formal complaints about a boy stealing from them. It would be significant amounts. The boy uses disguises, so he would appear different to each person except for his height and age. He is twelve, about yea high, gray eyes. He may pretend he's an orphan who's lost his parents to brigands while traveling. Sometimes, he gets kindhearted people to take him in and introduce him to those he plans on robbing."

"You don't say?" While the tone was faintly sarcastic, they could tell the man was interested despite himself. He studied the toe of his boots before saying, "Frank here'd have to look at the records for any mention."

"Any time you can spare would be most appreciated. We are willing to make another donation if any information is found to help us," Mica replied.

"Just what're you planning on doing if we do know about the boy?" the man demanded. "If he has broken the law, you do not get to decide his fate."

"I was informed by His Majesty's chamberlain we may bring the boy and our case before the king to have a judgment made. Of course, it would be with the cooperation of your office," Mica replied. "We hope that by finding him, we can recover any of our property remaining in his possession, or at least find out where and to whom it was sold."

"Can't go arresting someone on your own," the lawman replied, "and unless you have a list and description of what was stolen, I can't turn anything which might be found on such persons over to you."

"Of course, which is why we would be grateful for your help." Mica tapped the coin wallet again.

The lawman folded his arms across his chest, saying,

"The sheriff needs to clear your request first. I'll present your case to him. If he agrees there is time to look, it'll take a week before I have any information for you. Do the person and his accomplice have names they like to use?"

"Well, when he was with us, he told us his name was Michael Nicholas. I think he may like to use either a variation of it, or sometimes part of his name. We never did learn the name of his accomplice," Mica replied, noting the man's small, and quickly hidden, start.

"Come back in a week and ask for me, Saizar, specifically and no one else. I will try to have some information for you."

"You're most generous, sir. If I may request one other piece of information? Who in this town might take in orphans? We could inquire of them while we wait," Mica asked.

"The wandering priest, John, does. He has a small following, meets in an old cottage down by the free workers' quarters."

"Thank you," Mica replied.

As soon as they were out the door, Colin spoke, "I bet there are other slaves who'd probably help us find the boy for a price. We should try . . ."

"No, trying to gain a slave's trust would take too long. If we have a chance, fine, but I'm not pursuing it." Mica hurried as much as the streets would allow. "Did you notice Saizar start a little at the name?"

"No," Colin said. "You think he knows more than he's letting on?"

"I'd bet on it. Let's only hope the boy hasn't run off again."

"Well," Mica's brother said, "it is a common name. In the interest of fairness, it's possible there is another person with a similar name, and he thinks we mixed them up. We don't know if the kid is still here."

The brothers continued to walk as the afternoon slowly slipped away. While the mud had dried enough that they didn't have to fight for each step, it had also encased the garbage. The closer they got to the quarter, the more crowded the center became. The two men stopped at an outdoor food stall, buying heavily spiced sausages wrapped in bread, and also asked for directions. The cottage to which the food sellers directed them was halfway down a swiftly narrowing street. It was in need of whitewashing, and the priest had tacked a crude cross on the door. There was a shuttered window to one side of the door, and above it, two more.

"Perhaps you should make the inquiries," Mica offered once they had finished their simple meal, washing it down with some ale.

Colin shrugged, knocking on the door, which met with no response. He pounded again, waited again, then tried pushing on the door. It swung open. The only illumination in the murky interior came from chinks in the ill-fitting wood and an as yet unseen source of weak sunlight, nearly hidden by a rickety wall.

"Better leave the door open a crack." Mica cautiously nudged it open, propping it thus with a nearby rock. The watery light barely penetrated the gloom, but it was enough for them to see that the floor, hard-packed dirt, bore a broom's brush marks, and the table likewise had been rudely swabbed. The two men let their eyes adjust before cautiously moving farther into the space. Mica stumbled over a crude table, and he held an arm out to stop his brother.

"Hold on; this is ridiculous," Mica growled, fumbling in another pouch. He brought out flint, steel and the stub of a candle he had taken from the Bloody Knuckles. Colin held the stub. After a few tries, Mica got it lit. Mica held the candle aloft to better examine the wall against which the table was pushed. It didn't appear to be original to the cottage, but rather placed to divide what space there was. The brothers placed a hand against it for guidance, as only a small portion at a time was illuminated by the candle flame, following it to the far side, which was only a few paces away.

"Hello?" Colin called out to no response. Mica held a piece of long unbleached muslin away from the opening it concealed. "Hello? Father John? We wish to speak with you." There was no answer. Leading with the candle, Mica passed through.

"Humble indeed," Colin spoke in a hush. "Hard to believe the little boy would stay here even for a day."

"Mmmm," Mica said.

They stood in a space clearly intended to be a cooking area. A fireplace dominated the outside wall, crudely made with whatever bricks and stone could be scavenged. An open door filled in the rest of the wall.

Mica went over, looking out. "Manages to have a chicken coop, a well, and a small garden. He's not as poor as everyone makes him out to be."

He pulled his head back in, prowling about the room. The firebox filled with cold ashes. A covered bucket holding water, a tight corkscrew of stairs leading up near the interior opening. Against the separation, a straw pallet neatly made up with a threadbare blanket. On a peg above hung a crude brown cassock made of wool. The last wall had shelves nailed to it, holding two each of crudely carved wooden bowls, trenchers, and cups. On a second shelf were a wheel of moldy cheese, stale bread, and sausage reeking of garlic. Below sat three covered buckets. A bit of prying revealed grain, possibly for the hens, some potatoes and dried apples.

"Should we try the stairs?" Colin asked uneasily. It was clear no one was in the humble dwelling.

Mica looked around. "I think we've invaded their privacy enough. They should have heard us by now and made their presence known. Unless they think we're up to no good?" He approached the stairs, calling into the darkness above, "Hello? Father John? We mean you no harm. We are merchant men wishing to ask you some questions. The sheriff's men directed us to you."

He waited for an answer which never came. "I suppose we should go before anyone reports us."

The brothers walked back out to the front. Mica noticed a locked wooden crate under the table. It piqued his curiosity, being finer made than anything they had seen. The lock was simple, but he wasn't about to pick something belonging to a man of God. Behind and to one side of the table was a reed basket. Mica peeked in, saw something woven. He took it out and unrolled it. It was a thin square reed mat, just big enough for a person to sit or kneel on. He put it back, noting the basket held several of them. Colin was already at the front door. He followed his brother after extinguishing the candle and storing it back in his pouch. His brother was talking to an old woman leaning out the window of the cottage across the street. Mica joined them.

She was suspicious. "You better not 'ave messed with the good father's house. I be telling him about the likes of you two fancy men snooping around." Her voice was cracked, wavering with age.

"We are not here to cause the father problems, ma'am." At the title, the old lady cackled. Colin courteously replied. "We were hoping to find

Father John inside. Do you know where he has gone?"

"Why should I tell you?" came the querulous reply.

"Forgive me ma'am," Colin soothed, "we heard Father John helps orphans. We were once thus ourselves. We thought to see the good work he does and make a donation in remembrance of one who helped us in our time of need."

"Hah!" she challenged. "Liars! Now get before I send for the law." Her still-piercing eyes swept them both, no doubt to remember what they looked like.

Colin reached into his pouch, drawing out one of their precious coins. He held it out to her. "For you, if you will please tell the priest, when next you see him, that two parchment merchants wish to speak with him. We shall stop back in a few days to visit again."

The crone reached out a hand with twisted fingers and large knuckles to snatch the offering. She bit into the coin with her few remaining teeth, decided it was real. "Come back in three days, in the morning." She withdrew into the cottage, slamming the shutters closed.

Colin motioned to Mica. They returned the way they arrived, almost positive they were being spied on by other hidden residents. As soon as they turned the street corner, Colin said, "Three days!"

Mica turned to check they were not being followed; so far he saw nothing. "We should make inquiries of the prosperous merchants." He cast a glance up at the sky, the sun sinking down slowly.

"And what if they complain to the sheriff? It's sheer luck the man we spoke with either didn't recognize us, or hadn't heard of our problems with his boss." They turned another corner, leaving the poorer part of the quarter.

"What do you suggest, Colin?" Mica demanded. "We need to get back on track."

"We need to increase our store of funds if we're going to keep bribing people. Soon we'll be looking for a job, like Eron." It was the wrong thing to say.

"Damn traitor! He can go rot! I needed him! It'll take days to question all the merchants with just the two of us," Mica raged.

Colin sighed to himself, suggesting, "Okay. Fine, we'll start questioning. Besides, we still need to find a spot to camp, and it's getting dark. You've been having nightmares ever since you stumbled upon the clearing, which I take is in the woods. I know you'll consider it a waste of time, but we should try and find it. Some event happened at the grove to disturb you. Looking at it in daylight would put those fears to rest."

Mica scoffed, remaining uneasy, furtively looking around to make sure they were not being followed. He didn't understand why he should have terrifying dreams. Every enemy he had fought and bested, he lost to them again and again throughout the hours he slept. Sometimes they killed him immediately, but mostly they made him suffer, and each had red glowing eyes, spoke in guttural tones. His brother was still talking, and with an effort he tried to listen, catching the last sentence.

"I know you think it make-believe nonsense. Nicky does like to pretend he's an occult leader, showing his acolytes the true meaning of depravity. What if he's back to his old games and using the grove?"

Mica scowled. "It's bullshit! Playing at evil."

"Yes, but remember the Hellfire Club, The Skull and Bones and, oh, every other gathering of like-minded people? It could be another version of it," Colin cajoled.

Mica snorted. "It's a waste of time, forget it, I'll think of something else. Let's just head out of town and find a spot to camp in before we do anything."

Chapter Seven

The bell clanged over the door as my guide, Bre, escorted me inside. I breathed an internal sigh of relief as I stepped out of the direct sun. I had covered myself in the enveloping black cloak from the tavern so I could move about and not burn, though the weak light left me enervated. Our ride here had given me glimpses of what the everyday people wore, but not what a person calling herself a duchess would. There was another group in the shop as we entered. Domiano had his hands full with my stallion, who did not like standing about when he could be running free.

"These are the best tailors in the town, according to the nobles," the woman was saying as I took my time to look around. "It's just . . . they . . . . well, the whole town is not always welcoming of foreigners, so . . ." She trailed off.

The floor was varnished wood, polished to a high shine. Light came in from the two generous front windows, across from which were three doors and a platform. There were various groupings of chairs and sofas scattered about sitting on fine rugs, side tables between them. Two fireplaces flanked either end of the shop, and above our heads hung two brass- and glass-ornamented chandeliers holding a wealth of lit candles.

"I understand," I replied, moving farther inside so we were not blocking the doorway.

The front room was already in use by an older woman with her family, attendant slaves and guards. Bre saw my glance, explaining, low-voiced, "Countess Elizabeth, her children, Lady Caroline and family, Lady Sally, Viscount Martin."

They stared at me in a mixture of insolence and fascination as my companion murmured in my ear, "She is a cold one. Right proper too, but she is the most powerful of the noble ladies."

I stared back just as insolently, Bre hurriedly dipping a curtsey to the family while murmuring a greeting.

Immortalibus Bella

I pretended to look over the shop as I assessed the ladies' clothes from the corner of my eye. There was no way I could cover myself head to foot in something bringing to mind shapeless sacks. I had no illusions as to whether, once I took off my cloak, I would shock and dismay all present.

A man with a slave came up to us. "Good day to you ladies. I'm sorry someone was not able to greet you properly the moment you arrived. Please accept my apologies, as we are not accepting new accounts." There was no hesitation even though his thoughts gave him away. *The girl knows better, we do not serve commoners.*

"Your pardon, Master Tailor. Yours was the first shop I thought of when Her Grace, Duchess Maison du Corbeau, engaged my services as guide."

The man kept the surprise off his face while asking, "Duchess? I did not know we had one."

I replied with my cover story, adding, "I am not sure if I am going to settle here, but I will need more than the outfit I have on. His Majesty so far has been most gracious in his welcoming of me." It wasn't technically the truth, but they didn't really need to know.

"His . . . Majesty . . . and bandits, did you say? Stole most of your goods?" The man was at a loss for words, glancing toward the woman helping the countess, all of whom had stopped to stare at us when he came over. "I—an honor, Your Grace." His bow was deep and deferential. "If you will allow me to help you?"

He showed us to a set of chairs off to the side, out of the sun, sending the slave for refreshments while motioning for his wife. *She could be an excellent liar, but Master Nathan is not often taken in by false titles, or gives permission for his daughter to provide guide service to those he considers suspect. This bears further investigation.*

As we were settling in, the woman who had been waiting on the countess excused herself to come over at the signal. The man hurriedly explained matters. The noble ladies had expressions of displeasure.

"A thousand pardons, Your Grace. My husband and I own this establishment. It has been too long since we had a duchess, even one on a visit."

I smiled to show I was not offended. "No doubt it will not be the first nor the last time until I am known. Have you a name?"

She gave a deep curtsey. "Your Grace, I am Emilee. How may I serve you?"

I let my cloak fall open, and she gasped at my outfit. "Oh, my!" slipped out before she could pretend what I wore was typical for a noblewoman, or any non-slave/warrior woman in this town.

"As you can see, I am in desperate need of a complete wardrobe and all its accoutrements. Most of my possessions fell to the depredations of bandits. I shall also require an outfit or two for wearing immediately, as what I have on is all the clothes I managed to escape with." I drew my hand down my body, making sure the bag on my waist clinked. I continued on as if I hadn't seen the proprietor's eyes light with greed. "I shall also require the services of a jeweler."

I opened the large leather bag, drawing a smaller leather sack out before plucking out a large emerald and holding it up. "Have you anything to go with this?" I asked, ignoring further gasps at the sight of the gem.

"Of course, Your Grace! At once, Your Grace!" Emilee turned, clapping her hands and shouting orders to bring more slaves out.

Beside me, Bre had trouble holding her mirth in as she leaned toward me, murmuring, "I don't think those two have ever been so shocked before. I can see why the king would want to see your misfortune in coming here does not taint your image of us, if what is in your pouch is but a fraction of what you managed to save."

"Yes, and when I send for the rest of my wealth, I shall make sure to take better precautions."

"Your Grace, at the risk of offending you, I suggest you burn that outfit with all haste. It is enough to make you an outcast among the noble-born and those considered respectable. As it is, I fear you may have lost any chance of winning over the countess if you do plan on living here. Without her 'unofficial' endorsement, I'm afraid only the most desperate or grasping will receive you," Bre counseled.

I studied the rigid, older woman who was doing her best to ignore us, replying, "Duly noted." I had no intention of conforming, planning rather to play up my "foreignness" to flout customs of dress.

The longer I spent in the shop, looking at fabrics, discarding some, choosing others, the greater the ecstasy of the tailor and the less of the countess even though it was I who had to make do with another seamstress. Bre proved invaluable, knowing the latest mandates on clothing, colors, and fabrics, and pointing out tactfully what the Countess and her daughters wore was considered proper fashion for a noblewoman's station. I did not care, and I made modifications to every dress pattern presented, and insisted on having some of my ideas drawn up. This would have caused problems with any other seamstress in the shop. I had been assigned a newer girl, who was eager to make a name for herself. Fabric came and went in a steady stream. Endless pots of tea and dainties were pressed upon us. I was standing on the raised dais being measured, noticing the young viscount eyeing me when he thought his mother wasn't looking.

I was deep in a discussion of one of my designs when a loud ripping sounded, and the countess's sharp voice rang out.

"Stupid slaves!" A slap followed. "This is the last time I put up with you two! Martin! See they are placed on the auction block immediately!"

"Oh please, Mistress! My lady! Please! I didn't! I'm sorry . . ."

"Mama! She ruined it! What am I to wear now?" wailed the younger daughter.

I turned to Bre. "If you would. I am in need of personal slaves. Seeing as they served a countess, they will do. Would you please broker an agreement? I shall reward you for it."

Her mouth dropped open, Bre muttered, "She won't like you for it, nor thank you."

"Tell me, Bre, how is it a daughter of an inn keep is so well-versed on the machinations of the nobles? You have information which comes from more than listening to rumors."

She blushed in embarrassment, mumbling, "I will not spread tales about you, Your Grace, if that is what you mean."

"No, it's not. Tell me how."

"I listen, that is all, and keep what is told to me in confidence. I am considered reliable enough the nobles confide in me and use my services as a guide."

"You are a very clever girl; tell me, what is your ambition?"

"My ambition? Madam?"

"Yes. Will you take over the running of the inn when your parents are no longer able?"

"I . . . I," She licked her lips nervously. "I expect I will marry and support my husband and bear his children. My older brother will inherit."

"And if you could earn a living for yourself, without being dependent upon a man, would you take it?"

"I don't want to be alone forever. The men here are not looking for a woman who does not need them."

"You mean they don't want to pay a slave for what they want, when they could have a wife instead. Funds of your own would give you the luxury of choosing whom you wished to marry and when." I inspected another bolt of fabric a slave held, glancing out the window.

"I . . ." She struggled with how to respond.

"Do not take distress over my words; I did not mean for you to have any. I shall say it again, you are a clever girl—too clever to be wasted on a man who won't appreciate you. You should have one who will, is all I meant."

"Thank you, madam, but I do not know what kind of well-paying job besides being a guide I could get without my father's permission."

"I suppose you are right. I shall need a permanent place to live while I decide if I want to make a petition to stay. I wonder who would know what is available," I mused.

"There are many homes on the way to the palace which do not have masters. The crown may consider renting, or one of the nobles might. My father and I made it a point to know them all. Often times they would house some of their guests with us. It may be faster if a person with more power were to intervene." She cut her eyes toward the countess. "If they were so inclined."

"Please ask her ladyship if she will come speak to me, along with selling me her slaves." I sent her off.

She was soon back with a young man in tow whom she introduced as Lady Elizabeth's son, Viscount Martin. He took my proffered hand, bowing, and kissed the back of it.

"A pleasure to make your acquaintance. I do hope I have not heard your lady mother wrong, but she did say they were to be sold at auction. As it happens I am in need of slaves. All mine died when bandits attacked."

He gave an apologetic smile. "Yes. Mother says many things when she is angry, but I am sorry to inform you she doesn't want to sell." He paused, continuing, "My family usually does business with Karstin or even Gri for our slaves. We have found them to be the most trustworthy and have the healthiest stock."

I thanked him and returned to the business at hand.

* * *

We could hear the shouts from the slave market while still a block away. Domiano rode ahead, trying vainly to clear a path for us amid the throng of buyers and sellers.

Bre had to shout over the commotion. "If you plan on staying long, madam, you may want to consider purchasing men who can clear a path before you."

"Is it common practice?" I inquired.

She confirmed it was, and I could see for myself with some of the richer townspeople. We rode through the press of people toward the two buildings connected by a smaller one. A small crowd before the building's veranda was attending to the auctioneer bawling out his song. It took a minute to get the rhythm.

"I shall want to see the pens," I told Bre.

She started visibly. "The-the pens? Oh, I don't advise it. They are mostly new arrivals or so sick they aren't expected to survive."

"Nevertheless, I will see them before I take part in the auction," I stressed. I had asked Domiano about the slave markets, and despite his obvious hatred of them, he had provided me with valuable information.

It took a bit of haggling, and my gold, as even Bre's knowledge wasn't enough to grant us entrance to the maze of narrow streets behind the main buildings. I could see why the owners didn't want many buyers back there. The new slaves were kept in what amounted to roofed-over animal pens. As we rode closer, it seemed a commotion was going on at the men's area. A worker spotted us, stopping our forward progression.

"What is the matter?" Bre called down.

"A new slave is causing problems, ladies. It would be best to return the way you came. We have sent for the sheriff."

There was no time for a reply; the shouting turned more frantic as a single man, sword in hand, came running toward us with a host of armed guards chasing. Some of the slaves in the pens he passed yelled out to him. I found it odd he didn't open them to create a distraction. I spotted the chains keeping the pens closed and had my answer.

I heard Bre gasp in alarm beside me. "Madam!" Her voice held a note of panic as the worker scrambled to avoid the no-doubt-stolen blade of the slave.

I saw at once why he had run our way. He wanted a horse. Bre had been trying to turn her mount to ride away just as the slave made to grab Windstorm's bridle. The beast wanted none of it, trying to bite the man who danced out of reach of the equine's teeth.

I was trying to give my guide a chance to move away, but it was too late. We were already surrounded by shouting guards. The slave took the opportunity to vault onto the back of my horse. Windstorm didn't like the sudden addition, rearing as men shouted while I tried to keep him from bucking.

A muscle-hard arm crushed me to the slave's chest as he hissed in my ear, "If you want to live get, this beast—"

It was all he had time to yell as my mount's front hooves came crashing down and his rear quarters rose up in a spectacular midair buck. A confused sound of voices mingling reached our ears as I felt myself jerked from the saddle by the slave's weight as he went tumbling. We landed in a tangle of limbs in the mud as I screamed at my mount.

"Windstorm! Hold! Domiano!"

I was furious. I had not fallen off a horse for thousands of years, and I must admit my pride was bruised. Angry squeals coming from Windstorm let me know he was not happy, nor were the men near him, judging by their terrified shouts. I could feel the piercing rays of the sun on my unprotected face, pain beyond words as my skin began to burn while I freed myself from the slave who was the cause of the commotion. The smell of cinnamon, vanilla, and ambrosia curled in my nose. The scent from the tavern and Nicky! I stared into rich brown eyes for a moment in shock as the world around us seemed to swim and waver.

The time was long past, in a city of modern era which no longer existed. The slave beneath me now stood across from me in worn jeans, boots, and a long-sleeved T-shirt. His arms were folded across his chest as he seemed to be listening to someone out of range. He turned to look at me and shook his head. The picture melted as I blinked—or was it the mud coating us both, dripping in my eyes, or my sight being burned from the sun? I heard the man grunt as hands yanked me away from him. The world came back into focus.

He was being kicked and pummeled by armed men. A pair of black eyes peered into mine while a familiar voice asked, "Madam, are you hurt? Did he hurt you?"

I couldn't concentrate; the scent! I had to know why he had the same scent! "Stop!" I yelled, forgetting myself for a moment, letting the force of my power flow out to halt the beating.

The guards all froze, turning angry faces to me. Saizar scowled, and Bre stammered out, "Madam, he caused you harm and tried to escape; either offense is a hanging crime."

"And hang he will, and right now!" the seller growled out, signaling to his personal guards.

"Nothing was harmed except my outfit and my pride," I grudgingly acceded. I easily shook off the man supporting me as I brought my hood up over my head to shade my face, taking a step toward the man now curled in a ball in the mud.

"Show me your face, slave; I demand to see the man who unhorsed me."

"Your Grace—"

"How can she be a duchess when she's dressed like a whorish warrior?" I heard the slaver demand of no one in particular.

"Perhaps we should send for the sheriff? Impersonating a member of the nobility is punishable by death too," a guard growled.

"I am a member of the law," Saizar growled in frustration.

I could hear Bre telling them the story I had made up as Saizar squinted at me, as if to say, *that voice sounds familiar.* Not wanting to be overheard, he leaned in close to ask, "Your pardon, madam, but by any chance were you the lady I warned in the tavern last night?"

A quick calculation was in order. I confirmed his suppositions. He turned to the other men, vouching for me, ordering I was to be obeyed. The slaver made no move to recall the man he had sent off to bring the sheriff.

I made a sharp gesture to the guards. They grabbed the man, hauling him, groaning, up to his knees. Another grabbed him by the hair, yanking his head up so I could see his face, fast swelling and turning colors. I stepped closer, to the displeasure of those surrounding us who crossed their swords in front of me so I would not go any nearer.

I stared at him a moment, breathing in his scent, realizing his mind was a blank to me; I could not read it. "Where was he captured?" I demanded of the slave seller, all discomfort from my soaked, muddy state ignored.

"Your Grace?"

"You heard me. Where. Was. He. Captured."

A moment of silence before the answer. "He broke the king's peace most grievously."

"That is not what I asked," I replied coldly.

"Inside the town," came the resentful answer.

"How did he break the peace?" I demanded as I tried puzzling out the man before me.

There was another pause and muttering before the seller said, "He was arrested while defiling a noble's daughter."

I could hear the ring of truth in what he said, but the man before me groaned, spitting out through bleeding, swollen lips, "Lies. My friend and I—"

A guard plowed a fist in his stomach to shut him up. His breath wheezed out in a painful whoosh. I turned my glare on the man, commanding, "I did not order you to touch him. I will hear his tale."

The seller cleared his throat, spitting, "Madam, I wouldn't waste time with the lies from the likes of him. Let me show you to my private quarters where you can have your maid tend to you and I will personally exhibit whatever slaves you need for your household."

I turned to Saizar. "Why is he not in jail if it is the truth?"

The man had the grace to look uncomfortable. "I was told he escaped and made for the foothills. As he has shown up here, he must have run into a band of slavers who captured and sold him. Either way, slavery or prison is a fitting enough punishment. Escape, however, is punishable by death."

My eyes itched, my exposed skin throbbing from the burns the sun inflicted, the scent of blood pumping through veins making it hard to think. "It won't matter if I hear his tale." I turned to the slave seller. "You will escort us to your quarters."

I ignored the grumbling, taking Windstorm's trailing reins as we made our way to the slaver's lavishly appointed space. When he found out I had no maid, this being part of the reason for coming, his eyes brightened. He snapped out commands to his slaves and helpers, especially when he heard the jingle of my money pouch. Bre stayed with me in his private rooms.

Two burly guards stood to either side of the door outside. The women slaves sent in to help me repair the damage my fall in the mud had wrought understood not to try any escapes. I knew he meant this as a sort of working test for them, as did they.

One of the women, who looked all of seventeen, busily brushed what mud she could from my hair, while a wooden tub and bucket after bucket of hot water was brought in. Two others helped me out of my clothes before proffering a variety of soaps, smooth and smelling of herbs, along with a cloth. Another slave held jars of scented oils, all but one of which reminded me of a whorehouse; the one acceptable to me had a light, clean scent of lemon verbena and rosemary. I had already gotten rid of a few women when they began fighting over who would do what. A knock on the door came and lowered voices between the slave who answered it with the guards outside. One of the middle-aged women came around the screen with an armful of clothing.

She curtsied. "Compliments of the slaver and his wife, who wish you to know they want this to be a gift for Your Grace."

The slave brushing mud from my outfit thrust them into the woman's arms, snatching the new offerings, turning to me saying, "I have your dress ready, Your Grace."

I saw anger tightening the older woman's mouth. She took my clothes, carefully folding them so what remained of the mud didn't get on the few clean areas left. I made to quit my bath, stopping when a pain shot through my head from the hair brush. I merely looked back over my shoulder. The young woman blushed red, mumbling an apology as the other women giggled in pleasure at the perceived rebuke. When I was once more as clean as I could be and clothed again, I inquired the names of the slaves before leaving the room to rejoin the seller and Bre.

"Ah, madam! As lovely as ever!" The slaver Gri leapt up at my entrance to escort me to another chair close by the crackling fire. I was more chilled from my unexpected mud bath than I realized. The heat felt good. Bre choose to seat herself near the left corner of the room. My gowned status, even borrowed, along with the elaborate hair style the slaves gave me, and the delicate scent, seemed to mollify the men enough they started treating me as a noble lady instead of a potential suspect.

"Your Grace, I would be remiss in my duties as a lawman if I didn't insist you forget about questioning the slave and let me see to his punishment."

I sat calmly, saying, "If you wish to profit at all from my business, you will have him brought in at once." I watched the smile turn into a grimace as he bowed, giving a brief command while I waved off another several slaves proffering food and drink.

"I trust the females I sent in to serve you exceeded your expectations?" he delicately probed. *One of them had to after you dismissed four of them for fighting and kept five to wait upon you.*

"For the most part," I answered, knowing he knew part of the answer already.

Soon the strange-smelling man was brought in by no less than half a dozen guards, clanking from the addition of wrist and ankle chains attached to a central chain running from the iron collar around his neck to between his bare feet. Saizar was the last to enter the room. He made his displeasure known before coming to stand by my chair, ostensibly to protect me if the slave tried another escape attempt as the guards forced him to kneel before me.

The room was silent as I studied the man, noting he met my gaze boldly. I could have sworn he had been more badly beaten the first time I saw him. It must have been the mud. I had ordered him cleaned up for my benefit. Lean and muscular, dark brown hair and eyes. A straight Roman nose, strong brows, a thin oval face and high cheekbones with little hollows below them made his face arresting.

"By what name am I to address you?" I coolly asked.

His eyes narrowed as he replied, "Eron."

"Very well, Eron, tell me why the guards lie."

His eyes continued to probe mine. "Why? Will it help me or convince you to have me freed?"

A sudden blow to the back of his head sent it pitching forward. "Watch your tongue around nobility, scum."

I held a hand up to halt any more blows, watching as he turned his head slightly to the side to see who had delivered it before he looked back to me. His expression told me the man who had hit him would be dead if Eron got his chance.

"You seemed eager enough to have your story heard when we stood outside in the mud. It appears I was wrong." I turned to the seller in dismissal of the man before me. "Ask the corrupt toad of a sheriff, or the men I was with if the pig hasn't killed them or sold them into slavery also."

At the accusation, Saizar spoke, "I would be very careful what you accuse the sheriff of."

"That pig wouldn't know actual law and order if it bit him on the ass."

A snicker or two was quickly squelched from a few of the guards, telling me the sheriff was not well liked nor universally respected.

"It does not tell me how you came to be here."

His lips lifted in a sarcastic grin. "Surely you remember giving the command for these apes to drag me here?"

"I say, madam, such cheek should not be encouraged," Gri protested. "He will be better for another beating."

I regarded the man before me calmly, while he said, "Get these cuffs off; I'll show you a beating."

"You won't be so mouthy swinging from a noose."

I interrupted their bantering. "What inn were you at?"

"The Bloody Knuckles," he ground out.

I turned toward Bre, acting as if I hadn't already been inside it, but only Saizar knew.

"I am given to understand it is a tavern?"

Bre hesitated, glancing swiftly around the room before saying in cautious tones, "It's both a tavern and a brothel, and its owner is said to be good friends with the sheriff. Sheriff Jake sees to it his men keep an eye on the property as some of the town's rougher elements have been known to frequent it."

A guard snorted in derision.

Eron's eyes glittered in suppressed anger. "One of my employers had invited me to sup with them in the common room. As we sat there, the sheriff and his men came up with some made-up story about the other merchant having stolen some horse. As he was not back from trying to see the king, we couldn't ask him. The sheriff decided to hang the man I was with, and me, as sufficient compensation. I fought them to give my employer time to get free and go for help." He stared defiantly at me.

I deduced he wouldn't speak more on the subject. "Your tale should be easy enough to verify." There was something intriguing me, even though the man could be lying if I hadn't been inside the Bloody Knuckles myself and seen what went on. I turned, saying, "Saizar, you are the sheriff's man, I have been given to understand."

He turned to me after glaring in disgust at the chained and kneeling man. "I am, madam, although I was not on duty that night and have no personal experience of what he speaks, nor have I heard anything about it."

"If they are even alive," Eron spat.

"Surely you don't believe a word of his story?" Gri protested. "It sounds the wildest tale ever. A bunch of lies told by a man desperate to escape his well-deserved reward for his crimes. I only buy from other reputable slavers."

"If there ever could be such a thing," I sneered, catching the quick amused quirk of the lips Eron gave at my words.

I contemplated the man. I should just forget about him, and the odd flashback. Instinct had me saying, "Surely there is some place he can be placed temporarily while inquiries into his story are made?"

The men protested, not knowing the tale had a greater ring of truth behind it than the one I had been given earlier, even without my being able to read it from his mind. He had none of the non-verbal tells most liars had when they spun their version of events. Of course, he could be a well-trained spy momentarily caught unawares, or an excellent liar. Eron and I had been staring at each other as the men argued around us, trying to convince me their way was best.

I gave each man a look. One by one, they fell silent. "I see not what the problem is. You claim he is a criminal while he does not. Saizar and these guards can take him to the jail while these so-called merchant men are found and questioned. If he is a liar, he can either be hanged or returned here to be sold."

"I paid good money for the bastard!"

"Yes, from only the most reputable of sellers," I replied pointedly. "I trust the slaves you have to sell me are not known criminals as well?"

He reddened, saying no more.

"If this man's story is true, a grave insult has been done to him. He will be deserving of the king's pardon; reparations will have to be made. You may inform the sheriff I shall be taking a very close interest in his case, Saizar."

Bre crossed the room, kneeling beside my seat to speak with me in lowered tones. "Madam, I fear your decision is not entirely wise. I feel beholden to counsel you on this topic. As you are one newly arrived and not fully aware of our customs, I can assure you most all in the town will take a dim view of such rebellious leanings. Lord Nicky will see it as treason of the basest and vilest sort. He is not a man you want to offend; he is a personal friend and advisor to His Majesty."

"Is that so?" I murmured in amusement, already planning what I could do with this new information.

She leaned nearer. "Everyone in town gossips, at the risk of offending you; a foreign duchess is a rarity and a source of curiosity. If you continue insisting, you will be ignored, and life will not be pleasant nor enjoyable. You may even be asked to leave before having the opportunity to properly reequip yourself." Bre moistened her lips. "Once put in jail, his fate is sealed, and not for the better—no matter what good intentions or motives you may have toward wishing to help."

I sat back, contemplating her words before turning to the seller. "I will give you four silver coins for him, no more, no less; certainly more than you paid for him, along with his papers of ownership. Attempt to bargain with me, and I shall take my considerable business and wealth elsewhere; after all, I do have an entire household to staff."

I let my overly generous offer hang in the air as greed leapt into the seller's eyes.

I should push for more coin if she's hot for the bastard. She must have liked the feel of him beneath her when they tumbled. But what if she isn't bluffing? An entire noble household, one belonging to a duchess? She will need a small village of slaves properly attending and supporting her higher status. Not to mention she will need guards she thinks she can trust. I can put spies if need be. But if the bandits got to her property, how has she the coin left for all this? Loans? Yes, she must have taken loans from the money-lenders. As long as I am paid in coin, it doesn't matter to me if she bankrupts herself.

"Madam, no!" Saizar hissed in aggrieved tones, moved finally into saying something.

I pulled out the coins, holding them above Gri's hand as he reached, I closed my fingers. "His papers."

The seller hissed but sent for them while Eron glared at both of us. Paper and money exchanged hands as the guards hauled the man up. "Saizar, a word before you go."

He turned to me with a barely concealed grimace which changed when he saw the silver I held out to him. "I expect you to discreetly inquire around for me. May I trust you?"

Dark eyes meet mine. *Trust her, she brings much-needed change,* I whispered in his mind.

"I . . . It is extremely foolish and ill-advised. I fear you put your life in danger. I ask once more to please forget about the subject of his arrest."

"Your objections are duly noted. Take the silver anyway with my thanks for your honest counsel. I trust you to escort the man, as is, to the stables at the Silver Thorn." I dropped the coin in his palm, turning in dismissal. "Now, as to my household needs . . ." I directed to Gri.

The day was well-advanced when I and my now-enlarged party returned to the inn. The slaver was not glad I only bought a handful of people, taking it as further proof I was unfit for the station I held. I was considerably weakened by now and in need of a brief nap.

"Your Grace," the owner greeted me reservedly. *I hope she does not stay here long, not with her anti-slave sentiments.*

The story had already spread through town. I wondered how many versions there were, and which ones he'd heard.

I held out more coin. "I shall need lodging and meals for my slaves.

I will want hot water for a bath in several hours. Until then, I am not to be disturbed." I ignored his gaping mouth and continued upstairs.

Chapter Eight

The small room was dark when I woke. For a moment I couldn't remember where I was. It came flooding back. I needed to feed. My exposure to direct sunlight had left me weakened. I rose as a soft tap came upon the locked door. I opened it to behold my new body slave.

She gave a brief curtsy before saying, "Your bath water is ready, Your Grace. Shall I have it sent up with the tub?"

"Yes."

The woman headed back down the hall, several minutes passing before she returned with several bundles and a lit candle. "The owner of the tailor shop, Mistress Emilee, had these delivered. Where shall I put them?"

I looked about the room, realizing she could not see in the dark as I am able. "The table shall do until my trunks are ready."

"Yes, madam." She carefully laid the bundles down, before using the candle to light the oil lamps. She stood with hands clasped before her and head bowed as I came over to see what the seamstress had been able to ready for me.

I stopped at the sight of my once-muddy clothes, picking them up. "Have I you to thank?" I asked, knowing other slaves might have presumed to toss them out, as either not worth cleaning, or because in this town, a woman, especially respectable and/or noble, did not wear such things.

"Yes, madam."

"I see I have chosen well. Thank you. Has there been any news while I slept?" I set the articles aside, noting a green dress, a blue one, and one outfit guaranteed to cause consternation.

"The inn keep, Nathan, says one of the sheriff's men, Saizar, has information for you of the utmost importance." She had a frown, but she continued, "Lord Nicky requested an audience, as did Sheriff Jake, and the king!" Her tone became wondering though she sent me a sly-eyed look. "He sent a slave with a missive." I held my hand out for it. Susafan drew the king's missive and several others from the single pocket in her thin, worn, short dress, placing them in my palm.

I broke the royal seal to read what was written. "Damn the man!" I whispered to myself. I was being summoned to answer questions about my title and my family along with other rumors.

"I need parchment, ink, and where is my bath?"

"I will see to it at once. Madam." She curtsied before bolting from the room.

The bath and the rest of my items arrived together. Susafan was scrubbing me clean with more enthusiasm than called for as I tried to scribble a reply to the king using a wooden stool for my ink and penknife while balancing the parchment on the narrow lip of the tub.

"I am not a spot on a dress," I warned her as I had to blot another blob of ink.

"S-s-sorry, madam," she squeaked, making sure to take more care.

I finished the note, folded it, and using the candle to melt the sealing wax I'd purchased today, sealed it with an imprint from my signet ring. Susafan sent it off with the little page, Rolf. She held a linen towel up as I rose from the tub, wrapping myself in it to dry off. She brought over the layers of my outfit. First was a low-cut shift. Next, the silk-lined corset. It's a good thing I don't have to breathe anymore, and my internal organs were impervious to the damage such a garment produced. To think, when the world went back to a second dark age, so did the clothes! Susafan helped slide fine silken hose up my legs, fastening them with garters. She placed the tight green silk-linen blend shift over my head and shoulders, tweaking it to get it to lay correctly.

Next came the medium-weight linen underdress, also green, over my head and into position. Lastly, the overdress of silk-linen blend dyed an emerald green, which highlighted the green in my eyes. Susafan fussed with the bodice of the gown as the neckline was squared off and quite low, showing off a wide expanse of bosom. The corset had pushed my breasts up into mounds. I would have to be careful not to lean over too far. The gown had long, tight-fitting sleeves; the bodice itself fit my torso like a glove but the skirt flared out slightly to a demi-train. The bottom two inches of the dress and the cuffs had been heavily embroidered with bright blue silk thread in a design of roses and leaves. I stepped into the low-heel shoes that matched the color of the dress and had the same pattern as my hem.

I sat at the small table as Susafan opened the various pots of crushed minerals and plant mixes passing for makeup in this era. I began the laborious process of applying them to my face, for I was unused to working with them and didn't want to end up looking like a clown, as the slave began to brush my hair, pinning it into an elaborate updo.

"You have been a slave for how long now?"

"I belonged to an earl, but he was accused of treason. He was stripped of land and titles before he was killed. His lady eventually was forced to sell me back to the slavers. I had been in their service for twenty years, all of them here."

"You must know all the good gossip," I remarked offhandedly.

I caught the hitch in her breath when she continued. I could tell tears would fall soon. "I wish I had never come here." Her eyes grew large, and horror-struck, realized what she had let slip.

I replied, "I hope you do not speak so freely when other nobles can hear you; not everyone is as tolerant as I am."

I could have told her I had no intention of keeping her as a slave, but I wanted to make sure when I freed her, she would be protected.

She dipped a curtsey at the warning, meekly going back to my hair as I switched the topic.

"What can you tell me about the king's man, Saizar?" I asked. Slaves are the best source of information. They know everything going on.

"He takes his job very seriously," she replied. "I heard he prefers whores, so he can't be trapped into marriage and worry about supporting a wife and kids."

I half-turned, arching a brow, as she hurried to hold a polished bit of metal up for me to inspect myself in as she continued. "One of my old mistress's slaves tried getting him into her bed, and he turned her down. He was very polite about it, she says, and she demanded to know if he liked men. He said he will not dally with slaves of nobles or merchants."

"Is that so?" I inspected my face, making a few adjustments to the cosmetics as Susafan continued.

"He is very dedicated, madam."

I indicated my approval of her efforts with my hair, standing so she could finish adjusting how the dress's demi-train lay. "What else about the man?"

"He is different from the other men the sheriff employs. They all want a feel or a quick toss from us slaves if we need their help, but not him."

"Is it true, Susafan?" My eyes bored into hers. She stammered a bit but stood by her assertions. "What else of Saizar? Besides his bed habits?"

"Well, madam, I heard how he doesn't extort money for the services he performs, which makes the sheriff angry. He almost never takes bribes, but occasionally he will accept small tokens or favors."

"Why would his boss care, Susafan?" I asked, though I had a good suspicion as to why.

"The king doesn't pay the lawmen enough to live on. I suppose they think they have to make extra coin as they can. O' course Sheriff Jake is careful only to extort from those he thinks will let him get away with it, and if he doesn't, well . . ." Her shrug was very matter-of-fact.

I would have greed, corruption, and bribery to deal with, subjects I was familiar with.

"Why is the king not concerned?"

"Oh, no one can say why with any certainty, madam." She hurried to mollify me. "Most seem to think as long as he gets his taxes and whatnot, he does not care. It is also said Lord Nicky turns a blind eye toward any complaints against the man."

I noted the small shiver Susafan gave at the mention of the name, and the surreptitious warding away of evil she made as well. Hrm, interesting. "What of Lord Nicky? What can you tell me about him?"

The older woman soberly replied, "He is the king's advisor, an outsider who's an orphan, although he doesn't like to be reminded of the fact. If I may be so bold as to warn you, madam, he is a very powerful man, not one to cross lightly. The last family I worked for made the mistake." She hesitated before continuing in a rush, "I don't wish to repeat things which may not be correct, but shortly afterward they lost their fortune, land, and lives. It was the king who ordered it, but at the time it was attributed to Lord Nicky. I shan't say more, madam; I shouldn't have said what I did. I'm just a slave who's ignorant of the truth. Please forgive me."

She bowed her head and curtsied in apology, falling silent, fearful I would order her whipped for spreading lies and rumors. I had no intention of doing so, but I let the silence go. Susafan tweaked the dress into place as I gathered the front up enough not to trip as she arranged the small train to hang correctly before opening the door.

"Thank you; make sure you get supper. I will send for you when I need you."

She curtsied, murmuring assent as I swept past. It had taken nearly two hours to get ready. The little page was waiting for me at the bottom of the stairs along with the inn keep. The small common room was packed with minor nobles and monied burghers who had completed their town business and returned to dine with each other or any family they had brought.

"Pardon me, Your Grace, but a lawman is here and wishes to speak with you; shall I tell him you are unavailable?"

I looked over the room, seeing only the back of the person. I really did need to be going but decided to spare a few minutes.

"Rolf, tell Domiano I shall want Windstorm saddled and ready immediately. Stay with him and have him send you inside to get me when the horse is brought round." I had purchased a sidesaddle that its owner had pawned earlier. I could only hope I did not have any more embarrassing falls off my horse.

The child ran off, to the innkeeper's *tsk* at the lack of manners and respect he showed. "I will want food and drink for my guest, sir."

"Of course, madam. Shall I serve something light?"

"Bread, cheese, meat, fruit if you have it and whatever wine is available." His attitude was slowly warming toward me, no doubt helped by my gold and new wardrobe, unconventional though it still was.

He bowed as I made my way across the room, approaching from the man's right side as he sat at a table near the fireplace. Saizar started when he realized I was near, hurrying to rise, making a deep bow.

"Your Grace, forgive me for not noticing you sooner."

I seated myself, adjusting my skirt as I waved him back into his chair. "Have you reconsidered my request?"

The scowl on his face grew. "I have thought it over."

I waited for elaboration, but none was forthcoming. "And?" I prodded him.

"I am sorry, but it would not be wise, discreetly or otherwise."

"Very well; thank you for coming to tell me." I rose. I would have time to snag a quick snack.

The inn keep delivered the meal I had ordered for the lawman before I was able to leave, startling Saizar. "I did not order this."

"From Her Grace." The inn keep bowed, showing the wine.

"Thank you, but it is not necessary." Saizar said to Nathan and me. "Please, madam, I have a few more questions if I may."

"It is not a bribe, Sir Guard. You do me a great dishonor to consider it such."

The scowl got more pronounced as Nathan hovered uncertainly by us. "Very well, I shall partake of your generosity, madam. Thank you."

I dismissed the inn keep, reseating myself while Saizar poured himself a cup, and tasted a few bites. "I do not mean to insult you with my questions, madam, but I am afraid I must ask them."

When I didn't respond, he shifted. "You must not obtain any more slaves accused of running away."

"Why not? I hardly think it is an uncommon occurrence. In other lands I have been in, they were whipped or severely beaten the first time it happened, as a warning, and only killed as a last resort. Am I to understand that the slave has done such more than once?"

I watched his surprisingly sensual lips thin as he fought to retain his disapproval. Saizar replied, "Our laws are different here. Runaway property is put to death as an example for others thinking to follow. And he dared to harm a noble."

I arched a brow, smiling in amusement as his lips thinned further. "Be that as it may, what's done is done."

"Forgive a servant of the crown his boldness in speaking thus to his social betters . . ." His hands clenched into fists briefly before forcing them open. "I do not mean to question your judgment, but I do not trust a word the slave said." He hesitated again before venturing, "Sheriff Jake is not a man who takes accusations against himself lightly."

"I would imagine not many would, especially if they are innocent as the man claims he is."

Saizar shifted, not liking our discussion. I could see he wished he hadn't brought the subject up. "That is the other thing." He fumbled. "I should not be getting involved investigating my boss."

"If you think he should know, by all means tell him. I do hope he will not impede any requests for clarification. I would hate to have to involve the king. I suppose I shall have to hire an impartial third party to determine innocence or guilt, or look into the matter personally."

He winced. "I do not recommend either course of action."

"Why?"

"You must not undertake it," he insisted. "Forgive my forwardness. Let me speak with the sheriff first. It could be this was all a terrible misunderstanding, and a way can be found to clear it up."

Saizar lowered his voice as if he didn't want anyone to overhear him. "I will find the merchant men, whether they reside in the tavern or not. Madam must stay out of drinking establishments inside the town itself, any of them, but especially the one called The Bloody Knuckles. And madam must not pursue the matter herself."

His eyes caught mine again briefly, drilling into me in an effort to convey a hidden message before he looked away. I tilted my head while lowering my voice. "What are you not telling me, guardsman? I command you to tell me." I punched a bit of power behind the last sentence, watching him waver for a moment.

Saizar looked around, as if expecting to see spies hiding behind the furniture and window coverings. He leaned closer to me. "I should not say, but if it will help madam understand, I shall." He paused again to sip some wine, continuing, "Decent women do not frequent the taverns or pubs here at all."

My imagination was piqued. "Surely there are merchants who might bring their families with them?" I asked, wondering if he would tell me the truth the way Mary Elana had.

He looked ill at ease. "Not many do."

"I am not some shrinking violet. What are you not telling me? This is a town. Where do travelers stay when they are here? Certainly not all of them are men."

I should not tell her, the sheriff would not like it known. I could see him wavering on a decision. Swiftly, he said, "Those who have local contacts, or have been warned, stay at particular inns only or with other guild members who live here. They never stay at that tavern."

I narrowed my eyes at him. "Are you telling me the owner of the Bloody Knuckles encourages his patrons to cause harm to travelers?"

He gave a slow nod, briefly flicking his eyes my way before returning them to a spot on the wall. "Look at me. It's hard enough having this chat without being treated like I don't exist." My hunger making me irritable.

Saizar scowled, looking me in the eye as I continued my intelligence gathering. "The king, does he know? How can he expect to have trade if the very people he depends on for it are harassed?"

"In certain circles, The Bloody Knuckles is known to cater to the criminal element."

I did not care for his implications. "What if the unwary do happen to stumble upon it?"

He hesitated, uncomfortable with the direction our conversation had taken and what he was about to admit. "Rumor has it they are more than just harassed, madam. Your slave was lucky he was sold into slavery; he could have been killed."

"You are part of the law, guardsman. Why are you letting it happen? Is it not your responsibility to protect the people who live here, including those who visit?" I was angry.

His face flushed at my admonishment. "It is not so simple, madam —," he began before I interrupted.

"Bullshit!" He blinked his eyes in astonishment as I continued, "You are admitting the sheriff is corrupt and chooses to ignore the situation." I had a theory. "Or perhaps he is told who to protect and who not?" My eyes bored into his.

He looked around, quickly nodding once, not speaking, still trying to convey a meaning with his eyes. I sat back in my chair for contemplation. "My slave may have been telling the truth." My tone was low and menacing.

"I was not there for the event. I could not say with any certainty. It is not something which happens on a regular basis. The tavern is frequented by rough men, and on occasion, equally rough women, all of whom are considered lawless."

"People who wouldn't mind how they earned an extra coin or two. Why is the tavern still open? Why has word of what takes place inside not leaked out?"

"Decent folks are encouraged to go elsewhere, and most do after spending more than a few moments inside. The ones who refuse? Who is to say they were ever at the tavern? Who will vouch they safely made it through the mountains? You claimed to have come overland and ran into the outlaws plaguing our area, did you not? I was given to understand it's why you needed to purchase slaves."

I saw no reason for him to know the truth: I'd run into the bandits because I had hunted them down and fed off them. "I do not go out of my way to cause harm to innocents. The slaves I own are well treated."

He looked down, then back up. "Be that as it may, please stay out of the Bloody Knuckles, and forbid your slaves to frequent it if you do not wish them harm. It is not a spot to be overheard asking for the merchant men or particulars on what happened the night your former freeman was attacked. The tavern is riddled with those looking to make a quick profit."

My tone remained low and terrible. "Guardsman, why do you warn me? You are part of the sheriff's band, meaning you to take part in those crimes."

Now he did look me full in the eyes without flinching. He was enraged. "I do not partake of those activities. It was by accident I did learn of them. I should not even be telling you these things. I wouldn't if —"

"Don't give me your excuses. You are just as guilty as the others, if not more so, as you know what goes on and you do nothing to stop it!" I had to change my censorious sounding tone to cajoling. "Please, Sir Guard. Your actions today and before in the tavern toward my safety show you are a man of principle and well-meaning intent. I am honored you chose to confide in me. Please, tell me the true reasons why such evil continues unabated. I want to help you as a way of showing my gratitude."

He slammed his hands down on the armrests, his fingers tightening around the wood while hissing, "I have sent a report to His Majesty. I was told the matter would be investigated. When it seemingly stopped, I thought the matter resolved. Months later, I discovered that they had only become more careful. When I again reported it, I was set upon and warned to keep my mouth shut and do nothing if I valued my life. I was told it was not only the sailors who needed a place in which to unwind and relax."

Saizar grabbed his goblet, gulping the wine down before pouring more. "Had I but known what the sheriff's men were like, I would never have joined. As it is now, I have seen too much and cannot leave, expecting to live."

He sat back with mouth clamped shut, his lips almost vanished from anger. *Why have I told her any of it? She is just a woman. Now she will blab about what I have said, endangering me. They will kill me.* He had never confided his knowledge since the day he had been attacked.

I had to let him know he had not erred. "I have a slave who should not be one, and lost coin. I will have to think what shall be done."

I almost missed the look of panic and distress crossing the face of the man before me. "Madam, I can do little to retrieve the coin you paid. The rest is a job for men."

I gave him a searing look. "Yes, and see how well the men seem to be doing," I remarked in a dry tone.

He colored red, opening his mouth to say more when I cut him off with a wave of my hand.

"Should I choose to help you, don't dismiss my proposal. I may be a woman, but I can hear things you won't. As you have shown, men discount women. There are males who don't think to censor talking of their plans around us, but love to brag when we are about."

He was stiff, gulping from his goblet. "Not all men think so little of women. Not the smarter men."

"I have yet to see an abundance of those around," I mused.

His expression turned alarmed as he practically begged me, "Please, madam. I should not have spoken of it with you. My intent in coming here was to warn madam about the nature of the tavern and to ask that she drop your inquiries into the subject of the slave."

I gave an imperious wave. "You are becoming tiresome, guardsman.

Now you have delivered your message. Let us speak no more of it."

Saizar struggled to keep his face neutral, but his eyes failed him. They had crimped in anger, as he bit back any additional arguments. Rolf came inside for me; when I left, the guardsman was staring into the fire, brooding over the remains of his wine and meal.

* * *

I didn't need to use my powers to gain entrance to the throne room on my second visit. The guards must have been told to expect me. They led me directly to King Maceanas. He sat in a small audience chamber where the remains of a meal was being cleared away and attended by a few of the royal harem. Also present were two men I was unfamiliar with. I made my curtsey, and when no offer of a seat was forthcoming, it seemed I was to remain standing during the ordeal.

We all waited for the king to start; he ordered more wine, dismissing the harem.

"Aranthus, read off the title the woman before us gave when she arrived."The chamberlain did so."That is the title you claim is yours, is it not?"

"Yes, Sire."

"What country did you say you are from?"

"The one I just left, or the one my ancestors lived in?"

"Both."

"I have recently lived in Gemica, and my ancestors came from a place once called Illthanthia."

"Once? Are you saying it no longer exists?"

"Yes, Sire."

For someone who claims to be a victim of outlaws, she has been spending coin freely, including on rebellious slaves.

I did not care for that thought.

Why would a woman calling herself a duchess dress like a mercenary and hang out in taverns known to be frequented by lowlifes? I think she is but a common trollop out to deceive the royal court; it must be stopped now.

Nor that one.

The king looked toward the man with the casket, whom he called Dascis, as he cleared his throat. "If I may?" Dascis turned to me. "Where was this country supposed to have existed?"

It seemed some records had survived after all. I needed to be cautious. I had a prepared cover story for in-depth queries. "I only know what I have been told by my deceased mother. It was a city built upon the banks of a river with mountains to guard her back, and partook of the seasons as they came in turn."

The king scowled. "That could be anywhere. Did your mother say which countries Illthanthia bordered?"

"She may have, but I cannot recall the names she used for them."

"How terribly convenient," Dascis muttered under his breath.

"You have no country, no home, no one to vouch you are who you say you are. How can I be sure you were even attacked by bandits?" Maceanas demanded.

The third man had yet to say a word, but just watched me with his piercing sapphire eyes.

I arched a brow. "I have no way of proving the veracity of my title to you, only my word, my honor, and my family signet ring." I held out my hand to show the age-worn ring.

I needed a new one made, I noted. The men leaned forward to inspect it, sitting back as I continued my faradiddle. "I heard of the beauty of your land from passing travelers. It reminded me of my mother's descriptions of Illthanthia. I decided to journey here, and if what I saw agreed with me, to make it my home. In the few days I have been here, I do not know if I have made the correct choice. Despite your kingdom's potential, it is becoming clear I should gather what wealth remains to me and leave. It seems people are attacked regularly for no discernible reason."

Aranthus and Dascis sucked in a breath. Maceana's face turned purple in rage.

"What!?" he bellowed. "You cast a slur upon my country and expect me to help you!"

"What else should I call it? Your hills are infested with scores of bandits who robbed and kill with impunity. The law is a joke. You enslave people with no regards to who they are, what they've done or whether they are really innocent or guilty.

There was dead silence in the room, all eyes on the king after my brazen words. He gurgled, turning even redder. I feared he would expire from his emotions; wouldn't that throw them all into a tizzy?

"Insolent bitch!" Maceanas sucked in a breath. "You—you—I'll have you thrown in the dungeons and then we'll see how you like my laws!"

The sapphire-eyed man spoke up. "Your Majesty, may I?" He did not wait for an answer. "How can you have money if you were attacked by outlaws? I have heard rumors you lost all your people and possessions to them."

The king was chugging his wine, slamming the cup down to glare at us both.

"Yes. I escaped because my guards insisted I travel disguised as one of them. I carried my funds on my person. The bulk of my wealth is safe in other countries with money holders. I plan on sending for it when I decide upon a place to stay."

"And you have already bought slaves, I am told, or tried to?" If he had a spy network, he could be a potential ally.

"I'm afraid you have me at a disadvantage, sir. I do not know who you are, nor how you come to know these things; if you would be so kind as to tell me?"

I wanted him to underestimate me at first so I could get a better measure of the man.

He hesitated briefly before saying, "I am Earl Sydney. My countess tells me you tried to buy her body slaves from her when she was displeased with them. As for the rest, rumors spread quickly, especially when you buy a rebel slave and show up in inappropriate clothing for one who claims to be noble-born."

"There are no rebels!" Maceanas screeched. "I will have them killed! They will not plot treason and murder or overthrow me the way my family was!"

Dascis rolled his eyes, grimacing and decided to join His Majesty in drinking.

"I do not know of any rebels. I did buy slaves. There is one who is insisting he was a freeman before men claiming to be a part of Sheriff Jake's office ambushed and sold him."

"Sheriff Jake has faithfully served me for untold years; he is a man of integrity," Maceanas insisted.

I saw the look of disbelief pass between the other three men. I inclined my head. "As it pleases your Majesty."

"It does," he grumpily snapped, waving for his cup to be filled. "As for the slave, you should not have bought him but left him to his fate. I am told he was trying to escape, grounds for execution. How dare you interfere with our laws? How do I know you are not leagued with the miscreant and here as a distraction so an assassin may try to kill me?"

He was on a path I didn't want him to pursue. I was at my most logical, persuasive best. "I have no way I know of to convince you that what you speak of is not correct. As for the slave, his story was so far-fetched, that I cannot comprehend how anyone with a measure of intelligence would consider a tale like that a lie. I have no wish to displease Your Majesty by circumventing your laws. If they decree he must die, I can only be content to obey." My tone implied otherwise.

"You should have been informed by the slaver from whom he attempted to escape. The slave who you purchased should have been executed immediately, not allowed to be sold."

"The fault is entirely my own. I found his story intriguing. I convinced Gri to sell him to me."

"You must have paid a goodly sum to make him so daring."

My head inclined in a nod as I named the price, which had the men blinking and exchanging glances.

The king could not help himself. "Just how much of your wealth did you have concealed about your person?"

The way I phrased my reply had the men understanding it was a considerable amount. I had two saddle bags full of flawless gems, gold and silver; along with rare spices. They could not hide their shock or greed. The king decided to ignore the problem involving Jake and Gri. No doubt visions of the tax I would have to pay to the crown if I was granted residency had something to do with the decision.

"Now, about the news you were seen in a tavern no respectable person, especially a woman, would frequent. How do you explain?"

"It was the first open one I happened upon. I was not in there long before I realized my mistake. I met Saizar inside, who confirmed my suspicions and warned me to leave. Shortly thereafter, I came to present myself to you per his advice."

"We do not want to hear complaints of you being in places you shouldn't be," the king remarked.

Dacsis had not stopped regarding me with suspicion. "I would like to hear more about why you have no homeland."

"I was told my ancestors roamed the world after the country they called home fell to invaders, and they were forced to flee if they wished to live. I had not expected to find proof of the lands they visited."

Dacsis still was not pleased. "I don't think it speaks well of a family who is unable to settle down and is always roaming. How can descendants show or understand the meaning of loyalty if they haven't found a homeland after all this time?"

"Yes! Loyalty! I want no malcontents, not even ones from other countries." Maceanas seemed more concerned with drinking than the proceedings, a fact the men were quick to pick up on.

"I am the last of my line. It is true we all had wanderlust, but at one point or another we find a place we wish to settle down in. I am tired of traveling, and want a place to call home. I thought I would prefer your country. The numerous problems I have encountered, however, have caused me to reevaluate my situation," I stated.

Sydney turned toward the king, saying in a lowered voice, "She can help refill your coffers. Already merchants have benefited from the lady's stay. You mentioned you needed support to get rid of the bandits. Offer her full citizenship, after meeting certain provisions; until then, make it temporary."

"Do you really wish to have a foreign woman bearing such a title, a citizen?" Dacsis muttered. "What if she wants to marry? The man may demand he be granted her higher title and the standing it confers."

"Lord Nicky is the only one I would trust absolutely, but he has refused to marry," Maceanas mused.

"You could assign her a sponsor, one tasked with seeing she learns our laws and cultures. Ask for a portion of her wealth as surety against fleeing," Dacsis muttered.

"Forgive me, Your Majesty, but those rumors—," Sydney began.

"Do not bring it up again! I will hear no slur against my childhood friend, who has been more loyal than any of you. He will do as I command." The king's voice rose at the end.

Both men winced, falling silent as I acted as if I couldn't hear every word they tried to keep from me. I stood still, the perfect picture of a model future citizen waiting to prove her loyalty.

The men looked at me as the king said, "I must think on matters. I do not like the rumors which swirl around you and your actions. I do not advise you to get too comfortable here. I will grant you a three-month temporary citizenship, but not leave to use your title." My brow quirked up. He hastened to add, "At least until inquiries into your claims can be verified."

"Thank you, Sire. How long might that take?" I curtsied, waiting for his response as his brows contracted in a V.

"It depends on what difficulties we encounter. If your behavior has not given offense, and all other replies are satisfactory, I shall consider making it permanent. You will need a sponsor while you are here. Who will teach you our laws and customs? I will send word when I have found one for you."

I curtsied again. "And my title? Will I be given leave to use it then?" I asked for form's sake.

"We must think upon it." The king made a gesture of dismissal.

I backed away until I could turn and leave, deciding to investigate the advisor, trying to determine why he smelled the way he did. I would find a method to break the seemingly impenetrable wall around his mind.

* * *

The hall was silent, the torches used for light having long since burned away. I paused outside the room of Lord Nicky, listening to the young man breathe. He was sunk deep in sleep. I had fed off one of the many palace slaves, ripping from his mind where the young man slept.

Now here I was wasting precious time dithering outside his room. Did I dare go in? What was with this sudden indecision? Why shouldn't I? But I felt a flutter of fear just the same. *This is ridiculous! Stop waffling and go!* I raised a hand to the door, gently pushing. It was locked. I sent my power out to undo the small hindrance. It swung inward on silent hinges. I wrapped myself in shadows, gliding through rooms, past sleeping slaves until I stood before his bed.

The advisor mumbled, turning over as I approached. I inspected him closely, taking in a deep breath, inhaling his scent. Under the smell of sweat was an odor of rotting eggs, cinnamon, ambrosia and vanilla. The same unidentifiable scent from the bar. I knew he had not been inside when I was there. He didn't seem the sort to frequent such places either. Was he related to someone who had been? Tentatively I reached out a hand, brushing a finger across his cheek. He felt warmer than most. It didn't necessarily mean anything. There was nothing unusual about his skin tone or texture, but I still felt somehow he was not mortal. I tried to slip into his mind, but could not. It was strongly shielded and locked to me, even in sleep.

Nicky mumbled again, turning onto his back, his eyes moved rapidly beneath his closed lids.

I drew the shadows closer around me. I had a feeling I shouldn't linger overlong. If I planned on biting him, I should get on with it. I took a deep breath I didn't need. The idea of what I contemplated sent a frisson of fear through my being. I should not. *No, stop.* Just a little drink and I would know if his blood would be poison to me or not. One of his arms lay on top of the covers.

Gently, carefully I picked it up. Nicky mumbled without waking. I brought his wrist to my mouth, keeping my eyes on his face, gently bit into the vein. The blood leapt into my mouth, scalding me. Involuntarily my eyes widened in shock. Even the flavor of it was different; besides the metallic tang, it also tasted the way he smelled. I wanted to drink deeper. I had already started to swallow when a warning ping went off in my brain. It was with great effort I stopped drinking, swiping my tongue over the wounds to heal them. An instant later, I felt a cramping in my gut so overwhelming I curled to the floor. It was like the death pains I had experienced when my body first transformed. I could feel my hold on the shadows growing tenuous. It would be disastrous to let them go, even though the pain was excruciating. My whole body flushed with heat. Blood-sweat broke out lightly on me. My lungs burned as I took in sharp breaths, panting, trying to remain silent. I could see my skin instantly turn pink, flushed with humanity. The pain left as suddenly as it had come.

I stayed crouched in the shadows, looking back up at the young man. He had turned over but had not wakened. Slowly I stood, hearing a thumping. Where was it coming from? The door? Was someone pounding on it? No! It was my heart, beating as it had not in centuries, beating as if it were still mortal! Ye gods! What was this boy that his blood had such an effect! I tried slipping into his thoughts again, ignoring the growing unease that I had to get out of there right now!

* * *

The clearing was shades of gray, black and silver. A circle of men stood chanting about an altar, not quite drowning out the screams of the terrified men and women in pens behind them. A man was chained to the altar. Nicky carved symbols into him as the victim attempted to flail about. Suddenly the background melted, the altar blurred. The chanting never stopped, but the voices, the altar, the voices, were different.

The scene reformed, the advisor now a boy who sat at a heavily carved wooden table, reading from a large, ancient-looking book. An old man with gray hair and beard instructed him. "No, you do not pronounce it right! Repeat after me: Acfantamin! Manopeo! If you mispronounce it, the spell will not work correctly, and you won't like what comes through, much less what will happen to you." The little boy's eyes lifted from the pages, seeming to glare into mine as he grated, "I understand, Master. I will do better."

Now Nicky sat sobbing on the ground in a pair of jeans and t-shirt. A man with sandy hair and brown eyes had hold of his ankle with one hand, and the other pushed up his pant leg to reveal a strange mark. "But you are one of us! Where did you get it?"

A second man knelt, big and blocky with dark brown hair and tired brown eyes. "We'll help you any way we can, but please tell us, who marked you?" Nicky continued to sob; the men missed seeing the hatred and calculating look flashing behind the tears as the boy answered. I felt a shiver of tension run through me; I knew one of the men, somehow, but before I could guess from where, the scene flashed again. The little boy was in a robe, fighting the two men, fighting dirty. The air rippled in a disturbing way about him as he brought pain to his adversaries. I could feel a deep, long-running hatred in the boy toward the two, along with fear. He wanted them dead; they knew too much about what he could do.

The scene shifted yet again; the little boy was now a young man, sitting upon a horse. To one side, a cloaked figure stood, and before him a man dressed in filthy leather and furs. "How long will it take you to recruit the men and march upon the city?" Nicky coldly inquired.

"It'll go quicker if'n I have some gold to give 'em. Ain't none of them gonna march all that way on just a promise."

He swore under his breath. "Very well. Gant will ride with you and make sure you are doing all you say you will. He will be the one to receive payment for the men and dole it out. I want two thousand men . . ."

The person before him snorted, but Nicky continued, "I told you I will pay handsomely. I don't care if you have to collect every murderer and cutthroat on your way to the town. You will show up with two thousand men, and several companies of them had better be mounted. Try to keep the raping and pillaging to a minimum on the way. I don't want the king to get wind of this. Here, for you." Nicky held up a leather bag, the pouch chinking as he tossed it to the man.

* * *

I lost my connection to his mind, all my senses screaming danger. The young man snorted, giving a shout of fear, sitting up. I froze, watching. Nicky's eyes stayed shut, but his breathing had speeded up, lashes fluttering. I could feel him starting to wake up. Swiftly but silently I ran toward the door and eased it open enough to slip through. As soon as it shut, I used my power to lock it. I heard Nicky call for someone. He was fully awake. I started running, a blur amongst the darkness. I waited in a clump of trees for Domiano and my horse. What I planned to do next was tricky, but I had to know if my presence had been detected by the advisor with his strange powers. I left my body to float near the ceiling in the boy's room. He was talking to his hooded companion.

"I swear I felt someone in my room!"

"The wards are in place and undisturbed, the door remains locked."

"I don't care. Someone was in here! Find out who!" Nicky's face contorted in fear and hatred.

His companion bowed his head, beginning to mutter and pace the room. It felt like a long time before Nicky demanded, "Well?"

"I sense someone tried to disturb your wards; perhaps a rival you thought you had killed?" the companion inquired blandly.

The young man seethed. "No. No one is better than I. They will not get away with trying. Leave me."

The companion bowed, turning to go. I swear he looked right at the spot where I hovered. I saw a gleam of red eyes, a cruel smile, and I felt as if I hurtled from the room. I slammed back into my body painfully, not realizing I was on hands and knees until I focused on the ground inches from my nose, my heart pounding, wanting to beat its way outside my chest. Slowly I stood. I would have to be very careful around the young man, awake or sleeping. Most of his images showed him as a young boy of twelve. Suddenly, I didn't feel well. My stomach gave a grinding lurch as I shuddered, almost doing a face plant in the ground. I waited for the pain to pass, but it didn't. Instead, my head seemed to swell, my veins felt on fire, and I could feel the heat rising from my body. It was time I went back to my hiding place. I didn't know what else his blood was going to do to me. I felt vulnerable and exposed. I could also feel the coming dawn more keenly than I ever had in all my centuries.

Chapter Nine

I awoke from my dead sleep abruptly. My dreams had been even more twisted than usual. Ever since I awakened to my new life, centuries ago, they have never been the same. They are not dreams, but one ongoing nightmare. My resting spot remained pitch black, no scent of intruders, undisturbed. I still had on the green silk linen gown from last night, somewhat worse for wear. I walked up the tunnel, coming to the iron door set into the side of the mountain. I opened it, not understanding what was wrong. I listened to the downpour, saw how it silvered the world. Thunder growled across the sky, lightning brightening it in flashes. I stepped out from under the rock, looking up. The dark clouds parted to reveal a glowing orb in the sky. No! I scrambled for the door, the security of the tunnel. I was panting in terror, my back against the cold iron as the rain trickled down my face. I brought my shaking hands up to my face, but they only had a golden sheen, making me appear more human. For once there was no pain with that exposure. Okay, think. Why was I able to go out into even this modest amount of daylight uncovered and not suffer for it?

Calm, the trick was to remain calm and think about this rationally. The only change on my end was the blood of the young man. Surely it couldn't . . . could it? First things first; open the door. I made it back out under the rock overhang. The rain still poured down, the sky was still terrifyingly light. I stood there with my cloak held at the ready, just in case, but my eyes didn't burn out of my head. I took a step into the thunder and lightning. I was immediately soaked, but I didn't burn! I felt strangely energized! Did I dare? I slowly held a shaking hand out; steam curled from it and I snatched it to my chest, taking a hasty step back under safety. I inspected my hand. It was no more burnt than it had been; the steam was because my skin was so hot, the rain so cold. I couldn't help it; I laughed in delight. I could walk in daylight uncovered and not burn! I could see colors in all their brilliant glory, not the muted shades appearing to my night-seeing eyes. I could not waste this opportunity! Be bold! I walked out from my shelter feeling the rain soak into my hair. The blood of the advisor kept me from burning in daylight. I had to discover what he and his kind were, and if there was a way to bottle and store their blood.

I wrapped the cloak around me in an attempt to save the dress. As I walked, I smelled wet horses I had stolen from bandits. A few of the animals grazed on the grass and looked up in curiosity as I approached. I whistled for Windstorm, who was "talking" to himself and the mares while trying to mount them. One of them lashed out with her hooves, and followed by biting him. I whistled for him again, and he decided to leave them alone. He came at a trot, nuzzling my hand for treats I didn't have. I was thoroughly drenched by now, but I didn't care.

I found Domiano underneath the crude lean-to the horses sheltered under when they felt like it. He was sorting through bags and trunks of stuff I had stolen along with the animals.

"Is there not anything of use in what I liberated?" I asked the boy as we dried, brushed and saddled our horses. Windstorm turned his attention toward snuffling and biting at boxes and bags, still "talking" to himself.

"Lots of stuff. Looks like they raided several merchant trains. You're going to need a dwelling, or this will all get ruined by the weather. Plus, the horses will need hay soon, or moved somewhere they can graze unless you plan on selling them."

The path into the sheltered valley was treacherous even in daylight. I wasn't worried about anyone finding my spot. Even when airplanes and helicopters and such had ruled the air, the rift was near-invisible. The only technology which could have detected it had no doubt fallen out of space by now. Plus, there was no one who could manipulate such technology if it still worked and existed. The path resembled a treacherous goat trail. Domiano sucked in a breath as we threaded between stone walls so tight they looked as if they would crush us. My current haven had been in use by brigands before I woke. I was lucky they had a leader who had been stupid, refusing to leave, even when his men slowly started disappearing one by one. Him I had saved for last. Their remains littered another, smaller canyon with no way to it except to fly down, or rappel for the adventuresome. My hunger was a faint thing inside, one I would have to feed sooner or later depending on how well the day went.

We rode out of the hidden valley, taking a different path down from the stony mountain hills which would bring us to the plateau the nobles and royals had built their homes upon. We came out on the cliffs, the river flowing swiftly past below us, an abandoned, tumbledown stone mansion before.

"What do you know of the property?" I asked Domiano as we rode up through what had once been paddocks to a crumbling brick wall with a closed gate. I slid down off my mount, reaching for the latch, leading Windstorm.

"It would let you control access to the valley, but it's a wreck, haunted, and too close to the bridge."

"Haunted? We shall see," I murmured, and louder, "Go about your business. I shall be at the inn later." He bowed, riding past me toward the front of the ruined hulk.

The gate had lost all its paints, and it no longer sat its hinges correctly, so I had to muscle it open. Shells crunched under my feet from what remained of hidden garden paths, Windstorm crowding me, snatching at wet mouthfuls. Our trail through would be easy to see. The overgrown hedges, trees, and grasses showed a muted yet glossy deep green. The colors of the closed petals themselves! I wandered amid the wet plants, bending to smell their soggy scent, in love with their rainbow hues.

I touched the coldness of a statue covered with patches of bright green moss and laughed. Movement at my feet had me peering into a dirty, near-clogged water basin. I saw the flick of bright gold, orange and red of a few remaining fish. I had been trying to catch one and inspect its colors up close when I almost missed hearing the footsteps which stealthily approached. I pulled my hand out of the water, letting go of the fish. It frantically swam off to hide beneath a lily pad as I straightened up.

I whipped around, my sodden cloak spraying water, but I saw no one. I could pick out the scent of unwashed skin and clothing, the sound of a beating heart, and the slow, careful breaths of a hidden watcher.

Silly maid, this is no place to meet a lover, not on a day such as today. I caught the stray thought from the hidden person.

Gradually I resumed walking in no particular direction, trying to see if the person would be content with just watching. The wreck of the mansion loomed before me. I scanned the building with my mind, picking up many persons hiding inside. Squatters. Windstorm nudged me in the back; he was tired of being soaked. The house was a dark gray stone flecked with mica, so it sparkled, even in the muted light of day.

The empty window frames had been boarded over or shuttered up. Leafless vines crawled over all. I came to a door with rusted hardware, but something wasn't right. I studied it, realizing there was a perfect, hairline outline following its dimensions, running through the concealing vegetation. Someone had gone to a lot of effort to make it appear there was no way in.

I would hold off going inside until nighttime, continuing my inspection, aware of careful footsteps following, only stopping when I turned the corner to the central courtyard. The iron-studded wood gates hung crookedly, my mount and I managing to squeeze through onto the main street. As I rode out from the remains of the mansion, I received a few shocked stares, some sniggers and a few glares I ignored as I crossed the road, entering the Silver Thorn's courtyard. My body slave was horrified at my sodden, bedraggled state, and upset I had chosen to stay somewhere else for the night. It took all my remaining strength just to stay awake as I stripped, drying myself. I dismissed Susafan, locking the door. Suddenly, sleep was dragging me down, the deathly sleep all my kind fall into when the sun is high. I let my limbs relax on the bed, tumbling into the nightmares I knew waited for me.

* * *

When next I woke, the rich smell of blood assaulted my nose. The room lay in darkness; I could hear each heart beat in the inn and nearby stables. *Drink me*, they thumped. My fangs ached with the need, a hollow feeling in my stomach. I felt like a newborn vamp unable to control her need. *Drink me.* I had to keep control, however impossible it seemed. Only my centuries of life saved me. In a sudden rage, I yanked out the pins holding my hair in place, so the whole mass fell in long curling waves down my back. *Drink me.* I clawed open the shutters. They slammed against the building in a crash, but I didn't care. I balanced on the ledge. *Drink me!* The sound was maddening. I flew onto the roof, landing in a crouch. The noise had attracted attention. I was up and running, the folds of my gown floating behind me, keeping to the shadows, a blur of darkness. The mansions behind me would be too well guarded for what I needed. The cliffs loomed ahead, the bridge with the palace guards. On the opposite bank, the main town side, the stinking mud flats held hovels. The very poorest of the freemen and women lived there, slaves too old to be of use, beggars, dumped like so much garbage.

Forbidden to live anywhere outside their quarter. Ignored, expendable, they had no guards, looking out for each other as most have nothing worth stealing. Nothing of value except to a vampire. The guards never saw the flying blur I became as I landed beneath the bridge. Soon, death visited. *Drink me! Drink Me!* *DrinkmedrinkmedrinkmedrinkmeDRINKME DRINK ME!*

I stumbled from a hovel, the aching need inside me gone at last, my gown streaked with dirt and other filth from the few occupants who had woken and tried to fight me. The memory of what I had done flooded into my brain. *Shit! Bad me! That's how Van Helsings are made.* My immense age should have made me immune to a newbie's feeding frenzy. I had drunk more than any average vamp, even the newly turned. I felt fat and bloated, like a tick or mosquito. I would have to do something. I just wanted away from the dead, with their staring eyes, asking why I wasn't one of them. I had lived too long; I should be dust, murderer that I was. *Stop it!* I forced myself to go back inside, looking for flammables. Old grease, tar and pitch there were aplenty. I poured cooking oils over the bodies. The few bits of furniture and loose wood I broke up, stacking together. I did this for each hovel. They would have to burn together. The only problem would be those made of mud bricks. I raced from each dwelling starting with the furthest, lighting fires. I couldn't risk flying across the river with the illumination from the flames. I climbed the bank, hiding in the shadows of the bridge as the fires kindled, growing brighter. I listened as the guards smelled the smoke, debating what to do. In the end, they did nothing. After all, what does it matter if the hovels of the poor burn as long as they don't catch the rest of the town on fire?

I slunk into the shadows behind them, crossing the bridge to turn into the haunted mansion's grounds. Now that the worst of my unexpected thirst was slaked, curiosity about the house rose in my mind. I used the shadows to conceal me as I quickly inspected the outbuildings lining the drive to the central courtyard. They showed old signs of use as I could see repairs. What did these "ghosts" do to make previous owners flee? The cliff side of the mansion remained bathed in the flickering light of the fires I had started. I avoided that side, hidden by the bulk of the building, made my way to the door with its ingenious concealing vines.

Inside, I listened for the squatters. They all seemed to be clustered toward the half-exposed upper rear of the mansion—watching the fire, if their thoughts were any indication. I was free for the time being to inspect the main floor without them knowing, I did so quickly, noting repairs. The last owner had left some furniture and window coverings. Time had made the furniture only good for kindling, and spiders spun webs between the faded, shredded fabric. Some of the rooms still had dirty, slimy rushes covering the floor. Rats, mice, and bugs continued with the business of living as I walked with my usual soundless, light-pressured steps. A normal being's footfalls would have made the old clay tiles crack. I avoided the cobwebs draped over every surface, between every gap, not wanting any evidence of my passing. I mounted a still-classic, dirt-encrusted marble staircase. A faint scent of mold and damp, rotting wood clung to the air from wall paneling.

I ran into the first squatter just past the landing. He had no chance to warn the others as I struck swiftly and silently from the shadows to snap his neck. I set him down gently, continuing my hunt. Two more times I killed before I heard voices of the remaining squatters.

"Something's wrong, Mia. They should have come back up." The hushed voice was an older male.

"Who would dare after all this time? We didn't hear anyone break in." The other was female.

"The noble-looking woman from earlier. Ayden heard she's looking for a mansion."

"A young woman meeting a lover or on a dare to view the house. Go see what has happened. I will hide myself until you get back." I heard the sound of sliding wood, then soft, careful footsteps.

I watched from the darkness as a middle-aged man with a limp, holding a bow and arrow half nocked, glided past me on the creaking wooden floor, smooth even with his impediment. *Twenty years we've held this mansion, scaring those who we were able, killing those who wouldn't leave willingly. Who is inside, and how, without being noticed or heard?*

I let him pass, ambushing him. His instincts good, he managed to get a shot off before my fangs sank in. The arrow thwacked into the wall, chunks of rotting, loose plaster crashing down. His blood sprayed into my mouth in a gush, tasting of hot metal. I drank down several mouthfuls as he struggled futilely in my grasp, reaching with my powers into his mind.

The man before me was young and healthy, clad in bright armor over which hung a surcoat with his lord's badge upon it. He was bellowing orders to his fellow guards as the alarm bell rang out. Men in dull metal plate armor forced their way inside the many buildings, as the clash of steel upon steel rang out over the screams of the dying. "Yield! Yield to the king and he will show mercy!"

"Like the same mercy he showed the great heart oak? I'll send you all back to the dead lands with him!" the lord of the manor roared out as he met the invaders in nothing but nightclothes and sword.

The lord hacked and slashed, bringing down a number of knights until an arrow pierced his shoulder. He let out a roar of pain, but didn't stop fighting. The man took another arrow, this time to his side, and he crashed to one knee. A knight took the opportunity to come up from behind, slamming his sword down on the back of the lord's head.

The young man lay on the courtyard stones. He could feel his life slowly running out of him. He looked up defiantly at the ring of hooves on stone. Lord Nicky stopped, staring at the remaining men and women of the mansion coldly. "Lord Fishton, you have been condemned for treason. You shall hang on the morrow."

"Fuck you! You evil pissant! I don't know what magic you worked, but I'll take you with me, even if I have to come back from the dead to do it."

The younger version of Nicky sneered, "You should be begging me for mercy, for you or for your family, unless you care not they share your traitor's fate."

"You will not touch the likes of them. Already they are beyond your reach." The lord laughed at the flash of hate and irritation on Nicky's face until he was clubbed unconscious.

"Take the slaves, kill them, kill the remaining guard, find his family and bring them to me."

The young man woke in darkness, the sound of a woman crooning as she fed him broth. He was in pain, but she nursed him back to health, hidden in the remains of the once-elegant mansion. They stayed that way, he half-lamed. He made every person who tried to inhabit the mansion believe it haunted by the ghost of Lord Fishton and his murdered family. If they refused to leave, he slowly poisoned them with the help of the woman who had once been Lord Fishton's daughter, and who had healed him. Years passed, and soon no one came anymore to claim it—none but the most foolish, and they were quickly dealt with.

I let the body fall to the floor, nourished and warmed by his blood even as a voice behind me screamed in fury, footsteps pounding my way. I turned eyes shining with a sulfurous amber honey glow to see a prematurely aged woman charging me with a sharpened stake. She moved swiftly, but I was swifter. I caught her arm, squeezing, heard fragile bones grind together as she shrieked now in pain, the wood falling to the floor. My other hand, I wrapped around her throat, drawing her close as I sunk my fangs in.

Unnatural creature! Crueler than the man who loved me once, her mind shouted. *A man so gorgeous he put all others to shame. He had the most abundant head of wavy black hair, eyes green enough to make a cat envious or an emerald pale in shame. His silky cold lips and skin which would warm when he kissed me. I thought I could make him stay, but his heart belonged to another. He called himself Philippe. The advisor's slave did something to him. He turned feral, driven from the land.*

I did not like what her mind told me. There was nothing on this earth I knew of which could cause such a thing to happen to us. If something had, it did not bode well for me. Her body joined those of her companions on the floor, their blood warming me. My burned skin pricked slightly as my body began to heal the damage the sun had inflicted from yesterday morning.

It would not do for the corpses to lie out and rot; the scent alone would bring people looking for its cause. The nobles' street is the cleanest and best-smelling of the entire town. That, and it would be bad manners to scare my small household with the discovery of corpses. I was a bit peeved I was unable to get more information out of the lady on Philippe. I had not seen my mate since before my long sleep, and if his mind had been twisted by an unknown being in this town, I would have to take care. Dawn was not far off as I carried the bodies to the cliff edge after searching them. There was little of value on the corpses except the bow and arrows, a small, ornate lady's dagger, and two short swords which I shoved under moldering hay in the tumbling-down wooden stables. The remains I dropped over the cliff, hearing the dull splashes as they landed in the river far below while I used the last of the shadows to hide my return to the Silver Thorn.

* * *

I woke from my brief nap feeling better, sending for Susafan and a bath. She arrived first, clucking and shaking her head over the discarded, ruined garments.

"Really, I don't think there has been a day go by when you did not return soaked or dirty. A cloak would have helped." She shook the garments out and abruptly stopped at the sight of the blood and gore.

She inhaled sharply, froze and then slowly looked up at me. I merely raised a brow, staring at her, daring her to speak.

I watched as she wet her lips. "Shall-shall I burn the outfit then, my lady?"

My head tilted to one side, assessing her like a bird of prey. "You are not going to blackmail me? Or speak to the advisor or authorities on what you have seen?" A small, cruel smile curved my lips up. "Surely by now you must know how my garments came to be the way they are. You are a smart woman, and rumors and gossip fly fast."

Her throat moved as she swallowed, hands involuntarily tightening on the gown. Her bosom rose as she sucked a deep breath in. "I reckon if you wanted me dead, I would be so."

"But this is the first you have seen of such . . . evidence," I purred.

She nodded slowly, eyes never leaving my face, afraid if she looked away it would be her undoing. "There are monsters, my lady, and then there are monsters. The earl I once served? His daughter had an affair with one she thought she kept secret from her family. He did me no harm as long as I wished him none. I have not lived this long by being stupid. You are more powerful than he."

I evaluated her response, deciding it was sincere. "A wise choice. I shall have to reward you with more than your life, but do not let it make you over-greedy. I despise grasping, over-greedy servants."

She bobbed a curtsey, still caught in my gaze, her brown eyes dilated a bit in fear.

A knock on the door heralded the tub. I released her gaze. Susafan hurriedly thrust the offending garments into the small stove, where they caught fire. It showed great nerve and internal fortitude as she had to walk close past me. The inn's footmen carried the heavy wooden tub inside, followed by maids with pails of steaming water. They all gave quick, curious sidelong glances as they left. Rolf was the last to enter. His hands bulged with folded papers he offered up to me.

I took them. He dashed out to go join the children to whom the innkeeper's wife taught the rudiments of reading and writing. Once in the tub with my back and hair being washed, I opened the missives. The king had yet to assign me a patron and tutor. There was various notes from merchants welcoming me, begging to be allowed to be of service, or inviting me to stop and view their wares.

"Tell me, which nobles are considered the most powerful?" I idly questioned as I dried off and applied scent. Susafan brushed my hair dry, pinning it in another elaborate style.

"The Sydneys, the Marquis Jenabram, Viscount Nicky, who is also the king's advisor. I would not offend Lady Sydney. She can make life difficult for you, sway the other nobles to either accept or condemn you. I would advise having some dresses made up which will meet with her approval."

"I am not wearing what amounts to a shapeless sack just to appease her. I'm not married, nor an old maid."

"Noooo," she drawled out, "but you are foreign, unmarried, wealthy, and good-looking. She will see you as competition with her daughters, even with the king's refusal to uphold your right to your familial title."

We finished my dressing as a tap on the door brought an inn slave with a message that the sheriff was downstairs asking for me. It worried Susafan.

"I do wish you would drop the topic of that slave. No good can come of it."

"If it had been you instead, wouldn't you want to know someone was trying to help you?"

"I would not have been so foolish as to run away," she primly replied, and left, carrying the clothes that needed tending.

When I descended the stairs, I saw a tall, fat, unkempt man, disgruntled in appearance, sitting at the bar, drinking. Nathan, the inn keep, caught my eye, tilting his head toward the man. So this was the sheriff. I made my way over to the men, saying:

"I trust one of your private dining rooms is empty?"

"Yes, my lady, the same one you had yesterday. This is Sheriff Jake. Shall I have food and drink brought in?"

"If you would, please. Sheriff, come. I have much to do." I turned without a hello, striding off to the room I had used before.

The king had the town crier announce my status and name. I was not allowed use of my title; however, word had already spread of it. Those hoping to curry favor with me still addressed me as if I were nobility, while others ignored it according to decree.

Behind me, the stool scraped, his rough voice muttered, "Fucking nobles, piss on the lot of 'em, 'specially uppity bitches."

I swept into the room, pleased to see a fire burning merrily behind the flower-painted screen. It was a cozy room, with bleached muslin curtains embroidered with silver thorns, hanging over the diamond window panes. The sand-scrubbed, pine floor had a large oval braided rag rug covering it. A wooden table for four stood against one wall with chairs pushed underneath. Two silver candlesticks with unlit, new candles on top. A small fireplace opposite the table, another rag rug before it. Two carved wooden chairs with bright green cushions faced each other with small side tables. The stone hearth had been scrubbed clean. Another pair of candle sticks sat on the mantel. The weather in this hemisphere varied. It was fall now, with cool mornings and evenings; the days did not become very warm. I seated myself regally before the flames, observing the man who stomped in after me. He was large, at least six feet, muscular, but covered with a layer of fat as evidenced by his gut straining his tailored, lace-up white blouse, and hanging below his leather breast plate.

He gave a sloppy, barely-there bow, making to sit but paused as I raised a brow.

"Please, have a seat." I gestured as he lowered himself with a grunt.

A knock on the open door heralded the arrival of a serving slave with a tray of food and drink. I motioned for her to enter and set the offerings down, which she did before pouring a cup of wine for the slovenly man. I dismissed her with a wave.

"Thank you for coming, sheriff. I trust you have been informed as to why I want to speak with you?" I started after he had tasted the victuals.

His face became more peevish. "Yeah, somethin' 'bout some slave." He leaned forward, big beefy hands on his knees as he tried to take control. "Let's get somethin' straight: I be th' sheriff, an peoples respects me. They don't question me word or me methods. 'Specially not some disgraced noblewoman what ain't allowed to use her title and ain't got nothing and nobody."

"You will get used to it," I calmly replied, ignoring the rest of his statement as his face purpled even more. "I want to know what your excuse is in regards to the claims against you."

"Youse should be minding yer own bizness, and not listening to lies. 'Specially from rebel slaves that's suppose ter hang fer trying ter escape and not being sold again. I don't hafs to explain meself to the likes of youse. 'Sides, I heard youse a foreigner whose only gots temporary citizenship."

"When it comes to my slaves, accusations of corruption and misadministration of justice, I demand answers." *So I know whose minds I need to control.*

He stood, looming over me, sneering, "He weren't youse slave when he gots inta trouble. If'n youse knows what's good fer youse, youse'll ferget 'bout him, and remember it's me and me men who protects youse. A lotta harm can come to a single, foreign woman alone in a strange country, 'specially if'n she don't know nobody."

"I will overlook your poor attempts at a threat, treating them as the courteous warning you mean them to be. It does, however, make me wonder why such simple questions provoke such a strong reaction."

"Lissin here, youse uppity bitch, no one blames me for nothing. I can goes to the king and lets him know youse being a troublemaker, and youse should be thrown outta town."

"There were no accusations made by me, sheriff, only a request seeking answers. As you have pointed out, a rebel slave was sold to me who by law ought not to have been. I wish to know exactly what caused the problem between the man, his friend and you, so I may determine what I want to do with him. In the short while I have owned him, he has shown no rebellious tendencies or otherwise indicated he is willing to create the types of disturbances which are said to have resulted in his current condition."

A reasonable request easily explained away.

Sheriff Jake still loomed, trying to intimidate me, face red as his breath huffed out forcefully.

"Please," I gestured to the food and his seat, "is the meal and wine not to your liking? Shall I ask for something different? I had hoped we could have a civilized conversation."

The man glared at me; clearly temper control was not his strong suit. Slowly he sat as I waited calmly. "The only thing youse needs to know 'bout the slave is he broke a law, and tried escaping when me men tried bringing him to justice. If he ran into slavers after, ain't none of it me's fault." He crammed food into his mouth, swilling it down with gulps of wine.

"Very well. Thank you for the time you have taken to come and speak with me on the subject." I rose, offhandedly remarking, "I trust I will not have to worry about you or your men trying to cause harm to my slaves as they go about their duties. Enjoy your meal, sheriff."

He shot out of his chair, moving to block my path as his eyes crawled over my body while a nasty sneer grew on his face. He thrust a hand out, attempting to grab my arm. I blocked, twisted and squeezed. He dropped to his knees, yelping, tears of pain welling in his eyes.

"Are all your moves so ill thought out? I am not without resources, sheriff. I trust you will remember to treat me with respect should we meet again."

"Youse bitch!" he panted out. "I's could have youse hanged fer harming a man of law."

I bent down, so we were eye to eye and allowed a bit of the monster to peek out. "A bit hard to do when one is dead, isn't it?" I replied, low-voiced. "All I need do is claim self-defense, and they will believe me." I calmly remarked, "Remember, I will be keeping an eye on you and your treatment of my slaves."

I let go of him, exiting the room, calling for my mount as behind me I heard him struggling to his feet.

Chapter Ten

Colin and Mica sat grumpily in The Bloody Knuckles. Their search was not going well. "I fear we may have to ask the nobles after all. I can't discover a merchant who will admit to hiring the boy."

Mica grunted in response, listening dourly to the rain pounding overhead. It had started pouring yesterday, showing no signs of letting up. He and his brother had been forced to abandon their camp in the woods and stay at the inn again. The only good thing about the turn of events was it gave them a solid alibi for the mass murder and burning of the undesirables' quarter. The sheriff was forced to retrace their steps through every dockside inn they asked at for lodging before ending back at the tavern. Mica glowered across the room into the fireplace. The fire popped and sizzled from water making its way down the chimney. Despite the wet, Mica wanted to be out doing something, anything, to find the little boy. "Let's go back to the priest's house. It's the most reliable lead we've had so far."

"I don't think it's been three days yet." Colin frowned as he took another sip of ale, glancing about the room. He was still worried about Eron. The man had gone to extreme measures to see his friend get free and lead the posse on a chase.

"In this downpour? Where else do you think he'd be? He's only got one church. At least we can stop off at the sheriff's office, remind him of what he promised to look into for us." Mica downed the last of his watery ale.

His mind elsewhere, Colin could have sworn he heard slavers mentioned when he was hiding, waiting for a chance to sneak away. "But we've asked the merchants ourselves, at least half of them, and gotten nowhere," he pointed out after realizing he had been asked a question. "Do you really want to go there and risk the sheriff being in? Let's give Saizar the week he asked for first." He finished his own ale, grabbing his pack as Mica stood.

"Haven't you noticed how paranoid and suspicious everyone here is? It's more than we've usually run into. Something is wrong with the town."

Mica glanced over at the bar, shouldering his pack while moving toward the door. Both men drew the hoods of their cloaks far forward over their faces as they stepped outside. The rain came slashing down. Bending heads, they sloshed out into the mud. The rain seemed to be keeping all but the most determined of townspeople inside. The two brothers could see those were people well off enough to have an animal or vehicle to ride in or on, keeping out of the filth and muck. The streets were a quagmire sucking at the feet. The brothers saw some slaves out, soaked to the skin, lower bodies coated in mud. The farther the two men walked to their destination, the deeper the mud became. Soon they were struggling to pull their feet from the calf-deep mess. Still Mica wouldn't give up and by Colin's reckoning, three hours later, they arrived in front of Father John's little church, soaked and coated in reeking mud. The street was empty, all the dwellings shuttered. The houses were close together, leaning into the lane, making it very gloomy. Mica pushed on the door to Father John's dwelling and entered. It was just as dark inside as the last time, but Mica had come prepared. He took out a taper and Colin got it lit. They dripped onto the dirt floor, which showed the remains of mud clumps and feet prints.

"Hello, Father John?" Mica called out as he headed to the cloth door in back.

It was lifted out of the way by a young man holding a lantern. "Yes? Who asks after the father?" he inquired of them.

Mica stopped. "Father John? My brother and I have some questions we would like to ask of you if we may."

"I'm not him. I am his helper, Thomas. Priester John is meditating; if you'll tell me what you want with him before I interrupt?"

"It's about a boy he may have helped years ago," Mica began.

"The priester helps many people. Do you have a name or a description?" He waited expectantly.

"The boy would have been about twelve. He may have claimed he was an orphan. In actuality, he is our sister's son. It is a sad tale, if the priest will consent to hear it. He might be able to help us." Mica spread his hands wide in an effort to look non-threatening. "I would give you a name, but I'm afraid he might not be using it," he added a smile.

"Wait here." Brother Thomas disappeared back behind the cloth.

Mica turned to Colin as his brother shrugged. They heard the faint sound of a knock, muffled voices. "He doesn't eschew wooden doors altogether," Colin whispered, jerking his chin upwards.

"The bed we saw behind the cloth must have been Brother Thomas's," Mica whispered back while a growing unease curled in his belly.

"Sister, huh? What's the story this time?" Colin was still whispering.

"Sis remarried to a man who didn't like the kid. Kid ran away, possibly stowed aboard on a ship," Mica replied in a lower voice.

"Um," was the reply.

They heard feet clomping down the stairs. Brother Thomas entered again while Priester John carried a wooden chair crudely pegged together, strips of bark flaking off, which he set down before lowering himself into it with a small sigh. Brother Thomas stood off to his right side, holding a lantern. The priest stared at the two men, taking in the measure of them. Colin and Mica studied the man in turn. His small, close-set brown eyes peered suspiciously under bushy brows in a heavily lined face. He had a large bulbous nose, chapped red lips and hands. The rough, homespun robe of nut-brown, crackled stiffly from dirt, dried sweat, and old meals, belted with rope, drooped around his thin form. His feet were hidden in wooden clogs. The stench of unwashed flesh filled the room; he apparently didn't know or care of the benefits to using soap and water, much less a comb or scissors.

"So," Priester John began in a gruff voice, "Thomas tells me you're looking for your sister's son? Who are you?"

"Yes, Father. I am Micathan, and this is my brother Colinsam Dugan. Michael Nicholas is our nephew, our sister Ella's child from her first marriage. We've been looking for the boy for . . . how long now?" Mica asked of his brother but before he could reply, turned back to John and said, "Well, I'm ashamed to say I don't know how long."

Colin murmured an indistinct response, casting his face into remorseful lines. "Please, Priester John," he implored, "do you know of a child who matches our missing nephew? Have you helped anyone of his description over the past years? He would have been a boy of twelve or thereabouts, gray eyes and red-blond hair."

The man's eyes narrowed further. Did he not believe them? Or was there a chance Nicky had told the priest men might come looking for him? Men matching their description?

"I've helped many children over the years, many people. How do I know you speak the truth?"

"I guess I don't have a good answer for you. You're right, we could be anyone. Our nephew ran away from home about a year after our sister remarried. His new stepfather gave him a very rough time, as we found out much too late. If only our sister had confided in us sooner, one of us would have been glad to take the boy in." Mica spun the tale out.

"And you agreed to be away from your families all this time looking for the boy?" Priester John spat.

The brothers felt their uneasiness grow.

Colin stepped in hurriedly. "We are merchants of paper and ink. Our business requires us to travel a lot. We've never met women we wanted to leave behind for extended periods of time, so we never married. We told our sister we would make inquiries after the boy in our travels. It was sheer luck a friend of ours heard the boy had stowed away on a ship. Unfortunately, it was too late to stop him. We heard of this about a year after it happened. We've been several steps behind him all the time."

"He must be a young man by now, old enough to be on his own," the priest snapped back.

Mica and Colin glanced at each other. Mica replied, "I suppose he must be. We just wanted to speak with him, give him the letters his mother never stopped writing to her boy. She is dying, the wasting disease. We hoped we could convince our nephew to come home at least long enough for his mother to see him one last time." He looked as sorrowful as he was able.

"Hrmp," was all the priest said as he tugged at his long, tangled beard, contemplating them through narrowed eyes.

The silence grew, stretching uncomfortably. Just before Mica decided he would have to say something, Priester John spoke. "I may have helped someone like you described. But he told me a very different story. I will have to speak with him first before I can say for sure it is this 'Michael Nicholas' you seek."

"He is still in the area?" Mica asked a tad too eagerly, hastily adding as the priest's eyes narrowed again, "It's been so long since we heard any news on the boy. We started thinking he had met his end and hoped it was not the case. Of course, you must speak with him first. I hope he is our nephew. When should we come back to hear your answer?"

"It will take time. The young man I think of is at sea and should be back within a month or so. You could leave the letters with me," the priest replied craftily.

"A sailor? A good job, hard work. I'm sure we can extend our business dealings, so we are here when his ship docks. We can be reached either through the Bloody Knuckles or the sheriff's office," Colin spoke.

The priest's eyes shifted his way, penetrating again as Colin maintained a grave expression.

Mica mirrored his brother's emotions as the priest's eyes shifted back. "Yes, priester. I'm sorry the boy is away. We will do our best to remain in town. Thank you, for hearing us out and we do hope you'll let us know when the young man is back." Mica shifted, feeling they had nothing left to say, the unease growing the longer they stayed.

Priester John stayed sitting, glaring. Mica reached for the money pouch at his belt—he had sold his pinky ring, giving the brothers a little more money. "Perhaps you would accept a small donation toward your church? After all, whether the young man you know is our nephew or not, you are helping those in need." He held out a stack of coins. Priester John rose, inspecting the coins suspiciously but, spotting the royal seal, he tucked them inside his robe. The men thanked Priester John again, blew out the taper, stowed it in their pack, and stepped into the pouring rain.

As they struggled to the center of town, Colin asked, "Now what?"

"He didn't believe us," Mica flatly stated.

"We can't know for sure. He was just being cautious, and given the state of things in town, I can't say I blame him." Colin gave a grunt as he pulled a foot free. "I think we should go back to the tavern, at least wait until this rain abates somewhat."

Mica's reply was a snarl.

* * *

The brothers cleaned up before ending back downstairs at a table by the fire. The room was quickly filling up with its usual assortment of riff-raff. The brothers tried to keep out of any fights. Mica sat scowling into the shifting flames, consumed by his thoughts. Colin sipped his ale absentmindedly as he chronicled the past few days' events, watching the ebb and flow in the bar. A loud, familiar laugh made the hair stand up on the back of his neck, a flush of rage rise, which he tamped down. Sheriff Jake and his men were in the bar, and none too happy from the sounds of it. His voice carried over all the other noise.

"I sold tha' fuck to th' meanest slavers I knew, an' what did those pricks do? Theys sold him to Gri. Wouldn't'a been a problem, onlys tha' stupid fuck goes an' lets tha' prick gets ahold a sword."

"Ya can't trust 'em slavers, I say."

"Those fucks should'a taken him overland, or stuffed him on a ship, but no. Gri says he pulled some noble bitch off her horse who was lookin' fer slaves; the dumb bitch, instead of orderin' him dead fer the insult, demands to know how he be a slave!"

"Maybe she liked the look of him; he did have a pretty face. Maybe she needed someone to service her." The speaker gave a nasty bray of laughter.

The sheriff didn't sound too amused. "Tha' bitch done bought tha' fucker; seems he be tellin' tales 'bout me and me men, and the bitch wanna find the truth, she says. I'll gives her truth. I'll shuts her up."

"Gonna look funny you doing it, being sheriff an all."

"I ain'ts gonna do it meself, youse dumb fuck! I gots men to do it for me, just waitin' for the right moment."

Colin nudged his brother, who scowled as they eavesdropped. They sat with heads down, hoping the long table of mercenaries was enough to hide them from the man and his group.

"Who do you think he's speaking of?" Colin muttered.

"Hopefully, a criminal." Mica looked disturbed, uncertain, as he glanced toward the voices.

They sat drinking in silence. Colin knew his brother would want to warn the noble lady. He wasn't so sure it would be a good idea. If Eron had stayed, their friend would have been better at talking Mica out of most of his follies.

"I hear she ain't really a noble. My brother's son's wife's father works in the palace. He heard they brought her in and questioned her about her so-called title and bandit attack."

"So? Youse think all them damn nobles tha' comes here from other places is true nobility? Theys probably no more'n common dirt with a bit o' coin, copyin' their betters. How many of them are still around, huh? We seen plenty corpses decoratin' the walls. She probably jus' one more of them; won't be long before she jus' like all the rest."

"Or mayhap a whore to the king. He loves the pretty ones, and my brother's son's wife's father said she better-looking than half them whores in the harem."

There was a burst of laughter, followed by crude remarks and jokes. The voices got louder as the sheriff and his men came into view. Colin looked up, meeting the man's eyes. He knew it was a mistake as Jake changed course, stomping over to where they sat.

"Shit!" Colin mouthed as his brother got a wary look on his face, letting one hand drop to his sword pommel. Colin hurriedly sanded the page he just wrote, wanting to get the journal secured before more trouble started.

The sheriff slammed his hands down on the table, looming over them. "I's thought I's tol' youse to get the hell outta here! Youse ain't gots no friend to help youse gets gone now."

"We are merchants; we have every right to be in town selling our wares," Mica fired back.

"I hears youse a buncha liars. Youse been heard going all over town asking about some damn kid. What kinda merchants do tha'? 'Sides, we don't need no filthy slavers selling little boys fer the likes of youse to bugger. Youse get outta here, or I's be shovin' me sword some place youse won't like."

Mica's face hardened in disgust. "You are a foul man with an even fouler mind. You keep the hell away from my brother and me, or I'll—"

"Go to the king again?" the sheriff sneered, tossing the contents of Colin's mug into Mica's face. "Go ahead and try, and youse won't be as lucky as youse friend and be bought by some rich bitch."

Colin kept his face a mask at the words, seething inside. His friend should not have to suffer being branded a criminal slave. He had no qualms that was whom the sheriff had been referencing all along.

"From what I hear, it won't be long before he's pardoned. I imagine it'll be your corpse decorating the walls," Mica replied.

"Mica," Colin hissed frantically. Why was his brother so incautious and reckless?

The sheriff sneered, "There's all kinda accidents can happen. Be a shame if one happens to him. Youse get outta me town, soon if ya gets me meaning, or I'll have three corpses to decorate the walls with." He signaled to his men, and walked off, but not before they heard him say, "Keeps an eye on thems two. I wanna know everything they do, and if theys ain't gone by tomorrow night, youse come gets me."

Colin glanced over at his brother. His brows were lowered, his mouth compressed tight in anger as he wiped the moisture from his head and neck. "We'll see whose corpse decorates the walls."

"Brother, we have to extricate our friend."

"Fuck him!" Mica growled. "He left us and broke his word. The honor-less bastard can rot. We need to find the damn little boy!"

* * *

The rain was still pouring down as Colin took the slaves' stairs to exit the Bloody Knuckles. He walked as briskly as possible, given the mud had increased in depth. It took him forty-five minutes to make his way toward the bridge, another ten arguing with the guard before they would let him pass. He knew from earlier jaunts about town that the inn he was making his way toward catered to nobles and the luckier, wealthier merchants.

The big gate into the yard was shut, but not the side door. His goal was not the inn itself, but the stables behind it. The darkened building held the warmth of horseflesh as the inn's gatekeeper took him inside and to the empty stall being used by slaves.

"Hey, Domiano," the boy called out, "a man says he wants to talk with the rebel slave."

There was rustling as someone rose; a dim light glowed as a young man with wavy shoulder-length black hair lit an oil lamp outside the stall. He surveyed the soaked man before him in contempt as chains rattled, Eron appearing. He had a glower for the others.

"I know him. I'll talk with him."

The boy protested, "Domiano, you sure your mistress..."

"She's not gonna know if you don't tell her and he don't do something stupid like running." Domiano shooed the gatekeeper back to his post, hanging his lamp from a hook on a wooden stall post before going back to his nest of blankets in the hay. "I'll be watching you." He fingered his dagger meaningfully.

Eron ignored the groom. "My notoriety extends, excellent. How long did it take you to figure out it was me?"

"Sheriff Jake is a loudmouthed braggart. He wanted us to know. The noble lady, is there no way you can convince her to free you?"

His friend held up his chains; not one link had been removed since he left the slavers. "It would seem my word is not as trusted as it once was."

"I will speak to her, vouch for you, and have my brother do the same . . ."

Eron's lips lifted in what might have been a smile. "It solves half the problem but leaves the small impediment of my slave collar and the king's pardon."

"But we need you to complete our quest!"

"Colin, if she's only a forty-percent bitch, I may still be able to help. But I'm stuck here, unless I'm executed first. She is a noblewoman, albeit temporarily de-titled." He let the meaning sink in.

After Colin left, Eron lay down, trying to sleep. Coming up with an escape plan wasn't the problem—it was the lady who bought him. He had the disquieting feeling, ever since they'd crossed paths in the slave market, they knew each other. But from where? And how?

Far away was the faint drip of water and street traffic which faded as they walked farther into the maze of underground tunnels. The light from the flashlights barely penetrated the darkness. To either side, the man knew, lay piled walls of bones and skulls. These were areas not on the map, areas forgotten and lost to time. They had to keep the woman in sight, or they would wander down here in the dark and cold until death claimed them.

She paused a moment to give them time to catch up, her eyes reflecting the light the way a cat's would. The black rubber of her suit made her a part of the darkness. Crossed behind her shoulders, the hilts of two swords stuck up from their sheaths. She put a finger to her lips, the flesh starkly white. The light from her flashlight picked the faint shimmer before her of some liquid around a solid mass.

Lights burned across the river and in the buildings around, like little stars or small blazing suns. The dark bulk of Notre Dame rose off to one side, the spotlights picking out the towers and famous facade. Occasionally a tugboat blew its horn. The water magnified the sound of traffic crossing bridges. He knew stars were up there, somewhere, beyond the lights of civilization.

A gentle wind blew the scent of a little garden to their noses. He wrapped his arms around her, pressing her icy silken flesh to his, wrapping them both with the silk sheet. He could smell himself on her skin, and she on his. He kissed her long, rich brown hair, the nape of her neck. "Lira, come back to bed, come back to me."

"Lira! No!" Eron screamed at her as Mica yelled, "Holy Mother of God! What are you?"

Illyria's face was a terror: her flesh translucent, veins and arteries red and blue shining jewels, her eyes honey fire in black pits, evil fangs a glowing white framed by her hair which writhed in an unseen wind. The immortal she held in both clawed hands screamed in terror as they slowly rose in the air past the steel catwalks and concrete pillars.

Chapter Eleven

Dusk was fast fading into nighttime when I entered the Silver Thorn. I needed a nap; the weak sun sapped my strength. Before I could ascend the stairs, the owner let me know I had guests in the private parlor. I was set to refuse them when he identified them. I debated the wisdom of sending them away, before deciding I had enough self-control to speak with the men. As Rolf ran ahead to announce me, I received the second shock of my day: the scent of cinnamon, vanilla, and ambrosia curled in the air. The two men I had spied in Nicky's nightmares, and the king's! How far did the acquaintance go? And more importantly, were they enemies or friends? I put the disquieting feeling that I had met them before to the back of my mind since I couldn't do anything about it at the moment.

"Good evening, gentlemen. I was beginning to think you did not exist." I seated myself, waving off food or drink for myself but gestured for the men to be taken care of. A quick flicker of questioning between them, an infinitesimal nod.

"It is you who should be thanked for taking the time to see us, Your Grace," the thin, bookish man replied.

The tall blocky man growled, "We were given to understand you had questions about a guard we had employed in the recent past?"

Really? He was all business, not a moment spared for pleasantries. I wondered how they managed any transactions, if he was always gruff. I saw two men with enough similarities in facial features they had to be blood relations, despite the differences in their height, though the milder one had sandy hair and a slight ascetic look.

I matched my tone to his. "Only if you are indeed Mica and Colin Dugan."

The austere man replied with a bow, "We are, Your Grace. I am Colin, and this is my brother Mica. I trust our former guard, Eron Adams, is in good health?"

"Other than running afoul of our beloved sheriff and a band of slavers."

"I am most sorry to hear of it. He was never the reckless kind to get into scraps of that nature," Colin was quick to reply. I could tell he cared more for the man than his brother did.

"What is it he is supposed to have done?" Mica was blunt to the point of rudeness. I could see it upset his brother.

It grated on my nerves too. *Ack!* I should have taken that nap first. I was having difficulties controlling my emotions. I managed to squelch the urge to teach him the meaning of respect.

"I am hoping you will be able to tell me. There seems to be some confusion. I am told there was an incident involving the sheriff, which your guard witnessed."

Mica leaned forward as the chair creaked. "I don't wish to be insulting—"

Colin sighed in weariness as I let a thread of steel enter my voice. "Yet you continue to be so. I can assure you, no one else is likely to care about it, nor see any reparations be made. Speak truthfully, before I decide it is not worth my consideration."

Mica glared, about to reply, when a knock sounded on the door, and I held a hand up to stop whatever they were about to say as the door opened. A tavern slave entered with full tankards of ale.

He set them in front of the men, removed the empty ones, making as if to stand against the wall but I sent him back outside. *Bitch. Whore. I'm not some lesser slave to fetch like a mindless dog.*

The stray thought startled me, although I didn't reveal my reaction.

Colin hurried to make amends. "I do apologize for my brother's rudeness; he is not normally so out of sorts. Our trip has been fraught with dangers and bad luck. Would it help to start at the beginning of our tale? My brother and I are merchants of parchment and ink, as you already know. We came here to establish another trade route for our wares."

"Adams was your guard, he told me."

"Yes, he was," Colin replied as his brother snorted belligerently, arms crossed. He continued his tale, which was much the same as Eron's had been.

I couldn't understand; he spoke truth, yet it sounded false. Just like the others who shared his scent, I could not read their minds to determine which.

"Interesting," was all I replied, thoughtfully.

"If I may, when last I saw Eron Adams, he was fighting the sheriff and his men to give me time to escape. We are still unsure how he came to be a slave." Colin gave the briefest of pauses as if not sure to continue. "We mean no disrespect, but I must confess I find myself curious as to how and why he garnered your attention."

His brother smirked. "I take it he is an unsatisfactory slave?"

Coolly, I replied, "He was attempting to escape his bondage when we met. His story intrigued me enough that I purchased him to prevent his death. I'm afraid it did not sit well with the sheriff or the man you seek. I have been trying to ascertain the truth of the matter in a way which can be satisfactory to all parties. You are the only other individuals involved I have been unable to speak with."

"Oh, so that's what you call being a nosy, prying woman?" Mica challenged me, glaring at his brother when he murmured protest. I gave him a steely-eyed stare he more than returned. I had to fight to contain my rage at his tone.

"Is . . . pardon me, but is there not some way to free him? We know he is not guilty of whatever crime he has been charged with. We will swear under oath to His Majesty if we must, and recompense you for his price."

"It doesn't please me," Mica growled under his breath.

I couldn't help my eyes narrowing. Why hire someone multiple times if they caused problems? Unless it was something current, and thus was why they had made no effort to discover what had happened to their former guard?

"I am sure he will appreciate the oath-taking on his behalf, but I do not intend to sell him."

Colin cleared his throat and took a sip of ale. "May I ask what you do intend?"

"The king has decreed an end to the matter, officially, whether or not the man is innocent."

"Please, we have spent many a year with Adams as our guard,

enough to appreciate the value of the man. He is of high merit alive, and nothing if dead or a slave."

I merely inclined my head. "I suggest you visit the royal court scribe and make sure he witnesses your version of events." I waited a beat or two. "If I were you, I would keep a copy. I doubt it will change His Majesty's mind, however, or grant your guard his freedom back."

I rose as if to go as Colin spoke. "If we may, there is one other matter we wish to discuss with you." At my gesture, he continued, "We had not expected to come across it when we landed upon these shores."

He paused looking to his brother, still glaring at me. "It is of a delicate nature."

"What my brother is trying to say is we have received word a person who has stolen from us is now living here," Mica spit out.

My eyebrow winged up. "And what would I have to do with a thief?" I haughtily inquired.

"We believe the thief has made his way here, and attached himself to a member of the nobility," Mica replied. "The person stole something valuable from us, and either hid it or sold it. We need to find out where, or to whom, so we may retrieve it."

I reseated myself. "Ah, and you are wondering if—what? I am unknowingly shielding the person? He is perhaps a member of my household who came with me?" I asked. "Surely you are also aware bandits killed my people?"

Again they looked to each other. "We realize you are newly arrived, and have just been granted leave to become a citizen. It is why we thought to trouble you with the issue of the theft. Nobles prefer to mete justice out for injustices against them, even those not granted leave to use their titles. We are asking if it would be possible for the person to be handed over to us instead. We implore you to consider our plea." Mica's mind was closed to me, just like Eron's and the little boy's had been, unless I could find a way to take blood from him. "What does it matter who metes out justice as long as it is done, and why should my being a relative newcomer be a help to you?" I looked to Colin, but it was the other brother who answered.

"We believe because you are new, you would not give offense by asking questions persons of greater familiarity with the culture cannot."

"In other words, a foreigner would be excused my minor gaffes.

This significant object, it is business related?" I inquired. There was something about the story which just didn't sound right.

"Family and business related, and very dear to us," Mica said.

"Have you heard of the thief?" Colin asked.

"I am sure there are many thieves in and about town. You haven't given me particulars; would you care to rectify the situation?" I replied.

I heard Mica's heart beat faster, felt the rise in heat washing off his skin, a few other minute changes letting me know his anxiety level rose at my response. Strange reaction!

Colin spoke, "My we have your assurance we'll have some time alone with the thief to ask our questions? Before we describe him."

The whole conversation was definitely off. "Why would I agree to become embroiled in your problems? What is it about the person which makes you ask after him in such a strange manner?"

"When we tell people the whole story, they do not believe us, and he goes free," Mica said.

"He is brilliant, and as the law in this town may be corrupt, we do not know how he could be captured."

"I should like to hear more before deciding if it is a cause I wish to allay." It was the most I was willing to commit to before I heard more.

"Thank you," Colin said.

The brothers looked at each other again, and Mica began. "The thief is not a man; he is a . . . a boy. A young boy."

"Most people are inclined to believe a child's story over two grown men's; I begin to see your difficulty." I said. They sucked in a breath, but had not relaxed. "Which means of course I must ask why I should believe your version of events over a child's."

They looked miserable, defeated. Colin answered me. "We have no answer. We only ask if you know of, or run across the boy, to be careful of him. If you ask him his side of the story, he will know we are looking for him, and he will run again."

"And you shall be back to square one," I added.

"Yes, we shall." Colin regarded me steadily.

"Perhaps rightly so," I said as an afterthought.

They inclined their heads. Mica began to talk. "We took the child in when he was eight or nine. He was an orphan at the time, trying to survive on the streets. We started to teach him what we knew of our business. We did not realize the boy had already been taught a trade by another man, was still being taught: how to steal. We noticed stuff missing. At first it was just small objects, small amounts of money. We believed it to be other apprentices, or dishonest servants."

Colin took up the story next when his brother paused to drink some ale. "We began to travel, setting up our trade routes, taking only the boy with us, at which point we realized our thief was the boy himself. One night my brother and I discussed what we should do: cure him of his stealing, or turn him over to the authorities. He must have overheard us. We went to bed undecided. That night, we woke to find a strange older man in our room tying us up. He and the boy stole everything we had. He would have killed us, but Mica managed to work himself loose and called for help."

"We found the boy's accomplice, but not the boy himself. We managed to retrieve some of our possessions, but not our family heirloom. We've been tracking him down, and each time we think we're close, we lose him again," Mica finished the tale.

I looked at each man in turn. Seriously? That was the best they could do? "What is the family heirloom which makes you chase it down so—the crown jewels?" I asked in jest.

"Near enough." Colin gave a wry smile.

I heard Mica give an exhalation as if relieved that was all I was going to ask. Did they really have nothing to do with the young man carrying the same scent as they, having nightmares of them? I was missing something crucial; time to proceed ever more cautiously. "What does the boy look like? And what is his name?"

Mica told me.

Swiss cheese had fewer holes than their story. I thought back to the man I saw and his dreams of being a boy in pre-cataclysmic times. I wondered if their precious object was a grimoire. Were they witches? They were not kin to me, nor did they have the faint scent of animal which denoted a were-creature. Was that why they all smelled the same? What did you call male magic handlers? I had never met a witch before, but it didn't mean they didn't exist. I needed them to leave the town before they found out what I was. I had no way of fighting true magic users. Was this why the man's blood had affected me the way it had? I would have to tread very lightly.

"It is possible I have seen the boy you speak of. The name sounds familiar, although there are any number of nobles and adjuncts to the royal court who could fit your description. I will inquire discreetly for you." The name, coupled with the man's nightmares, made me think they did know each other, and were enemies. I could use it to my advantage.

I watched as Colin glanced at his brother, who was struggling to remain neutral. "Not to challenge you or your methods. But could it be executed so the boy doesn't flee if he is here? Or hears he is being looked for?"

I spread my hands wide. "Of course one can't always be sure word won't get to the wrong person. Be that as it may, the person I'm thinking of may no longer care, or think his position is unshakable."

The expression on Colin's face made me think of alarm bells going off in his brain.

Mica leaned forward. "You have seen the person?"

"I will have to rendezvous with the person of whom I am thinking before I can be positive." I let them infer what they wanted from the statement. How long had they been looking for the boy? Why did they persist in calling the kid a boy, if Lord Nicky were the same person? The advisor was a young man of nineteen, not twelve. I also didn't like the fact that if their story wasn't true, they'd be as long-lived as I. Only those who had lived pre-cataclysm would dream or know of modern clothes and inventions. "It would explain in part why we have not heard from the king about our query," Mica muttered to his brother.

I pretended I didn't hear. Any royal court is riddled with spies, and trying to keep a secret in court is akin to holding water in a sieve. What kept the boy from using his influence to neutralize men who were a threat to him?

"Has it occurred to you, asking after the child could be dangerous now on a more personal level?"

Mica's nostrils flared in anger. "I would hope His Majesty and the court would be glad to rid themselves of a snake in their midst."

I watched as he blew a frustrated breath out, sipping from his tankard. "We are at an impasse; none of us wish to bring the king bad tidings."

I inclined my head. "I agree. Let us not get ahead of ourselves. It all may be a moot point if the person I am thinking of is not the right one."

Colin spoke. "Is there a way you can arrange for us to see the boy or boys without him knowing?"

"Let me see what I can do," I said, wondering what was in it for me. "It will be safer if there is a plausible reason for us to meet confidentially on a regular basis."

Mica's scowl deepened. "I'd think your imprisoned slave reason enough."

Colin appeared worried as I continued, "I do not see the problem of my rebel slave dragging on much longer; therefore we cannot use such an excuse. As I recall, you mentioned you are looking to establish a trade route here, and the concessions needed to sell?" They nodded. "As new merchants in town, you will need help. I will get what you need to set up your business faster than the local guilds can, as a silent partner for a cut."

"We seem to be the ones taking the biggest risk, and now you demand a part of our business? Just what are you suggesting we give you?"

"I am not insensitive to your doubts. I shall be risking much in making sure the boy I know is the one you pursue, and he does not escape should he prove guilty. It is only fair I have a chance to recoup some of the costs. Say forty percent?" I ventured.

"We merely need to see him fully to confirm his identity. No doubt you can arrange it with none the wiser as to your role. Twenty percent."

I continued, "Are my sources incorrect when they say the sheriff confiscated your possessions in his zeal for upholding the law, as he sees it? And that attempts to retrieve those items have been unsuccessful?" I was fishing, exaggerating what Eron had told me, but by their reactions, I'd touched the truth. The brothers' faces froze as they drew back from the table.

"Have you not the funds for even the most basic of living expenses? I shall loan you what you require."

Colin bowed his head to me. "You must be a hell of a gambler, and a winner." He had a small smile of amusement at realizing they had been out-bluffed.

"Thirty."

"Twenty-five, on the conditions already discussed."

I had a feeling it would be his last offer. "Done. When will you have the agreement drawn up?"

"When will you arrange for us to see the boy?" Mica insisted.

I wanted to move cautiously until I had a little more information and this dolt wanted to go full tilt. "When we are satisfied he meets each of our particular requirements, the ideal time to grab him would be when the king hosts a harvest ball. It is a tradition here I have learned for the tradespeople to attend the Harvest Ball if they have received invitations and can afford to come in court dress. One may mingle with one's betters, if only for one night."

Colin blinked. The distaste on Mica's face indicated he hated cloak-and-dagger shit. "I fail to see how it's useful. There will be too many guards about, and we would need invitations. Besides, how will you know we are the injured party without questioning him about the specifics, which will make him run?"

I nearly gritted my teeth in vexation. *I'm all but handing him to you on a silver platter, and you want to quibble!* "I will not kidnap and hold a minor against his will if there is a chance he is innocent. Let me use my plan first. If I think there is a chance he will bolt, I shall detain him."

If this doesn't do it for the big lunkhead, what will? I needed them all gone. If the Nicky they sought was the same as the king's advisor, holding him against his will would escalate matters to a level I wished to avoid. I should have been able to sense the boy as I can everyone else, yet I had not. Only his footsteps and voice. If he as well as they were magic users, that made him an even more dangerous threat to me.

Mica answered, "Very well." He did not seem happy at my refusal to kidnap the kid. "However, there are problems."

I tilted my head inquiringly. *Of course you would think of more!* "Other than the invitations?"

"He could spot us and slip away, or somehow convince His Majesty or the noble he's with to have us arrested."

Colin buried his face in his mug to keep from laughing.

I used my most imperious tone. "None but the most foolish would think to question and risk alienating us when we bring wealth and much needed goods into the kingdom. There are gardens outside the ballroom where you may hide. I will lure the boy outside to you, at which point he can be grabbed and spirited away. I can further ensure the guards will not interfere. Any other objections?"

Colin decided to come right out with it, "The fancy outfits for the ball . . . I imagine all the tailors are extremely busy?"

"I will see to it a tailor has clothes ready for you as part of our bargain."

It is too easy. What we have to offer can't match the level of generosity and support if she is serious. Mica spoke cautiously, "Your generosity knows no bounds; it is worth more than what we have agreed upon."

"Believe me, even with papers for twenty-five percent of the trade route, I can recoup any expenses incurred in our venture over the course of my lifetime. Do we have a deal, gentlemen?"

Colin said, "I see no overt reason why we should not agree."

Chapter Twelve

Laughter and shouts from drunken patrons came through the kitchen door. Mary Elana stirred the pot of stew, hoping she needn't serve with the tavern slaves. A familiar name pricked her curiosity; the servants were gossiping about the new foreign woman, who'd been denied the use of her title by the king. How she had bought the merchant man the sheriff and his group had sold to the slavers.

Catya was bragging, "I heard it from the sheriff hisself when he wanted a little tussle. Said she even went to the king's advisor."

Laughter rang out; no one with a regard for their long-term safety put themselves in the position of needing or requesting a favor of the king's advisor.

"Marya from the Whale Tail, she heard it from a slave who heard it from the slaves at the Silver Thorn. That nob got the advisor to promise the sheriff would leave her slaves alone."

The young girl kept silent as she stirred; so the woman hadn't lied when she said she could help. Why would a member of the nobility want to help a nobody?

"I heard she be needing slaves, and freeborn, skilled workers. She ain't got none." Catya had all the best gossip, as the owner's favorite slave.

"Like you'd be sold ta the likes of her; what she want with a slut anyway?" a blonde called out as she snapped to the girl, "I need four bowls of stew and hurry up."

"She bought the smart-mouthed stable slave from here, didn't she?" Catya snarled before pushing through the door with her refilled tray.

Mary Elana's mother barely looked up from the meat she was carving. "Don't you sluts be thinking my Tom will sell the likes of you if you misbehave the way Domiano did. Highborn ladies want female slaves who know their place and ain't gonna be competition. Now get outta my kitchens. There's men out there be needing drinks."

The girl left off stirring at her mother's command and began to wash the used dishes. The water was cold, greasy and needed changing. She knew her Ma would not let her out of sight while the tavern itself and its yard teemed with patrons. Mary Elana went about her work, the night wore on, and slowly the tavern emptied.

Tom banged the door open. "Wife! The sheriff and his men wants food. Send yer daughter out with it."

"And why can't one of the others do it?" she yelled back.

"Cause them sluts be upstairs earning us more coin, that's why. Now send her out; he's already in a bad mood."

Jenfry turned to her daughter. "You heard him! Hop to it." She swatted the girl's bottom with the broom.

Mary Elana scurried to fill bowls, her stomach rumbling in hunger. She had not been allowed to eat yet, and it looked like she wasn't going to, either, as her father continued on complaining while he shoveled down stew.

"The damn foreign woman be in here, the one claiming she be a duchess."

Jenfry grunted, "Probably a lie if she likes to frequent places such as ours; she got coin?"

Tom gave a nasty laugh as their daughter dawdled, eavesdropping, until her parents caught sight of her and ordered her back to the kitchen. Catya's earlier words about food came back to Mary Elana. She felt a curious sensation start in her belly. The girl brought the tray out, the men grabbing the bowls and platters of bread. She only had time for a quick look around the tavern: the usual assortment of patrons, a few hooded and cloaked to conceal their identities. When her tray was empty, Mary Elana retreated into the kitchen, glad the sheriff's men hadn't paid much attention to her.

Her mother said, "Eat your food. They shouldn't need you for a while."

The girl nodded, sitting on a wobbly three-legged wooden stool, looking at the meal before her with new eyes. A not-quite-clean plate held chunks of meat too fatty or gristly for the stew, a burnt heel of bread. A mug held tepid buttermilk.

She hadn't managed to eat much when Tom yelled for his wife to send their daughter out.

"Go see what the other patrons want, tell 'em last call," he instructed her. The typical complaining from the drunks began at her words about Tom closing an hour or two early. The girl approached the last table that held a hooded and cloaked patron.

"F-father says it's last call. Can-can I get you one more?"

"No, thank you, child." The girl recognized the voice of the woman called Lira. She lingered a heartbeat, wondering if she dared vocalize *help me,* just two little words. Mary Elana flinched when her father shouted for her to get back into the kitchen, and scurried to her mother. A pail of scraps for the pig, destined to become dinner for tavern patrons, waited to be taken outside. Mary Elana huddled in her ragged, threadbare dress and shawl as she passed the stable, its doors shut to keep the heat inside, the expanse of yard almost pitch black and silent. The cold ground made her unshod feet burn with pain. The slops in the bucket were better than what her mother had given her to eat.

A squeal from the hog—she realized in horror she had been cramming food from the pail into her mouth. Her stomach roiled, the pail dropping into the pen, spilling what remained. Mary Elana clutched the top rail, vomiting up all she had just eaten, the hog snuffling and grunting as it ate. She sniffled, wiping at the snot running down her nose, dizzy and swaying with fatigue and hunger. What if the merchant man were wrong? What if there was no opportunity for a better life? Even her father's slaves were better treated than she; they needn't eat from the pig's slops What if she had just thrown away her only chance by not asking the lady for help? She sobbed out loud, cramming a fist in her mouth as she leaned against the side of the building. The coins she'd sewn into her dress hem rapped her knees as the wind whirled. Perhaps Mary Elana could warn the lady of the danger she was in—would she hire her in thanks? A sharp sound brought her head up; the side door to the tavern thrust open, a large, dark shape stumbled out, cursing. The girl huddled down, trying to make herself smaller, listening to the sounds coming from the tavern. The shouts from the tavern sounded different. She was too late. Her father and the sheriff's men must have already attacked the noble lady.

A hard hand yanked her up. "What's this?"

The sheriff breathed a combination of ale and bad breath onto her as he squinted. "Ain't youse supposed to be inside, girl? Yeah, I thinks ya are. Yer father thinks he gonna make his fortune offa yer hide." He gave a bark of laughter at the terrified look on her face.

"Well, ain't no harm if I's sample the goods first, make sure they ain't gone bad, hey?" the man slyly put forth.

She felt his fingers ram somewhere they shouldn't. The jolt of pain brought her out of her frozen numbness. She screamed, loud and long, barely taking in breath between screams. The pail dropped unnoticed from her hands.

"Damn bitch! Shut the fuck up!" the sheriff roared as another large dark shape hurtled out the still-open side door.

Voices shouted around her, blood was in her mouth, face pressing in the dirt.

"Damn it, Jake! The damn foreign slut be causing trouble! Git in here and takes care of it afore she kills half yer men!" Tom roared, missing his daughter on the ground.

The sheriff cursed. "She be one woman. How much trouble can she produce? Me's men can take care of it!"

"The stupid bitch knows how to fight! And it ain't any kind I ever seen before. She already disabled or killed half the damn bar! Just git in here!" Tom spotted two other men walking in the yard as Jake stomped toward the doorway. "Hey! You two get outta here! I told you before not to come begging around here or spouting your stupid religious beliefs!" It was Priester Joseph and Brother John. The men gave her uneasy feelings despite what they preached.

"Whore monger! Sinner! The death lands will have you for your sinful ways! You and your slattern of a wife and daughter selling their bodies," Priester Joseph yelled in outrage.

Her father's hobnailed boots stomping across the dirt yard. "Stupid bitch! I told you not to leave the tavern! You better not have tried fucking selling yourself like the whores. You stupid bitch, you're just like your mother! Neither of you listen!"

Mary Elana sobbed out denials, crawling away from her father's hands and feet slapping, punching, kicking. He was wild-eyed in rage, a look upon his face she'd never seen before. A revelation came to her: her Pa didn't care if she lived or died. He thought she was damaged goods and thus worth nothing. A sharp pain lanced through her head, vision growing hazy before she blacked out.

Tom would have continued the assault upon his daughter if he hadn't also hit the two holy men, purely by chance. They took instant offense and managed to subdue their attacker, alternately praying over and shouting accusations at him.

* * *

The girl lying in the dirt woke slowly, moaning in pain as voices continued to rage at each other. *Oh no. Where am I? This doesn't feel like my bed! Why can't I see?*

She shifted on the cold ground, the motion sending waves of agony over her. *What did he do? What has my father done to me?!*

"Nooooo!" she moaned fearfully. "I can't! Please, I can't be sightless!" The undernourished girl broke down into wracking sobs, sending a searing pain all through her body.

A cool, rough hand touched her brow, another grasped her hands, a man said "Shh . . . shh now. You'll be fine. I'm Brother John. You're outside the Bloody Knuckles, and you've been badly injured."

It took a while before he could get her calmed down. "Let me get you some water."

Mary Elana heard her father shout, "You leave the slut alone! I told you two to get off my land! What I do to her ain't no concern of yours."

She felt something wooden against her mouth. Tentatively she sipped, her split lips making drinking a new agony.

"Please, Brother John, what's wrong with my eyes?" Her voice quivered in terror.

"They are swelling shut. Can you try to open your eyes?"

Mary Elana did her best. She managed to open the lids a mere slit. Everything appeared hazy, and she said as much.

"It should get better."

"Please," Mary Elana whispered, uncontrollable shivers wracking her. "How-how long have I been here? Lying down?"

Brother John remained silent a moment, before gently replying, "Only for a few moments. Would you like to come to our temple with us? We can heal you, both bodily and spiritually. When you are ready, you can take vows to join as a Sister." He patted her hand kindly.

"Fuck you! You leave the slut alone. She ain't going anywhere with you or taking any of your crazy vows! Jenfry, get the hell out here and deal with your disobedient slut of a daughter!" Tom yelled.

"You have put the girl's soul in mortal peril of the wastelands, doomed to burn and wander after death in darkness." Priester Joseph replied harshly.

The girl heard sounds indicating Brother John getting up. More footsteps joined the group.

"Damn it, Tom! Didja have to beat the stupid slut half to death? He ain't gonna pay fer her now, looking like that." Sheriff Jake snorted.

"What the—? Jenfry! Get him a wet cloth! I wouldn't have to discipline her if you hadn't tried to make the stupid slut think she could fuck you the way the other whores do. I told you, he wants her untouched! Besides, I need the foreign slut outta my tavern. You should be dealing with her!"

"You get outta here, priest, my daughter isn't in danger of anything," Jenfry added to the din.

"It's ended," the sheriff replied in snarling tones. "Don't know where the damn foreign whore learned to fight, but she better watch her back. Damn bitch nearly cut me face off."

A deep, oily voice sounded near Mary Elana's ear as the two men continued to argue. "I see by the Great One's grace you shall live. We must pray and thank Him, for He has sent me to help."

Priester Joseph launched into a long prayer as the girl blinked her lids painfully, vision starting to come back. Some of the things he said had her frowning, but she didn't want to interrupt.

"Please, Priester, please help me."

"You must tell me everything, what caused your punishment, so I may help you."

"I-I don't remember, what-what happened."

"Start at the beginning of the night and go until you get to the parts you are unsure of. Think of it as a cleansing, and believe the Great One is merciful, my daughter. If you are free from sin, he will grant you your memories back."

Mary Elana took a breath, which made her ribs ache. Her parents seemed to have forgotten about her for the moment in their argument with Jake. Haltingly she went through the night, bits and pieces floating up until with a flash she could recall it all. When the girl began to describe the assault upon her by the sheriff, the priest interrupted with an enraged yell.

"Worse and worse! Have you so forgotten yourself, you thought to lure a married man and play the whore like one of your father's slaves?"

"But-but I didn't! I-I never said or did anything! He-he pushed himself on me! He always does," Mary Elana replied in bewilderment, tears starting to leak out.

"How dare you tell such evil lies about an officer of the law?! Wicked! You should beg the Great One's forgiveness for your lies!"

She tried to deny any thoughts or attempts of luring the sheriff, but the vitriol Priester Joseph spewed at her made her do as she was told. Priester Joseph was satisfied with her attempts, demanding, "What happened after?"

"My-my father came out yelling. He-he started to beat me."

The tears came faster now, burning her eyes, scalding her cheeks; her voice broke, unable to continue.

"And you swear before the Great One that is all?" There was something dreadful in the sound of his voice.

"Yes! I'm telling the truth."

It seemed he had not heard her. *How dare she tell me lies?!* The yard silent except for the sound of breathing. Her father raging at the priest and Brother John. His daughter barely aware her father and the sheriff were trying to force the two holy men out of the yard.

"Stupid slut! How dare you lie about your father and Jake?" Jenfry snarled. "Get her up, you useless sluts."

Why had Priester John not helped her? Two pairs of strong hands yanked her off the ground, unmindful of her bruises and hurts. The girl briefly blacked out, held between two slaves.

"Your pardon, Mistress Tavern Keep, might I have a word with you concerning your daughter?" A smooth female voice joined the group.

"Fuck you, whore! You get outta here before I have Jake arrest you for smashing up my husband's tavern and harming our patrons," Jenfry spat back.

An amused laugh was the answer as Mary Elana cried. Tears dripped down her face falling on her clasped hands. She didn't understand why no one would believe her. Priester Joseph was always going around telling people he met he could help them. Why wouldn't he do the same for her?

"'Tis no more than any of your other patrons have done before. As for the sheriff, I doubt he is going to be so foolish to try attacking or arresting me after tonight. At least for a little while. However, if it will ease your mind, I shall pay for the damage done." Coins clinked.

Jenfry sounded extremely greedy. "It ain't near enough to cover costs."

"It is most fair, considering the condition of your tavern earlier tonight; however, if you don't want it…"

Jenfry spluttered, "Give it here. What about my child?"

"I take it she is troublesome to you, not worth what it costs to feed and clothe her. I am in need of a house slave. If she can clean, I hope to engage her services, either as an indentured servant or slave."

"Noooooo!" Mary Elana moaned, weeping harder. Why was this happening to her? How could she have been so wrong about the woman? Was there no one she could trust? Was it fate because she hadn't warned the noble lady about what her father planned to do to her?

"Rent? Or purchase? She is freeborn." Her mother's voice was suspicious, despite the greed.

"I am told such things are of little consequence here. She is your daughter . . . your property . . . thus you may do what you desire with her."

Jenfry would not be put off. "Why would you want a troublesome slave? I heard you already got yourself two of 'em; one of them used to work in the stables here."

"Let us say problem slaves are my specialty. Will you sell her or not?"

"Well," Jenfry started, but footsteps interrupted as her husband and the sheriff came back.

"Why's the slut still here?" Tom complained.

"Hush!" his wife replied. "The lady," she sneered, "wants to buy your daughter. She's nicely compensated us for the damage she done to the tavern. I've a mind to consider it."

"Here now! Youse can't! Youse two know the slut be promised to Him! Youse know what'll happen if youse try a double-cross Him." The sheriff hawked, spitting as he glared at the composed woman. His humiliation at being outfought silenced him.

Tom snatched the coins from his wife's outstretched hand. "Quit your sniveling, slut; you've caused enough trouble for tonight. Well now, it's a right nice gesture on your part to pay for what you did to my bar. An' even nicer if I don't ever see you in my tavern."

No response was forthcoming; through her tears, Mary Elana could see the calculating look in her father's eyes. The sheriff's lower face, covered in blood from a diagonal cut running from beneath his right eye, over his nose, and to the left side of his jaw, made him even scarier. Tom crossed his beefy arms, facing the woman squarely. "What kind of price we be talking about?"

His daughter moaned, blood-laced snot dripping from her nose. She couldn't even wipe it away, her father's slaves had such a tight hold on her arms. The woman proffered an amount.

"You trying to insult me?" Tom demanded.

"I trust you will have more sense than your wife. The price is fair for one accused of being trouble. Given her current condition, I shan't be able to make full use of her until she heals."

Jenfry whispered something to her husband. He named another price. The lady countered the offer, still not close to what Tom hoped to con out of her.

The haggling went on; finally Tom gave in, only to bellow a moment later in outrage. "Papers! What you mean you want me to sign papers?"

"It is merely a precaution, nothing more. I should hate to have the sheriff show up on my doorstep claiming our transaction was invalid due to previous agreements. He seems convinced you made arrangements with a gentleman to have access to your daughter." She gave a thin, sharp smile, causing more than one person to shiver in fear involuntarily. "I trust you are not trying to sell me another man's slave."

"Do it!" Jenfry hissed at her husband. "You don't have any such paper from Him! And she's offering twice what He did."

Tom hesitated a moment, clearly torn, not liking the request but with no real way out. He rubbed a hand over his thinning brown hair, scowling. An oily smile crossed his face. "I'm afraid we have no writing paper or ink. If you be true nobility, we can have a gentleman's—er, gentlewoman's—agreement on it, can we not?"

She merely smiled, reaching for another leather purse on her belt, "What good fortune I happen to have both upon my person. If there is some solid surface I may write on, the sheriff, as a king's official, can provide witness." Her tone made it clear that refusal was not an option.

Tom scowled even more, and with ill grace, muscled an empty beer barrel over. The note was written, wax and a taper fetched from the tavern. Seals and signatures affixed, coin changed hands. There were even a few silvers for Jake as a fee for performing his office's function. It did little to ease his hatred of the woman.

A low, continuous drone of, "No, no, no, please, don't," spilled from the girl's chattering teeth.

The barmaids holding her captive laughed cruelly, shoving her toward the woman. Eagerly they took the bronze pieces she gave them for their efforts of restraining the girl. Mary Elana thought of fleeing. The lady's slim hand closed with surprising strength around her elbow, dragging her, stumbling, away from her parents. She began to cry again, not caring if it made her face ache more.

The trip away from her home became a blur. Hands hoisted the girl up into the saddle of a black stallion, Mary Elana clutching desperately at the mane as the woman led them out of the yard into the dark, narrow streets of the town. She would have tried to jump and run, but the horse was so big, the ground so far away, and the pace seemed faster than a walk. The girl was hardly aware of amazed stares, curious comments of the palace guards at the bridge. Nor did she notice the clop of stone under the horse's hooves after a turn into another courtyard.

She felt herself hauled down, this time by work-roughened male hands. A concerned, masculine face surrounded by wavy black hair glanced pityingly at her as he whispered, "Don't cry; she is as nice a mistress as we could hope." He and the horse moved off.

Mary Elana was pulled along by her new mistress into a clean, well-lighted public room, up to a shocked-looking man.

"Your pardon, Your Gra . . . lady! But-but!"

"Send for my body slave, please, Nathan. Is Cook up yet, or any of your slaves? I shall want a hot bath, along with beef broth, and mulled wine delivered to my room."

"Not-not for another hour or two," was his response.

"Very well. See it is done as soon as they awaken." Without another word, she hauled the still-crying girl after her into a small room tucked under the eaves. Shutters blocked the approaching day from a frost-covered window.

Mary Elana didn't know how long she sat, stunned, silent, morose, before a knock sounded on the door. An older woman in a thin, patched dress with a slave collar entered, momentarily shocked.

"My lady! Master Nathan mentioned, and Domiano, but I—," she gestured helplessly.

"As you can see, the girl has been much abused by her family. I have sent for a bath and broth. You will make sure she is cleaned up and fed. If any of her injuries need professional attention, send for the doctor. I will have to impose upon you further, Susafan. She will sleep on the floor of your room until we move into my new dwelling."

"Yes, my lady," Susafan dipped a curtsey.

"Later, we shall be going out, all of us. In the meantime, you may use my room to get ready." Lady Illyria stopped in front of the girl.

She lifted the tear-, blood-, and snot-stained face up. "Do not cry, little one. I do not harm those under my banner without reason. Be that as it may, you will not attempt to run away. I doubt you would care for the dungeons or the attentions of the head questioner."

Mary Elana said nothing, too disheartened over losing her freeborn status and becoming a slave with no rights when she had been almost certain the lady wanted to hire her. She let her head fall onto her chest when the woman let go of her chin. She stared numbly at the smooth, clean wooden floor as the two women exchanged words before the door shut. She was barely aware of a pair of patched and tattered brown shoes in front of her.

"Well," the older woman said briskly, "no sense boo-hooing over it anymore. You understand me, you've had better luck than half the slaves in this town. I don't know what she'll have you doing, but if you do it well and without complaint you will have no reason for worry. Now, the king says he won't allow a foreigner asking for citizenship to retain their titles, so we aren't to use Her Grace's title. But mark my words, she is a duchess, no matter what oddity she does or wears."

The new slave girl still stared in silence at the floor as Susafan gave a sigh and walked away. There was the sound of water being poured, her voice chattered on, still brisk.

"Until the bath is brought up, the water basin will have to do. I suppose I'll have to clean you as it looks like you haven't the gumption to do it yourself. Mind you, it is the only time I'll do it. You must be sure to bathe yourself daily. Lady Illyria requires it of us. She won't have any insect-ridden filthy slaves in her house. It's a queer request and takes time, but I confess I do feel better for it."

Mary Elana let her face be lifted, automatically closing her eyes as a rough, wet, cold cloth was applied to her skin, and the worst of the filth removed. She continued to sit silently, letting her dirty hands and feet be cleaned in turn. Her extremities burned as they slowly warmed up. She didn't know how much time passed. The little candle in the room was soon blown out. The weak morning sun streamed in with the wooden shutters folded out of the way.

Susafan chatted of unimportant topics mostly, some of her life of slavery, interspersed with what their mistress expected of them. The inn's slaves hauled in a tub, buckets after buckets of hot water, and more wood for the little stove. The girl stood when tugged at and commanded, but made no move to help nor hinder the other slave when she removed the girl's shawl, dress and shift.

"Now you just climb in." The older woman guided her charge to the large wooden tub, helping the girl in and gently pressing down on her shoulders until she sat. The warm water felt surprisingly good on her cold, bruised skin and helped to soothe some of the ache inside her. Susafan put a softer cloth and a bar of soap into the young teenager's hands. "And don't forget behind your ears and between your toes and every little spot betwixt." She peered closer.

"Your hair is ridden with lice. Ugh!" Susafan shuddered in horror.

Another knock on the door heralded a giggling slave with a tray and clothes which she placed atop a small table. She stared unabashedly. "Mother Moon Goddess! I heard your father beat you, but that's the worst I've ever seen! Bet you're glad to get away from him. Is it true he whored you out?"

"Lisello, shut your mouth please and go; you know Her Grace wouldn't approve of your nosy questions."

Lisello sniffed. "You know she's not a duchess, not according to the king. You shouldn't call her that if you don't want to be arrested and sent to be tortured by the head questioner."

"Either way, leave the girl alone. I reckon she's been through enough. Not everyone is lucky to have a master such as yours," Susafan retorted.

"I suppose so. Well, the stable slave, the handsome one of hers? He said for me to tell you he put a straw pallet in your room for her." On those words, the door to the room banged shut behind Lisello.

The bath continued in silence. The older woman decided she had done all she could for the girl's hair, including washing and cutting out the worst of the mats and burning them. She got the girl out of the tub and dried before smearing some kind of ointment onto the bruises. Mary Elana was given some cast-off clothes deemed too worn for the inn slaves to wear but still serviceable for those who had nothing else. She watched her old clothes burn, not even given a chance to retrieve the coins hidden inside the hems.

The former tavern-keeper's daughter ate mechanically. She distantly noted the beef broth was rich, hot and flavorful, the mulled wine strong with spices. She found herself unsteady after drinking it, following docilely behind Susafan down the slaves' stairs and into the tiny room she now shared with the older woman. She lay down upon a clean, sweet-smelling, crackling straw pallet and drew the generous, heavy wool blanket under her chin.

She lay staring at the whitewashed ceiling, tears leaking out. Susafan stood over her a moment in exasperation, before saying in a kindly tone, "Don't cry."

"She . . . she bought me, like a slave."

"If you want to blame anyone, blame your father for being greedy enough to sell you. Now try to sleep. Life will look better after you've rested."

It still seemed a long time before Mary Elana tumbled, exhausted, into a dreamless sleep.

Chapter Thirteen

A slave escorted the sheriff into Nicky's royal suite of rooms, boots ringing on the multicolored marble flooring. He knew trouble was brewing when the young man snapped out, "The Bloody Knuckles."

"In fine form," Jake oozed.

"Not from what I hear. You failed to inform me of an incident there." Menace curled around each word.

The sheriff kept his head bowed a moment to gather his thoughts. *Shit! Fucking cocksucker! Damn the thing with him.* "No slight meant, Lord Nicky. I's don't wanna be a bother to youse lordship with me small knowledge."

The tone became even more hostile. "I determine what is paltry."

Motherfucker. "Yes, youse lordship, beggin' youse lordship's most humble pardon. The, uh, incident. Uh, well, which one we talking about?"

"Which one?" Nicky asked incredulously. "How many have you not told me about? Start with those and if your answers please me, I may not order you flogged for your insolence!"

The sheriff scowled, wishing he could shove his sword through the young man's gut. "Most of 'em is petty stuff, not worth yer time; youse told me before not to bother youse with 'em. Slave women what won't listen and have t' be hurt, or some piece of scum causing trouble."

Lord Nicky's jaw clenched. Why was he surrounded by idiots? "Think, even though I know it's hard for you to do. Think if there was another. An important one you have forgotten?" His voice promised pain.

"No, me lord, I can'ts think of anything." He scratched at the scabbed sword cut running diagonally across his face.

"You can't think of anything? YOU CAN'T THINK OF

ANYTHING?" Nicky screamed in rage, tossing a nearby gilded chair at the lawman.

The sheriff ducked, bellowing, "I ain't lying yer lordship! If'n youse just tell me whats one youse talking abouts, I can tell youse." He dodged as a chunk of amethyst being used for a paper weight came at his head.

"Try TWO MERCHANT MEN AND A GUARD!"

"Uh, uh I don't know 'bouts two buts I knows about three. Maybe someone lied abouts 'em?" he asked hopefully.

The young man slammed his hands flat onto the marble desktop hissing, "I don't care about the number. What happened? DiJinn, help our man of law remember."

The sheriff felt a wave of terror wash through him as the robed and cowled slave began to walk toward him. "Waits, waits, gives me a minute!" He put his hands out.

Nicky motioned, and the slave stopped, waiting. Jake inched warily away from him, bringing him closer to the young man.

"I was in the tavern one night when three men come in looking fer rooms. Not the usual scum. They had on nice clothes, packs, and swords. They said they merchants looking to sell their wares."

"What kind of wares?" Nicky interrupted.

"Does it matter?" he snarled, but at the gleam in the lord's eye hurriedly added, "I don't remember. Theys so many of thems. They needed rooms fer the night. I toles 'em Tom had some. Mary Elana was serving 'em, and I warns 'em not to mess with her like you wanted. If'n youse be a lord, whys youse want her? She just a common tavern slut."

"Shall I drag you to the grove again to show you why? Maybe you'd remember then?" Nicky replied, silky-smooth.

Jake's face went pale, and he gulped; once at the site had been quite enough. "No, me lord, no need. I remember now."

"What about the men? The merchants? I doubt they were stupid enough to cause trouble right away."

"N-n-no youse lordship. They didn't do anything that night. The next time I seen 'em, Tom sent for me. He said one of 'em was grabbing the wench and interfering in her work. So I go to warn them and learns one of 'em had stolen a horse offa one o' our bandits, and he weren't back yet. While taking care of the two tha' was there, they gots uppity and started to threaten me and me men."

He stopped to scowl at the memory. "I was just gonna string 'em up a little, have a little fun with 'em is all. Scare 'em kinda like. Only . . ."

"Only what?" Nicky prompted.

"One of them fought back, and in the commotion, the faggy one gots loose, so I just took the one I did have and sold 'im to the slavers as a warning to the other." Jake trailed off weakly, his eyes shifting to make sure DiJinn hadn't moved closer to him.

Nicky interrupted to demand, "Why didn't you send me word when it happened? How many times do I have to tell you, you don't sell merchants to slavers in town?"

The law man shuffled his feet uneasily. "Youse said to sell 'em to the slavers with ships to take 'em elsewheres, or to the bandits to take 'em overland."

Nicky cursed long and viciously. "When did the incident take place? Who were they? Surely you remembered to get their names?"

The sheriff paused to think, his tongue pushing against the gap missing teeth made. "Uh . . . um, it been done bought a day or two, I thinks," he lied.

It was as far as he managed before Nicky threw a jewel-encrusted gold goblet at the man.

He ducked the missile as Nicky hurled objects at hand. The overweight sheriff ducked, bellowed, "Runty pissant!"

"You dare to speak to your betters thus?" the young man screamed, and with a tremendous heave he overturned his ornately carved dark wood desk; it crashed to the floor, everything flying off to smash or spill.

Sheriff Jake jumped back as shards and papers headed his way. The slave sighed; Nicky grew more mentally unstable day by day. It might be a good idea to intervene. The fat, lazy officer of the realm could still have information.

"Calm yourself, Lord Nicky," he spoke in cool tones. "The problem is still fixable."

The young man whirled, "How dare you! I'll punish you later! What the hell good are you if you don't protect my interests! Fix the mess this asshole left? There is no fixing the mess!"

The lawman babbled, "Looks, I knows whats the other twos looks like. I can send some men for them . . ."

"Damn you!" The young man seethed while looking for something else to throw at Jake.

The sheriff started to inch out of the room, but Nicky caught the movement. "You dare to leave? Have I said you could go?"

"Uh, pardon me, Lord Nicky, but uh, if I's—"

The young man's face suffused red again. "You incompetent idiot! You've fucked it up enough already!"

Jake was beginning to get an inkling that more had happened than he realized. "Ain't nothing wrong. One of 'ems a slave; I'll just makes sure he put onna boat as a galley slave to some port far away from here."

The boy snatched a piece of parchment from his belt and held it up, demanding, "Do you know what this is?"

"No, me lord." The sheriff's eyes darted from it to the advisor's face.

"It's a letter asking for you to be investigated, due in part to 'incompetence, conflict of interest, and collusion.'" Nicky ranted. "You moron! You pus-filled, useless sack of shit! I thought you had better control over the townspeople!"

Jake shuffled his feet, his face growing red in resentment. He tried to protest, but Lord Nicky would have none of it. "His Majesty commanded me to investigate the charges. You'd better hope no one else comes forward and add to it."

"I's can make sure they don'," the lawman sullenly replied, realizing what the advisor had said. "Hey! Why's some bitch be writing youse? I done tol' her I look into it." *An' it ain't been so long I talked wit' her, neither.*

Lord Nicky stood still, the rage in his eyes making them appear black, and Jake knew he was in terrible trouble.

"You spoke to this 'bitch' as you call her, about the problem? When were you planning on telling me?" His voice was icy, deadly calm.

"Uh . . . um . . ." Jake stuttered as he realized who'd sent the letter.

"You pea-brained lout! His Majesty has forced me to suspend you from your post while I investigate. And why? Because the woman who you call a 'bitch' is a duchess! Sammy is sheriff until I can manage to convince His Majesty the charges are false."

"We's can jus' visit the damn woman an' make her take back what she wrote," Jake suggested. "She ain't gots no duke, no fighting men—just three slaves, an' I heards she ain't allowed to use her title anyhow. King said so."

The withering look the young man gave him should have had him curling up on the spot. "That's your solution? Assault a member of the nobility without provocation?" Nicky stared for a heartbeat before letting loose with a blood-curdling scream of rage. He snatched his sword from its scabbard, leaping over the desk at the lawman.

The sheriff barely got his sword out in time. The force of Lord Nicky's blow sang up his arm. He could do nothing but defend himself from the furious onslaught. "DiJinn, get 'im off me! Get 'im off me!" he squealed.

The hooded and cowled slave stood humming, soaking up the waves of rage and fear. It was not long before Nicky had forced the lawman to his knees.

"Please, please, please youse lordship," he begged. "I can make it right. I can cleans the mess up. Don't-don't kill me! Ain't no one's gonna be able to keep the lawmen on yer side buts me." He was babbling, he knew.

Nicky had exhausted himself, burning out the worst of his rage. He couldn't let the man go unpunished. He slashed both sides of Jake's face with the tip of his sword, on top of the cuts the sheriff had received from the foreign whore. "Consider yourself lucky it's only a flesh wound. Fail to inform me of anything else ever again and I'll let DiJinn punish you."

"I swear I won'ts, thank youse, thank youse."

Lord Nicky turned away from the sheriff, who had never before been so anxious to get back to his job in his life.

"I need a spy in her household. Who can we use?"

"Uh, um, well . . ." Jake began.

"I wasn't asking you. You can't find your dick with both hands and a map. DiJinn?" He turned back to his slave, missing the look of hate from the chastened man behind him.

"She needs slaves for her household; why not talk to your contacts at the market? They can pick out several who will agree to be loyal in return for promised freedom. When and if they are no longer useful, you can always kill them."

Nicky scowled. "I suppose it could work." He paced the room as he thought. "Damn bastard! Nine years I've spent undermining nobles with more power than I, trying to get a decent title, and he goes and lets a duchess stay here."

Jake made the mistake of saying, "But she ain't a duchess no more; king said so."

Nicky's voice was wintry sharp. "What did you say?" His eyes bored daggers into the man before him.

DiJinn whispered for Nicky's ears alone, "She is a woman. Perhaps a personal visit is in order? You have put off meeting with her several times already."

The young man glared at his slave. "Why should I lower myself to visit her? I will command her to see me here, so she understands how powerful I am."

"It will keep her off guard! She will believe you are sincere in your intentions. If it's a display of power, take her to the hanging grounds and explain what happens to rule breakers." *Must I think of everything for the idiot holding my reins?* DiJinn sniggered; an encounter with the immortal woman could be the opportunity to free himself of the young man and exact his revenge for all the humiliations and mistreatment.

Nicky rounded on the sheriff. "As for the slave you have failed to dispose of properly—"

Jake took a chance to interrupt. "I'll have the man killed if you like!"

"You should have taken better care of the problem when you first knew of it," Nicky hissed virulently.

The man was rattled enough to stammer, "I's thought I's had." He was eager to curry favor again. "We's just send some men to kills him."

Nicky stared at him in loathing and spat, "Idiot! We can't kill him! Not when the bitch has made the king aware he exists, and she is expecting him to find the truth of the matter. Are you trying to expose us? Get us killed? You will do nothing to him until I can figure out what the bitch thinks she knows. There has to be a way out until I can tell His Majesty she is overreacting or some other equally believable lie."

Jake didn't have an answer, and it didn't seem one was required of him. "Go," Nicky commanded, "and do what I've told you to do. And sheriff," he warned menacingly, "you had better not fail me again."

"No, me lord. Of course not, me lord. Right away, me lord," He my-lorded himself out the door to do as he was bid, thinking it was lucky the little bastard hadn't heard how his bandits were being attacked and killed.

* * *

"What is the holdup?" Nicky snarled. No one made him wait; he was the king's advisor. He picked a nonexistent piece of lint off his black velvet gold-braided riding coat. Fawn-colored leather breeches tucked into tall shiny black riding boots, a crop, and pristine white thin leather gloves finished off his outfit.

Horse hooves rang out. A groom came around the side leading a big black stallion. The animal reared, striking out with his front hooves, scattering men. He pranced in place, tossing his head, while his constant neighing sounded like the beast was talking. He forgot his complaints at the sight of the animal. The horse was all glossy muscle, with a flowing mane and tail.

"Whose beast is he?" he demanded. He wanted the horse. He would look good on the brute.

"Do you like him?" a velvet voice asked. "He likes to get his own way, and he is in need of a good run."

Nicky looked over to see a woman who could only be the foreign duchess, and blinked, "Your horse is a stallion?"

"Yes," she replied simply, walking over to the rearing, snorting beast.

She spoke to the animal while caressing his nose and spent a few minutes inspecting tack and saddle—he calmed down long enough for her to mount him.

Nicky had resigned himself to meeting the woman, expecting the tales of her good looks to be grossly exaggerated and for her to be mannish and ugly-looking. The riding costume belied that expectation: tight black leather pants, paired with tall, shiny black riding boots with red tops, a split-tailed riding coat of crimson with intricate black embroidery over a white shirt, and a tall black-feathered hat perched at a jaunty angle, the net veil accentuating her pale complexion. It explained why so many men fawned over her and agreed to her whims. Well, she would find he was not weak. She had found someone to fashion dark glass into eye shades she could wear. Her long hair was in a curling tail lying over one shoulder.

Her groom let go of the bridle as she called out to him, "Where do you propose we ride?"

He narrowed his eyes, tempted to see how well she could stay on the beast. "Follow me. I know a place where we can ride without being bothered." He snickered to himself.

The path would take them past some hangings, only a bonus. His chestnut gelding tried to rear, wanting to show the stallion he was just as good, but Nicky curbed him sharply and rammed his heels into his mount's side. The horse arched his neck as they passed the stallion, who shrieked and stomped his right front hoof.

Their small party set out through the town center, she bringing her groom while he had at least a dozen retainers in his colors of black and gold. They trotted out the courtyard gate across the bridge, his herald and two outriders, one holding a banner emblazoned with his coat of arms, clearing a path for them. She kept up easily.

"I am told you lost most of your household to bandits," Nicky said.

"Yes, but I was fortunate enough to save the bulk of my wealth, and the slave markets have given me ample means to replace them."

He could hear the roar of a crowd. "I must tell you, it would not be wise to purchase slaves who are known rebels. Our laws state they are to be put to death for such crimes. It would be a shame if you were indirectly indicted for encouraging such behavior amongst them."

He was mildly disappointed when she showed no emotion at his warning, only arched a brow. "I am not so sure he should even be a slave, Did His Majesty not send along my note?"

Their party stopped at the edge of a crowd. Children played off to one side, enterprising vendors hawked various foodstuffs and drinks. A few participants already appeared drunk, and he ground his teeth, snapping, "Since you have brought it up, we must discuss it." The rest of his sentence was lost to the roar of the assembled townspeople.

A tucket of trumpets announced the arrival of a cart carrying condemned prisoners. The noise from the crowd swelled tenfold as drummers started to beat out the final march. Rotten vegetables, spit, and curses hurled at the occupants. The palace guards pushed townspeople out of the way so the cart could stop next to the gallows. Roughly they hauled several prisoners up the stairs. The screams of pain or pleas for mercy only served to excite the crowd more. Two of the guards had to hold up a woman as she couldn't stand on feet ruined by torture. A scrawny man with long, scraggly, greasy hair and beard, wearing a filthy brown robe tied with rope, stood off to one side making strange hand gestures and muttering. The herald stepped next to the condemned and, facing the crowd, raised his hands for silence.

"Good citizens, hear me!" He waited for the noise to subside, continuing when it had.

"These criminals stand before you, good people, for actions most heinous." The crowd shouted and cheered. The herald had to hold his hands up for silence.

"This slave who stands before you attempted to escape his bondage. He shall be drawn and quartered!" The crowd booed as he worked his way down the line of condemned.

"This one conspired with an enemy of the king against his rightful master! He will be flayed alive then hanged for the crows!" The herald paused again for the crowd's reaction, smiling.

"This slave dared to set herself up in her master's place after brutally killing her." Once more the crowd roared for blood.

"For being an enemy of the king and Lord Nicky, she is sentenced to forty lashes with a cat o' nine and imprisoned in the hanging cage until the flesh do slough from her bones.'"

The crowd screamed madly as the guards raised the woman's hands over her head and tied them up, stretching her body so all her weight rested on mangled feet. The herald moved back as the executioner stepped up with the cat o' nine tails held loosely in his hand. He shook out the metal-spike-tipped braided leather tails. The sound of leather on flesh brought screams of joy from the crowd, drowning out the cries of pain from the slave.

Nicky looked over at Lady Illyria, an ugly smirk upon his face. He was hoping for some sort of emotion: disgust, horror, anything. No, she merely observed the proceedings for a moment before turning her attentions to the crowd, smiling slightly in amusement. He could have sworn her eyes flashed honey golden flame in hunger.

He looked to see what had caught her attention and almost missed one of his thieves cutting a fat purse loose. It angered him enough to say, "Take a good look at the woman, my lady."

"Which one, Lord Nicholas?"

"Why, the one being flogged." He gave a particularly nasty laugh. "I have heard she was not really a slave either, but some freeborn."

"I take it the poor woman had to rely upon the ineptness and incompetence of Sheriff Jake. I feel for her. The people should not have to suffer because he cannot do his job."

The advisor's face twisted up in rage; it was not what he wanted her to get out of the display. "Are you criticizing me?"

"Did you hire the lout?" she fired back. "If you know the woman to be innocent, would it not be better to pardon her and place the sheriff in her stead?"

He stared at her in shock, not sure he had heard her correctly.

"I think it would be a morale booster for the town, punish the corrupt, and restore faith in the populace. It would serve as a warning for the next sheriff such behaviors won't be tolerated."

The young man glared at her. "The sheriff is not in charge of finding the truth. The head questioner is."

"How unfortunate for us all. I would image after enough torture, anyone would break, saying anything particular parties wanted if it meant a release from pain. Would it not be better if there were no head questioner, and other methods employed in discovering truth or guilt?"

He did not like the smile she gave him; it seemed to mock. She would pay dearly. "If I were you, I would hold my tongue and not offer opinions on matters you have no understanding of. You are a foreigner here. Our ways have always worked. Nothing goes on in the kingdom I don't know about!"

He nudged his horse closer to hers, hand clenched around the handle of his riding crop. He so wanted to use it on her for her insolence he could hardly think straight. "You would do well to look again at the criminal. Her fate could be yours, the fate of all who displease me grievously, and because I can, and no one can say or do otherwise."

They searched each other's faces a moment. "I do not easily scare, my lord, nor do I care for those who abuse their power."

"I don't give a damn what you care, cow!" he shrieked, unaware of the stares he drew from those nearest in the crowd. "The only thing you should concern yourself with is in following and obeying our laws and customs. Fail to do so and your fate will be worse than hers. I trust we understand each other?"

Her lip curled, the look of disgust she gave him angered him even more. "I am no slave to bully, no weak-willed maid to cower in fright. What law or laws am I supposed to have broken, if you would be so good as to inform me?"

"Your rebel slave! I had better not hear of you buying any more and acting as if they have a cause to champion. Nor will you go around accusing the sheriff of being unable to do his job. Do I make myself clear?"

"As I explained to Jake, I was concerned with parts of the story and what he had done, being as the slave is quite strenuous in protesting his innocence."

"I will have your citizenship stripped from you for daring to defy me! You ignorant sow! Have you not heard a word I said?"

Nicky had the unsettling feeling she was trying to peer through his eyes and into his thoughts before she spoke, "I do not wish to give undue offense to His Majesty's advisor. I apologize. We seem to be at cross-purposes. I have already settled the matter of the slave's story to my satisfaction. My intent was to ask you for the favor of making sure the sheriff does not unduly target my slaves. If you could assure me he can be made to understand and comply, I am more than willing to forget any previous complaints I had against him."

"Understand?!" Lord Nicky spat, unable to decide if she was truly brazen or just stupid.

Nicky fumed at the audacity of her request as DiJinn hummed happily to himself. He couldn't have planned the argument better if he tried. He spoke low-voiced in a tongue only the advisor understood, and received a glare for his efforts.

"You insult me and expect a favor? Why should I?"

She tilted her head at him, arching a brow. "It would put me in the position of owing you."

The young man sneered, deciding she really was stupid, but he did like being owed favors, and her eagerness to fix the mess his moronic sheriff made by putting herself square in his hands left him feeling generous.

Lord Nicky smirked. "Very well. I shall meet with Jake on your concerns. In return, I will choose when and how you owe me." He twisted in his saddle to address his slaves.

"Let her go. DiJinn, see to my orders." He ignored her fulsome thanks, turning back to the platform in time to see the nearly dead body of the female slave being placed in a hanging cage. He noticed a familiar figure on horseback at the edge of the crowd and froze. He didn't realize he'd made a sound until his slave spoke low in his ear.

"My lord, what is it?"

Nicky started, causing his horse to shy. He fought to get the beast back under control. That pain in the ass, Mica.

"Do you see? That man there! Guards! Guards! Arrest that man there!'" Nicky pointed to Mica, squirming in rage and fear, forgetting he had a demon to help him, so upsetting was the man's presence. *He has to be looking for me. It means the damn bastard must be trying to end my life again! How the hell did he learn I might be here? And where is my soul gem?*

A frown marred DiJinn's face as he looked. *Oh, it was only one of the visiting merchant men. Deny me the lives and souls of men I need to regain my power and survive, and regret it, little boy.*

Next to him, Nicky continued to gesture wildly, screaming for his guards, who had been clearing a path for Lady Illyria. The man left the town square with a wave of people.

Nicky turned to his protector in a rage. "He got away! How dare you let him get away! You're supposed to protect me!'" He drew a fist back.

"I am not one of your mortal peons, boy," the slave hissed for his master alone.

Nicky hesitated, staring in shock. How dare his slave threaten him! Had it finally found a way to break the protection the boy had from it?

"Calm yourself. You're attracting too much attention. I know what the man looks like. I will get information on him for you." *It is no big thing to give him. Keep him from guessing I am really working against him to free myself.* "You are not the little boy he thinks you are."

"I said I want him brought before me! You know my form isn't permanent! You refuse to make it so!"

"I have told you, that is beyond even my power. Why tip him off you are looking for him until you know the real reason he is here? You have changed; he may not even recognize you. It is what you wanted, isn't it?"

Nicky glared at the people around him until they looked away, concerning themselves with the punishments before them. *I must not make mistakes now—not when I'm so close to gaining everything I ever wanted. It's what I have a demon for: to protect me from other immortals.* He felt out of sorts; what should have been a pleasant outing and a showing of his power to a cow of a woman had instead ended in near-disaster.

Chapter Fourteen

"Youse traitor!"

The enraged shout was all the warning Saizar had before his arms were pinned behind him by two of his fellow guards. Jake stood before him, red of face, and gut-punched him. His breath whooshed out. If he hadn't been prevented from doing so, he would have doubled over in pain.

"I's should sell youse to slavers meself for what youse done," Jake struck the man's jaw. "Youse my man,"—punch—"not some lackey for a bitch of a disgraced noble!" Punch.

Saizar could do nothing but struggle, hoping his attackers' grip would loosen so he could mitigate the anger of the man before him as a cold, icy dread filled his belly. "Your pardons, ugh," he grunted at a blow, "sheriff. It sounded a reasonable request." He couldn't speak after another forceful punch to his gut.

The sheriff got a fistful of black hair, yanking his man's head back to bring their faces so close he was spitting on the other. "How many times do I's gots to tell youse. Youse only ask questions of stuff I's tell youse too. Anybodies brings questions, complaints, or anythings, youse tell me first. Youse don't go promising to look inta it." A flurry of punches to the face and body followed.

Saizar rocked with each blow, felt his nose break, spilling warm blood. He wasn't sure how long the beating went on, but found himself free on hands and knees, his blood dripping to mingle with the dirt-encrusted wood floor.

The big, hobnailed boots of his superior were before him. Saizar barely managed to look up at the man as he demanded, "Do I's makes meself clear? Or ares we's gonna have us a problem?"

The man spat blood out, panting for air. "No, no, sheriff. No problem. It-it won't happen again."

Jake snorted, spitting before he walked away to the far end of the barracks with the two men who had helped. Saizar kept his head down, turning it to the side as the men stopped to talk in low voices between themselves. Snatches of conversation floated back to him as he tried to breathe and determine if any ribs had been broken.

"Youse two get the master's mouthpiece to deliver the message. He has something special planned fer them."

"What about him? It ain't the first time he done something stupid," one of the men asked.

"The bitch trusts him. He's gonna remain as long as he tells us what she does. But if'n he's don't, I'll deal with him."

The voices moved off, down the stairs. Saizar didn't like what he'd overheard. He had to discover what they were planning, no matter how hurt he was.

As Saizar shadowed the traitor, he wondered how much good he was doing as a lawman. He was only allowed to continue because Jake needed a scapegoat, someone to lull the commoners into thinking themselves guarded by good men, and not a pack of wolves.

I am spit upon, treated with derision, fear, and hatred. I need to bring proof of who supports the sheriff to the king, without losing my life.

Saizar had ridden out early, while it was still light, in the hopes that he'd find the place he sought more easily; the valleys could be tricky— more so when dark—and risky, with all the outlaws and bandits plaguing the area. The sheriff's man left all known roads behind. He rode through forest, following one branch of the river. He had thought he was making good progress, but now, he wasn't sure. It was pitch black beneath the evergreens and trees, some still had a few leaves clinging.

The sound of rough voices floated on a breeze. He stopped his mount, listening. The valleys could distort sound and the distance it travelled. He was fairly sure the outlaws' camp remained ahead. It was only by chance he'd overheard where the meeting was taking place.

I must go slowly; I do not want them to know I am here, but how much farther? They could be off a mile or more, or right around the next rock.

He sat a moment before deciding to ride closer. Saizar rode a good while before the voices came again, louder. He stopped, tying his horse to a low-hanging branch. He continued on foot, expecting a few scouts to keep an eye on the approaches to the camp. He didn't need to be found. After twenty minutes, he saw the glow of several fires through the trees and outlines of some sentries, slithering as close as he dared. When the wind blew, he could smell animal and human dung.

Occasionally, laughter broke out, or the bark of a dog. Saizar crawled into a patch of bushes, lay waiting, hoping he was not being a fool. From the sounds he heard, the females were treated as slaves, made to wait upon the men, cooking, pouring drink, or being used by any man who felt like it.

These are not a band of wild, roaming raiders, but of outlaw men making their own place to live. By rights, Jake and my fellow lawmen or even the king's army should be hunting them down and arresting them. He recognized a few men who once belonged to the army, or thought he did.

Saizar learned what few townspeople knew: the kingdom had no decent standing army. After the last war, it had never been replenished, a fact few remembered. The king, in a fit of madness, thinking they were trying to kill him, had ordered the lot of them disbanded. Lord Nicky stepped in, stopping it, but even he hadn't been able to save everyone. Most of the men were dismissed; only a small number remained to guard the town's borders, receiving little pay or reward. Were the men former army or recent deserters who had taken to other means of making a living?

Saizar thought he saw runaway slaves amid the group, even a few criminals he recognized who by law should have been hanged. *What can the king be thinking, allowing this group to exist? They could loot the town, slay the king. I must warn His Majesty, but how to do so without losing my head in the process? Should I ask Lady Illyria to speak on my behalf? She championed the rebel slave's cause, even though he is now her property.*

He brought her ladyship's face to his mind's eye. Her eyes seemed fever bright in the sun, skin pale as death. He didn't know why, but he felt a shiver of fear go up his spine whenever he was around her. He also didn't care for Lord Nicky's pardon for her slave. The young man would collect, and that collection was always rumored to bring about a person's eventual downfall.

All the dogs began to bark, men rushed to grab weapons. The leaders stood to face the threat. It was only a small party of even rougher-looking men, escorted by some of the sentries. They made a wary peace, sitting to break bread and drink.

Saizar could tell Jake was not a part of the gathering. He didn't recognize any of the newcomers.

"What does our lord be wanting now?" the apparent leader asked sarcastically after the formalities had been performed.

"What you owe him for being left in peace."

"You tell the bastard we aren't scared of his threats. There's more of us than of him and his men. We won't be paying. The loot is ours by rights. We fought for it, and many of us got wounded in the process."

"He does not ask for loot. Only for your men, and cooperation in a private matter."

"What's the matter he speaks of?"

"He wants you to raid the nobles' street, but none of the nobles themselves must be taken or unduly harmed; just a little fear and chaos."

The leader laughed. "What is to be our reward? That street is the best-guarded of all. Many highborn have men of their own to defend their property and lives."

The speaker's voice betrayed anger. "It is to be a night attack. By the time anyone knows what is going on, it will be too late. The reward will be whatever you can carry off from their houses. Don't tell me you are scared of a few men with swords."

"And the palace guard? The sheriff's men? What of them?"

"My lord assures me they will pose no threat. He has willing spies placed to make sure. Do not go near the palace, and you will not lose."

"Why should we? We have it good here: food, shelter, security, and witless fools who ride into our traps to be plucked like the birds they are."

"His lordship does not tell me why, only that he wants it done."

"I bet he also wants us to spare his house?"

"No, that would draw suspicion. You will have free rein to raid his house as well if your men can overcome his defenses."

A rumble of voices rose, the leader shouted for quiet. "I would rather we raid the town. Some of the merchants are rich, ripe for plucking, and don't have as many guards!"

A roar of assent came from the sitting outlaws. The speaker who had come with the offer sat in stony silence until the noise died down.

"No, the town comes later. For now, he wishes only to cause discomfort to the nobles."

"What if we say no?"

"He will pay each man who raids ten gold coins."

"Ten!"

"Each man? Let me see his gold first!"

The stony-faced man again waited for the crude laughter and jests which came to die down. "After. You will receive your gold after . . ."

"What? So there are fewer of us to pay? He will show us his gold before, or maybe we should send you back in ten pieces."

Grumbles of agreement came; for a moment it seemed the hard-faced man and those with him would come to harm.

"Do so, and you seal your deaths."

"He can bugger himself trying to find us."

The other man said nothing, only raised one hand. A slew of arrows came out of the dark and found their marks. It seemed the hidden bowmen did not care who they hit. The outlaws roared in anger; the leader jumped up, drawing his sword. He was felled by an arrow through his throat.

"Now do you agree to serve my lord?" the hard-faced man cried out. "Slay me if you will, but you will all die with me!"

Some of the men charged; more arrows came raining down. The camp was a boiling mess with people crying out for the death of the hard-faced man, others yelling they would comply.

"Hold, hold, HOLD!" a different man shouted. A tall, massive, heavily muscled individual, he carried an axe upon his back and a large hammer on his belt.

"I don't care to do some lord's dirty work, but neither am I ready to die! You fools! Sit down!" It took a few minutes, but he cowed the others. "You will rue the day you fired upon us. We are free folk who don't take kindly to being told what we must or mustn't do. If we agree, we will be paid first."

"You must take my lord for a great fool. Pay up front only to watch you run away with his gold and nary a thing in return? I think not. You will show up three days hence at the darkest hour by the hanging tree. Then, and only then, will you get half the gold before the battle. Once it is complete, you shall receive the other half. If any of you think to make your profit greater by betrayal, I can guarantee a long, painful death."

More grumbling ensued, but the massive man spoke up, "We will consider all you have said and done tonight. You will receive our answer in three days. Now go, and leave us be."

The hard-faced man and those with him were escorted back out. Saizar still didn't know who he was, nor who the great lord could be. He didn't know anyone with so much gold at hand, not even the advisor. Except perhaps Lady Illyria. He heard she had already paid a fortune in coin for services. If she were behind the plot, why, and to what purpose? What would she gain by such a move?

The party who had come to treaty dressed plainly, and bore no crest. Saizar picked up two arrows which had landed near him. He hoped the fletching on the arrows would identify the attackers, but they used common goose feathers. He eased himself out of the bushes. Saizar had to get word of what he'd witnessed to the king, but how, and how to be believed? There was one person to whom he might go. Earl Sydney.

* * *

The earl tapped missives against one hand, pausing just outside a terrace door. His wife had elected to take her afternoon meal by herself.

"Countess, might I join you today?" Sydney stood by his wife's chair. When she nodded consent, he seated himself, waiting for the slave to serve him hot spiced fruit juice and meat pastries. "I have had a royal decree from the king, on the subject of the meeting with the new foreign duchess upon whom I had been commanded to attend."

His wife grimaced, replying, "I had the misfortune of meeting the woman myself." She sniffed contemptuously. "She was in Burkes, replenishing her wardrobe."

He made no reply. Elizabeth continued, "You should have seen what she had on! She thought herself some warrior woman! I find it hard to believe she even is a duchess. His Majesty must pass a law against such things."

"What would those things be?" her husband asked politely.

A withering look was sent his way. "Foreign commoners coming here claiming to be noble-born, the ass of a king believing them, allowing them to stay and dirty our country's noble bloodlines. Really, Chadrick, it's bad enough our daughters can't find decent men to marry, but to have a woman like her allowed to stay?"

The Countess sat back, disgruntled, as her cup was refilled, oblivious to the warmth of the afternoon, perhaps the last of the fall season. Oblivious to the last leaves turning colors, swirling down, the last flowers bravely blooming. If she'd cared to look beyond the garden wall, the highest mountain peaks already had snow. She had made inquiries about the foreigner, and had not been able to find out anything to her satisfaction.

"She had the gall to try and buy my body slaves!"

"Our daughter Caroline did say you threatened to sell them after they ripped Sally's dress."

"It was rude of her to presume. She even sent some nobody of a guide—a guide, I tell you!—over to bargain on her behalf. I let her know in no uncertain terms I would not sell to the likes of her."

"Which would explain the events at the slave market," Sydney drily remarked.

The countess gave an insulted sniff. "Well, with that behavior, it won't be long before we are rid of her. His Majesty will not put up with it."

The earl winced inside, knowing his wife would not like the news he had to impart. "I wouldn't be too sure, Elizabeth."

She paused, cup halfway to her mouth, her eyes narrowed in suspicion. "Explain."

He sighed, taking a sip of his juice to fortify himself. "His Majesty seems rather taken with Lady Illyria, and with the rumors of her wealth she managed to save from bandits."

"Nonsense. Wealth does not make up for supporting rebel slaves, or bad breeding, nor should it." Elizabeth gave a decisive nod. "She will have to go. Our king can't chance she may be here to provide distraction while assassins try to kill him again."

The earl opened his mouth to say more, but she ignored him, continuing, "And if he doesn't, Lord Nicky should. Either way, I don't see where we shall have to be bothered by such an uncouth savage."

"Mmmm," Sydney hummed.

His wife set her cup down with a sharp click, straightened her already-perfect posture as she turned the full force of her glare upon her husband. "I care not for your tone."

"Forgive me, my lady, but you will like even less what is being considered." He paused as her face whitened in rage, plunging on. "The king is granting the duchess a three-month leave to stay, with full citizenship and restored rights to her title, contingent upon certain conditions being met. Aranthus sent word I am being considered for the favor of sponsoring her ladyship; should I be chosen, I am to see she learns our laws."

"Is that so?" Ice was less chilly than her voice and demeanor. "Where is the letter? I demand to see it now."

Silently the earl handed it over, drinking his juice as his wife read the king's demands. Her mouth tightened, eyes flaring, whole manner stiffening in outrage. Elizabeth tossed the letter carelessly onto the ground.

"My lady, I must obey. She—"

"How dare you?! How dare you presume to lecture me on duty? I have always done what is correct. I will not have you instructing that woman on anything. I know how you get."

"Elizabeth, you're not being fair."

She held a hand up. "You say one thing and do another. I know what the woman looks like, even with the dreadful outfit she had on."

"I have kept my promise to you—"

The sound of a sharp slap rang out in the garden. The countess trembled in rage, her hand stinging from the force of flesh meeting flesh. "You still visit whores, only they are common ones now. When I say you will not be alone with that upstart woman, I mean it. Send your steward to teach her the laws, or better yet, tell His Majesty to command she place her money in trust to be administered by a loyal countryman."

A red handprint stood out on Chadrick's cheek; his sapphire eyes blazed bright as his lips compressed in a thin line. "Do not slap me again. I have done my best to honor our marriage."

"You will not be alone with her, or I will take my complaints to His Majesty. Do you understand me?"

A polite cough interrupted. Their daughters stood just inside the terrace door, and when they had imparted their message, the countess felt her rage flare anew.

* * *

"How dare she disobey me?! How dare she question why a slave was enslaved?! I will have her stripped of title and lands!" The king paced around, storming.

His slaves waited against the walls, quiet, eyes downcast.

"She does not have any lands, Majesty," Aranthus wearily reminded his sovereign. "You have not granted her any, she has not bought any, and you have already forbidden her use of her title."

"She will lose her head! And her wealth!"

"She is not from here; she can move to another country."

"Damn you, eunuch! What kind of advice do you dare to give me? I will have her arrested! She can't leave then!"

"I am merely pointing out the truth, Sire, which you have commanded me to do many times before in the past." Aranthus would have to somehow charm His Majesty out of his rage. He rather liked their new foreigner, and would be sorry to see her leave. He also had a feeling clapping her in chains would be an even bigger headache than tossing her out of the kingdom.

"I do not think arresting her will help. Perhaps her faults lie with the fact she doesn't seem to have had a proper home or upbringing; therefore she is ignorant of what is required of her as a noble-born."

Maceanas snatched up his goblet, quaffing deeply before signaling it to be refilled as the chamberlain continued.

"Your Majesty has assigned her a sponsor, now she needs a noble-

194

born lady who will gently teach her what is expected of her."

The king eyed his eunuch over the rim of his gem-encrusted goblet as he drank. "And where do you recommend I get such a paragon? Most of the females in my realm are silly, flighty women."

Aranthus thought a moment, as if he didn't already know who he would suggest. "What about Lady Elizabeth? Or her eldest daughter, since Lord Sydney is already in charge of teaching her our laws?"

"No, the eldest only looks for another husband after the knight she married died. Her mother is a rigid prune. I don't want our spicy lady turned into another turnip like the frigid bitch. I just want her to learn some manners."

"She will have no choice but to do as you command or risk your wrath." *If you admitted to Lady Illyria you only want her to warm your bed and fill your coffers with her gold, she would be more receptive.* The eunuch knew if he dared voice the idea, he might become a guest of the dungeon, and Rablias scared him.

"I should consult my advisor."

Aranthus winced; His Majesty caught the movement. "What now?" he demanded.

The eunuch bowed. "Your pardon, Majesty, but might he feel some resentment over what may appear preferential treatment and give you bad counsel?"

The chamberlain barely ducked the goblet hurtling toward his head. He scurried across the room should the king decided to follow with more objects. A slave hurried to fill a new goblet and present it to the king as another knelt to clean up the mess

"Tell Lady Elizabeth to attend me at once! AT ONCE! Do you hear me? Not an hour from now. At once!" Maceanas roared. "You will fetch her yourself after you have my ladies attend me."

"Of course, Sire," Aranthus hurried to do the king's bidding. Shortly, he found himself being ushered inside the Sydney household and greeted by the daughters.

"Aranthus! How nice to see you! Have you any good gossip?" Lady Caroline asked.

"Indeed, but I am here for your mother. His Majesty has commanded she appear before him, and I dare not stop with you lovely ladies. Is she at home?"

"Oh yes, she and father are having one of their discussions," Lady Sally rolled her eyes.

The chamberlain winced. Everyone at one time or another had been treated to one of Lady Elizabeth's "discussions." It was a wonder the man even stayed home, but, ever since he had lost his first love, he was a mere shell of a man.

"I pray you, send for her at once. His Majesty is in a foul mood and not disposed to wait."

They curtsied and hurried out, leaving him with a moment's peace. The household was cold and rigid as its mistress. The chairs and sofa all had hard, straight backs and seats. He refused to sit, knowing from experience it would be uncomfortable. The colors of the room were somber. The windows had the luxury of glass but they were closed to the beautiful day outside. The light barely penetrated the gloom. The floor was of varnished wood, and remained uncovered.

Aranthus could remember Sydney's first wife, Alise. She was given to smiles and laughter, not unlike Illyria. It wasn't long before the girls' mother came hurrying out to meet him, the earl not far behind. No doubt he had to look concerned about the unexpected summons, or she would have yet another "discussion" with him.

"To what do we owe this unexpected pleasure?" she asked calmly enough as greeting.

"Forgive the intrusion, my lady, but His Grace requires your presence immediately."

"I do hope nothing is the matter?" she probed carefully.

"Nothing of the sort, but he has a delicate matter at hand he needs a woman for." At her disdainful look he hastily added, "It, er, um, concerns another of his nobles, a woman as well." He paused to give her a meaningful glance. "He thought another female would be better equipped to help advise him on what to do about the problem. I am to take you back now."

She was quick to grasp his intent. "Another woman, you say? Noble-born? I . . . see. I am not sure what I can do, but I will do my best to help." She turned to the earl. "I shall return later, and we will continue our conversation." It came out sounding more a threat than a request.

He stroked his chin speculatively before returning to estate matters.

"Children, I trust you to look after our dwelling while I am gone. I am at your disposal, chamberlain."

The eunuch bowed, hurrying out to the royal conveyance and helping the countess in. Upon their arrival at the palace, Aranthus escorted Lady Elizabeth inside the king's private apartments. Her face gave away nothing of the honor, but her eyes gleamed as if she had spotted her holy grail. They only had to wait a moment for the king to finish with his harem, in which time the countess had swiftly absorbed the contents of the room to recount later at home to her daughters. Lady Elizabeth gave a deep curtsey, trying to keep her face neutral. Maceanas wore only a robe, loosely tied, and reeked of wine and sex.

He snapped his fingers at his slaves, seating himself as he said, "Rise and sit. I trust Aranthus has informed you what I want?"

"To some extent, Your Grace; he only mentioned you have problems with a noblewoman and wished for some advice on the matter?" Her tone was questioning as if not sure she had gotten it correct. "May I inquire as to who the noblewoman is?"

"I thought by her actions everyone would know of her. The Duchess Maison du Corbeau."

"I have encountered her, but I did not wish to presume."

He grunted as he lifted the goblet placed at his hand and drank. "Her . . . shall we say . . . less-than-conventional life seems to have left her ill-suited for the realities of being a proper subject and noblewoman."

"What would Your Grace have me advise you on?" She had yet to touch her wine, which the king could consider an affront.

"Aranthus thinks our noble lady might benefit from instruction on what befits her station in our country. Even though she cannot legally lay claim to her title per my decree, she is still of noble blood. I am making it a part of the condition for her to regain use of her title and live here."

The look on the countess's face turned so sour the king thought it would turn the wine to vinegar.

She finally picked up the goblet to take a sip. "Your Majesty, if I may speak freely?" At his nod, she continued, "Is it truly the wisest route? Gossip indicates she has the capital in an uproar. Her wild, unfounded accusations against the sheriff, her support of rebel slaves, her free ways, and her . . . dress. Would it not be better if she was thrown out, so she will not foment rebellion? All the single men—and some of the married ones—pant after her already, like dogs after a bitch in heat."

"I hope you do not include me in your estimation," the king softly warned her.

"No, naturally not, Sire. You are the one man sufficiently resolved to resist her...charms. Why, even Lord Nicky is rumored to be obsessed with finding out about her, and he a confirmed bachelor!"

Aranthus mused, *I bet Earl Sydney would even ignore his vow to his countess and bed her. Rumor has it he frequents the worst of the brothels just to spite his wife.*

The king made no reply, only drank some more wine as he thought before saying, "I will make it a royal command the lady attend such lessons. She dare not disobey. Not if it means forgoing the right to live here; I have my reasons for wanting her to stay."

The chamberlain had to turn a laugh into a cough as the countess's face looked as if she had spotted a large, nasty bug swimming in the dregs of what she had just drunk.

"I will do as you command me, Sire. I know my duty as a noble-born," she said in martyred tones.

"I am not unmindful of the amount of work required of you, nor the fact it will limit your time with your family. You will be amply rewarded."

She hesitated before inquiring, "Is there any particular area you want me to concentrate on?"

"I trust your judgment in these matters. If you will wait but a moment, I will have the paper drawn up so you may start immediately. The Harvest Ball is not far off, and I mean to have my jewel polished and perfect on my arm."

Lady Elizabeth's expression appeared as if she had bad indigestion. "As Your Grace commands." She took an even bigger sip of wine.

The king was scribbling upon a piece of parchment when the doors to his apartment banged open. Lord Nicky charged inside, king's guards on his heels.

He stopped short as he spotted the countess. "What the hell are you in here for, you sour-faced bitch?"

"You dare to enter my chambers without my leave, advisor?" Maceanas' face turned a dangerous shade of puce.

"Send her away; I won't be put off any longer!"

"Speak thus again to your king and I'll strip you of your title and station and have you clapped in the dungeon for such insolence." Lord Nicky gritted out an apology and bowed but refused to leave.

"As it so happens, the countess is here about her ladyship, the foreign duchess."

The look in the young man's eyes caused the countess to pale, but she met his eyes with resolve in her own.

"Is she now?" A dangerous purr in his voice. "And what would she have to do with our disobedient newcomer?"

"I am to teach her ladyship manners. Our Majesty's request."

"Are you now? What kind of manners do you think you can teach her? The kind that drives your husband to find his comforts in the lowest sorts of whore houses?"

Her face turned crimson.

"Even you cannot deny the woman is a little too free in her ways. She needs polish. The countess knows what is due someone of her station."

The young man sneered at the trembling woman before him. "She knows what's due a frigid lineage-struck bitch."

"Nicky, I begin to think the foreigner is not the only one in my realm needing lessons in manners."

The advisor bit back what vileness he was about to spit, bowed the minimum required for a countess. "Forgive me, Lady Elizabeth, my cruel tongue. I know not what I say at times when I am disturbed." He turned back to the king. "Our talk," he prompted.

The king sanded his proclamation and gave it to Lady Elizabeth. "Aranthus, see she gets home safely whilst my advisor and I deal with other matters." The chamberlain felt the hot, hateful gaze of the young man upon their backs until the door shut behind.

Nicky swung around to his childhood friend. "Exactly what kind of manners do you intend she learn?"

The king did not answer; instead, he gulped more wine, trying to give himself time to calm down. He wiped his mouth with his sleeve.

"You are my dearest, and most loyal of friends, Nicky. Should you ever enter my room again unbidden and behave in such a way before my nobles, I will have you stripped of lands, titles, and wealth, and given over to Rablias to learn humility. My father spared you when you were a little boy, an orphan," he stressed, "because you warned him of danger. You have learned enough to pass as one of us, but you were not born noble. So remember I am your king. I am your better."

The young man's face darkened until it almost looked black but knew he had no choice but to kneel, bow his head, and apologize. *I swear, you fat fuck, this is the last time you threaten me. Once my army is here, I'll show you humility.*

"My hasty actions and thoughtless words offended Your Grace and your guest. I let my damnable temper get the better of me. What may I do to atone?"

"Remember who you are, where you came from, and if it wasn't for my family's generosity, you would still be a homeless orphan."

Nicky nearly cracked a tooth in gritting his teeth, but he tried to look chastised. "I trust you will have time for me now?"

The king snorted as he seated himself. "Fetch food for us from the kitchens, and more wine," he instructed a slave who hurried to do his bidding, before irritably yelling at Nicky, "Sit, damn you! Sit! You think I enjoy making threats against the only man I know who has my interests at heart? But damn if you don't sorely try my patience."

"My patience is also tried. You tell me I must investigate the sheriff because of complaints from this unknown, this so-called noblewoman of whom we know nothing. How do you think I should feel?"

"You should feel grateful I support your decision to keep the man in his position."

Nicky's look was enough to curdle milk. "I do not think it enough. Not when we still have assassins to fear. I have inquired of other court advisors in the countries she has professed to have lived in."

The king waved a hand negligently. "I'm sure they will come back favorable, and if the countess does her job properly, she will be quite a prize. I may reinstate her title sooner if only to marry her myself. What has your investigation turned up if you are so concerned about her true motives?"

"I have not found the so-called merchants for whom the slave worked."

"I thought our lawman was beyond mistakes such as the one she wrote about. You assured me he had been properly instructed and trained."

His friend took another sip, to give himself time to come up with a lie. "He has been instructed. When I am finished, I will present my findings to you and the court."

"I will hear no more on the matter? That slave will not try to run again and cause trouble?" the king demanded.

"No." Nicky paused a moment before continuing, "We have both heard what a strong-willed creature she is. I doubt many men could control her. Do you really want to marry her? What if she insists she be given rights to equal a man's if the countess does not instill proper manners?"

The king shuddered in horror. "No woman will have more rights than men, nor rule my kingdom! Sons that my wife will bear me, yes, but not a woman; they are to provide comfort and family."

Nicky buried his sudden sly smile. "I would hold off on thinking of marrying her, or reinstating her title, at least until after my inquiries come back and we see if Lady Elizabeth can teach her that women cannot and will not rule your kingdom."

"What? Oh, yes, yes." He drained his goblet and held it out. "But she is so beautiful, and her breasts . . . I will make her my mistress."

Nicky nearly choked on his wine. *You bastard! I won't have her trying to winkle any more favors out of you. I'll make sure she refuses you.*

* * *

Lady Meanna greeted her sister-in-law with a kiss on both cheeks, waiting for the woman to seat herself. She could see Elizabeth was upset, figuring it had to be one of three things: her brother Chadrick, the new foreign woman, or some moral slight. She reflected her father had certainly been right in his estimation of her. She would have made a better second wife to him than to her brother.

Her childhood home had changed much since her parents had lived there. The portraits of Sydney ancestors hung in the main corridors but the countess had replaced Lady Meanna's mother's comfortable furniture with ostentatiously carved wooden pieces, the airy frilly window hangings with rich brocades, and the secular bric-a-brac with religious icons. Over the years, all the old Sydney slaves had become dour and humorless like their mistress, or been sold if they could not conform.

The two women exchanged the usual pleasantries. "Dear Meanna, thank the spirit that you, of all your father's children, inherited his sensible mien. I have received the worst possible news from the palace." Her bosom heaved as she drew breath. "Our Majesty is commanding Sydney and me to sponsor that ill-bred duchess. I am to teach her our customs and manners! Can you imagine? It's a disgrace! I will have to be seen consorting with a foreigner! One denied use of her title!"

The viscountess put a suitably grave look upon her face. "And my brother? What has the king commanded of him?"

"Teach her our laws. I told him in no uncertain terms he is not to be in her company. He can have his steward substitute. I won't have her trying to get her claws into him."

You mean you don't trust my brother not to be seduced by a beautiful woman despite the promises he made you. "A wise decision, my dear. I have seen her, and the types of things she considers clothing. She is hardly better than a whore."

"I'm glad you understand. I have refused to visit her, and let our peers know while what they do is up to them, I certainly don't consider it a good idea. Now I will look a fool, and all because of our king's command!"

Her sister-in-law shook her head. "The less powerful are already visiting her at the inn. The merchants are rumored to be fawning over her. It's quite a disgrace."

"I should say so, but they lack power because they support the wrong people. I don't care how enamored the king is of the whore. We both know it won't last long." The countess accepted a cup from her slave and took a sip.

"It is said she wrote to the advisor about her rebel slave." The viscountess gave a nasty laugh. "She may bring about her downfall much sooner than she realizes."

"Clearly she hasn't a brain in her head. Have you heard? She bought the old Fishton Mansion. A cursed, tumbledown ruin. How long do you think she will last in it before being driven out by the ghosts of the murdered Fishtons? It's too delicious to think of."

"I'm glad my girls are more sensible, although I do hope Caroline would find another husband, preferably one who won't go and get himself killed in battle."

"I know you want her to marry a man of good position, but have you considered one of the lesser peers you can direct and raise to power, who will do as you wish?" Meanna inquired delicately.

She watched as her sister-in-law's thin lips pulled tight in a grimace, and her demeanor grew frosty. The woman was too picky. The kind of men she wanted for her daughters didn't exist anymore, having been accused of treason and executed. Lady Sydney had scoffed at all of Meanna's suggestions; she'd have two spinsters on her hands if she wasn't careful.

Elizabeth replied sharply, "I have heard Lady Anne is ailing again, and not expected to live much longer. I believe Caroline has a good shot at marrying the marquis when he becomes free."

"She is encumbered by children. The man won't be pleased to be burdened with another man's get," the viscountess warned.

"The children prove my daughter is fertile. If he agrees to marry, I will include a caveat in the contract that my husband and I will raise her offspring from the first union, and they relinquish all claim on his title or property." The countess wore a smug smile. "All she must do is birth a living son, something his other wives have been unable to do."

"Do you really consider him a smart match? All those unseemly parties, the whores, the fate of his previous wives?" Meanna probed.

The countess's face twitched in annoyance. "Exaggerations. Caroline will reform him of any bad habits. He needs a woman with a firm hand and a strong backbone. It is true he prefers them young, but I'm sure he will see a lady of Caroline's ilk much more suitable for breeding."

"What of Lady Sally? Will you not be presenting her? She is of age."

"Yes, she has turned out to be more biddable than her elder sister, and a credit to her upbringing. I do believe she could change Lord Nicky's mind about marriage when he sees what an accomplished young lady she has become."

Meanna's brows raised to her hairline; though she adored her nieces and nephew, she had no illusion they could make the matches their mother dreamed of.

"How are your preparations for the event you're hosting for Harvest week?" she asked instead.

"Very well. I shall have a recital, to be followed by a supper. It will be an excellent way to display my daughter's talents."

The viscountess chose her words carefully. "Do you mean to have them perform the entire time? They will become exhausted and have no energy for mingling with the men."

"I have requested some of the younger, married ladies who wish to be socially acknowledged undertake the divertissements. My girls will not have competition for the hands of the single gentlemen present, and the husbands will make sure their wives don't try to enter any liaisons. I expect by the Royal Harvest Ball, at least one of my daughters will be engaged." Lady Sydney had a superior look upon her face.

Chapter Fifteen

The sun was a slowly sinking red orb in the sky when I awoke. Unlocking my door, I called for my maid, searching through the growing pile of clothes Emilee and Brent sent over. I paid my bills in full with gold and jewels, unlike the nobles who all maintained monstrously large accounts, which they slowly paid. The adage money talked meant the husband and wife had set three-quarters of their workers to sewing my outfits.

There was a brief knock on the door. Susafan entered, followed by Rolf, my little page, and Mary Elana.

They waited for my instructions as I took the few missives sent to me during the day. The royal tax collector sent the title to the former Fishton mansion. The builders' guild sent contracts to be signed so they could begin repairing and building. A few people in need of money begged me to consider loaning them funds. Lady Sydney was hosting a dinner tonight, but it was Lord Sydney requesting the pleasure of my company.

My eyebrow raised, wondering how he dared to ignore her wrath. After only a few lessons with her, I could well believe the gossip that she was the power in the marriage; clearly the slaves' gossip was true that she refused all contact outside our lessons until I'd learned proper noblewoman's behavior. I tapped the note thoughtfully against my hand. The countess had made no mention of the party to me earlier when we met. I had a feeling it was a last-minute invitation. If I planned on accepting, I had to get ready, and swiftly, or fashionably late would turn into unforgivably late, and as the earl had no doubt gone out of his way, I didn't want to offend him by not showing.

"Rolf, I shall require you to be my link-boy tonight, tell Domiano to have my mount ready for my usual ride." Translation: I would go bandit hunting in the wee smalls. "And also tell him and Eron we will delay our outing until tomorrow."

He bolted out the door, feet thumping on the stair as he jumped from step to step. "Lord Sydney has invited me to a supper party at his mansion tonight." I couldn't help the brief smirk crossing my face.

Susafan startled. "Her Ladyship will think you are trying to seduce him. I recommend not going."

"Nonsense, I have no wish to insult either of them, as they're my sponsors, though she denies it."

"Do not be surprised if she is still affronted by your gown. She is always advocating for high collars, long skirts and sleeves. You should have ordered Rolf to rent a carriage. Shall I see if Master Nathan will let you borrow the inn's coach?"

"Why ever would I? It is only a few minutes' walk."

I could tell when she slowly closed her eyes then opened them, I had committed another no-no. "Ladies never walk, no matter the distance."

"You and I know nothing will make me a proper lady in the countess's eyes. Which dress, do you suppose?" I asked.

Susafan hesitated a moment as she mentally ran through my wardrobe. "The black or the purple; they show the least amount of skin, my lady."

"Very well, the purple, with the silver shoes and my diamond jewels. I will want most of my hair curled up—use the diamond clips."

Two strips of satin-weave silk circled the dress, one at the neckline, one at the waist, framing the silver vine-patterned embroidery on the bodice. Brilliants accented the dress. Eight ornate diamond and silver clips between my waist and upper thighs gathered the full skirt up into a pretty design of soft folds and drapes. A row of tiny buttons held the dress closed in back. My earrings were three diamond drops. I wore a diamond collar and wide cuff, along with my signet ring on my right hand, and a large, square-cut diamond on my left middle finger.

As Susafan predicted, the purple mostly covered my breasts, except for the swell from the tops. I dabbed scented oil upon myself, catching sight of the girl when I handed the bottle back to my maid. She was silently crying, keeping her eyes on the floor. I looked toward my maid, who couldn't help but roll her eyes, grimacing.

"You'll want something to cover your shoulders and hands with later; it does get cold this time of year."

"The black fur drape and muff." I turned to address Mary Elana quietly. "You asked me for help. If I could have given it in a manner allowing you to remain freeborn and safe from your family's clutches, I would have."

I saw the jerk her whole body gave at my words, although she remained staring at the floor. Susafan handed the garments to me as I carelessly tossed the drape over one shoulder and held the muff with one hand as I exited the room.

The inn's common room was full of minor nobles, knights and a few wealthy merchants. Most of the men stopped to watch as I made my way across the room, to the displeasure of the few wives present.

I returned the greetings graciously as I swept out the door. Domiano and Eron stood with Rolf, holding a lantern.

"I do wish you would change your mind," Susafan complained once more as she huddled in her cloak, shivering.

"A walk in the crisp night air will be refreshing. Rolf, careful with the lantern; you don't want to spill the oil." I turned to my remaining slaves. "I trust you will have everything ready for our move on the morrow." They nodded as my maid gave a long-suffering sigh as we set out.

True to her word, our walk garnered much attention as carriages slowed in passing, the occupants hanging out of windows to gape at us. Susafan held her head up so high I thought she might trip. A spot of red dotted each cheek. I inclined my head to each gawking person if I happened to catch their eyes as I strolled along.

We approached the brightly lighted façade of the Sydney mansion. A large covered carriage with several outriders bore down upon us. A slave ran before, shouting, "Make way for the king!"

Hell and Damnation! He hated for anyone to arrive after him. If I ignored him and went before, he would think I thought myself more important than he.

"My lady," Susafan whimpered.

"There is no help for it, either way he shall be displeased," I replied as we approached the entrance. The royal coach pulled up at the carriage block, ignored by both the royal and Sydney slaves who were gawking at my approach.

"Why the hell aren't the slaves opening my door?" came an angry bellow from inside.

Aranthus poked his head out, spotting us, but a furious roar from the king had the chamberlain hissing at the royal slaves to open the door and lower the step.

His Majesty alighted, glancing our way.

"What the hell is this?"

A slave kowtowed before me. "My lady, the king demands to know why you arrived on foot and are tardy."

"You may tell him my invitation arrived late, and I saw no need to borrow a carriage for a walk of a few minutes."

"Bring her here!" the king demanded, overhearing my explanation as slaves hovered around, uncertain if they should grant entrance to someone who arrived in such an unconventional manner.

I made my curtsy. "Your Majesty."

"Did Lady Elizabeth not inform you that only slaves and commoners walk?"

"I suspect that my dress alone would scandalize her." I gave a roguish smile.

He guffawed, roaring out, "You will have to wear the most scandalous of your dresses for me at my next party."

I smiled. "I shall have one made, just for you."

He held his arm out to me. "Come, I want to see her face when she spots you."

I laid my fingers on his arm. He escorted me up the short flight of stairs as a different slave held the door for us. I knew word was already spreading to the house slaves inside.

Oil lamps flickered and candles flamed throughout the hall, but still a sense of gloom reigned. Dark carved wood paneling covered the walls up to head height. Dark portraits of unknown ancestors hung above. I left my furs with Susafan as she followed a slave to another part of the house, Rolf having been taken around to another entrance. The Sydney slaves greeted us, bowing low.

"Gloomy, is it not?" Maceanas said, "The old earl was a loyal friend of my father's. A very rigid man who I always found dour and humorless. Chadrick, the current Earl, is his middle son."

I matched my pace to the king's lazy amble as Aranthus and the Sydney butler preceded us down the hall.

"How many brothers did he have?" I asked.

"Two, and a sister, were all who survived to adulthood. The sister is a close friend of Elizabeth; they are like peas in a pod. The brothers . . . we will not speak of them."

It meant they had done something to anger the king, exiled if alive but probably dead. He transferred my hand to the crook of his arm, keeping his left hand over mine as we continued down the hall. "I understand my advisor has finally met you?"

"Yes, Your Grace. He was kind enough to help me with a terrible entanglement and explained the slave laws to me. I am most grateful for his compassion and sensitivity for my gaffe."

The king snorted. "How goes the sponsorship?"

"I fear her ladyship is most displeased with me. I find the history fascinating while some of the customs and dress are vexing to learn and memorize; I am trying to do my best for you." *My progress satisfies you, I whispered in his mind.*

He gave me a piercing look. "You should try a little harder to conform. I have been receiving reports from the countess. She is most unhappy." *The woman has not ceased to complain—rolls and rolls of parchment, more than the damn council ever sends me.*

Conformity is boring, you enjoy the spice added to an otherwise dull existence. "As you wish, Majesty," I lied, barely managing to keep the amused smirk off my face as he waved Aranthus to begin announcing us when the hall opened into a large reception area.

Each end held a fireplace, between which groupings of uncomfortable-looking chairs and sofas had been arranged. The paneling continued into the room. The upper walls had been hung with all manner of weapons. Heraldic banners hung down limply. Lord Sydney towered above most of the gathering, talking with three other men.

A silence slowly rippled across the room as we were spotted. The butler pounded his staff against the dark wood floor and didn't stop until the crowd was facing us and the whispers died out.

Aranthus bawled out, "His Royal Majesty, King Reginald Warren Maceanas and companion, the Lady Illyria Sasha Caladonea Maison du Corbeau."

All the assembled guests slowly sank down in curtsies or bowed low and didn't rise until the king gave them leave. Earl Sydney came forward. "Your Majesty, thank you for gracing my home with your presence."

"Yes, yes . . ." He waved him off. "Has Nicky arrived?"

"No, Majesty, he sent a note saying he was unsure if he could attend. Lady Illyria, I am glad you found time to come."

I inclined my head as the king scowled. "He should make time. Aranthus, see the lady is told some background on everyone."

I winked at him, causing him to turn rosy red in pleasure as I whispered, "Make it extra juicy."

The chamberlain bowed, shifting to stand behind me, saying just loud enough for those nearest to overhear, "If Lord Nicky doesn't want the honor, you could marry her yourself."

The earl appeared embarrassed, remaining silent as his countess made her way toward us, her eyes shooting daggers at me, mouth crimped tight in anger. Her two daughters and another woman trailed, as the king patted my hand idly. A move not lost on those who overheard the chamberlain.

"I do not recall inviting her! Damn Chadrick! Disgusting the way she flaunts herself! I bet the scheming baggage did it on purpose. Look how she clings to him! And he allows it!" Lady Elizabeth hissed to her companion.

The other woman made a noise of contempt, whispering back, "I heard from my body slave she walked! I'm sure we all know how she 'persuaded' him to let her stay here. You had best send her off, with a warning to stay away from your husband, or you'll complain to the king. Have both the sponsorship and her residency terminated."

They stopped their cattiness before they got within normal human's earshot. They curtsied, greeting the king. He spoke a few pleasantries as Aranthus stood behind us whispering tidbits in my ear.

"Ah Lady Elizabeth, a pleasure, I hope your lessons with her ladyship are going well?"

Her eyes flicked contemptuously over me as she said, "Welcome to my home, Lady Illyria. I am happy you came, though it is clear we need to expand your lessons. I don't recall inviting you."

"She wishes you to the dungeons so her daughters will not have competition, and her husband won't try seducing you," Aranthus murmured in my ear, laughter barely suppressed.

"Are these lovely young women your daughters?"

Her mouth thinned further; the older woman was amused. "The lady to my left is Earl Sydney's sister, wife to Viscount Tottenham, Lady Meanna."

"Pride and Propriety," came the murmur.

"This is my eldest daughter, Lady Caroline; and my youngest, Lady Sally."

"Lady Caroline was married to one of the king's knights, but he died a few years back. She is looking for a new husband and father to her children. Lady Sally is desperate for a title of her own. She is always trying for any bachelor nobleman, or the king," softly in my ear.

We stayed chatting a bit, or to be more precise, I ignored the barbs both women tossed my way, until they realized they couldn't ruffle my composure. The earl caught His Majesty's eye. A tall man, patrician, sneering, blonde, was the first to greet us as the king and I approached our host's group. "The Most Honorable, the Marquis of Jenabram."

We exchanged greetings.

"He has been married three times; all of them died fairly young. Rumors say he has them poisoned when he becomes bored, or they don't give him sons. The small, thin woman with mousy blond hair speaking to the baroness is his current wife, Lady Anne."

She was barely out of her teens; shadows under the rice powder covering her face spoke of bruises.

"I thought you didn't trust foreign nobles?" Jenabram drawled. "How can you be sure she will be loyal and not a traitor."

"I am thinking of marrying her to one of my nobles to ensure her loyalty and reinstating her title."

"My apologies, Sire, I meant no offense." Jenabram bowed. *A dukedom! With land and favors owed, I'll marry her myself. 'Twould not be so hard; she is gorgeous and rumored to be rich.*

Another murmur: "Sycophant. His nose is so far up the king's ass, he shits for His Majesty. Rumor also has it he and the advisor participate in degenerate practices."

The second person in the group was on the shorter side, and very rotund with thinning blond hair and a full beard. He possessed merry brown eyes, a florid face, in his mid-thirties. "The Right Hon'ble Lord Rothsbury."

"His wife is just as rotund, although quite merry and ten years younger. They have the best food, and the most money problems."

The butler led us in to the dining room, with His Majesty and me right behind our hosts, much to her daughter's displeasure. Countess Sydney was relegated to the opposite end of the table with her daughters and the earl's sister.

"Cackling hens."

I was given Earl Sydney's spot to the right of the king; he was shuffled to the king's left side.

"Your Majesty, there have been rumors of people going missing again," Jenabram said, as the slave-footmen began serving mock turtle consommé.

"Who is being blamed now? The river pirates?"

A man whose name I did not know replied, "That was last week; this week it is the ones upon the sea."

"Yes, they annoy Lord Nicky and are called treasonous," someone replied sotto voce, which caused nervous titters amid the guests.

"Lord Nicky has a difficult task," the king snapped. "Not all the murderers of my family were brought to justice. They are still hiding, as are some of the individuals who tried murdering me. It is treason to say such words, may I remind you? Should I find out who said it, I will strip them of lands and title."

A brief moment of deadly silence settled over our end of the table. We could hear the chatter of the women at the other end.

Baroness Rothsbury broke the silence. "Where is Illthanthia? Was it a terribly long trip? I would love to travel, but the bandits hereabouts make it all but impossible. It was very brave of you to come overland."

I faked eating while replying, "Its location has been lost to time. I have been living in Gemica. If I had known how bad the bandits were, I would have increased the size of my guard."

"Are you saying my army does not do enough to curb the banditry?" Maceanas demanded angrily.

"I have not been here long enough to form an opinion on the army, but if the talk around town, and size of the group who attacked me is any indication, the army is outnumbered," I replied.

The smirk grew on Jenabram's face. "Even if you had been born here, a woman still would not have an accurate opinion of the army."

"It would depend on the woman, wouldn't it? I have known quite a few female warriors." I needled him.

He snorted. "Amazons. Our women who are raised properly, you will find, let themselves be guided and guarded by their menfolk. Only those women who cannot get a man, or are too old for marriage, dabble in matters best left to men."

"Do you think I do not have enough guards to handle the job?" Maceanas would not be mollified.

The rest of the table avoided looking at the king. I stepped in, "Given the complexity of the mountain terrain, I doubt even a larger force would rid the area of bandits; there are so many unmapped ravines and gorges."

Jenabram sneered, "Are you implying that you know the art of war better than the king?"

I could kill all the bandits single-handedly—my powers let me find them easy enough—but that wasn't something he needed to know. Besides, they were a very convenient food source. "I doubt there would be many who would consent to be led by me. How often do they raid?"

Jenabram goaded me. "Even those amazons you speak of were defeated. Women don't have what it takes to fight."

"If they were trained properly, as the men are, they would be just as formidable," I replied.

The men laughed. The king still stewed. "Since you seem to find my army inadequate to the task, you would not mind contributing more men and money, so the problem can be properly taken care of."

Jenabram looked smug, the baron alarmed and panicked. "Well,
I . . . I would, Your Majesty, but I have not the resources to spare.
Indeed, I have had to sell some of our slaves as it is."

Jenabram muttered something disparaging about minor nobles, and
the baron's color heightened, but he did not reply.

"And you, woman, rich and beautiful you may be, but you should
keep your mouth shut on subjects you know nothing about."

"Give me leave to choose a squad of women, train and equip them,
then we will see," I snapped back.

"I need men, loyal only to me, not some noble trying to raise an
army which could be used against me!" His face was going from red to
purple with rage.

"Naturally, Sire, but why not let me try with some women? After
all, the general opinion seems to be we are weak and easily defeated. An
army as experienced as yours would have no problem subduing a unit of
women."

The king gurgled speechlessly. Jenabram couldn't help himself. "I
would take the bet, but you shall be gone in three months and even I
could not train men that fast; unless His Majesty changes his mind?"

"A year to train. It takes the army at least that long to get the green
off its new recruits. Not all of them handled weapons before joining," I
countered. "If it please the king."

"And the prize?" the marquis recklessly continued, his eyes
gleaming in unholy lust. "Your hand in marriage when you lose, with
title to be duke."

"You are not free to marry, sir, if I am not mistaken."

"Trifles; she is sickly and hasn't given me a son. I'll divorce her if I
need to. Marriage, and the title."

His poor little wife sat farther down the table, eyes downcast, pale
enough I thought she would faint.

"If you tire of me, or I give you no son, what will you do?"

Those nearest us fell silent in shock at my audacity as he snarled at
me, "Marriage and a dukedom is all I will consider."

I turned to the king. "You could make him a duke if I fail, supposing he actually wins."

"You would have to give something up in return. You have nothing but wealth and your life," the marquis shot back, goaded into believing I was trying to get out of our bet.

"What would Your Majesty consider a fair exchange if I lost?"

"Are you trying to mock me? Or stupid enough to defy me openly when I have not granted you leave to stay?" Maceanas hissed.

"Neither," I promptly replied. "If you make him a duke, and I a citizen with my reinstated titles, I will pay and equip the entire army for two years, including new recruits, should I lose."

The entire table gasped; behind us a slave dropped a platter. It clanged and echoed as it hit the floor in the sudden silence. All eyes upon us, the king sat staring at me for a heartbeat or two, weighing the benefits. I was hoping he wouldn't think to ask what I would want in return if I won. I could tell he was about to agree when an all too familiar voice piped up.

"Why should the marquis be the only one to benefit? Why not any man here try if it is dukedoms we discuss?"

All heads swiveled to Lord Stavic, who was looking angry and defiant. A peek at Jenabram's face showed the depths of his rage.

"You have not the coin for it! You would lose what little land you hold and be reduced to selling your title within a fortnight. We play a high-stakes game."

One of the earls spoke, "He may not, it is true, but I can. I can equip and train a squad for one year. At the end, they could fight the women in combat. Think of it, what better way to find out if their training is true?"

Agreement rang around the table as the women giggled cattily.

"Interesting," Viscount Ramsbottom said. "Would this battle be to the death? Or with blunted weapons until one side yielded?"

"If they are going to train and fight like men, they should be willing to die like men," the marquis snapped, gulping his wine down before signaling for a refill.

All heads swiveled back to the king, waiting for his permission. He sat glaring, chewing while he thought. We waited in silence; he swallowed, belched, then waved a hand irritably.

"Very well. Anyone with funds may join the bet. One year to train a squad, after which time they will meet in a battle to the death. The squad with the most men standing shall be declared the winner. Or women," he added. "In exchange, the winner will be made a duke, the losers will turn any remaining men over to my army, reequipping them to full standard for two years."

He took a gulp of wine. "As to the originators of the bet, lady, your loss will be your original offer."

I bowed my head, replying, "Should I win, I want land." I named a large tract outside the settled countryside.

Maceanas spewed out the mouthful of his drink that he'd managed to take. "You are insane!"

"Too much land?" I asked innocently, halving it.

"No! You will not hold it at all; it is an area of heavy banditry," he replied.

"What better solution for you, Sire? I will be spending my coin, time, and effort to wrest it from their depredations. You will be free to send the army to other areas," I pointed out.

"Madness, you had better hope you lose, 'twould be cheaper to support the army than to keep all that land free of those pests," Earl Ramsbottom advised.

"Very well. If you win, I will deed all that land to you," the king said.

The king turned to Aranthus as the men gave a roar equal parts dismay and admiration. "Aranthus, have the royal copyist make a declaration. All those wishing to participate will sign consent. We will put the official start after the Royal Harvest Ball."

"If I may? I do not know when it is."

"The ball is in less than a month's time," the baroness called down to me kindly. "We always host a weekend hunting party to start off the festivities. I do hope you will join us."

"I would be honored, Lady Lily; thank you."

"Perhaps you should host something, my dear," the king suggested. "Most of the nobles do." It was a gentle reminder I would be expected to adhere to duty, once granted citizenship.

"Of course; what would you suggest?" I asked the table at large.

"A ball is always good."

"We have a ball every night already."

"Lunch, then!" Roars of laughter greeted the speaker.

"Another hunting party!"

"For what? Game or bandits?" a wag called to laughter.

The mood at the table lightened, anticipation for the harvest higher than usual. The rest of the dinner passed innocuously enough. After desert, we all adjourned to a room where the younger daughters took turns singing for us, or played primitive stringed instruments and woodwinds.

Chapter Sixteen

"**My** dear lady, why would you want to live in such squalor whilst your mansion is being built? Far better to live in the Silver Thorn."

"It is not all bad; the bones are good. I can do much with it. Lady Anne, would you like to see what is left of the gardens? I am told they were quite grand at one time; a few of the statues are still present."

The reply was softly indistinct as the speakers continued on. Before them lay the tumbledown mansion, slaves and builders swarming over the site. A small army of slaves unloaded and stacked construction materials, doggedly chipped away at the ground with pick axes, digging a new basement.

"I would not like to live so close to the bridge and the cliff edge, all the noise it shall entail. The wind will be freezing in winter." Lady Elizabeth sniffed scornfully, looking about the grounds.

"I like to think of it as an excellent deterrent to any slave considering escaping," I replied. "My household is growing fast and frankly, I am tired of staying at an inn. I rather fancy my own place, humble though it is."

Indeed, after Aranthus' jest about the king marrying me had made the rounds, in addition to news of Lord Nicky's favor, my buying the tavern maid along with such a notorious mansion, a steady stream of merchants, builders, and slavers waited hours on end for me at the Silver Thorn, sent me gifts and invitations to dine with them. Paying my bills in full had all the warehouses open to me.

We walked farther between the piles, faint sounds of pounding growing louder.

"You will not get far with building; winter is a few months off." Sydney asked, "My lady, might I view what has been done?"

I turned to Lady Anne. "Are you sure you are not tired? I can have the slaves bring a chair for you, and victuals." She was wan and looked faint.

"No, I am fine," she murmured. "What about the ghosts? Of the murdered family who once owned this? Are you not afraid they will kill you as they have every other noble who's lived here?" It was the only sentence Anne uttered to me.

I caught the glare the marquis gave her as she lowered her head to study the dirt, or the toes of her shoes, it was hard to say which. Resentfully, Lady Elizabeth opened her mouth to give me corrective instructions. Her hatred of me had grown since her supper party, especially as the king seemed to be teetering on the edge of reinstating my title. I knew the bulk of the ugly rumors and slurs against me came from her and Lady Meanna.

"Not at all. I don't believe in ghosts. Any foolish enough to try will not succeed."

"She'll just put on her warrior outfit and scare them away with how unfeminine she is," Jenabram sneered.

I ignored the jibe; it angered him when he couldn't upset me.

We continued outside, following a trampled grass path to the new construction. A large wooden structure rising, before it an area trampled into dirt. Eron had a group of women, dividing them into subgroups.

"I thought we were not to start our bet until after the Harvest Ball," Jenabram inquired innocently enough.

I gave a trill of laughter. "Why, my dear marquis, they are not training. My man is weeding out those who are unsuitable for our little bet." I half-turned to him as I said, "Tell me you are not doing the same?"

He smirked, laying his hand upon my shoulder to lean close. "I would not tell any but you: yes. Why should I have to suffer with the dregs?" He straightened up, casting an arrogant eye over the women. "If this is what you consider the best, I shall easily win."

I caught the bitter expression Sydney sent us before he turned to observe the workers.

"It is a disgrace!" Lady Elizabeth would not let the bet go. "No proper woman should dirty her hands with such things." Her nostrils flared as she continued, "Proper women do not flaunt themselves or their wealth. Their financial affairs should be handled by their menfolk, and if they have none, by an elected elder."

The marquis sneered at her, letting the backs of his fingers trail from my shoulder down my arm as his eyes greedily feasted on the tops of my breasts. "Proper women, it seems, do not catch our beloved king's eyes, nor wrest thoughts of wedding from him." He turned to the earl. "I have heard you choose not to take part. I would think you of all people have the funds for it; you are so unfree with your wealth."

"I am wealthy because I am miserly, not wasting it on every fad and fashion," Sydney replied.

"Did you hear, Lady Illyria? We are a pack of wastrels," the marquis mocked as his hand rested on my shoulder again.

I moved subtly away from the marquis, so he had no choice but to let go, which put me closer to the earl. Lady Elizabeth's mouth was puckered up as if she was sucking on a lemon. I knew she had seen how grabby Jenabram was, and was offended by it.

"There is much to be said for being careful with one's wealth, just as one must spend some to gain some," I replied.

Sydney turned to me, his blue eyes piercing mine. "I do not see where it is being spent wisely. You will not be gaining any investments unless they can win. The risk far outweighs any reward."

"Yes, but there are other rewards. None, I grant, so satisfying as winning would confer, but useful all the same."

His eyes narrowed as he contemplated me. He gave a small bow saying, "As you like."

"What if the slave should incite the women to rise and slay you?" Lady Elizabeth continued. "You are alone, without male protection, with few guards." Sydney cast a worried eye back over the man.

"I would be if he were not innocent of the crimes he has been accused of. His story intrigued me, so I made inquiries. It seems he has been telling the truth. It is the sheriff who is in the wrong." *He would be food.*

Lady Elizabeth snorted derisively. "Jake always does a competent enough job. It is the riffraff flooding our town. The bandits keep honest folk away so only the bad sort come." She pointedly looked at me.

"He is a bully who should never have been trusted with the power he has. Half his men are thugs," I shot back.

How stupidly, willfully blind did she intend to be?

Sydney cleared his throat. "I have heard some of the wilder rumors about the man, but I would not credit them. If there were evidence, it would be another matter entirely."

"Evidence which no doubt is hidden, or witnesses forced to stay silent upon pain of death from someone who protects the miscreant."

The blue of Sydney's eyes darkened with worry; he made as if to speak, but it was his wife who replied, "I would keep such opinions to myself if I were you. You have not resided here for long, and are ignorant of our methods and laws. We do not coddle our lawbreakers, but treat them as the vermin they are. I see we should be extending your lessons."

"I have not said I believe criminals should be coddled. We should be careful innocents are not stripped of their rights by the overzealous, or those with a personal vendetta."

The marquis gave a shout of laughter. "My dear, you are starting to sound as if you have one against the fat lawman."

"I should hope I do not descend to such a level. Let us speak of more pleasant topics instead: the Harvest Ball, for one." I had plans for Jake, and being investigated for them was not part of it.

"Just so," Sydney replied; his worried eyes had not once left my face. Now he turned, offering his arm to his wife.

She ignored him, jerking her whole body away to gather up her skirts. She walked over to the marchioness, making quite a show of fussing over the fragile young woman. I alone heard the small sigh of frustration he gave as he moved aside to allow me to lead the way. I felt the marquis brush against my back as he came up to my other side.

He bent his head as he offered his arm, breathing in my ear, "Rumor has it you bought him and forced his pardon through after you fell on top of him." I waited for him to get to his point. "If you seek a man to satisfy your lusts, you need not buy an animal such as he; there are others of better birth."

"I do not know who started such a silly rumor or why it persists. Everyone's personal lives must be terribly dull for them to be so concerned with what goes on in my bedroom. If you will pardon me, Lord Jenabram, your wife does not look well."

His smirk crumpled. "You dare to sneer at my offer? Don't make the mistake of thinking the king's infatuation will lead to you becoming queen. He has whores, to be discarded the moment his lusts have been sated. I, on the other hand, would make you a cherished lover."

My pet, begging me to take you, calling me Master. Doing whatever I desire and thanking me for it. Always wanting more.

His thoughts marked him a closet sadist, the feeling behind them tipping toward the psychopath side. One night, he would meet my inner monster.

Jenabram saw my faint amusement as I replied, "Your lover, or your pet? We are not what we appear to others, so be careful where and how you tread, Marquis. Now, if you will excuse me, your wife seems to have fainted." I went to Lady Anne, crumpled upon the ground.

"Useless bitch!" I heard him hiss in fury behind me.

Lady Elizabeth crouched, patting the marchioness' hand and fanning her with a square of linen. Rolf was hopping anxiously from foot to foot. Lord Sydney knelt by the girl, turning her onto her side for the countess's and marchioness's slaves to loosen the laces of her gown.

I sent the page for wine and slaves to help carry Anne back to the mansion.

"No need. I will be glad to bend my back to the task if the marquis will permit me. She is such a little thing."

"There is no cause for concern; she does this all the time. She is infirm." Jenabram's mouth twisted up in condemning lines.

"It is still no reason for her to lie in the grass while she comes round," I chided him. "If you will, Lord Sydney, my slaves will have a spot ready for her inside."

The earl gathered the marchioness up as we started back to the building I used for temporary housing. At one time, it provided shelter for ground slaves. Susafan and Mary Elana met us at the door, but the earl insisted on carrying Lady Anne to what passed for seating. I had only the basics of my newly purchased furniture delivered for the small space.

My slaves bathed her brow and hands in lavender water, managing to loosen her stays as the men stood outside the room. "Mary Elana, she should have some wine to drink when she comes round, if we have any, and a bite to eat. She is too thin by far."

"Half-starved is more truthful. The marquis was ever a cruel boy; he has grown into an even crueler man. His slaves whisper he starves and beats her when she displeases him," Susafan furiously informed me.

"I doubt the laws of town would support our keeping her here, and she has to want the help for it to be effective."

Mary Elana silently fetched some wine and food. I left the two women caring for Lady Anne, and stepped into the room where the men waited.

"Would you care for some refreshments while we wait for her ladyship to recover?"

"A most welcome proposal," Sydney replied.

Jenabram stared at me, lust and anger warring in his eyes as I sent Rolf for food and drink. My guests sat enjoying a light repast as we chatted.

"I do hope our seamstress will have time to make you a decent dress for the ball," Lady Elizabeth began. "We must go see her soon, so I may instruct you on what is proper for our balls."

"She has already started on my gown," I assured her, laughing to myself.

The older woman's face thinned a moment as she frowned. "You may think you are being creative with your clothes, but you are only disgracing yourself and insuring you will remain without respect or social standing." *Attention whore!* She turned to the marquis. "Tell me, what delights have you planned for us?" The faintest hint of sarcasm in her tone.

"I mean to make my ball a mask; my wife is such a child still it will delight her." *And the dancers will pucker up your lips, you ice bitch. If you opened your legs, your husband wouldn't be so joyless.*

"I despise masks. It is merely an excuse for people to hide their identity so they may act badly. We shall not be attending. Your little balls tend to get out of hand. I cannot have my daughters subjected to such wantonness to which rumor has it your balls descend."

"A pity," he remarked lazily. "I have invited what is left of the single, noble-born men and women; no military allowed." *Your eldest has been bedded, numerous times. She enjoys a good, long poke.*

"Let us not be too hasty, Lady Elizabeth," Sydney spoke. "We should show our support for our fellow peers; there are so few of us left. We need not remain the entire night."

"How nice to see you still know where your balls are at. If only you used them now and again more often, you might gain more favor from our king." Jenabram's eyes glittered in malice. He turned to me as the countess went white in rage.

"And you? Will you come? Or are you going to turn into a frigid snow queen like dear Elizabeth?"

"I quite enjoy a good masquerade; I shall attend." *The easiest way to seek a delicious morsel of prey to snack upon.* "Do you plan on your guests wearing costumes? Or just masks?"

He gulped his wine, slamming the cup down, signaling for a refill. "I think I shall request costumes. Thank you for the suggestion." He toasted me, downing the refilled cup.

The Sydneys looked at me in displeasure as Rolf came pelting into the room. "My lady! My lady!" he shouted, breathless from running. "His Majesty comes!"

The marquis turned to glare at the interruption as I thanked the boy, sending him to bring another chair along with more food and drink. We could hear the tramp of booted feet as the palace guards entered, fanning out to make sure no assassins hid. We made our obeisance as he entered upon Aranthus's announcement, waving for us to attend him, the small room now crowded.

"Your Majesty, we were discussing the harvest ball. I plan to make mine a costume party. I do hope you'll attend," Jenabram said by way of greeting, always the suck-up.

"Forgive me, Jenabram. I want to speak with Lady Illyria alone."

The marquis' face froze into a smile, his eyes glittering angrily as he bowed consent. The king paid no attention to the earl or his countess; I could see how insulting she considered the slight.

"As you wish, Majesty; shall we go outside? The marquis' wife is in the next room and has not recovered from the fainting spell she had earlier." I offered.

He appeared startled. "What? Oh, very well." He waved a jewel-encrusted hand. Aranthus gestured for the guards to go first, making sure no one lurked to do the king harm.

One of my slaves poured a cup of wine and held it out, which Maceanas took after offering me his arm. Three glares burned holes into our backs as we exited.

"What is it you want to speak of, Majesty?" I asked.

"I have had some complaints about you." He made a negligible hand movement.

"What is their nature, and I shall do my best to satisfy," I replied.

"Trifles."

"As you say. What do you want me to answer?"

"The sheriff is displeased you are still claiming he is unfit for his position, as is Lord Nicky. I was told the two of you had come to an understanding in regards to our lawman."

Why were my careful manipulations not working as they always had in the past? Finessing was needed. "I do not care to keep dwelling on the man. Lord Nicky and I did come to an agreement. I am stymied as to why they claim otherwise. I am satisfied with the outcome."

"So you say, but I have heard otherwise from them. I am tired of your incessant whining about the sheriff. I see a man trying to do a difficult and dangerous job with the men he has. So dangerous is it, most people do not voluntarily join."

I merely raised a brow. "I fear we shall not see eye to eye on the subject."

"Then find a way," he curtly replied, scowling around at the activity.

I acknowledged his words with a bow of my head. My plans for Jake needed the right moment to move forward.

"The countess does not think you are learning our customs and manners fast enough. How dare you disregard my favors? It is enough to order your imprisonment and execution."

"Her ladyship is much mistaken. It is true I do not know all your customs yet. I am meeting with her, doing my best to remember. I would not presume to break them knowingly, nor show such ingratitude," I soothed.

Elizabeth was not conscious of the topics we discussed during our sessions. I used my power to make her think she instructed me, while all the while I gained intelligence on the townspeople.

Maceanas swung around to face me fully. "I have been thinking over Aranthus's jest."

"He makes so many, I lose track. To which do you refer?" The sudden change of topic unwelcome, I couldn't tell from his thoughts whether he believed me or not.

The king ignored my words, carefully evaluating me. "You are rich," he muttered to himself. "You are more than pleasing to the eye, and you were titled and are of suitable birth, despite the accusations against you."

I didn't like his musings. None of my plans included a legally binding contract with another man, king or not.

"I would not press the issue, especially since he is the only one I can trust, but . . ." he trailed off, walking around me, inspecting.

The weak sun beat down when the clouds parted, burning my exposed skin golden, sapping my strength and ability to influence his thoughts. A throbbing in my veins began, my dark hunger rising. I didn't have time for nonsense; continuing exposure meant true death when my flesh ignited.

"What can I do to put your mind at ease and have the accusations dismissed, Sire?" I asked, hoping it would give me months to work upon the king, bending his mind and will fully to mine.

Maceanas stopped in front of me, eyeing the tops of my breasts as he drank the last of the wine.

"Shall I call for more, Sire?"

He threw the cup down before attempting to grab me and smashing his lips against mine. I evaded his clumsy attempt while retreating into shadows. For a moment, anger sparked in the king's eyes, before he got a crafty look.

"Oh ho! So it is a chase! Very well, I have not had a good chase in a long while."

The denial was sputtering out while he lunged toward me once more. I maneuvered out of the way, conveniently leading us closer toward the concealing bulk of raw materials nearby.

"Your Majesty, I am not worthy of the high honor you wish to give me." Inside I fumed.

What was going on? I never had trouble seducing men, when I willed it. I did not will it now, nor with the marquis. I would have to use drastic measures; I preferred not to do so when I could be easily interrupted.

Maceanas grasped my shoulders in an effort to bring me closer, the lust in his eyes flaring. I needed to bite him. I let him thrust his tongue in my mouth, piercing it with a fang as I used the last of my sun-depleted strength to prevent him from recoiling at the pain. His blood pooled in my mouth as I swallowed, twisting his mind. Shouts rang out from guards, giving me just enough time to erase the marks along with the memory of the bite as I shoved His Majesty back. I made it look as if he had flung me away as he stumbled backward tripping and falling.

"Your Majesty!" I played concern to its hilt as I knelt on the ground beside him.

His guards hustled over to help us back up. The king dazed, whatever gripping him before I bit him gone.

"Is His Majesty all right?"

We all turned toward the doorway, saw Aranthus goggling at us, Nicky glaring murder. The tops of other heads could be seen behind them or crowding the windows. I wondered how long the young man had stood watching.

The advisor stomped down the steps to us. "What is the meaning of this?"

"Your lordship," the guard began before being cut off.

"I know what happened, you idiot!" Nicky screamed at him. "I saw the whole damn thing! Everyone saw!"

"Your pardon, advisor, but . . ."

Nicky stopped his forward movement long enough to make a motion, cutting off the man's words. The guards all took an uneasy step back.

The advisor and I stood nose to nose, his cinnamon and ambrosia scent curling stronger in the air between us, along with a heavy under-note of sulfur, turning the whiff rotten.

"Now, now. There has been no harm done," the king snapped, irritated at being thwarted.

I ignored the renewed leap of rage in the young man's eyes. "Your Majesty," Nicky snarled, "I trust you have not been hurt from tripping over the debris in her ladyship's deplorable grounds."

Maceanas drew himself up, outrage upon his features. "I am your king. I trust you will remember next time I must have a private discussion?" He addressed us.

"I have no intention of forgetting," I informed him. *Asshole!*

"Shut up!" Nicky hissed at me. "Sire, if you want a woman for a quick lay, there are any number of female slaves here." He lowered his voice. "You can't just assault what noble-born we have left like they're common whores and expect them to remain loyal."

"I will not be made a fool of!"

"Of course not. They will not question what we tell them. You tripped on some rubble."

They were all arrogant assholes. The taste of the king's blood meant I could control him better should the need arise.

"Very well. Guards, attend me." The king snapped his fingers. "Lady Illyria, you will hold your tongue."

I only bowed my head as we followed the king back inside. The doorway and windows hurriedly emptied of onlookers. Everyone sunk into a deep curtsey or bow as we entered the room.

The king ignored them. "'Tis a pity your grounds are strewn with litter. I expect you to have it set to rights before I visit next."

My curtsey was deep. "As you command, Majesty."

He bellowed to Aranthus to announce his departure, his retinue following. The moment he left the room, people straightened up, looking toward the advisor and me avidly. I could tell they didn't believe a word of what happened. Most saw how the king pursued me. I kept a neutral expression on my face, though inside I gloated. A new round of rumors would be a hot topic.

"My lady, we should be going." Lord Sydney bowed to me.

The tightness of Lady Elizabeth's lips gave them the illusion of having disappeared. *Scheming viper. You will not steal either of my daughters' chances to become queen.*

Lady Anne's cold, trembling hands clutched mine briefly. "Thank you for your hospitality." *Beware my husband. He is dangerous.*

Lord Jenabram bowed, his eyes never rising above my bodice, leaning closer to my ear. "Lady Illyria, thank you for such an entertaining afternoon."

Saizar was the last to take his leave. He wore an unhappy, speculative expression as he bowed and strode from the room. Nicky's body slave stood, near invisible, in the darkest shadows. The fight-or-flight response washed over me, along with a sensation of pure evil. Unwelcome thoughts started crowding my mind. I pushed them out of the way to concentrate on the advisor, who ran his eyes over me. I didn't need to read his mind to know he felt jealous of my relationship with the king.

Rage flamed up in Nicky's eyes. "So you think to trap the king into marriage."

My brow raised. "If I may be perfectly frank, Lord Nicky, it is not my intention to marry anyone, not even His Majesty."

The advisor answered with lip-curling disgust, "Don't lie to me!"

"It is no lie. Why would I want to marry? Unwed, I control my money and property. I can go where I please and when. A husband only interferes."

The young man's hands curled into fists; he made an involuntary motion before stilling himself. "Women are meant to be guided by men."

Oh, hell, another one of those damn patriarchal women-haters. "I find your attitude antediluvian. I am not one of those women who must have her life directed by a man. Why such concern over the subject?"

"I will not have you marrying the king and trying to usurp my authority," he hissed. "Don't think I can't see what you're doing. You think you can look down upon me? You think you can outwit me? I will see you dead first! You have no idea with whom you are trifling!"

I sighed as he ranted on, voice rising to a shout, veins in his neck and head pulsing. Had he listened to a word I said?

"Help me convince His Majesty I am better off remaining unmarried. We shall both get what we desire."

"You stupid woman! No one says no to the king!"

Or you? I wanted to say but didn't. "I am sure that the pair of us can persuade him I would not make an acceptable queen. You need not fear for your power, and I will be left in peace."

"You will have to marry someone."

"Why? What harm is in my remaining single?"

I could guess what he left unsaid. They did not like the enormous wealth I controlled. Once my title became reinstated according to their laws, I would have near-unlimited access to royal power and the ability to wield it. I had yet to find a man worthy of being gifted with my secret.

"It will have to be. You cannot remain single."

"If I should feel the need to join in a permanent union, I will pick out my mate."

"No, you will not. You know damn well that nobility carries certain obligations. The countess should have already seen to that portion of your education."

His tenaciousness irritated me. "I am well aware of what they are. I shall fulfill them as I see fit. I grow weary of this conversation, Lord Nicky. I shall have a slave escort you out."

I could hear the audible grinding of his teeth. "You will make sure you are never alone with His Majesty."

"I can hardly ignore a royal command, now can I?"

"That is not the point!" He stopped what he was going to say, changing it. "Jake has complained that you were in a place you shouldn't be. When he tried to explain, you attacked him unprovoked, causing severe damage."

"I am unaware of any laws forbidding women to frequent certain establishments. Which establishment was it?"

The young man gripped the edge of the table, head down as he tried to control his rage. "That tavern, the Bloody Knuckles; and there is no law forbidding women certain establishments . . . officially." he gritted out.

"I stopped in to speak with the owner about his daughter. I had been told she would make an acceptable maid. I would leave such dealings to a steward, but as of yet I have not found a man trustworthy enough to hire for the position. If anyone were attacked unprovoked, it would be me, by Jake and his deplorable men."

"I can find nothing remiss in the sheriff's behavior. You will cease your campaign against the man. Need I remind you of the commitment you made in exchange for your favor? "

"Oh?" I quirked a brow in disbelief. "I trust he will keep his notions of law away from my people and not go out of his way to harass them."

Nicky raised his head. "He will continue to uphold our laws. Your slaves had better hope they don't break any."

"Pray he has enough brains not to make up excuses to arrest and harm them. Or I will start to think it is you who doesn't care for a friendly alliance," I replied.

Our eyes clashed. "You should remember you are a female, one refusing the protection of a husband. Refusing the man with the most power in the kingdom: me," he softly reminded me, fighting his rage.

I answered, "I am not some breeding creature to lay upon her back, spitting out children, and bowing to a man. I will be treated as an equal."

We stared at each other a moment more, until his slave whispered something to him. Nicky took a deep breath, and stood straight to address me more convivially. "Tom wants to see his daughter. He is concerned for her well-being."

His abrupt change in attitude disturbed me. I wondered what new game he played. Caution would be needed: I still did not know for certain what flavor of supernatural being he was. He was right in that he was the second most powerful man in the country; he was also the most mentally disturbed.

"I do not so permit. I find it hard to believe he wishes to assure himself of her well-being, as he is the cause of her injuries."

Lord Nicky's face turned beet red. "Slave or not, he should still be allowed to see his daughter if he wishes."

"He signed papers giving up all rights to her in exchange for coin when he sold her as my slave. If I understand the laws correctly, slaves are under the complete control of their owners. She must have my permission to leave the property for anything not related to the work she does."

He narrowed his eyes at me. "I shall send someone to give the man your response. In the meantime, you will stay away from His Majesty until I can convince him you are unfit to be his queen."

Abruptly, he called for his horse to be brought round; the floorboards quivered under the pounding of his feet. Susafan brought the two merchant men in. They bowed as Mica spoke first, going straight to his complaint.

"What makes you think that the king's advisor is he whom we seek? He is considerably older than the boy we described."

I had about had it with men today. I didn't understand why they insisted the person they wanted was a child. Plus, the other information I received was disturbing me more than their problem. I decided to see how they would explain the discrepancies.

"You said Nicky was a little boy when he left you how many years ago? Wouldn't he be older by now?"

The men subtly tensed. Mica answered, "I don't believe we did say when he left us, but it was not long ago."

The casually given reply, lacking specificity, increased my suspicions. The recollections of images in the advisor's dreams made me uneasy.

I said, "When I was speaking with His Majesty, he let slip Lord Nicholas, or Nicky as he calls the man, has been his childhood friend for about ten years. His Highness recalls being thirteen at the time of their meeting. He says the boy was maybe eleven or twelve."

I watched Mica look at his brother; subtle gestures passed between them.

Mica replied, "We have a problem, for our Nicky is about twelve. The young man we saw today can't be he, but the resemblance is striking."

He was lying; I could see the microphysical changes. My unease slowly intensified. The four men shared the same scent. "I am sorry for wasting your time." I felt a clear, sudden sense of danger, though neither man had offered an overt threat.

Colin inquired, "You've shown us the advisor, whom I'll admit looks eerily similar to our boy, including the name. Is it possible they are in league with each other?"

It felt ten minutes past time for them to be going, not only from my dwelling, but from the land too. The sense of danger pulsing through my being meant extra caution, even if it included keeping the men around longer than needed. I paused as if weighing my words.

"I have never seen your little boy near the advisor. I could not say with any certainty, but it is entirely plausible Lord Nicky is hiding the child, protecting him."

They were disturbed, unable to hide it. "A bigger problem than we have anticipated. We do not want to risk accusing the wrong person; however, if the young man is actively participating in the masquerade . . . I imagine the king would not be pleased and would want to prevent it from continuing," Colin voiced their views. "His Majesty is temperamental. One never knows what prompts him to call for the execution of his unlucky subject without a fair trial. The boy's duplicity would be enough."

As an aside I casually mentioned, "But it would take care of your problem for you, would it not?"

"No. He is a child, even though he is a thief and a liar. I cannot countenance his death, not if there is some way to help him become a productive member of society," Mica spoke for them both.

My brow quirked up. Nicky, whichever version they searched for, was already a hardened criminal and nothing was going to change him. "Your ideas of justice are admirable. I only hope they are not ones you will live to regret. We still have time before the Harvest Ball. If I discover further information, I will send word."

I did not care for what happened next. I saw pain lance through the older man's eyes, and a feeling he was no longer fully present in the room with us.

* * *

Mica suddenly doubled over, clutching both sides of his head, groaning in pain. Images flared before his eyes, of a lady he had known during his long life. She had the same facial expression as the noblewoman before him now, and a naughty streak in her which somehow got him tangled in her escapades, to his detriment.

Mica was looking down into yellow-brown, green eyes peering up at him mischievously. "Stay away from the boy."

She pouted at him as he whirled her out and back in a tango. Her bright yellow, belted halter-style dress billowing. "Chéri, I am only being friendly."

"No, you're trying to seduce him. He doesn't need you to be playing with him when you have no serious intentions."

"He knows we are having fun. It makes him feel better about himself when I flirt with him. What is so unkind?"

"No, Lira, leave him be. The more you flirt, the more he believes it's for real. I will not have you destroy his heart."

"Oh Mica, such a stick-in-the-mud. I promise, I will not harm your young protégé."

"Mica! Mica! Mica! Are you all right?" Colin attempted peering into his brother's face.

"I'm fine; nothing's the matter." He gasped, standing straight. "Your pardon, my lady. I am bothered lately by searing head pain, which comes and goes."

He breathed a moment, steadying himself. "In response to your question: Yes, it would be immensely helpful. Thank you." His dark eyes bored into mine, intently studying.

I scowled to myself, wishing again their minds were not closed to me. "Gentlemen, you are quite welcome. Now I must take my leave of you. My slave shall show you out. I have much work to oversee."

Chapter Seventeen

Mica sat scowling as he broke his fast. Each day ticking by brought him a little closer to the guardian coming for the boy's soul-gem. He and Colin had finished questioning the merchants, at least the ones willing to talk. No one would admit seeing a boy of twelve around town who matched Nicky's description. The closest they had come was a sighting over ten years ago. The man took a drink of ale, ate some more. Colin entered the room; he grunted a greeting as his younger brother went to the sideboard to serve himself.

Colin had just sat down when a slave brought in a scroll, offering it to the men. Mica took it, breaking the wax seal, noting there was no imprint in the wax. Whatever was in the text of the short note had him snarling and crumpling the paper.

Colin smoothed out the paper, reading, "Sirs, information has come to me about a mutual acquaintance and certain activities I think will be of interest to you. Rites of a religious nature will be performed in a grove within the forest, in which the little boy is known to participate."

A crude map had been drawn underneath the note, which was unsigned.

"Huh, it seems someone knew something after all, just too scared to come forth in person." Mica muttered something. "Sorry," Colin replied, "I didn't catch what you said."

"I said," Mica repeated louder, "this is a bunch of bullshit. Religious rites in a grove? Sounds like hocus-pocus nonsense to me." Something was nagging at the back of his mind, something trying to get out. He felt a searing pain in his head. Mica clapped his hands to the sides, squeezing, as if it would help.

"I'm sure it is, but it will give us another opportunity to view the person, whether it's Nicky or his double."

"How are we supposed to get close enough out in the damn woods?" he shot back.

His brother continued looking at him in concern. "We won't know until we look at the area, will we? If we can discover it. The map is pretty crude. I hope it's not a false lead, or a trap."

The sharp pains were slowly fading, leaving a feeling of nausea behind. Mica rubbed his head again at another stab. "I ran into a grove, a group of people. Damn! Why won't these pains go away?"

Colin looked at his brother worriedly; due to their nature, they were not plagued by ills the way mortals were. There had to be something wrong.

"I don't care what it could be, it's more than we had. We'll just have to be careful. We both know a trap when we see it. I don't think it is one. It would have been easier to lure us into a trap when we first arrived. It must be Lady Illyria; just accepting her hospitality and staying under her banner is enough for the townspeople to place their faith in us."

"But she is a newcomer herself; I thought you didn't trust her?"

"I don't, but as she is the only one of the nobles who will speak with us. What choice do we have?"

His brother looked at him expectantly as Mica pressed the heels of his hands to his eyelids, then removed them as the pain finally let up.

"What about the marquis?" Colin asked.

Mica shook his head. "He sent word he was mistaken, mentioning the king's advisor is investigating the duchess." He watched the disbelief spread across his brother's face.

"What if it is all some elaborate plot by the boy to lure you in, smashing your soul-gem to destroy you once and for all?"

His elder brother shot him a disgusted look. "Since when has Nicky ever had enough coin for something so large and elaborate? He's a twelve year old boy whose only real skill is thievery and lies. What adult is going to listen to his advice willingly and follow it? No, I think she has gotten sucked into something she doesn't comprehend and is a pawn."

Colin was alarmed. "Should we not warn her?"

"And tell her what? She seems smart enough; she's managed to charm the king into supporting her," Mica snapped back.

Colin shrugged, standing to ring a bell, waiting for a slave to answer. "My brother and I have to go out on business. We will need the horses saddled. We're not sure how long it will take. Please have cook pack some food and drink for us."

She murmured assent; Colin called after, "We'll need the horses and food ready in twenty minutes. Thanks." He bounded up the stairs after his brother to change into riding leathers.

It had taken the men longer than usual to ride out of town, owing to the fact they were trying to find the correct orientation of the map. After several false starts and an hour of wasted time, they were on the right track, entering the clean green scent of the forest.

"The more I think upon it, the more I'm sure the map refers to the grove I stumbled across. It looks to be taking us by the most direct route. If this is a trap, we should try finding the little track I originally used. That way we can sneak up on any watchers and ambush them."

Colin kept quiet, content to let his brother search while he gazed at the forest. The growth was thick on both sides, the rutted road stretching before them, wending its way through the trees. He had never been this way during his searches. The sight of the road reminded him of the ruined castle hiding deep inside the kingdom. Was is possible to find the remnants of a way to it, no matter how overgrown?

Mica signaled to him, interrupting his thoughts. They plunged off the track onto something resembling a deer path. After about a half hour, Mica growled in disgust, remarking it wasn't the right trail. They started back to the road, repeating that pattern many times throughout the afternoon. The sun had turned a mellow color before Mica finally found the right path. Branches and shrubs brushed their legs as they picked their way down the game trail. Colin lost track of how long they rode. Both horses stopped dead, whinnying in fear, trying to rear and plunge back toward the road, though there was no apparent reason for the spooking. The riders had their hands full, keeping the mounts reined in.

"This happened the last time I was out here," Mica gritted out as he finally got his horse to hold still. He slid off, patting her nose, calming the jittery mare whose eyes rolled to show the white. "Better lead them back toward the main track before we tie up. I couldn't get the mount I was on at the time to go any farther, either."

The brothers tied their horses to a branch, leaving enough slack for them to reach the grass. Then, shouldering supplies, the two men began walking. After a while, they came to a tangle of shrubs.

"Here," Mica quietly mouthed, while scanning the tree line to see if he could spot any watchers. Colin could see how the bushes were broken and trampled by a large mass moving through.

"Here's where it gets tricky. I remember crawling through." Mica was puzzled, then suddenly collapsed to his knees, bowed over with excruciating pain. As suddenly as it had come, the pain disappeared.

"Don't worry about it," Mica panted out, carefully standing. "No, I don't know what's causing it. Let's just forget about it and keep moving," he brusquely answered the unspoken question, starting to walk around the brush, looking for an end or break.

Colin followed as they fought their way to the edge of a clearing. Both men stopped, sweating and breathless, to look around. When they were satisfied no one was lurking, they stepped out into the open approaching the center. Immediately both men's skins itched as if hundreds of tiny, unseen insects crawled over their flesh. The men slapped and scratched to no avail before setting their minds to ignore the sensations as best as they were able. A sweet stench, reminding them of decay, hung heavily. Despite the sun overhead, the grove was gloomier than it should have been. Colin set his pack down, taking out a small, slim box. He opened it up, noting the wax tablet within was still intact as he removed the metal stylus that went with it. It was one of the better presents her ladyship had given them, in his opinion. He would have to keep his notes brief, so as to take advantage of the space.

"Clearing of medium size, say, sixty feet around?" He shook his head. Noted an altar in the center covered in dark stains looking suspiciously like dried blood. Likewise, the ground all around was black and hard. Colin crouched down and, using one end of the stylus, scraped up reddish-black dirt. He poured it into a small clay bottle, stoppering it with a wood cork before replacing it in his jacket pocket.

"Blood drained from the altar? Maybe." He noted a path with the remains of burned torches tossed to either side of the path, and a wagon track. "It looks like the main track on the map we were given. We'll have to take the horses around to find the start."

"The path, do you know where it goes to?" Colin asked.

"No," Mica answered, looking around once more. "If you want to find a spot to hide, I'll follow it a bit, see where it ends."

"Sure," Colin replied, eyes drawn back to the altar.

Mica left. Colin could see the bones of animals piled around the altar, the carving around the entire rim, obscured by dark stains. As he inspected it, he realized they were symbols. Some even looked familiar, yet he couldn't recall where he had seen them before. Colin started at one side and began copying the symbols in order. He was afraid he would run out of room on the tablets before he finished. He didn't have too many of the portable tablets with him.

* * *

Mica followed the path with its faint imprints left by footwear. He reckoned that he'd gone about half a mile into the forest before the path emptied into an overgrown lawn, across which sat a two-story, squat stone house. Mica saw no watchers or other signs of life. The air was still and heavy with the same sweet smell of decay as the grove. The man felt uneasy but couldn't pinpoint why. The windows were all shuttered tightly. Did he dare go closer? A terrace ran the length of the back wall, a trellis hung with dead vines centered against the wall. The trail from the grove continued across the lawn, the grass beaten down in a line to the patio.

"This must be where the men meet to leave their mounts. A private lodge for the boy?" he muttered to himself as he cast a glance back down the shadowed way he had come.

"Colin should be fine; they probably don't come until dark anyway. Plenty of time to explore." But still he felt unsettled without knowing why. The sensation of wrongness about the house increasing as he gained the terrace; was it possible the stench was stronger?

Mica tried the shutters, all locked from the inside. He headed around the corner and spotted a dark shape shuffling around the other side. Other dark shapes rustled forward out of the forest, slowly following the scent of the intruder. Mica passed through a walled courtyard past a stable; he ignored a door opposite, more interested that the front was unguarded. Just as he opened the far door, he thought he heard a thump on the one he had just come through, thinking he heard a shuffle and a moan.

"Hello? Anybody here?" Mica called out. The moan grew louder.

It sounded as if someone was in pain inside the stables. What if it was a clever trap by the little boy? But then again, what if someone were being held prisoner, hurt and needing help? He couldn't remember much from that night, though he could have sworn there was human sacrifice. He walked toward the big door, slid the wooden bar back, rolling the door to the left. A foul stench of rotting meat and body fluids assaulted his olfactory endings. He fought down the urge to throw up as a cold, rubbery hand clamped on his arm. Mica's brain froze. The person—no, the thing—before him moaned again, drawing him toward the remains of its mouth. That broke his inertia. Mica tried to tug free, a shout of horror bursting forth, but the hands holding him were like steel bands.

"Holy Mother of God! Get off me!" Mica hollered, swinging at the creature.

His punch landed with a splat, clotted blood flying out, skin breaking and slipping. His attacker ignored the blow, dragging the immortal's arm closer to his gnashing teeth. They danced around the courtyard as Mica struggled to break free. He backpedaled, drawing his sword, but the creature before him moved closer, hands grasping, moaning, taking no notice of the warning cuts Mica gave him across his arms and legs. He saw they didn't bleed the same way as a mortal—clots of a thick smelly dark ichor oozed and dripped out.

"This is fucking crazy! I've got to get the hell out of here." More moans came from the darkness of the barn, men/things spilling out, reaching out, as Mica tried not to cast his breakfast on the ground.

He sliced a hand off but the once-man relentlessly pursued. Mica could feel hands and arms all around, trying to grab hold. He sliced and stabbed; he needed to get back to Colin, but how to kill these things? Frantically he searched his mind, couldn't remember anything, deciding to open the man from stem to stern. It wasn't hard to do, only...

"Damn it!" Mica swore, losing the fight with his stomach as a wave of foul gases engulfed him.

The once-man kept shuffling toward him, coils of intestines falling out.

"Fuck it all!" Mica managed to trip the body up; it fell back, squirming like a helpless beetle or upturned turtle. The other creatures bumped against it, momentarily held at bay. Mica dived between the legs of the mob, managing to come up behind them. He began to hack heads off, always moving, trying to keep the group off him. He was panting, sweating and worn out by the time he got the last head off. The bodies lay still on the ground.

"Okay. Great. So the damn things can die after all."

Mica lifted his sword up to gaze at a head impaled on it. The grisly lump looked and smelled long dead. "The thump I heard on the courtyard door. I bet that there's more of them waiting."

The door into the house was locked tight, the surrounding wall high enough he couldn't see over. *Do I dare try the door to the front? How many of those things might be waiting? Can I circle around? No, better to not chance it.*

Cautiously Mica walked toward the stables, sword at the ready, stepping just inside the entrance. He stopped to let his eyes adjust to the gloom. Carefully he explored, finding the ladder to the loft. Fast and silently he climbed, making his way over to peek out the barn loft door through which hay was loaded, using the pulley rope to lean out farther. There was a small crowd of the things, all standing still, staring at the door leading into the courtyard. Mica silently cursed to himself. They hadn't tried to break down the door to swarm him, but he didn't want to get stuck here until nightfall. It was only the thought that Colin might come looking which drove him to more action. What little he could see of the front lawn was clear of the creatures. He scanned the visible tree line; nothing moved but he saw another road leading away from the house into the forest.

"Think, Mica, think," he muttered, climbing back down, walking over to the gate leading to the front of the house, avoiding the corpses. The problem was he hadn't watched those damn horror movies humans had so loved pre-cataclysm. "Colin would know what to do, I bet; this sort of shit is just up his alley, debunking myths and legends. Shit!" He ran a hand through his hair.

"I have to get back to the clearing. I don't know where the road goes. Maybe I can go around the house, behind those things, and make the trail before they notice me? It's worth a shot. I need a shield, something else to help bash them out of the way." Back to the stables he went, but nothing he saw looked helpful. New torches in holders gave him an idea. "Fire. Everybody in their right minds is afraid of it; 'course these things don't seem to have a mind."

He paced some more, deciding to take one anyway. He searched out his flint and steel, after a couple strikes managing to light it. "Okay, Mica, here goes nothing."

Mica led with the torch, opening the door with his free hand. It was still clear, no moans of greeting as he slipped out. Silently he shut the door behind him, and jogged across the front lawn while drawing his sword out. He chanced a quick look back, and saw more of the things shuffling toward him from the tree line. He nipped around the corner, still in the clear, picking up the pace a bit. But another thing stepped out just as he rounded the far back corner of the house. The group by the courtyard was slowly turning his way.

"Shit!" He was going to get caught between the two groups. Mica put the after-burners on, breaking into a flat-out run. He sliced with his sword, batting with the torch before making the path. He ran, the horde moaning and shambling after him.

Colin had just started down the wagon tracks, oblivious to his wheezing brother bursting into the clearing.

"Colin!" Mica bellowed. "Move, we have to leave! Now!"

Colin stared in horror at the group which had split to come after new prey. His brother reached the tangle with the horde. Mica thrust with the torch, miraculously still lit, deep into the brush, which caught easily.

Both men concentrated on trying to get free of the tangle, the things moaning and following. The flames grew higher, the heat unbearable, the smoke choking. They fled down the path, back to their horses, hoping the animals were still there.

* * *

The men galloped back to town, casting uneasy glances around them, waiting for horrors to burst forth from the forest.

"I've been thinking, Mica: how do the men use the grove if those things are there?"

"Are you crazy? They don't!"

"Think about it . . ."

"I'd rather not!" Mica interrupted. "I'd like to know what the hell is going on around here! This shit never existed before!"

"Oh, I don't know," Colin replied, "there were zombies in Haiti back in the day."

"The Haitian zombies weren't dead, they were living men under powerful drugs! Those damn things chasing me today sure as hell looked dead to me! No one can live with those sorts of wounds!" Mica couldn't help the shiver of revulsion.

"Still, there are things in this world which can't be explained even to this day."

"Don't even start such bullshit with me! There. Is. No. Magic!" Mica gritted out.

Colin merely sighed, resuming his train of thought. "It's possible the men are under powerful botanical drugs, and their bodies are slowly breaking down. You said you smelled a sweet scent? There could be some plant perfuming the air causing hallucinations. The drugs in the zombie's system clearly make them impervious to a lot of damage and pain. I have a feeling, though, the participants use the house before the rituals. I think we should go back."

"Are you insane? We don't know how to stop those things!" Mica bellowed.

"Actually, we do. Destroy the brain. Face it, we don't know what kind of drugs were used so the best thing to do would be to put them out of their misery. Look, there's another way into the grove. You still have the map, right? Why don't we find it?"

Mica stared at his brother in disbelief. "No!"

"Why not?"

"Uh, look behind you, toward the sky," Mica replied.

Colin did, seeing a column of smoke rising several miles behind them. "Ah. Whoever uses it doesn't know their grove is on fire. They may send someone to check it out. We can lie in wait for them as we keep an eye on things. They might lead us back to whoever is hiding the little boy."

"The damn forest is on fire! You want to get caught in it?"

"No, but this is the best lead we've had in years. What if they have to abandon the site? We could be wasting an opportunity."

"I don't fancy burning to death! A forest fire is nothing to mess with. Do you realize how long it'll take our bodies to regenerate? And how excruciatingly painful the process will be?"

Another sigh from Colin was his answer. They got the horses moving again, each man lost in his own thoughts. When the road forked, instead of taking the turn leading back to town, Mica took the opposite way.

"I thought . . ." Colin began.

"Shut up. I see flames, and we're out of here," Mica spat.

Colin only smiled.

* * *

The men found the track leading into the grove as the sun set. A heavy scent of smoke, mixed with charred meat, greeted their noses. Cautiously they rode down the path, nerves keyed up, expecting an ambush. Unexpectedly the road split; the brothers reined in to confer.

Colin squinted, catching a nose full of sweet scent.

"Not that way; mayhap we should leave." Mica hastily snatched the reins up, turning his mount around.

"The horses are calm; they're not disturbed. Remember the burial pit I saw? What if I didn't realize how close to the grove it is? There's what appear to be bloodstains all over the altar. We know Nicky used human sacrifice before," Colin theorized.

Mica objected, "And what if it's not? These horses need water; they're not going to be able to gallop far."

"I'll go down on foot. It's starting to get dark; someone's going to be here soon," Colin pointed out.

Mica ran his hand through his hair. "No, you're right. We'll go together. I'll lead, though."

He nudged his horse down the path, just two dirt tracks worn into the grass from the repeated passing of wheels. A small brook intersected, deep enough for the horses to drink from, but not so deep to prevent wagons from crossing. The smell of decay grew stronger, but they didn't see or hear any shuffling movement or moans. The brothers tied cloth over their mouths and noses at the unbearable stench. The trail opened up; before them, in the gloom of dusk, appeared a pit. The men got down, lit the lantern they had brought, holding it high. The wagon tracks crisscrossed a cleared space. The removed dirt formed a wall around the far side. Colin was barely able to see the break he had used before. On the far right side, tangled roots and tree stumps had been piled up to form a type of barrier. The brothers held the light out over the pit. The sight horrific: bodies lay in a tangle as far as they saw, all in various states of decay.

A choking sound came from Mica, hushed tones of dread. "I remember some of the clothes the men and women wore. They must have been sacrificed at the altar." A vision roared through his mind with the strength of a train, bringing red burning eyes, a guttural voice, and one hell of a headache. "These foul murderers must be stopped."

"I've seen enough; let's go." The men mounted up, extinguishing and securing the lantern before starting back down the path.

The sky above the tree line held the last dying rays of light, but they rode in darkness. Voices along with the creak of wheels alerted the brothers they were no longer alone. Hurriedly they guided their mounts into the foliage, hoping the other men would pass by.

"Of all times to wanna come out here," one of the voices spoke.

"You ain't the only one. Crazy bastard, if'n he didn't pay so well, I'd tell him what he could do with his orders. You smell smoke?" the second asked.

"I tol' you we all saw smoke from the forest. Some damn bandit accidentally set some of it on fire."

"Naw, man, it looked awful close. Smells like it too."

"What, you think someone found this place and set it on fire?" the first voice asked. "Probably them damn poachers. Haven't got the sense to go elsewhere."

"You think we should check it out?" the second asked.

"Naw, I think we should get the cattle to the pens afore the brat starts wondering where they at."

The voices faded along with the sound of wheels. Mica whispered to Colin, "We need to secure the horses somewhere, follow on foot."

Then his mount gave a nervous whinny. The noise ricocheted in the still air. The brothers froze, but when no one came to investigate, they hurriedly secured the animals out of sight before slipping back to the grove. The trees around the far side had been blackened by the fire, the underbrush burned away. It was a bit eerie, one side green and growing, the other gray and lifeless. Tonight, four torches burned by the altar, and only a handful of people huddled in the caged wagon. There was no sign of the men who had driven it. The ground inside the clearing appeared untouched by the flames.

The denuded branches provided scant protection. Mica hoped no one chose to walk around the tree and look up. They waited, breathing in the stink of smoke. Out of the inky darkness came a cloaked, hooded figure carrying a torch, followed by twelve others. Every supplicant set their torch in the ground in a wide ring behind them. The leader stood before the altar, speaking words in an unknown tongue. The brothers held their breath. Chanting filled the space, while the leader began waving something shiny about. Fog boiled out of the heated, charred ground as the cold night air met it. A sudden flash of bright light scored Mica's vision along with a sharp blooming pain in his head.

Oh no! Not now! He fought to stay conscious and maintain his grip. The world moved past in slow motion as he found himself falling toward the ground—or it was moving up to meet him? The last thing he saw was the figure behind the altar turning in his direction.

Chapter Eighteen

Dark clouds blotted out the sky; their undersides glowed red, orange and yellow as shouts and screams drifted on the wind. I reined my horse to a stop, smelling fire and death. I should have just stayed at home. My food would have come to me; I wouldn't have to go out to the countryside to hunt. A shape hurtled from between the buildings, howling in victory, sword covered in blood. The man spotted me and charged, battle madness shining in his eyes. I deflected his sword with my own, cutting him down, not recognizing him. It would be madness to enter a burning town; fire was deadly to me. I put my mount to a trot. We entered the drifting smoke, shapes appearing and disappearing in the flicker of light and darkness. I headed toward the center, a jumble of thoughts letting me know bandits and townspeople clashed together. I hadn't had a decent fight in a long time.

Windstorm shied as we dashed past buildings fully engulfed, the heat near-unbearable. I guided him away so we wouldn't be singed, killing those with evil thoughts who crossed before me. I left behind the shouts of townspeople I helped, passing through the engulfed center of town. The heat lessened, as did the fire. We burst from a cloud of smoke and ash to see bodies of the palace guard. A hard wind blew down the river, toward the sea.

A mix of people fought in a roil at the base of the bridge. I paused for a quick look. The cliffs loomed across the river; shouts echoed in the flickering fire amid the warehouses at their base. I could see thick smoke from farther up the hill, letting me know noble houses burned. A horn blasted out. I saw another group of fighters at the top of the street before the inn.

"Move! Fall back! To the hills! The palace guards have been alerted!" a big bearded man screamed over the noise. He sat a horse in the middle of the bridge.

I doubt his fellow raiders heard but they seemed to know what the horn meant, as the tenor of the battle changed. I wanted him; I could use him. I put heels to Windstorm; he leapt forward, knocking over a pair of fighters. It had been a long time since I fought from horseback; I used the smoke and flickering shadows to help hide my super-fast reflexes as I rode closer.

I wheeled around, cutting down fleeing robbers whose arms were full of booty, while I waited for the fight to come down off the bridge. On my side, townspeople chased after them. The horn blew again. I was temporarily alone with the dead. The apparent leader spotted me sitting my horse, letting out a roar intended to terrify, but he didn't ride closer. He could see the firelight shining on my bloody blade. I was glad of my black leather; it would hide the stains.

"Looks as if I'll have a bonus after all!" he screamed.

His men reached the top of the bridge, running down it toward me. The foolish fleeing thought to pull me off my mount by sheer numbers. It only took a few seconds of my flashing blade, Windstorm's teeth and hooves, and my exponentially growing pile of dead bodies to have the rest deciding I wasn't worth the trouble.

I continued holding my ground, cutting down those I could reach. I shifted my balance to stay seated as Windstorm trampled on fallen bodies. Finally, the big man had no choice: the last of his men streamed past, the guard behind with their pole arms and swords.

We met in a clash of steel and rearing horseflesh, while around us the last of his comrades flowed into the smoke and flames.

The man let out a wild laugh. "Come with me lady; I could use a fine fighter and mate such as you."

I made no reply as the palace guard pounded past us, intent on chasing and capturing any bandit they could. My opportunity came just as the captain of the guard came riding up to help. The big man fell unconscious at my feet, the horse he rode galloping off before realizing he was riderless and stopped.

* * *

"Open the doors! We demand to see the king!" The crowd screamed and yelled outside the palace gates as the guard looked on nervously from the battlements.

"Coward!" A dirty-faced woman grappled with another in the ashes, both of them pulling on a lumpy sack; with a rip, it split, spilling bread and cheese as the two dived after the food.

A black-haired man in a leather breastplate with a sheriff's patch on his sleeve ran from a bunch of men and women, who were brandishing ropes and weapons. He tripped on debris, went sprawling, and scrambled back up. "There's one of 'em! Come on! Grab him and we can hang him!" The man turned a corner and ran into another pursuing mob. They swamped him; he was dragged through the streets and hanged.

"Don't you leave us here to pander to those commoners! Your family needs you! Let the advisor deal with it if the king is too scared." Lady Elizabeth's nostrils flared in anger, her pallor making bruises stand out.

I surfaced from my nap with the tumulus thoughts of the townspeople threatening to overwhelm me. I still wore my leathers from the attack; the stale smell of smoke rose off them. I descended from my room, finding my slaves clustered near the front door in a state of agitation. They turned at my approach.

"I hope there is a reason why no one is working?"

They looked at each other, Eron stepping forward. "Nothing to worry about, just a mob forming." His dark eyes challenging me to chastise him.

"If it is not outside our gates, I expect everyone who wishes to continue receiving food and shelter to get back to their tasks." After a moment, they went back to their daily chores. "As for you, come with me." I crooked a finger at Eron. We headed down the drive.

"How many of the warriors did we lose?"

"A handful, along with the new barracks, oh great Mistress."

"Sarcasm? Really? I know I am considered a kind owner, but don't let it give you false confidence. Morale is low enough without my having to order you punished."

Eron followed me as I threaded my way past burnt wagons, and a row of bodies neatly lined up near the closed gates of my courtyard. Two slaves guarding them drew open the gates enough to let us out.

A cold wind smacked into us, angry steel gray clouds boiling overhead as we stood in the middle of the nearly empty street. A look left showed me bodies littering the road, most of them bandits, with a few sporting the uniforms of the palace guard or of noble houses with a sheriff's man or two. I couldn't see the entrance to the palace because of how the street twisted, but I could make out the dull glint of metal from pole arms atop the wall. A few drifts of smoke curled from various noble houses. The scent of charred bodies and organic material lay heavy in the air. I saved the view of the town for last, just standing there. A few of the guards turned, but as we provided no threat, they faced back across the bridge, except for one man who came striding over.

I recognized him from last night as the captain of the guard: Mathias. He stopped abruptly in front of me, hands on hips. "What did you think you were doing last night with your display? You should have left the battle to the men, to us guards—"

"You're quite welcome for the save," I interjected into his rampage as I surveyed the hastily erected barricades at both ends of the bridge.

His uniform was sweat-, smoke-, and dirt-stained, as were his face, hands, and neck. His brown brush-cut hair lay matted to his head. His hazel eyes were sunk in dark circles of exhaustion.

An angry mob comprised mostly of townspeople, with a few groups of slaves, milled around a large bonfire. Bodies were tossed in a pile off to one side, the ground a churned sea of bloody mud. From our vantage point, it was easier to see the damage. The center of town lay in drifting ashes; the path of flame had radiated out in a circle, slowly dwindling to spokes on a wheel. Smoke continued to hang heavy, blanketing the remains, with the occasional crash of an unstable building drifting to our ears.

He hawked, spitting, "I want your prisoner. He needs to be questioned. Give him to me or I'll be forced to arrest you."

"Why are they not searching for survivors, clearing the wreckage, and burying the dead?" I answered.

"Damn it, woman! No one wants to address the rabble. It took all the men we had just to push them away from the palace and back across the bridge. They want the king, and he hides with his harem, crying about assassins trying to kill him again." He snorted in contempt. "You wanna risk your noble neck by talking to them, be my guest. After I get the prisoner."

I finally faced him, noting he also had a horn slung around his torso.

"What of the advisor? Why is he not addressing them instead?"

The captain crossed his arms as he regarded me, a muscle next to his mouth pulsing in annoyance. "He can't be found."

"What of the other nobles?"

"They refuse to come out, or lend their personal guard, citing the need to protect themselves if there is another attack."

I had a plan forming. "Get me into the palace, and I'll bring my prisoner. We can all hear what he has to say."

Mathias just stared at me. "I was warned you have trouble obeying our laws. The prisoner goes to the head questioner, who will report his findings to the king."

"Tell me, captain, just how far up the social class do the rumors of treason go?"

He frowned at me, his eyes shifting to the man behind me, then to the mob. "The king isn't going to come out of his rooms, and I'm not risking execution to try and force my way inside."

"Very well. What of the sheriff and his men? Should they not be helping to disperse the mob?" I gestured to the lower half of the bridge. I could hear the lawmen and the crowd exchange taunts and threats.

The captain snorted again. "Why do you think we have a mob? Half of 'em are crying the sheriff and his men helped the bandits. The other half wanna blame other townspeople they got a problem with."

"At least take a note to the chamberlain, Aranthus. In two hours, I will bring the prisoner here. I trust you can keep the mob at bay at least that long?"

Mathias regarded me even longer; with a sigh he relented, sending one of his guards.

* * *

Two hours later, as promised, I had the prisoner with me, weakened from blood loss. The big man stood, wrapped in rope between Eron, who rode on my left, and me. A horn wailed from the palace, low and mournful. It wasn't a warning of attack, but an announcement that the royal presence was emerging. After a few minutes, the call came again, and the mob, which had grown in the meantime, crowded closer to the barricades. I was very conspicuous as I sat still on my mount. The crowd muttered and shouted at us, which we ignored. A third time the horn blew. My household was lined up before the entrance to my property, bundled against the cold. Windows on the top floors of the inn facing the road opened the guests who had those rooms leaning out to see what was going on. The stable hands opened the inn gates; more guests and workers came to stand and gawk.

The horn came a fourth time, closer now, along with the sound of hooves and boots trampling. A fifth time the horn blew, sounding right behind me. Palace guards marched past as their comrades got a space open in the barricade. With barely a pause, they continued through and onto the bridge, lining the length of the bridge on both sides. Mathias rode up next to me. Eron, following my earlier instructions, rode back to stay with my slaves, and Aranthus took his place on my left, clutching his pommel as a palace groom led his horse.

"This will either earn you much prestige, or a trip to the dungeon," he muttered to me through clenched teeth as the three of us rode onto the bridge, my prisoner stumbling beside my mount.

"Did he ask where you were going, and demand you stay with him?" I asked.

"Yes. I used my best persuasive arguments. He was cursing us as I left."

"The important question is: will it be enough to make him decide to come out and let his people see him?"

"If not, Lord Nicky will clap us in chains."

"I thought he was missing."

"He turned up just as I was leaving. Wherever he had been, he was gloating. I heard him questioning the slaves as the horn rang out the first time. I think it would be safe to say you probably single-handedly ruined the best mood he's ever been in."

The last of the mounted guard had formed the other three sides of a box. Aranthus, the captain, the prisoner and I stopped on the hump at the middle of the bridge. Behind us, the clatter of hooves stopped; the captain had raised the horn to his lips, and before he blew, he said, "I hope to the death lands you know what you're doing."

A sixth and last time he blew the horn until his breath gave out. He was red of face from the effort, but the mob realized if they didn't quiet down, they wouldn't hear what we had to say.

"Good citizens! Hear me! I speak to you on behalf our glorious ruler, King Maceanas, may he live forever!" Aranthus's voice quaked as he spoke. There was some booing and derisive jeers, which died down as he continued.

"Thanks to the due diligence of our royal guard and the Lady Illyria, we have the leader of the bandits before you now as a captive."

Screams of joy, cries for him to be hanged or other creative deaths, came from the crowd, while a few insisted he hadn't acted alone. I saw the sheriff turn to glare up at us, his mouth moving as he talked to his second-in-command. Jake must have made a crude joke as a few of his fellow lawmen turned to look my way, laughing and leering.

"For far too long we have been harried and tormented by the lawless hordes who hide in our hills and mountains, raid our town, steal our animals, rape our womenfolk."

"Are we talking about the bandits or the sheriff and his men?" called a voice from the mob.

Laughter and other voices yelling in agreement followed. The captain of the guard held a hand up, bellowing for silence as the sheriff and his men spluttered denials and retribution to the speakers. Several tense minutes passed as the two groups heckled each other; it looked as if a fight would break out. Mathias sent a man to tell Jake to shut up and get his men under control. He did so, turning to look at me, searching behind as if expecting someone.

"Are you sure about this, my lady?" Aranthus took the pause to question me as he cast a worried look at the man between us, who was swaying, sweaty, and pale, mind firmly in my control.

"History is in the making, chamberlain, let us hope the townspeople recognize an opportunity. That those in the mob are less afraid of change than of the sheriff."

The captain was directing some of his men to bring wooden crates, forming a makeshift platform upon which we could have the bandit stand for better visibility. The palace guards took the lead rope from me, prodding the man, forcing him to mount. He almost toppled, but two guards leapt up to help him stand upright.

"The man before you calls himself the King of the Bandits!" Aranthus shouted. The prisoner stood, looking around, half-defiant, half-afraid. "Today, we shall deal a blow against those who have preyed upon us!"

A voice called out from the crowd, "I still see the sheriff in charge! One bandit ain't gonna help none when the biggest one of 'em wears a badge!"

"Shut it! I'll have youse hung!" Jake screamed, wildly looking over the crowd for the person who had spoken. His men and the townspeople hurled accusations against each other.

Mathias was calling for order, Aranthus cast a nervous look back up the hill as the crowd jostled and swayed. A few of the townspeople tore at the barrier, trying to make a way through it while others tried to climb up it. The chaos was exactly what I needed. I had not planted the speaker; whoever they were would have my gratitude.

"I don't like it," the Chamberlain muttered. "We should get back to safety before a riot breaks out."

"Aranthus, it seems the people have a grievance against our good sheriff; it could be legitimate. We should let them have their say before they take matters into their own hands." I suggested. *Either way the man will die.*

The chamberlain quivered beside me, scented linen held up to his mouth and nose, eyes wide with terror as he watched the crowd becoming increasingly agitated. A few enterprising townspeople made it to the top of the pile. They leapt upon members of the sheriff's men as Jake scrambled up the bridge toward us. His men began using their clubs and swords to subdue the jumpers as the Palace Guard tried to hold the barricade in place.

"What is the meaning of this? How dare you!" a voice thrumming with rage rang out behind us.

Aranthus turned, moaning in terror, "Sire! We, we have caught a bandit, the . . . the king of them, as . . . as the man proclaims himself."

I half-turned in my saddle, noting Lord Nicky beside the king with his slave as he gazed in hatred at the people massed below us.

"He should already be in the care of Rablias. How dare you place His Majesty in danger?! How dare you think to exceed your position?! You have no authority for such matters!" Nicky hissed at me as he transferred his eyes to mine. If looks could kill, and I can assure you mine can when I want them to, I should have been long dead and buried.

Speak! Now! I commanded the bandit mentally while the noises from the crowd began dying down.

"You promised us we wouldn't get caught! Traitor!" the prisoner screamed at the sheriff, pointing a finger at the man.

Jake's mouth dropped open in panic, eyes widening in alarm. The accusation echoed across the excellent acoustics afforded by the river.

"We were promised ten gold coins from your master!" the bandit continued howling out. "We were promised the palace guard wouldn't interfere!"

"No!" I heard in a near-silent hiss from Lord Nicky. "Shut him up, DiJinn!"

The mob went wild, the bandit continuing to accuse the lawman. Jake stood gaping stupidly for a few moments before adding his own denials to the rising din. He stomped closer to our location.

"A tad too suspicious, my master," DiJinn, equally low-voiced, replied.

"Aranthus! We are going back at once! Lady Illyria, I will deal with you on the morrow!" Maceanas shouted at me, terror in his voice. He seemed more afraid the mob would break through the barricades and try killing him.

"These are your loyal subjects, Majesty, the very backbone of your kingdom. Would you deny them their right to redress wrongs? To deny them a chance to take part in rebuilding the town and their homes?" My tone a gentle rebuke. "I should be ashamed to call this my homeland if we cannot work together for the betterment of the land and Your Majesty's might."

The king bristled at my tone, his florid face turning redder. He opened his mouth, but the chamberlain came to my rescue.

"I would not mind listening to what the people have to say, in a more controlled setting, of course. It is a great job we have ahead of us." He put the linen square back to his mouth and nose. Only I heard him mutter, "Finally a chance to rid ourselves of the damn sheriff."

"What?" Nicky snapped, looking toward us. "Nothing is needing redress. Captain, get the man down and escorted to the dungeon now!"

"He has already spoken of what he knows, of who delivered the orders for the raid. Hang him now, for the townspeople, and question the sheriff." I spoke drily, earning a vicious glare from the advisor. "The more important matter is who gave the orders for the raid to be carried out."

The captain frowned. "An excellent suggestion, Sire. I wondered why they were so bold."

"I, too, see no harm in it, I suppose, Your Majesty." Aranthus looked at us uncertainly.

"Without us," my gesture including the people and surroundings, "Your Majesty will not have a kingdom. Many townspeople are ready to leave, seeking fortunes elsewhere, I have been hearing," I added.

"NO! His Majesty is too exposed here. There are traitors in the palace guard if what you're insinuating is correct. That's the only way they could have made it across the bridge without an alarm being raised," Lord Nicky snapped out.

Mathias bristled. "I can assure Your Majesty all my men are loyal to the crown."

The advisor intended to keep the king in a state of panic, keep him from thinking. The young man turned to me. "Or else you helped them across somehow. Isn't that your mansion to the side of us?"

"How could I possibly manage it? As you have stated, I have no authority, no power for such a thing."

"But you have gold, much gold. Men have betrayed others for less," the advisor craftily replied, the chamberlain gasping in shock.

"Why would I want to help them sack the town? Or the palace and its grounds? His Majesty is and continues to be more than generous to me. I have no need nor desire to see either destroyed." I countered, the roaring mob's voices swelling. "I would lose what little I have to the ensuing power vacuum."

We turned as one to see people actively attacking the barricade, tearing it apart, palace guards and sheriff's men trying to brace the pile while fighting off their attackers. The bandit lay on the ground, curled in a fetal position, Jake over him. The horse guards clattered into position, their captain yelling orders.

"Sire, if you don't at least grant them a forum to be heard in, here and now, they will certainly finish what the bandits began." I slammed my power into the king.

His eyes rolled back in his head, gurgling as I forced my command through unknown barriers freshly overlaid in his mind. An angry sound as of a kettle hissing came before being cut off. Maceanas swayed in his saddle, while royal guards hurried to support him as he blinked and coughed.

"Where are the archers?" Lord Nicky yelled.

"Majesty, what happened, are you all right?"

"Hold the line! Hold I say!"

Be a king! Command your peoples to obey!

"SIIIIIILLLEEEEEENNNNCCCEEEE!"

The king managed to stand up in his stirrups, his great roar echoing over sounds of shouting and fighting. Combatants broke off, casting about in shock. Many of the people were sporting cuts and bruises, a few had to be helped up from the ground as others dropped pieces of debris meant to be used as missiles. Bridles jingled, saddle leather creaking from men repositioning themselves.

"I will have order! I am your king! How dare you think to attack me!" Maceanas was breathing hard, trembling in a mixture of rage and fear.

His words only had the effect of starting the grumbling up again. *Soothe them. Promise them justice.*

"You want justice?" the king yelled out fiercely, the mob roaring back just as fiercely in the affirmative.

I sneaked a look toward Lord Nicky; his face was a thundercloud. "We should not do this here; they are too close to you," the young man said but was ignored.

"I will hear you, but you must maintain order."

There was some shifting and muttering from the crowd before they subsided, eyes glittering in the torchlight. It would not take much to set them off again. The king gestured to Aranthus to open the proceedings officially. The chamberlain's voice started out squeaky before firming up.

"We are here to garner the truth of how our town was raided. Those of you who have direct, personal knowledge will be the only ones from whom we need to hear."

Eager volunteers shouted out.

"It was those damn bandits! They came out of the hills!"

"There was too many of them!"

"I'm telling you it was the corrupt sheriff and his men!"

"Someone had to let them across the bridge! Damn palace guard! We need to bring the army back and strengthen it!"

Aranthus banged his staff on the stone bridge, shouting, "Silence! His Majesty said truth, not lies! The next person to speak out of turn will be fined!"

Slowly, the voices began subsiding, chastened. The king continued, "Lord Nicky, what have you heard?"

"Many rumors, as these men were so kind to point out," he needled them. "I am sorting through them. I will have your answers before morning."

I let a smile curve my lips saying in my sweetest voice, "Let me ease your burden. My slaves can help you. They were nearby for the first of the attacks. As Your Majesty is aware, I am restoring the old Fishton grounds, which sit at the head of the bridge."

Eron's mouth firmed in annoyance as he strode over at my beckoning, bowing to the king. "With Your Majesty's permission? My fellow slaves and I at first mistook the attackers for part of the sheriff's men."

"Outrageous!" Jake bellowed. "Youse lying no-good, worthless slave."

"A serious accusation for a slave to make," the king reminded.

"Nevertheless, Majesty, it is what I saw with my own eyes."

"How dare you accuse a man of law!" Nicky spat. "Have you and your mistress not been warned? For your sake, I hope you have proof."

"We could ask the man himself," Eron recommended. His sarcastic tone brought sniggers from the crowd who knew the lazy sheriff well.

"Your pardons, Majesty, Advisor," a merchant yelled to be heard. "My shop was burnt and raided, my family killed in the attack despite my attempts to protect them. I saw the men clearly. They were sheriff's men and wore his badge. I know them well from their rounds of the town."

A deadly silence fell at his words. Those nearest him drew away a little. It looked as if he would be on his own when another tradesman spoke up.

"He speaks the truth. I too witnessed the sheriff entering a shop, dragging out both of its owners and putting them to the sword before several of his men looted it."

"He might have been serving justice to a traitor," Nicky gritted out, trying to see who else spoke.

"If the cobbler is a traitor, we all are!" a third merchant yelled out.

The townspeople began calling for the sheriff and his men to answer for their role in the raid. The lawmen added to the din, yelling out their innocence and denials. Aranthus began to bang his staff against the bridge to bring order back. Mathias murmured orders to his men as the shouting subsided.

The king turned to me, an unhappy look in his eye. "My lady, the timing is most convenient for you. I have not forgotten your crusade against Jake. I hope you have not bribed honest men to tell dishonest tales. I would hate to order you taken to the questioner."

"I have no need of such despicable acts, Sire; the man is corrupt. He is reaping what he has sown; if you doubt me, ask him to explain where he was and what he and his men were really doing."

Unexpected help came from the crowd as a man forgot himself enough to yell, "My money is regularly stolen by the sheriff and his men."

The din rose again, all the merchants pouring out their woes to the king. Mathias directed some of his men to maneuver closer around the cluster of lawmen. I could see the sweaty faces, the combination of fear, and bluster. If they could have, I had no doubt the sheriff's men would have tried running. Each tale highlighted misdeeds. The townspeople had waited a long time for a chance to air their grievances against Jake to the king. And be believed. Nicky could do nothing to stop the proceedings without seeming to support the sheriff and his men. I almost hummed out loud; another step in my plan set in motion.

I cut my eyes to Nicky. It was a wonder he didn't burst a vein. I didn't know if he was a wizard, if he truly had the power to cause harm at a distance like I am able, but his anger was sufficient. I felt the old familiar rush of exhilaration I got against a worthy foe.

The king sat, dazed from accusations. The merchants brought up every time the lawmen had done them harm. He realized he would not be able to ignore their words as mere hateful tales, or my dislike of the man as a personal vendetta.

"Advisor? We need a sheriff." Maceanas turned to Nicky in a barely concealed panic.

The young man looked murder at me. I stared back, daring him to try and protect the men. I hoped he wouldn't be able to think straight, thus making a fatal decision. His slave leaned close, whispering something in his ear. Nicky gave him a brief glare, his mouth moving as he spat something back.

"Jake and his men should be given a chance to answer these accusations at a tribunal," he gritted out between his teeth, trying to stall.

The response did what I wanted, enraging the merchants. "Are we not good enough for a tribunal right here?" one called.

Another shouted, "To hell with that! The man is guilty!"

A third bellowed, "When the sheriff accused my son of wrongdoing, he was not given the same consideration! He is a commoner as we are; he should have to answer the same way as us! Let the king's questioner get the truth out of him!"

This was met with many cheers, Nicky bellowing, "No! We need a sheriff!"

"If I may, Your Majesty?" I interjected, waiting until he acknowledged me before continuing. "If you will recall, when I lodged my complaint against Jake, I recommended a man named Saizar be elevated to the sheriff's position. I still stand by the recommendation, even if it is only temporary until a new sheriff is found. Would that be acceptable to all?" I swept our group with my eyes. "Furthermore, I believe the people when they say they have been grievously harmed by Jake and his men. The slave with me tonight," I gestured to Eron, "and a free man with him were almost hanged by the sheriff for no reason other than he didn't like the look of them."

"Thanks a lot," Eron hissed so low only I could hear it. He bowed to the king, "It is true, Majesty. Your own guards even intervened. You wrote my friend and me a pardon."

The king appeared flabbergasted, groping in his memory. "Yes," he said slowly. "Yes, I do remember. How is it you are now a slave?"

"Jake did not obey your command, Sire. I fought for my freedom and that of my friend. My sacrifice gave him time to escape, but the sheriff's men overwhelmed me. He sold me to slavers who then sold me on the auction block. My mistress has been trying to get my pardon recognized so I may have my freedom back." *Bitch, throw me to the wolves. I'll play the game, and you'll lose.*

The merchants discussed my proposal, confirming the rumors about Saizar being reluctant to force bribes from the townspeople. Slow nods of approval spread. A few wanted the posting to be temporary, while others suggesting the whole pack of lawmen needed replacing.

Nicky signaled for Aranthus to stop the quarreling. "Majesty, as your advisor, it would be best if we cleared this up here and now before she unwittingly commits another act that starts a war. Have Mathias find this Saizar while we get to the truth. Any lawman refusing to cooperate can be declared guilty and ordered killed." *Nicky despises that woman; does she realize that her actions could get him dismissed?*

The merchants, emboldened by His Majesty's support, blocked Nicky's every suggestion to rescue Jake. Finally, the young man quit. He could see to continue protesting might make a connection he was the one supporting the corruption or another reason he didn't want revealed. The lawmen, including Saizar, had a sheen of sweat on their brows as the palace guard surrounded them, nudging them forward a few feet. The sheriff's eyes skittered about the bridge, spotting me, hatred growing in his eyes. They landed the longest on Lord Nicky, who ignored the sheriff.

"You," the king pointed to Saizar when a guard singled the man out. "We don't need you just yet. Go stand back there." He waved his hand, concentrating on Jake.

Saizar bowed, waiting for the guard to let him pass before walking the few paces afforded by the bridge away from his comrades. He caught sight of me briefly before turning his attention to the sheriff and his fellow lawmen.

Jake remained kneeling, head down. "Youse Majesty, they's all lies, everyones of thems."

"I demand the truth of you and your men, sheriff. We have heard some serious accusations which must be answered," Maceanas rapped out briskly.

"Uh, er," the man before him stuttered, trying to catch Lord Nicky's eye again. *Shit! Fuck! Damn asshole said I's wouldn't be asked any questions about anything, what the hell's this shit? Fucker better not be double-crossin' me.*

"Look at me! Nobody else! I am your king!"

Some men smirked, others yawned as the sheriff stammered out an apology. I concentrated on him, trying to read his thoughts, to no avail.

"Where were you the night of the raid by those bandits? And where were your men?"

"Where . . . where was I?" Outrage plain in his voice. "Me and me men were guarding the town, like we's supposed to be."

"More like guarding the ale and slaves at the Bloody Knuckles as he does every night, all night long," Eron muttered just loud enough to be heard.

The sheriff raised his head to glare at us.

"Who said that? Speak up!" the king demanded. My slave remained silent, and His Majesty went back to asking questions.

"How did those raiders get by you?"

We all watched Jake lick his lips, eyes darting around the bridge, pausing on Nicky's face. The young man sat, stone-faced.

"The fact you have to think about your answer tells me all I need to know." The menace in the king's voice had the man before him sweating profusely.

"No, no, Youse Majesty! I . . . I . . . we, I mean we, were, um . . ." He fumbled, plunging on. "We was making rounds. They must have slipped past us after one of our patrols took us away from where, where ever they slipped in at," he finished lamely.

"How is it you didn't notice a band of armed raggedy men trying to get across the bridge, running amok, burning, and pillaging in my town! It was no quick job!"

Sheriff Jake struggled to come up an explanation. Sweat poured down his face. "Majesty, I, we's . . ." His eyes went back to the advisor's, but the young man was busy assessing the crowd.

"Look at your king! I shall not tell you again!" Maceanas screamed in anger. His horse whinnied, prancing in place before settling down. The sheriff flinched; everyone in sight of the man could see what an effort it was for him to obey. "You have not answered my question, Jake." The menace thrummed in the king's voice.

"I's . . . I's." He gulped, turning to look at his men.

It was the wrong thing to do. "If you are in charge of your men, you should not look to them for answers! Or lies, as it seems to me!"

Help came from an unexpected source as Mathias spoke up from his place, turning heads. "Forgive me if I'm wrong, Majesty, but what would have happened if the bandits had overcome the palace guard and entered the palace itself? All because the sheriff and his men decided it would be better drinking and whoring in some dive of a tavern?"

We all saw the thought hit home, the slow blooming of horror on the sheriff's face as his rival's words sunk in.

"He would be responsible for your death, Sire; they would no doubt have killed you." Mathias all but gloating to serve some revenge on a hated foe. "By failing to do his job, he committed treason, as did his men."

"No!" the sheriff screamed. "Me men and me was doing our jobs, we was! We was patrolling the town, I swears it!"

Lord Nicky's brow furrowed in concentration as if trying to determine what revenge to get upon the man. His men shot looks to one another, and one spoke up to support their leader. When he wasn't chastised, more chimed in to support the sheriff's story.

"Silence!" Maceanas roared. "I did not give your men leave to speak! Silence I say!" Gradually they subsided into sullenness.

I cocked a brow at Nicky, daring him to say anything in the man's defense when I spoke. "It seems your patrols, as you call them, are not very effective. Dare I say, useless? Dereliction of one's duty."

"Perhaps he was attending to other duties," Nicky snapped out, still scrutinizing Mathias. "Was there a fight at the tavern requiring your presence?"

The sheriff stared in puzzlement, before nodding in assent. The king looked suspiciously at Lord Nicky, who gazed back as innocently as possible.

"A fight taking all the men away from their patrols for hours at a time? Preventing them from stopping bandits when it became known they were setting the town afire while killing and plundering it?" My scorn for such bullshit was clear.

"Lira?" Now King Maceanas turned to me, asking me for advice while the sheriff stammered denials.

Jake and his lawmen tried changing their stories, sending pleading looks toward Lord Nicky.

Nicky cut his losses and turned from the sheriff, sitting, clenched of jaw and fists; the look of vituperation he sent me meant I would have to sleep lightly and in my hidden spot else I find my un-life being ended. I was not about to let the threat stop me as I announced,

"The people should have their day. Allow your head questioner to see what he can get from the man and his band on the other accusations. As we have heard, he was not working alone, and the matter needs to be cleared up. Otherwise, people will never be able to trust any of the men who swear they are protecting them."

I could feel Nicky's eyes boring into my head, the approving nods of men. "We shouldn't be hasty," the advisor began, when Mathias jumped in.

"An excellent idea, Majesty. I concur." He hummed with happiness, his agreement shocking me. I had to dip into his head to find out why. Ah, he hated Nicky more than he did uppity women. If siding with me meant pain and humiliation to the young man, he gladly would do it while figuring out how to pay me back for not handing the prisoner over to him straight away.

"Let me think on this and advise you what is best for the kingdom," Nicky spat out, muttering, "It is still my job."

"What is there to think on? There are sufficient witnesses of misdeeds and misconduct. You have heard firsthand of one from my slave, Majesty. Now is the time for questioning, not release so they can flee and never be brought to proper justice. Or worse, join the bandits who seem to want you dead," I urged.

The merchants agreed with me, drowning out the protestations of Jake and his men of their innocence.

"Why not also bring in the owner and whoever tends the bar at the tavern—what was it called? The Bloody Knuckles?—that the sheriff and his men are supposed to frequent for questioning."

"Er," Maceanas recovered quickly. "Very well. Guards, deliver these men to the questioner . . ." He didn't have a chance to finish; apparently some of the lawmen had concluded escape was the better option.

"No! No! Please! My lord!" Jake broke down, guards moving toward him.

One of the sheriff's men unsheathed his sword and started swinging. It didn't take long before chaos reigned.

The king started screaming in terror like a child at the closeness of the fight. His horse reared from the noise and commotion, sending His Majesty slamming to the ground as the mare bolted. The grooms on either side stumbled back as the panicked animal rammed into a mare I was riding today, as I was turning the horse's head around. Her hooves slid on the slick cobbles of the bridge, nearly toppling us both.

More horses caught the scent of fear, beginning to whinny and rear. Less experienced riders lurched in saddles or fell upon the ground or over the low stone bridge rail to splash in the raging cold waters below. Those left on horseback tried maintaining control of their mounts. A few screams rang out; whether from the conflict behind us or trampled riders, I had no idea. I grabbed the royal mount's bridle, only my super strength keeping the horse's head down. The mare kicked out with back legs, narrowly missing a groom as Gray Ghost gained purchase.

"Protect the king!" a man bellowed over the madness.

"Get your mounts under control and off the bridge!" Nicky screamed, fighting to keep his horse calm.

His slave raced off. Guards leapt off their mounts in an attempt to help manage some of the riderless horses. Gray Ghost attempted to buck. Her hindquarters mashed against the side of the royal guard's horse next to me. Lord Nicky and I faced each other. My mare reached out to bite the horse in front of her in an effort to get it to move.

Familiar shouting made me risk a quick look. Domiano and stable slaves from the Silver Thorn came running. The king lay winded. Aranthus had thrown himself over the man. The royal grooms ran up to grab the mare's bridle from me. A torrent of abuse at my back came from the royal horse guard I had inadvertently trapped.

"Shit!" Eron swore near me, lending a helping hand.

Once the grooms got hold of the mare, I was able to turn my attention to my mount.

"Get that blasted animal away!"

Nicky swore, trying to get his mount to back up so he could turn the gelding without my horse attacking. I knew Gray Ghost would rear and kick out as soon as she had space, thus adding to the problems. Domiano and the other slaves began throwing pieces of cloth over the heads of the remaining mounts, helping their riders lead them off the bridge and farther up the road.

Aranthus, Saizar, and Eron helped the king up. Those of the royal guard who were now dismounted ran onto the bridge to help His Majesty. I gave my mare the command, turning her head sharply to the right. I galloped off the bridge and up the street before Gray Ghost would slow. I turned her around, letting her canter back. We stopped, seeing more clearly the fight taking place between lawmen and palace guards.

Due to the constraints of the bridge, the fracas was short. Even so, a fair number of bodies lay bleeding on the ground, most of them lawmen. One or two royal. Many of the royal horse guards already remounted. Shouting across the river let us know some townsfolk had gone to the rescue of people who plunged off the bridge. Folks streamed through the breached barricade up the bridge before meeting the wall of mounted royal guard.

"Hang them! Hang them all now!" Lord Nicky was yelling.

"I want answers! Put them to the questioner!" the king bellowed.

The guard shuffled uneasily, pole arms and swords held at the ready should any of the lawmen break free again. To everyone's surprise, His Majesty turned, clouting the advisor upside his head. The young man was caught off guard, swaying in the saddle before righting himself. The look of loathing he directed toward His Majesty plain for all to see.

"I AM THE KING!" Maceanas was red-faced, huffing. "You will take the lawmen to the questioner and have him find out all their secrets. As for Sheriff Jake, I strip you of your office! You too will face the dungeon. When Rablias is done, you will be flogged and hanged in the center of town, your carcass left to rot as a warning for the next sheriff."

A throaty roar of approval was heard, along with a scattering of "Long live the king!"

Mathias saluted smartly, barking out orders to his second-in-command, who got the men moving. Townspeople crowded behind with their makeshift weapons and torches as further insurance against the prisoners' escape. I guided my mare to the side of the street, letting the procession by while moving closer toward the king. Jake struggled with his guards, blood streaming down the side of his head while he screamed at Nicky.

"Youse bastard! Youse runty, lyin' bastard! Youse tol' me we's never gonna get caught! Youse tol' me youse swore..."

Lord Nicky's expression of hatred transformed to panic and shock a fleeting moment before the guards clubbed the sheriff to his knees. Jake suddenly fell silent from a blow to the back of his head.

"DiJinn," Nicky commanded his slave so quietly only I could hear it. "See the traitor makes it to the dungeons and enjoys Rablias's talents for a long time."

The king sputtered. "I want answers! How the hell was this nest of vipers allowed to flourish without anyone bringing it to my attention?! Nicky! You are my advisor; you're supposed to protect me from such men! You have failed me grievously! I have no law and order! No protection from bandits! I should replace you!"

Nicky hissed viciously, "He has duped us all, it seems, even me. I promise you, he will pay for his crimes. No one makes a fool of me!"

"It could be, Majesty, the man didn't work alone; someone with authority might be covering his crimes, maybe more than one," I mildly suggested, receiving a sharp look from the young man as I reined near. "I am sure Lord Nicky will discover their identities soon enough."

"He had better," the king muttered, glaring at his friend who returned the look with interest.

I could see my slaves bunched to one side, avidly staring, along with various other onlookers who hadn't accompanied the prisoners.

"Where is the man who helped save me during the revolt?" Maceanas asked.

"Saizar, Your Majesty," Aranthus said, as the lawman stepped forward, kneeling before the royal presence, bowing his head.

"A man of the sheriff," he flatly replied. "What am I to do with you?"

"You could elevate him to sheriff by royal proclamation as a means of wiping away the evil deeds revealed today."

"You bitch!" Nicky hissed like steam escaping a teakettle, hands balling into fists around his horse's reins. "Keep your damn mouth shut! I am the advisor!"

"Lord Nicky, you dare speak to a noblewoman thusly in my presence when she is giving me good counsel, when she saved me along with this man?" The warning was mild, the look wasn't.

I raised my brow in my most supercilious manner, giving the advisor a shark-scaring smile. Nicky paused, fear and confusion briefly crossing his face. He sat staring at me uncertainly.

"You were mistaken in your remarks toward me, were you not?" I asked in flat tones.

"Of course he was," Maceanas glared at his childhood friend.

Nicky cared not for the public reprimand, especially when he saw who was listening. I watched him swallow before he was able to choke out, "Of course not. Please forgive my hasty and ill-thought remarks. These events have upset me more than most and made me forget my manners."

Our eyes still clashed, but the king seemed satisfied, turning to Saizar. "You are one of the sheriff's men, although we heard no mention of you taking part in their treason. Why should I trust you? Why should I not have you questioned?"

Saizar's face whitened, but his voice was steady. "If my liege lord commands, I pray my answers bring him peace."

Nicky gave a nasty chuckle, which died away as I spoke. "If it pleases Your Majesty, I can vouch for his whereabouts on the night in question. He was helping defend the Silver Thorn from attack."

"What?!" Nicky snarled, giving me a look of loathing.

"Why didn't you say so earlier?" Maceanas asked irritably.

"It's a lie. He doesn't want anyone knowing he was ducking his duty," Nicky spat.

Saizar's face hardened. "I was bringing information on a missing person to guests at the inn. Her ladyship's slave was there, the guests I wanted were not. I was preparing to leave, when the bandits attacked."

"What's the man's name?" The king demanded of Saizar.

"Eron."

My slave stepped forward, bowing and confirming the matter before the king could bellow for him to show himself.

"Nicky," the king said.

The boy bared his teeth at me in a smile. "He has some honor after all; make him sheriff. If Saizar fails to find men to reform his office, or can't control them, and they betray you as the old one did, make the price of his failure a long, painful death."

"And to whom should he report? Who should keep an eye on him and the new men of law, so it does not happen again, going unnoticed?" Maceanas demanded.

"Why not your captain of the palace guard?" I suggested. "Have Saizar report weekly. Your royal heralds can announce any complaints be given to Mathias. You can decide who will investigate to find out the truth."

Nicky glared at me harder, missing the speculative looks among the crowd, as whispers spread of Saizar's elevation while the king continued. "My capital is in ruin! My subjects reduced! My slaves scattered and on the run!"

Mathias cleared his throat as he stepped forth, bowing. "I believe I have some answers, courtesy of your loyal subjects, if I may? I am afraid, Majesty, except for the warehouses, the buildings on the nobles' street, your palace, the outlying farms, most is a complete loss."

He gestured to the crowd, continuing over the king's spluttering. "Your subjects will be able to tell you if any family members are killed or still missing."

His Majesty ordered any townsperson who lost family or property, or been grievously injured, to present themselves at the palace. I saw the quick shudder pass through the minds of the guards at his proclamation, knowing many sleepless days and nights were ahead of them. The king intended to tour the remains on the morrow. Aranthus gestured to Mathias; the captain strode forward with his remaining men.

"All right, disperse! Go back to your homes if you have them, or wherever you are staying. You heard the king: everything else must wait."

An immediate outbreak of protests and shaking of fists or various implements greeted his commands. His Majesty's grooms led his horse next to me while the people were slowly forced across the bridge.

"Might I speak further on the subject of rebuilding, Majesty? I believe our biggest concern is for food, shelter and protection. It is doubtful any can replace what they lost before the snows and ice of winter arrive," I said.

Lord Nicky cut me off, his tone as sharp as his glance. "I hardly think we need advice," he stressed, "on what needs done. This has occurred in the past."

"May I inquire what we plan on doing?" I needled him.

Nicky sneered. Maceanas asked, "You are volunteering to help over-see, under my advisor's auspices?"

The young man would make it difficult with many pitfalls. Yet the rewards outweighed the negatives.

"She has no idea whereof she speaks. I will assign men to the task."

How dare the asshole belittle me? "What about the palace and its grounds, Majesty?" I queried as we rode in a group toward the palace. I had motioned for Eron and Domiano to stay at my grounds with the rest of my slaves.

"What!?" he barked in alarm.

"The public rooms can be used dormitory-style to house and feed the displaced. Or we can erect temporary shelters on the grounds. The food laid on for the Harvest Week festivities can be used for their sustenance instead."

"No." Nicky spat, "you will be putting His Majesty's life in danger with so many people having access to the palace."

"In exchange," I continued, "the people can select which of their numbers would be most suited for guarding the actions of their fellow townspeople. If any should threaten Your Majesty's person and safety, hang them as a warning to the rest. Should they continuing being foolish enough to let it happen a second time, banish them to the town or forest to try their luck with the outlaws and the winter weather. The palace guard can be used to keep people from the private apartments." I needed to protect my food source.

The king looked in alarm at Lord Nicky, who himself was incredulous.

"Care for them now on a temporary basis, and they'll expect to be taken care of permanently, and none of them will want to work." Nicky snarled.

I gave a merry peal of laughter, teasing, "Don't be mad you did not think of it first." I continued over his protests, "May I suggest, Majesty, we take the opportunity to build a bigger, grander town. A city worthy of being called Macinas."

Scoffing and rude noises greeted my suggestions, but I could see the king liked the ideal.

"I doubt the people have funds for it." Lord Nicky sneered. "I certainly know the royal coffers cannot support expenditures when many will plead poverty to avoid paying taxes. Keep your mouth shut, woman. You cause enough problems. I will advise His Majesty."

"Your Grace, I know I have only resided here for a few months, but I have seen many cities of the world. I am ashamed to say my newly adopted homeland cannot expect to compete or survive without drastic changes. Yes, it will take several years and lots of hard work, but which would you rather have? A town of empty, rotting buildings, dashed hopes, and a dwindling population? Or a bright, prosperous, growing city of wealth?"

"How dare you heap scorn on my country! You are under probation and have yet to swear oaths to me!" Maceanas roared.

"Pardon my poorly chosen words; it was not my intention to slight. Only to proffer some ideals for your consideration. I'm sure if we enlist influential merchants to help in exchange for certain concessions, it will make the task less onerous."

"No!" Lord Nicky protested.

I looked the king in his eyes, using my power to control him. "Let me do this for you, prove my loyalty, help ease the burden while you guide and direct your kingdom. I can report progress to you directly, or Aranthus if you wish, each day. I can carry your commands directly to the people." *Remember the shining white city of stone, the acclaim of your neighbors, more trade and wealth.*

"Shut your mouth, you stupid bitch! Women have no concept of what needs done!" the advisor ranted.

Aranthus whispered to the king as we paused outside the opening palace gates. "Very well, Lady Illyria, I will give you a chance tomorrow to prove to me you can handle such a task. You shall accompany me and the advisor as we tour the town."

I bowed from the saddle to the king at his dismissal, as Lord Nicky fumed. I left the royal party at the gate, returning to my home.

Chapter Nineteen

Mica pounded in hot pursuit of the little boy, barely feeling the slap of branches against his face and arms as the horses tore through the forest. He cast a quick look over his shoulder and saw Colin and Eron as dim shapes behind him, turning back in time to avoid being swept out of his saddle by a branch. Up ahead, the boy broke from the trees, able to spur his horse to greater speed. The immortal followed the boy into a white mist. Mica urged his horse on. He could hear the thunder of waterfalls around him and the ring of horse shoes on rock. Mica burst from the mist in time to see Nicky racing up an incline. Mica leapt off his horse before it could come to a stop, continuing after the kid on foot.

Mica found himself in a long tunnel suffused with a soft, yellow glow. Up ahead, Nicky dashed through a door. It swung shut behind him. Mica slammed into the closed door. He reached for a knob only to find his hands scrambling over glass. He saw the Duchess Illyria standing on the other side. She had Colin strapped down on a table, Nicky next to him.

"Noooooooooooo!" Mica screamed and drawing his sword, struck at the glass.

It shattered into a million pieces. Mica charged through, ignoring the shards cascading around him. "Colin!"

"You shall not interfere with Her Grace!" Eron appeared suddenly in front of Mica with his sword at the ready, preventing him from reaching his brother.

"Get out of my way, traitor!" Mica yelled, and after a brief clash of weapons, Eron fell to the ground, bleeding from a stomach wound.

Nicky was starting the Ritual of Undoing. Illyria moved to block Mica's path. "I cannot be stopped. It is too late. See how my will is done?"

Behind her, Colin cried out in pain as Nicky chanted.

"'Colin! I'm coming! I swear, I never meant for this to happen!'" Mica pleaded through the glass which had sprung up from nowhere; cutting Her Grace and him off from the other two. "This was not supposed to happen! I'll get you out"

Mica charged, ramming the blade of his sword through the duchess's gut. She looked down at it and then up at him; only it was Colin he saw in her place.

"What have you done to me, brother?" Colin whispered painfully before sliding off the blade and onto the floor, blood blooming.

Laughter rose up around him as the red continued to spread in a widening puddle around Colin. Mica stumbled back in horror and looked to Her Grace and Nicky.

"I'll see you both dead for this! I'll tear down heaven and hell to reach you if I must! I curse you! In Colin's memory, I will strike you down! I give my solemn vow by my blade and blood!" Mica slashed his arm with his sword and his blood flowed over his brother's body, raining down to mingle with the rapidly spreading pool on the floor. "By my blood and the blood of my kin. By the steel forged from the earth," Mica thrust his blade into the dirt and a goblet appeared in his hand. "By the air I breathe and the water of life." Mica drank. He held the goblet up in a salute before pouring the remaining contents over his sword. It mingled with the blood and earth. "By this solemn vow to spirit, guardian or daemon I make, I will see you dead!"

Lightning crashed around him as Illyria and Nicky faded from view, still laughing. The sky darkened and for a moment Mica couldn't see. The skies opened up in earnest, a deluge soaking him. Mica jerked upright with a roar, hearing strange sounds around him as if people were laughing, screaming, or babbling. He stared around uncomprehendingly for a moment. The sights and sounds of his location flooded back. The icy air struck his skin harshly after the still closeness of the dungeon, the gleam from burning torches hurt his eyes used to the darkness. Droplets trickled down his face and neck, working their way under the soaked collar of his shirt.

"I must have it," came a hissing from the dark.

Mica figured he was about to be tortured; he could take it, he could take anything they did to him. He knew it wouldn't be long before his brother broke him from this place, assuming his brother remained free.

"Without it, I cannot control the boy. He will tell us where it is."

"Why? Not to question you, Master, but I thought you had more power than he," a second voice asked.

"I am weakened, trapped on this plane. He wears protection from prying eyes that blocks even me from being able to control him."

"Don," the other voice commanded, "start with the nipple pinchers." The speaker came into view. He was a drab looking man, one of those utterly forgettable types, except for his eyes; there was something in them saying he enjoyed his job. Enjoyed it perhaps a little too much.

The first hissing voice spoke. "No, apprentice, they will harm him more than we want, and we must not allow the boy to know we are working against him. You must begin with a delicate touch first."

"Yes, Master," the second man replied, and to the man hanging in chains, "Ah, you are awake. Excellent. I am Rablias, the head questioner; soon you and I will get to know each other very well. You have something belonging to Lord Nicky; where is it?"

"I don't know what you're talking about," Mica ground out while frantically trying to think what their strange conversation meant.

The man gave a nod to whoever stood behind him. They began violating him. Mica struggled and cursed to no avail, lances of pain spearing through his body.

The question was repeated once more, Mica denying any knowledge. Once more he was violated. The immortal wanted to vomit from the pain and humiliation. He needed to take his mind off what was being done to him, keep his sanity. Mica writhed, tried to question them on allegiances to the boy, but they only wanted to know one thing. He would not give it. He didn't know how long it was before they gave up. The two hulking brutes shoved a funnel in his mouth and poured a noxious liquid down. He felt himself losing consciousness.

Mica came awake curled up into a ball of pain, the hurts inflicted on him already healing. He shivered in the freezing air, could only guess how much worse it would get when the men saw not a mark of torture on him. He had to get out. He couldn't understand why Colin wasn't looking for him, or her ladyship. Unless . . . unless it was true that she was working with the little boy. But why, and for what purpose? Surely she didn't think Nicky would treat her any differently than he had all the others he had betrayed. He shivered himself to sleep.

* * *

Mica paused in the doorway of the bar, partly to let his eyes grow accustomed to the dimness, partly to look for his protégé. He could see heads turning his way; most gave him a quick glance before dropping away. Only a few lingered longer. He ignored them, making his way through the tables as he continued scanning. There was a bunch of young, muscled youths slouched at a table in a far, dark corner. They were all heavily tattooed with gang symbols, wearing the baggy, ripped clothing and flashy jewelry in style with today's youth. One of the men had a bandanna to hold his hair out of his face. He sucked on a toothpick. His flat, dead stare trying for intimidation. It didn't work on Mica.

The immortal made his way to the bar where he sat and ordered a drink. He wanted to piss off the little punks, Toothpick being the main one. His protégé said he was a friend of his, and it was easy to see the miasma of jail time enveloping the boy.

The bartender set his customer's drink before the man, and retreated to the far end of the bar, where he picked his conversation back up with another patron. He looked like an ex-con, heavily muscled, jail tattoos, bald head, scars crisscrossing his skin. It didn't take long before the group in the corner became loud in their derision of Mica and his jeans, pressed button down shirt, shiny brown leather loafers. He let the mockery build, smiling to himself as the bartender kept a wary eye out. Mica finished his drink, waiting for the bartender to notice its emptiness. By and by, the man did and lumbered over.

He refilled the glass, and setting it down said, "Yo, man, I don't wanna be all up in your business, but you might not wanna hang around here too much longer."

"I'm waiting for someone, but thanks anyway," Mica replied politely.

The man gave him a dubious glance, muttering, "Your funeral," as he walked back to his post.

The heckling got louder. Just as Mica decided Devon wasn't going to show up, he came swaggering in the door with a few other of his juvie friends. "Aw man, what a downer," Mica heard him say to his friends, and they sniggered.

One of the kids bumped into him hard, trying to knock him off the stool. Mica stayed firm, sweeping his leg out, causing the punk to trip. He crashed to the ground as Mica casually laid out tip money, turning to the group who had now stopped.

Mica ignored the teen swearing on the floor, and his buddies who had crowded around to help him up. The group in the corner leaned forward intently. "You realize you're going to wreck your last chance by being in here," he addressed his protégé.

"'Hey man, what are you? Some kinda social worker? My boy here don't need your handouts, so get lost, gramps, 'fore you get hurt."

Mica ignored the speaker, keeping his eyes on Devon, who rolled his. "Quit hasslin' me, man. I told you, I don't wanna buy what you're selling no more. Go peddle your bullshit somewhere else."

"Man, I'm gonna fuck you up for disrespecting me!" the punk who had tried to knock him off the stool yelled as his friends helped him upright. He shrugged his oversized clothes more or less into place, reaching behind him.

The bartender came over, trying to defuse the situation. "Hey now, this is a clean joint. I don't need no flashing lights in here. We don't take kindly to do-gooders, man. I think you oughtta just get out now. Come on now J, let 'im go, he's not worth it."

"Fuck that shit, don't nobody disrespect me like that and get away with it!"

Mica continued to ignore the screaming youth, "I couldn't get hold of you any other way, but I thought you might like to know." He swept a jaundiced eye over the watching people before turning toward the door, but some of the crew stood blocking his way.

"I have no quarrel with any of you; it would be best if we didn't start one."

"Let 'im out," the bartender said. "Now. Or I'll bust ya heads myself. He won't be coming back in here."

Reluctantly, the youths parted, letting him go. There was a lot of jeering at his back. He ignored them; as he left, he heard his protégé say, "Man, I don't know why he gotta be hasslin' me. I told him his shit wasn't for me no more."

* * *

Mica woke, screaming, to his limbs being stretched. The gruesome twosome used knives to carve slits all over his body.

The entire time, the hissing, sibilant voice asked one question, and one only. "I want what belongs to the boy, to Nicky. Where is it?"

But Mica wouldn't tell. He didn't know why, since they seemed to want to kill the boy, only something held him back. He didn't think he could trust them to end Nicky's life. He gritted his teeth against the never-ending pain, casting his thoughts back to better times to wait out what they did to him.

When he was dumped back into his cell, it was as a bleeding, screaming mass of agony. He closed his eyes briefly, opening them again at the sound of the door thumping shut. A stump of a candle burned next to a wooden bowl steaming with some kind of stew, and a mug of water. He dragged himself over to the food, using his forearms and elbows. It took a long time, blood smeared the filthy floor, muscles spasmed. Mica couldn't help himself; he scarfed everything down before realizing it was tainted. He forced up what he could of the meal, but it still wasn't enough as he fell into a drugged stupor.

* * *

"Devon, I know you think those guys are cool and all, but you and they are heading to an early grave."

"What do you care, man? You're gonna live forever, so what the fuck's it matter if I die now or not?"

"Because," Mica patiently replied, "being what I am is both curse and blessing. I see how brief your lives are, how easily snuffed. If I can help make them better, even just one person's . . ."

"Aw, man, you guilt trippin'? Well I ain't gonna be your road offa' it. I'm outta here! I don't need or want your stupid salvation. Keep it!" He swung away from the kitchen counter, heading out of the loft as Mica called after him fruitlessly.

Mica and Eron walked along the rain-slicked pavement. His friend listened to him complaining about how the teenager had seen Mica come back alive from a fatal wound, how he was trying to get him out of the life he was in; he showed promise if only he would straighten out.

"You can't force him, unless and until he wants to change; you might as well forget about him. Find someone else to be your protégé. Trust me, if he hasn't ratted you out by now, I doubt he will, but if you keep pushing him . . ." was all Eron would say, leaving Mica to infer what he wanted from the statement.

The phone in Mica's pocket rang; he would have ignored it but was hoping it was his protégé. He didn't recognize the number but answered it anyway. Eron waited patiently, watching the flow of pedestrian and vehicle traffic.

"Mica!? Mica!? Holy fuck! Holy shit! Man! Oh man! You gotta come help me! I swear, man! Ohhhhh, sweet Jesus!" the teen moaned in panicked whispers.

"Devon?" Mica said. "Calm down, I can hardly hear you. Where are you?"

"She got 'em, man!" The teen babbled on. "She-she fucking got 'em! J an' T-bar, and . . . and all of 'em, man! Oh fuck! Oh Christ! Ya gotta help me! I'm dead otherwise! She . . . she fucking killed 'em. Slaughtered 'em like . . . like they-they were nothing, man!" Devon's voice rose into a hysterical squeal before breaking down into sobs.

Eron was giving Mica questioning looks; he held a finger up and spoke into the phone, "Devon, tell me where you're at. I'll come get you."

"Now, man! Ya gotta come now!"

"Yes, now, where are you?"

Devon gave instructions hurriedly, hanging up on a sob. Eron accompanied Mica reluctantly. When they got to the youth, he was so shook up, he rabbited into the car. He lay on the back seat, shivering in fear and cold, sobbing, as Mica drove them to his loft. It wasn't until they got inside and the teen was wrapped in a blanket, drinking coffee, before they were able to pry the story out of him.

"We was at the club, man, just hanging, ya know? And J man, he was drinking and stuff, ya know. We had all these really tight chicks hanging around and stuff. T-bar, he was just chillin' and he spotted this really hot chick come in, like supermodel-hot, all dressed in Gucci an' shit. Man, there be some sweet bitches in there but ain't none of them lookin' that fine. Well, T-bar, he go on up to her and she, like, brush him off like he ain't nothin'!"

"I think I like her already; she's got taste," Eron murmured, earning him a glare from Devon and a shushing motion from his friend.

"So he hit on her and got turned down. How did they end up dead?" Mica tried to speed things up.

"Yeah, so like, he didn't like that . . ."

"Imagine that," Eron interjected once more, earning another glare.

"I dunno what happened. He got all offended and tried to grab her or some shit. She musta' known some fancy kung fu moves like you, man. 'Cause he went sliding across the floor 'afore anybody know what going on. He slammed into the wall, and when he get up, she be gone an' shit. He was all cussing an' stuff at the table, and J, ya know, tried to calm him down. Said he didn't need no stuck-up bitch when he could have all the fine bitches with us."

"Yes, 'cause nothing says 'I want you' like an assault," Eron added.

"Anyway, we leave when it be getting lame, and T-bar sees the chick, the hot chick that dissed him. Well, he kinda all jacked up on shit and stuff—"

"Naturally," Eron commented but was ignored.

"He just, I dunno, we told him to just let it go. He didn't need no stuck-up bitch like her that didn't know a good thing when she see it, just ignore her, ya know? But T-bar, he was real pissed, 'cause everybody pretty much saw her wipe the floor with him, ya know? So he go after her, all cussing and yelling and stuff."

Devon paused to drink more coffee. The men sipped at theirs, waiting for the kid to go on. He brought his arms and fists up in front of his face, moaned and rocked for a minute before bringing them back down to huddle in the blanket as if what he had seen was one thing too many for him.

"She just kinda look at him, an' tilt her head to the side and just smile. Then she turn real calm-like and walk into the alley! Like, who does that? She didn't look all alarmed or anything, and she was like, right by her ride too! Man, it some sweet, tricked-out road bike. But T-bar, he just think she scared of him and go charging after her. J he was all like, man, I too tired for this shit. He was just gonna leave but then like, T-bar scream, man! I ain't never heard him scream like that."

"So we had to go and see what was up, like, maybe the bitch had set T-bar up to get beat by a rival gang or something, 'cause everybody know T-bar got a weakness for the ladies, ya know? So J an' me go over to the alley, and T-bar be lying on the ground with the bitch standing over him.

"J, he bring his piece out and shoot at her. But it's like he didn't hit her or nothing, ya know? She just look up at him and laugh and he goes to shoot her again, but she ain't there no more! It's like she disappeared or something! J, he just go running up to T-bar and, man, he be dead! He all staring at the sky an' shit with this look a terror on his face. His arm be all broke an' shit, bone poking out. I dunno how she done it, but she twisted his head right the fuck around on his neck! He laying on his belly, but he be staring up at the sky!

"I'm all like, man, let's just go, something ain't right with this chick. But J all pissed now she killed one of his crew, and he all ranting and raving about how he gonna find her and cap her ass an all. Show her not to fuck with J, ya know?"

Devon shivered, his voice dropping lower as he told what had happened to the gang, and how he alone had escaped. Mica wanted to report it to the police, but the teen didn't. Eron thought what was the point? The little punks only got what they justly deserved. Mica anonymously reported it, but he never heard any newscasts on bodies being found. The incident itself would have been enough to scare Devon straight, if only for a little while. Until he became the hunted, until he began to be afraid to leave Mica's presence when darkness fell. He claimed the bitch who killed his friends kept showing up everywhere he went; he even woke once to find her standing in his room, staring at him like death itself.

Mica surmised drugs, and wanted Devon to go to rehab if he expected to continue staying at the loft, but the teen refused and left. One night, Devon showed up shivering, strung out, at Mica's loft. He took the two of them to hear Steve play. That's when the teen saw his personal nightmare, and pointed her out to Mica.

She had sent drinks to their table, smiling in a sly, knowing way, freaking the kid out. Mica had calmed him down and gone over. That's when even his life took a turn for the bizarre, the first time he met Illyria.

* * *

"Illyria!" Mica woke up screaming her name, hearing the echoes of it fading in the small, filthy, cold cell.

He didn't understand what his dreams meant, who Devon was, or how her ladyship could show up in modern times in modern clothing. Mica rolled over on the stone floor and vomited bile up, his head throbbing viciously. He crawled as far away from the spot he had soiled as his chains would allow.

"Oh no!" He didn't realize he moaned it out loud.

Where was Colin? Why wasn't he helping to rescue him? Mica didn't know how he was going to get himself out. They kept drugging him so much his body had trouble throwing off the effects, including healing from the repeated torture. His captives were being very careful to keep him chained up. Could he overcome them somehow? But how to get out? He wasn't certain where he was.

The immortal knew he would have to try staying awake. Try to see in the darkness what his surroundings looked like. He didn't know if it was night or day, or even how much time had passed. He only knew his brother should be coming for him soon. Mica waited, composing himself, but they never came.

Chapter Twenty

The two guides ate their meal in silence while scanning the open area around them, though other members of the party conversed softly among themselves, discussing the scout's news. It had taken six months to get as far as they had. This part of their journey was the most perilous; the bandits infesting the mountains around Macinas seemed to have doubled. They were half a day's walk from the town. The night air's reek of smoke and charred things wasn't from their fire alone. A merchant and his son opened another flask to continue drinking.

Farther off, a young woman took care of her oxen while her little brother lay on bales of wool.

"I've been thinking, Franz. I plan on staying. I'm getting too old for this, I don't think I could survive another large attack. It's the best I'm likely to do," Henrik announced.

Franz grunted, spooning more of the stew into his mouth, and tore a huge chunk out of the flat bread in his other hand. He kept one eye on the young woman and her brother. Another loud burst of laughter from the fat merchant intruded, and his son staggered up. He didn't trust the man, and was pretty sure he had already assaulted the woman once, though she had not spoken a word. Franz smiled grimly to himself as he ate, continuing to scan the area out of habit. He couldn't stand the man, and felt rather protective of the woman; she reminded him of his dead sister.

Henrik persisted. "What about you? I'm thinking a body could do a lot worse elsewhere.'"

Franz grunted again, swallowing the last of his bread. "I'm not interested in land like you, Henrik. Give me a place to sleep, food to eat, and some coins in my pocket and I be happy."

Henrik snorted, "I'd rather I had something in my old age. Something permanent, my friend."

"Ja, sure. To each his own.'' Franz slurped down the last of the stew and wiped his mouth on his arm. "I am thinking the town has more problems than bandits."

His friend snorted. "A lot of towns have problems with them, that's life."

Franz downed his one mug of ale he allowed himself at each meal while on a job and belched. "Those bandits had collars on. Collars mean slaves, escaped slaves. The one I killed? He was babbling about attacks against the ruler."

"So they attacked the ruler; if he is a good one, they will be taken care of soon." Henrik was unconcerned.

"Nein, he said there be fighting over the throne. I have no desire to be caught in such things."

The other man spat a bone out and grunted, more concerned with his meal than rumors from scum. Franz watched the son as he tried to corner the young woman. She was yelling at him as she tried to keep the oxen from lumbering off. The son had a hand wrapped around the woman's arm, trying to drag her off into the woods.

"Sie dort!" Franz came up beside the man. "Fräulein, you want help with those animals?"

The man turned, snarling drunkenly, "Mind your own business!"

The guide had seen the look of barely-concealed fear on her face. "Get off me, you oaf!" She was trying to pry the son's hand off her arm.

"You liked it well enough those other times," the man slurred, trying to get a better grip on her.

"I said get off!" She tugged, bringing a small dagger up to cut his hand.

The man swore at the sudden pain, letting go. He brought his other hand up to slap her when Franz intervened. "Nein, the Fräulein wishes to be left alone."

"Get your hands off me, you pig fucker, or I'll not pay you," the son threatened.

"Nein, not until you leave her alone," the guide replied. "And your father will pay us for bringing you this far, or he will have a eunuch for a son."

The man sneered, but it was weak. He was terrified of the much bigger man. "Guides who make threats to their employer don't last long."

"Perhaps," replied the guide, "but neither do ones who allow their charges to come to harm, no matter the source." He squeezed a little harder and had the son dancing in place from the pain.

"Lemme go! All right, all right!" The son threw a vicious look at the young woman, who still had her dagger out. "Bitch ain't a good lay anyway."

Franz shoved the man away, folding his well-muscled arms across his chest. The son spat on the ground before stumbling back to his father.

"I could've taken care of him myself," came the angry mutter from behind him.

Franz quelled her with a look. "Not with your tiny dagger. It's not big enough to do more than anger a man. I meant what I said, Fräulein. I would not be a good guide if I let harm come to the group. I wish you had told me before that he had assaulted you. I would have left him and his father behind."

She tucked her dagger back into the sheath on her waist, sniffing, "And he would have had the law on you. The law supports the actions of dung like him." She spat on the grass, turning away from the big man before her, saying as she did, "Thank you."

"Ihr willkommen," the guide replied. "I think I stay and help anyway, whether you need it or not."

She compressed her lips together, but thankfully did not argue.

* * *

The sun weakly shined down as the party came out of the forest, the half-ruined town stark against lowering gray clouds and an icy rain.

The man and his son were the first to complain. "You stupid men! You've lead us to a charnel pit! That's more than a little damaged! Stupid scout! I don't pay for incompetence!"

"You dumb ox!" the son added.

Henrik stopped, staring in dismay at the wreckage before them, but Franz turned and said, "Our agreement still stands. It was not dependent on disasters. You will pay us."

"The hell I will! We're going back, and you'll owe me money!"

Franz stepped closer to the man. "I still have our contract, and it still binds you. You may go back, but you will pay us before you go."

The man's mouth gaped open. "You're our guide!"

"No payment, no guide." Franz fondled the pommel of his sword meaningfully, looking between the man and his son.

They looked from him to Henrik, who remained silent, and then to the other members of their party. "You're not going to let him get away with this, are you?"

The other men glanced around themselves; they did not care for the man and his son. One of the men stroked his beard thoughtfully, saying, "I still see buildings, and a bridge; the town is still partly there, therefore he is correct. You owe him the balance for bringing you here."

After a brief moment of silence, the other members agreed. The man turned red, then purple while his son spluttered beside him but withdrew a leather pouch and carefully counted out coin. He hesitated a moment, contemplating flinging them at the big man before him, but at the last second dropped them into his hand.

"Danke," Franz replied.

"You'll never get another guide job when I'm through with you," the man hissed before barking at his son, "Get our stuff together. Now! I'm not staying with these dogs a minute more!"

The group watched in silence as the two started back into the forest. The graybeard said, "Let us continue so we may get out of the cold."

Trudging into what was left of the town provided a clearer picture of just how the fire had raged. The party could see groups of men and women working on clearing charred debris. Carts waited, pulled by a motley assortment of animals and slaves. The young woman even saw children helping out, and she grew anxious for what was left of her wool. Franz stopped by the first group to speak with them. They pointed toward the bridge, but were soon moving again. The woman thought some looked avariciously at their merchandise.

"Keep a sharp eye out, Hilel; we don't want to lose what's left of our goods."

Her brother gave her a sour look, sticking his tongue out saying, "I am the man now since Father is dead."

"Mind me now, you are not old enough," she replied as they continued on.

Her brother began to whine, which grated on her ears, until the graybeard spoke a few well-chosen words, and her brother subsided into a resentful silence. The place they were directed to was a swampy quagmire.

"I am used to the town lacking hospitality, but this is a new low," the graybeard commented.

Franz motioned with his hands for the complaints to hold. "I shall explain."

"You'd damn well better!" a wine merchant grumbled.

"A representative from the palace is coming to survey what's left of the town. The Harvest Festival will continue, but given the extent of damage, housing is a problem. All travelers with goods to sell are being asked to group in this area for safety."

There was much muttering along the lines of, "So it makes it easier to steal from us."

Franz shrugged massive shoulders. "If you disagree, feel free to find another spot."

Quarreling broke out between the merchants; it had taken them a long time to travel, and it wasn't safe to leave without being in a protected caravan. Their two guides and scout, having been given the other half of the payment due them, set out to find places to sleep.

* * *

The young woman didn't trust her brother to keep a proper watch while she hunted about. A son of the wine merchant had just agreed to keep watch for her when trumpets rang out. The newcomers saw the palace guard snap to attention as a small party started across the bridge.

"Raina, I'm hungry," her brother whined.

His complaints fell on deaf ears as everyone nearby stopped to watch the procession. Sunlight glittered off metal encircling the head of one obese man, and whispers of "His Majesty" reached their ears. People bowed or curtsied as the party approached. Raina lifted her eyes to watch, envious. It seemed the party would pass them by, when a woman's voice spoke. It was with some startlement that the wool merchant realized one of the riders was female and not an effeminate male as she had thought.

"Our tour is the town, not every displaced traveler," snarled a man, dressed in purple velvet, with red blonde hair.

"I take it you have come for the Harvest Festival?" the striking woman addressed them.

Raina noticed a small boy, around her brother's age, clinging to the back of her long, full-skirted black coat. The graybeard confirmed,

"I am sorry we are not properly able to provide food and lodgings; as you can see, we were visited by bandits."

Cold gray eyes swept over the group, pausing a moment on Raina. She didn't like how they assessed her. He reminded her too much of a person from her past who had ultimately driven her to flee with her brother.

"One of the palace guards shall escort you across the bridge. The accommodations are still spartan, but your goods will be safe." One of the men signaled, and a guard detached himself as the party rode on.

"Come on, you," the guard growled. "This way." He was starting back across the bridge even as people were scrambling back into their carts and wagons.

It was a steep climb; the animals nearly exhausted by the time the group made it to their destination. They were directed toward a patch of dead grass beside the palace walls and left to find spots as best they could. Piles of hay stood off to one side. The guard rode off before anyone could ask him about lodgings and human food.

Raina fed and watered her oxen, Hilel whining and being more of a hindrance. She secured the wagon, chewing on her lip a moment in indecision. If she thought for one moment she could trust her brother to do what was needed, she would send him, but she couldn't.

"Come on, Hilel, we need to find some food, and a bed."

Brother and sister slowly walked back down the hill. "Raina, when we gonna go home? When we gonna have servants again?"

She sighed. "We can't, not anymore."

The only inn they saw before crossing the bridge was completely occupied; even if it hadn't been, it was too pricey for her reduced circumstances. She and her brother would have to sleep with their wool, and enter the town proper for cheaper fare. Raina left the inn, her brother still whining behind her, dragging his feet.

"Come on," Raina commanded.

He promptly stuck his fists on his hip and stomped his feet. "No! I wanna go home! Now! I'm the earl! You're just my sister. You have to do what I say!" her brother insisted, bottom lip in a pout.

Raina felt her temper snap as her brother continued screaming and stamping his feet. The young woman slapped him, speaking harshly. He was so shocked he fell silent. She grabbed his arm and hauled him into town with her.

The palace guard had been correct: what inns had escaped the fire did not have room, and staying in the ramshackle buildings by the river would not be wise. Her brother had stopped his incessant whining once she found them some food and drink, but she knew it wouldn't last long. Raina had also taken the opportunity to seek out townspeople who might need wool. She had a few prospects; tomorrow would say for certain if anything were to come of it. Brother and sister began to walk across the bridge, dusk falling, the cold wind blowing a little harder.

"Raina, I don't wanna sleep outside. It's too cold."

"We don't have a choice; the wool will keep us warm."

"But Raina . . ." She ignored him, pausing before the open gates of a mansion being rebuilt.

The woman from earlier in the day stood talking to a slave. Raina was set to walk on when the lady turned her head, piercing the two outsiders with a disconcerting gaze. Even from their distance, the young woman saw the slight smile flit across the older woman's face, and her acknowledging nod to the pair outside her gate. Without knowing why, it bothered her, enough to have her snatching up her brother's hand and dragging him up the hill, back to their cart and oxen.

* * *

Franz felt uneasy about leaving the young woman and her brother to fend for themselves, but knew if she were determined on her present course, it were best she learned what she needed to know now. She seemed competent enough, but he still hoped that someone halfway trustworthy was looking after them. Once he'd found a place to sleep, Henrik left to go speak with some man about a tavern, leaving him at loose ends. The big bald-headed man prowled around the town, across the bridge, up and back down the steep street. Inactivity did not sit well with him. He was ready for something new after ten years of being a guide, though he knew not what else to do.

He stopped to watch a group struggle to dismantle a burnt building. He could see what needed to be done to make it easier. He drifted closer, one of the men yelling for him to get back before he got hurt.

"There is an easier way to bring this down. You have a big hammer?" he asked.

They paused and one man said, "This is the way we do things."

Franz shrugged, "I could do it easier. I need big hammer." He held his hands apart to show how big. "Like a large mallet."

The men and women muttered within the group. One man went and fetched a large hammer. The big man hefted it in his hands, getting the feel for it. Franz scrutinized the building again, finding the points he needed. The men and women watched in silence.

"If you stand back, I will hit here, here, and here," Franz pointed the areas out, "and the building should come down in pieces."

He lined himself up, and with a mighty swing, brought the hammer around into the support beam. For a moment he was afraid it wasn't going to fall. A shiver and a crash as part of the building collapsed. A cloud of ash, dirt, and other debris floated up as Franz went to work on the other two support posts and the building was a pile of rubble laying on the ground. The leader of the group clapped him on the shoulder.

"Thank you, stranger, I'm ashamed I ever doubted. Where did you learn how to bring buildings down?" he asked.

"I was in the army, and because of my strength I was given many such jobs," Franz replied.

"What brings you here?"

"I was discharged and became a guide. Now I look for something else."

"We could use someone with your talent; would you consider staying long enough to help out?" the man asked.

"What would I have to do?"

"Just what you did, on whatever is still standing."

"And would I get anything in return?"

"Food, lodging, a small payment at least. The king's requisitioner would be able to tell you. He is at the palace."

Henrik and Franz met back up later in the evening. They sat at a scorched table, eating what passed as fare for the tavern. Slave girls ran back and forth, answering the calls of the men and a few warrior women. A freezing wind gusted flakes of snow on those patrons unable to get a spot under what remained of the ceiling.

Fire pits had been dug in the now-frozen dirt, lined with chunks of a strange whitish stone called concrete. A big fireplace blazed and flared inside the remaining half, heating the fur-covered men before it.

"Have you found your tavern yet?" Franz asked his friend as he huddled in his cloak, keeping a watchful eye on the other patrons.

The grizzled man leaned closer, grinning. "I'm gonna be the new bartender here."

He paused spooning stew up to give the half-burnt wreck a disbelieving look. "But it is not worth it! It's a sty; look at the patrons."

"Nein, nein. You always did think yourself better than most. This is the place for me. I know these types of people; we fought beside those like them in our army days. The woman and her husband over there? They need someone to help, and if it works out, I have been promised part ownership."

"I don't know, I don't like the look of them. If you are sure?"

"It is a good deal," his friend insisted.

Franz merely grunted, keeping his thoughts to himself as he watched the patrons. He knew trouble when he saw it, and that's what the tavern catered to. He didn't like how his friend seemed willing to go back to the old ways, the army days.

"You could join us, just think! Men always find money for drinks and whores. We would have food, lodgings, women." He nudged the big man beside him with an elbow and chortled as he downed his ale.

"I think I will stick to knocking down buildings, my friend, but, should I get tired of it . . ."

"Sure, sure, you come look your old friend Henrik up. No hard feelings, good luck." The man got up, taking his empty stew bowl and mug, walking up to the remains of the bar.

Franz sat sipping his ale as a slave took away his empty bowl. The tavern had been decent sized before the fire, judging from the charred remains of beams poking out of the frozen, blackened earth. He felt unsettled, with the darkness and emptiness at his back. The big man watched the street before him, torches flaring in the wind. Night had firmly settled over the land, and the traffic of the town dissipated. There was supposed to be a curfew, but it wasn't enforced—at least, not consistently. Franz figured he had a little while more before he would be locked out of the men's dormitory and the sleeping spot assigned to him.

* * *

The former guide trudged in a line of other men in the pre-dawn darkness. He had managed some sleep, and now, his new life would begin. The townsperson in charge led his group past what had been the main street. It had sustained the heaviest damage from the fire; not a single building remained, only ashes and cracked stone or concrete.

"Time to get to work!" the man bawled out, sorting the group when they arrived at their destination.

Wooden shovels, rakes, hoes and other tools were passed out from the back of a wagon. Each small knot of people spread out to begin work. Wood too charred to be reused was tossed in one of the wagons, and what could be saved for reuse in another to be sorted elsewhere. Stone or concrete was stacked in piles for the stonemasons to inspect later on. As the sky lightened, Franz was pulled away from stacking stone and told to inspect the remaining buildings near the fire's path. A prominent townsperson accompanied him along with a slave carrying a bucket of paint and a brush.

The building they looked at had once been a shop, with living quarters above.

Franz took his time with his inspection, to the disgust of the man with him. "I will not rush," he told the town official. "If I overlook even the smallest detail, it could cause problems later on. Problems which would cost more time and coin and mayhap lives."

"You're not in charge of rebuilding, just of telling us if the main supports are still stable and can be used again. The owner will decide what he wants to do with the remains."

Franz sighed—these Macinas townspeople were so arrogant and impatient. "I will tell you now, it doesn't meet your requirements and should be torn down." Franz pointed out why, the slave marked the building, and they moved on.

"Nein . . . nein . . ." A whole street of buildings ruled out, onto the next block, "Ja . . . ja . . . nein . . ." In this way, he passed the morning.

At midday, a group of women came by with food and drink. Franz, the townsman and the slave used a slab of charred wood as a table. It was no surprise most of the buildings in this section couldn't be saved—they had been near the central path of the fire.

"What will be done when it gets too cold to work outside?" Franz asked. "You cannot build. The ground is already too hard for digging."

The man made a face. "The king's favorite-of-the-month will have some in the forests, cutting wood, others will be sorting what we salvage, and some shall be trained to provide support for the army under the earl's command."

He probed gently. "This person have any experience?"

"So she claims," the man flatly stated.

Franz stopped eating for a moment in surprise, "I didn't think your women educated enough to know of man's politics."

"She is foreign," the official explained to Franz, which made the man before him narrow his eyes a bit in suspicion. The townsman motioned for the other two men to start working again.

By the time dusk was falling, the former guide and soldier was pleased with the job he had done so far. The more buildings he inspected, the faster he got at identifying which could be reused, and which needed to be torn down.

* * *

The merchant and Raina shook hands after the successful completion of negotiating a price for her wool. It wasn't what she had hoped for, but she knew it was the best she was likely to get given the town's economic condition. Her thoughts turned to what she could do next, and if she wished to stay here. Raina took the oxen and cart back to the area outside the palace walls, unhitching and picketing the beasts. She began carefully exploring the town, mindful of the overheard conversations of kidnappings and people being illegally sold into slavery. She refused to go down the street of bordellos and whorehouses. Her violations were still fresh in her mind, both the ones received months ago and the recent. No matter what happened, she would never sell her body, even if it meant starvation or death.

She was good with numbers and enjoyed negotiating. Maybe she could convince a merchant to take her on as a bookkeeper? At least until she figured out what she really wanted to do and had the funds saved up. With this strategy in mind, Raina began another round of the town. Her initial optimism waned after an hour or two. Those who could use her services hadn't the funds; those who could afford didn't need them.

Raina collected her brother, who had been playing with other children on the muddy banks of the river. He didn't want to leave, but she ignored his tantrums and hauled him across the bridge. He was filthy, tired and hungry. She knew how precious their coins were; still, she stopped at the Silver Thorn and paid for a hot meal for them both, and a bath. She continued her quest for work, little brother in tow.

The palace had long lines of dispossessed people, many who were quick to set newcomers straight on which line a person needed to be in. Raina watched in envy as those who were lucky to score spots inside the palace walls went to the food lines. She shuffled forward, Hilel content for the moment to watch the bustle. Finally, it was her turn.

A fat blonde women, noble by her manner of dress, addressed them. "And who do we have here?" She asked.

Before his sister could answer, Hilel spoke, "I am Hilel Ian Rampling, Earl of Smirkin. Who are you?"

The woman raised her brows. The young woman felt her cheeks

flame in embarrassment as the noble made no attempts to smother her laughs.

She hissed a warning to her brother and murmured, "I am sorry, my lady, I apologize for my brother."

The lady inclined her head graciously. "I am the Baroness Rothsbury. You may call me Lady Lily. I was unaware we had an earl by that name."

"Pardon, your ladyship, we are not from here, and we no longer have use of our title. We are just simple folk now, looking for work and a place to stay. We have oxen and a cart."

"I have not heard of an earl who drives oxen, willingly or not."

"It's my sister's job," her brother replied scornfully as if it should be obvious to all. "I wanna go home! I want our servants back!"

"What is your name?" Lady Lily asked.

"Raina," the young woman replied.

"Is it true, what you say?"

"Yes, my lady. We are exiles now, our parents dead, their title, lands, and wealth stolen. There was much upheaval in our country. I thought it better to leave and make my way in the world than become a bond slave to another." Raina replied with some heat, shocked she could still feel anger over those events.

Lady Lily seemed surprised as well. "Had you no relations willing to take you in?"

Raina hesitated, glanced at her brother who was opening his mouth. "None who did not wish us harm."

"No future husband to help either?"

"No," she replied firmly, pushing the memory of his family's humiliating tearing asunder of the marriage contract out of her mind.

"Ah." *There seems to be a lot of that going around, first the duchess and now these two.* "We do have need of oxen and a wagon, but it is not the type of work for a young woman. Nor do we have anything we could utilize your noble upbringing for. Unless . . ."

"I know my numbers; my father had excellent tutors for me. I was allowed to learn things other noble daughters couldn't. I can negotiate, I can read and write." Raina rushed on, seeing the baroness open her mouth to offer something she wouldn't like. "I can lease the oxen and cart to His Majesty for use in rebuilding. I offer my services as a bookkeeper. I know how to run a manor, knowledge not so different from keeping track of what you do here."

"Well, I—we have slaves for the menial tasks."

The young woman felt her opportunity slipping away. She made one last desperate bid, "But do you have enough overseers to make sure they do not cheat the crown? Let me prove myself. Give me a set of books I can audit. A set which won't upset the balance already in place, and can be easily gone over by the royal bookkeeper."

Lady Lily frowned. "I don't think we have such a thing."

"Please, my lady, anything at all."

The baroness sighed, her bosom heaving, a crease between her brows. "I will ask around. It is the best I can do. Now, as to the oxen and cart you say you have?"

Chapter Twenty-One

Slaves cowered against walls, trying to avoid being noticed by the enraged young man destroying his rooms. That damn foreign woman! It had only been three days since the tour of the ruined town, and already she had organized groups, appointed leaders, even gotten the other nobles to help! Where once before no one dared do anything without clearing it with him, now they ran panting like dogs in heat after the bitch. In one move, she had decimated his power base. He had no influence with the new sheriff or his men. Yet. Thus, no way to use them to frighten the population into submission. She had also managed to place all the merchants out of his clutches.

He never heard the knock on his door, but DiJinn was before him with a slave holding sheaves of parchment in his shaking hands.

"What?!"

"Master, this man is a copyist with the royal tax collector, and he has some . . . interesting information." Nicky snatched the papers from the slave.

He flipped through them, a tax for the rebuilding of the sheriff's office, one for the rebuilding of the town, a credit to any noble or merchant who donated services or goods to the sheriff and the town. A reduction in taxes to any townspeople who rebuilt their shops. It was ridiculous and unheard of! He knew the damn king would not have thought of this on his own. Nicky would have blamed the bleeding-heart earl, who had managed to worm his way onto some committee or other, but it seemed more the work of that damn woman. He ground his teeth together. It was not worth the aggravation for a dukedom when the woman refused to listen to him. She had even managed to suspend her lessons on proper behavior from the countess.

Calm, I must remain calm. "I will speak to the king about such matters." Nicky stopped himself from crushing the papers in his fist.

"It came from His Majesty, signed and sealed. He said to see they were enacted at once . . ." The man trailed off at the vicious look from the advisor.

Nicky almost cracked a molar, grinding his teeth together to keep the rage at bay. "And did your master?" he finally managed to ask.

Droplets of sweat broke out on the young copyist's brow. "They . . . they came from the king. He . . . he . . . he had no choice . . ."

"Get out of my sight!" Nicky yelled. When the man stood gaping, he screamed, "I said, get out!" He grabbed a cup with his free right hand and flung it.

The man before him bowed before running from the room, the door banging shut after him. The young man turned to his slave.

"How dare the bitch think she can advise the king? I am the royal advisor! I am the only one! She needs to be brought to heel! I won't have her sneaking behind my back. How dare she think she can do a better job than me? She will rue the day she crossed my path!"

His slave remained silent, waiting, humming to himself while feeding off the man's rage.

"Where is my army? How long does it take to march across a few weak kingdoms? The asshole in charge had better be near."

Still DiJinn spoke not a word. Nicky paced, muttering to himself, scowling. Each year, he felt a little more of his powers slipping away. Soon he would be just like the rest of the sorry rabble cluttering up the pathetic mudball planet. He could never be ordinary again. It took what little remained to him just to stay as he was. If he unleashed his power to accomplish more deeds, he would use it up. Nicky would go back to being a weak, powerless twelve year old.

"I will go see my prisoner. He has something belonging to me he ought not to have. But that damn duchess—if I let this go on much longer, she'll soon have passed a whole new tax code!"

Indecision was not like him. He stopped by a table, picked up a cup of wine, downed it. "Everyone is against me, and I'm surrounded by idiots!" He paced and drank, muttering some more. "DiJinn, we have calls to make. The dungeon first, the frigid bitch, and lastly the foreign whore."

The years of unchallenged power had caused him to forget some of the very first lessons his master had taught him. He had been stupid, sloppy, complacent. Well, it was all going to change. Nicky turned to his demon. "Come. You want fed, I'll feed you."

* * *

The advisor stood glaring as the guard unlocked the heavy wood door leading down into the dungeon. He should have taken care of this when the sheriff was first brought down. But he noticed the palace slaves taking more interest in his movements than usual and clenched his hands in their leather gloves. This had to be because of the bitch's influence on the king. Once the door was open, a cold, noxious air escaped. The two slaves shivered, gripping the poles holding the lanterns more tightly and cautiously started down the steep stone steps. Torches burned in brackets at intervals along the long hallway. The space at the foot of the stairs was open, receiving light and air from small openings set high in the walls. A rickety wooden table with chairs around it was in the space behind. To the far right, a tripod-mounted brazier had been set up, on which the dungeon guards could cook the gruel for the prisoners and at which they could warm themselves. One of the men, noticing whom their guest was, nudged the others. They all made low bows.

"The former sheriff, where is he?" Nicky demanded.

"Uh, he-he's down a level, my lord." The man seemed unsure what to do. "Shall I have him brought up?"

"No," Nicky said, "Lead us down to him."

"Certainly, my lord. At once, my lord." The man bowed and went to a board holding a variety of keys. He picked one off and taking a torch up, lit it from the fire pit, motioning to the small party.

Nicky was quite pleased with the remodeled dungeons. Extra room meant more scum could be shown the error of their ways, and he was able to secrete another work chamber in the confines. Heavy iron-banded wood doors barred each level, with a separate key for each lock, something else the advisor had insisted on.

No chance for a mass breakout, or some silly peasant trying to storm the dungeons and free a family member.

The air got colder, the smell worse as they went down a level. The torch bearers gagged continuously at the mix of unwashed bodies, rotting flesh and food, urine, and feces. The floor was slimy, puddles scattered about. The guard stopped halfway down the hall at another wood door. A small metal grill was at eye level, a moveable flap near the bottom. Nicky's slave hummed faintly, his eyes gleaming in the dark. The guard avoided his gaze and with shaking hands tried to unlock the door. After several fumbling tries, the lock disengaged.

"I'll . . . I'll . . . be . . . be outside, should you need me, my lord," the guard gasped out. He didn't like being so near Nicky and his slave. He could have sworn the slave was actually happy to be visiting.

Nicky curtly commanded one of the slaves with a lantern to precede him, striking the slave when he hesitated. The slave yelped in pain and hurried inside. There was a groan from the figure curled up on the filthy, moldering straw as he tried to shield his sensitive eyes from the light. The slave's tremors caused the lantern to bounce around on the end of the pole.

Nicky struck the slave once more to hold the light still before he turned back to the figure as the slave hurried to comply. "Jake." The cold tone was cruel.

The figure whimpered, forcing its eyes open. Nicky could feel Jake's despair and misery. The sheriff, never a very clean man to begin with, was black with filth. Old blood, sweat, dirt, puke—all covered festering wounds. His leather armor had been taken from him, but he still retained his pants. Nicky could see they had dark streaks on them, front and back, stiff patches from where he had soiled himself during the torture. He was shirtless, his once muscular body starved, flabby chest and stomach showing burn marks and green pus dripping. A string of bruises around his throat, large scabby patches of missing hair on his head. Nicky enjoyed the look of recognition when it finally came.

Jake's eyes widened farther; gurgling frantically, he reached forward trying to grab the boots of the young man with broken fingers. He was still trying to speak through a jaw nearly swollen shut, pleading with gestures.

"At least one thing has gone right: you are unable to tell anyone not under my control who commands you. Good." An evil smile split the boy's lips.

The man before him shook his head from side to side frantically, clutching tighter at the young man's boots as Jake's gurgles became more insistent.

"Do you realize what your stupidity and incompetence has cost me?" Nicky hissed. The young man stepped back, using his booted foot to kick the older man in the chest. Jake screamed, clutching at the new pain.

"You should have told me about those three merchant men and the damn foreign woman sooner! You messed up the raid by the bandits and the burning of the nobles' dwellings! You can forget about getting out."

Nicky walked out of the small, filthy cell. He ignored the sheriff's efforts to crawl after him. The slave holding the light scrambled to keep up, barely making it out the door before the advisor slammed it shut.

"Wait," he murmured to his demon. "I'll have him brought to the chamber, and you can enjoy your feeding while I see to other matters." A bit louder, he said to the man accompanying them, "Where's the head questioner? I need to speak with him."

The guard all but dropped the keys as he was relocking the door. "Uh, um, he-he's down in his chambers with one of the other lawmen, my lord. Shall I escort you back to the waiting area and have him brought to you?"

"No, you will take us to him. I wish to see how his project is going."

The guard gulped audibly; visiting the head questioner at work was expressly forbidden by the king's orders. He had tried to tell the nobleman before him once, and he still had the scars from the beating.

"Right-right this way, my lord." He led the way farther down the hall.

Another heavy iron-banded door needed opening. His hands shook so much from cold and fright that it took him several minutes to undo the lock. The temperature dropped several more degrees as they continued down well-worn stone stairs, breath fogging the air. Water could be heard dripping from the ceiling, seen trickling down the slimy mold-covered walls and pooling on the sub-basement floor, wherein floated bits and pieces of unidentifiable things. Small stone islands appeared in the wavering torchlight, off to either side. Each one had a metal grate covering the top. Only Nicky and his slave seemed unaffected by the atrociously pervasive reek of advanced decay. The rest of the members coughed and gagged, adding their vomit to the sloshing soup.

The small party waded along the hall, flames wavering as they passed through strong currents of icy air flowing down from vents near the ceiling. Yet another stone island appeared in the uncertain light. It was just big enough for the group to stand on. The guard pounded heavily on the iron-banded door blocking the passageway, waited a moment, pounded again. The sound of sliding wood and a face peering out suspiciously before shutting the peephole had the guard letting off. A few moments later, the door opened inward, and the group walked inside.

A large stone room, barely lit from smoking torches and huge braziers, greeted them. The head questioner made an elaborate bow to the elegantly dressed young man.

"My lord, a pleasure to serve you. What may a humble servant do for you? May I offer you a seat?" He gestured to an area barely seen.

It was a viewing platform encircled by a low balustrade and set with chairs, reached by a half-flight of stairs. The slaves tried not to look at what else was in the room. Two hulking, bald, heavily scarred men fed more wood into a brazier nearby. They turned mean, glittering eyes on the small party.

"Stay," the advisor curtly commanded his slaves and the guard, turning to Rablias. "A word with you in private."

"Of course. If you would please follow me?" He led the way past the men and a human wreck on the rack deeper into the gloom to a door hidden in shadows at one side of the platform. Once inside the small office, the head questioner turned with an inquiring look.

"The man I sent you. How is he doing?" Nicky asked.

"Very well, actually. Better than I had hoped for, of course. Per your instructions, I have not started on the physical torture yet. The plant matter—hallucinogens? as you call them—work quite well to make him see what is not there. May I hope you are here to change your orders, master?" the man groveled.

"Not yet. Has anyone come asking for him?" Nicky demanded.

"No, my master, no one. Do you expect someone?" he inquired

Why does the young man seem so unhappy with the news? wondered the questioner.

"Perhaps. You will send word to me immediately if anyone does, and detain them without explanation." Nicky instructed, receiving a bow in return. "Those two outside, they do their job well?"

"Yes, exceptionally well. I must say, it was a stroke of genius to remove their tongues."

"What has the king ordered for Jake?"

"Just the standard torture, my master. I doubt you would like what he confesses to as he names you as the source of all his misfortunes. His struggles excite Don and Jon. It's a shame he cannot write, or I could have him sign a confession," the man continued.

"I want him to suffer!" Nicky snarled.

Rablias hurried to bow. "As he is. Would you like me to edit what he has said?"

No, you fucking idiot! I want him to name me so His Majesty can order me exiled or killed. Wouldn't that satisfy the foreign whore? "Naturally, only we will replace my name with another's."

The man before him was startled and pursed his lips, "Shall I make a name up?"

"No." Nicky replied. "For now, say he either can't remember or never knew. I have to consider who would be the best name to proffer. Is there anything else I should know?"

"Very good. As to the other, my master, no, there is nothing. I have a list of prisoners who expired and what they confessed to. Would you like to look it over before I send my report to His Majesty?" Rablias held a scroll out, but the young man waved it away.

"Not right now; I'll inspect it before I go," Nicky replied. "I need to spend some time with our special guest. DiJinn wishes to observe your work on Jake. If he wants to participate, let him." Nicky smirked to himself.

Rablias barely kept from flinching; if the advisor found out he was disobeying his orders . . .well, it didn't bear contemplating. He would kill himself before Nicky could carry out his punishment on those who defied him. His only consolation was the prisoner was not likely to tell. "The guard and your other slaves? What shall I do with them?"

"Send the guard back up to his duties. As for my two slaves, they can wait here until I am done," Nicky commanded.

"Very well. Which room would you like me to place our guest in?"

"Have him brought to the chair in the little questioning chamber. I will want wine sent in, not the piss water you give to others. This is for my enjoyment."

"Certainly, my master. I will send word when things have been made ready, if you wish to wait here."

"Fine," Nicky replied curtly, settling down to poke through and read the papers covering a table as Rablias and his slave left.

* * *

The light hurt Mica's eyes after days of unending darkness, making everything a blur. His guards enjoyed starving him, only giving him an endless procession of putrid drinks. The sour-smelling liquid had some additives in it, powerful ones, which gave the immortal nightmares and hallucinations after finishing every cup. He tried to refuse, but the assistants would force a funnel in his mouth and pour the drink down his gullet, sending him off to sleep.

The three living immortals galloped away from the clearing in pursuit of the little boy. He was three furlongs ahead, and spurred his horse for all the animal was worth. The men knew the horses would not be able to sustain their pace for long.

The little boy swerved off the rutted dirt road and onto a deer path. The men followed, tree branches reaching out to snag their clothing or slap them across the face and chest. A particularly nasty branch whipped across Mica's face, leaving a long score he barely felt.

"He's heading for the mountains! Don't let him reach the rock scree!" Eron shouted.

Mica bent lower over his horse's neck, urging his mount on to greater speed. Nicky hit the lower slope at a flat-out gallop, and his tiring horse stumbled, almost crashing to its knees. Nicky whipped the animal viciously, making his mount leap forward in pain and terror. The beast was gasping and floundering as its hooves scrambled for purchase on the scree slope, but stumbled and collapsed, dead.

Nicky was tossed over the horse's head, slamming into the ground. He lay stunned, giving Mica time to catch up. Mica scrambled up to the little boy, sword drawn, as Nicky sat up. The boy's eyes grew large with terror while he crab-walked backwards as fast as he was able before gaining his feet.

The little boy gave a sob of fear. "Stay away from me! You're just like all the rest who want to see me dead!"

"You murdered, enslaved and tortured people! I would hunt down and kill anyone who did that, no matter their size or age." Mica waited for Colin and Eron to circle around, while he tried to reason with the boy.

"I'm just a little boy! I've never known any other way to be! Maybe if you had been my teacher, I would have been different. I can change! I can! Just give me a chance!" Nicky was begging and pleading. The snot ran from his nose, dripping down his face.

Mica would not give into the sheer terror the boy's face and voice wore. He had seen the performance too many times.

"I . . . I'm sorry," Mica's voice was hoarse, and he had to clear it. "I can't let you go."

Nicky started to flee when he was stabbed from behind. The little boy looked over his shoulder into Eron's cold, pitiless eyes.

The boy jerked and gasped in pain as Eron withdrew his sword. Time seemed to slow for him; his head didn't want to turn. He was falling forward as he looked at Mica. He caught the disappointment in the man's eyes as the ground rose up to meet him. Hands took hold of his shoulders, roughly turning him onto his back. One small hand still managed to grip his sword. Nicky could see the cloudless blue sky above him. A shadow fell over him. Mica's head came into view, as he placed his booted foot upon the boy's wrist to prevent him from using his sword. Nicky heard Colin start the words of the Undoing. He felt his soul gem placed on his chest, knowing the ritual mixture was next.

Nicky kept his eyes locked on Mica's and spat, "I curse you for this! Do you hear me? I curse you! May you never know happiness again. May everything you touch wither and die. May love flee from you! I curse you for all eternity!"

A sharp pain tore through Nicky, starting in his chest. The last thing he saw was his enemies' red-rimmed eyes.

Mica felt a chill race up his spine at the boy's words. "Your curses mean nothing to me," he told the body of his foe.

The immortal looked toward Colin and Eron. "Justice has been done. Our quest is ended. Will you not share one last drink, enjoy one last feast with me before we part ways?"

"Aye, we will," the two men answered.

* * *

Mica woke to find himself sitting chained to a wooden chair. The potion forced upon him left him too weak to struggle, much less hold his own head up. *If they would let me die, I would be reborn, whole and strong. I could overpower them and get out of here, find my brother. Colin—where is he? What happened to him? Was he captured too?*

The man didn't like this change. It meant his captors grew tired of whatever game they played and planned on doing something different. Mica sat, waiting for a voice, for his eyes to adjust, for anything. If they thought he would speak first, they were sadly mistaken. Gradually the room came into focus.

He was in a circular stone pit; all around him rose tier upon tier of stone seats. A stone ledge before him, and underneath it a sloping tunnel leading into blackness. A young man sat behind the broad ledge, a cup and a flagon beside his left hand. Illumination was provided by hundreds of burning oil lamps. Even though the light and shadows flickered, a chill ran through Mica. The double Nicky must be paying to act like him, sat before him. *He is not innocent. He too must be brought to justice.* It was eerie how closely he resembled the little boy. If Mica didn't know better, he'd say it was the boy, but that was impossible. Once an immortal, they could not permanently die by any mortal means, nor could they change height, weight, or age.

"You have something belonging to me. I want it."

"How much is he paying you?" Mica said, watching irritation briefly cross the young man's face. "It's not worth it. He'll kill you as soon as he no longer has use for you. Let me go, and I'll see to it the boy brings you no harm."

"Still playing the role of a noble knight," the man sneered. "And still you know nothing. You have something I want. You know what it is. Don't make me ask again."

"You don't want to do this. This is not a game to be played lightly. People die—"

"People always do, you stupid, pig-headed bastard! Tell me where it is!" The man shoved up, descending to the pit floor.

"I don't know what he promised you, what mad tales he told you, but none of it is true," Mica began as the man drew closer.

A glint of silver flashed. Mica felt a burning pain from a cut, blood slowly welled and dripped down his face. *Oh no! Not now, it's too soon for this. The cut will heal, he will see; then will come the fear, or greed, or both.*

"I asked you a question, and I want an answer. Where. Is. It?" The young man's gray eyes bored into his.

"Where is what?" If he acted stupid, he could try and work his hands free. Or a leg. He tested the straps, but there was no give.

The man only sliced his cheek again, above the previous cut. "Tell me. You are not stupid; you know of what I speak." The tone was testy.

Mica remained silent; he needed the soul-gem, he couldn't get rid of the kid without it. "How long has he been paying you? If you free me, I can pay you more."

His words only earned him another cut. It felt shallower than the last. He only hoped the man would grow tired. He looked bored as it was.

"I should let Don and Jon work you over." The mutter was contemplative.

Mica hoped the young man did; they would have to unchain him, and he could defeat them in unarmed combat. His tormenter gave the man before him a sharp look.

"Don't think you'll win your freedom when they go to move you. Do I look stupid to you?" he demanded.

No, you look like someone who doesn't have the stomach for this, Mica wanted to say, but kept the thought to himself. He stared at his tormenter, daring him to do more.

The young man brought the dagger up, placing the point underneath one of the chained man's eyes. "I don't know when you stole it, so maybe your time is almost up, or maybe it isn't. Either way, I want what you stole. You will tell me, or your life will be one unending torment."

Fear gripped Mica. The young man talked as if he knew the secret. Was it possible Nicky had promised to make him an immortal if he found the kid's soul-gem? He could not let it happen. His only consolation was the thoughts of his brother remaining free, and looking for him. He fervently prayed his rescue came quickly.

The dagger point pressed a little harder, drawing a trickle of blood and pain. Mica would not show concern. They stared at each other a moment more. The man turned and moved behind him.

"So be it. Don and Jon it is."

Mica sat still, listening as the man walked off, trying to figure out where he left. The room's echoes made it hard to pin-point. He sat there, the blood drying and his cuts healing, waiting for the next level to start.

* * *

Nicky stormed into the torture chamber, where the sheriff was chained belly down over a table, being assaulted with various objects. The big man screamed, struggling and hollering. Tears and snot ran down Jake's face, and the two mutes had an unholy light in their eyes, enjoying their work. Rablias sat off to one side, calmly sipping wine, a sheet of parchment, quill, and ink before him, waiting, no doubt, to record anything of note.

The young man put his back to the spectacle, but he could do nothing to shut out the noise. If he stayed long, he risked a bad flashback.

"Rablias, you will have my special prisoner put back, and triple his dose. I want him to be dosed every six hours."

The head questioner's eyes popped wide. "Tripled? Every six hours? But-but, my lord, will it not kill him?"

"Are you questioning me? Are you thinking I don't know more than you on the subject?" Nicky asked softly.

"No, my lord. I didn't mean . . ." He fumbled for words. "I have found no one who knows more about poisons and plant matter than you, Master. I only hope one day you will teach me more of your knowledge."

"Then do as I say, and don't ever question me on my methods again." The voice was chilly, yet strained.

Rablias bowed, keeping silent as the man turned and left the dungeon. The head questioner noticed the advisor refused to look at what went on behind him. Terror lurked in the back of those gray eyes, no matter how well he tried to hide it.

He has been assaulted before, and more than once if I'm right. What was he before he came to me? An orphan, he claimed, no doubt about that, but not a noble one. Oh no, never, no matter how often he professed otherwise. A poor one I should think, a peasant. He is no better than I. Rablias felt a smoldering resentment rise.

Everyone needed his skills, but no one wanted to associate with him. They treated him as if he were scum. Their manners changed once they became his prisoners. He made them regret every slight, every sneer, every snub; down here, he was king. The questioner waited for the two men to tire of their sport, and took a break to drink from a bucket of well water.

"Don, Jon, we will leave the sheriff to contemplate his folly of disobeying orders. In the meantime, Lord Nicky wishes his special prisoner to be returned to his cell and given his drink again. I shall make it up for you, and after, you may rest for an hour or two. I will send slave women to attend you."

The two men grunted in anticipation, their excitement straining the thin fabric of their pants as they waited for the concoction to be mixed up. Behind them, the sheriff moaned pitifully, barely conscious.

* * *

Nicky stood waiting for the door to the earl's house to open. He should not be made to wait outside like some beggar. If he wasn't admitted soon . . . well, he would make them pay somehow. Finally, a slave opened the door, informing Nicky the earl was not at home.

"It's not he I wish to see. Stand aside. I'm not some peasant to be made to wait outside. You will fetch the countess for me." He pushed his way inside, making for the reception room, calling back over his shoulder, "And send in food and drink for me."

The refreshments came before the countess, accompanied by her eldest daughter. She directed the slave to put the tray down and serve their guest as she welcomed the advisor before seating herself.

"Your pardons, Lord Nicky. My mother will be down directly. She has not been herself lately, not since the attacks happened."

The young man sneered at her, "I trust she was not harmed by those savages?" He had expressly ordered them to not unduly harm the noble women. Harm to women would be a sure way of getting the king to make finding them a priority.

"No, they said some harsh things, slapped her around a little. Forced her to show them where her jewels and my father's money was hidden." She hesitated and said, "The Lady Illyria was here, inquiring after us." Her nose wrinkled in distaste.

"Was she?" he asked as he ate some of the food, enjoying the look crossing the woman's face. *She may not listen to advice, but she is more a lady than you,* Nicky thought, knowing Lady Caroline slept with every high-ranking officer of the mostly defunct royal army.

"She has no manners, no class. How dare she call herself a lady? She's nothing but a common trollop who tricks the king. I could be your viscountess. Why do you want a slut like her?" She pouted, leaning over to show off her bosom, one hand sliding up the inside of his leg.

"Because she is filthy rich, gorgeous, and a soon to be reinstated duchess to whom the king listens, you stupid little fool," Nicky taunted.

Lady Caroline's hand suddenly stopped. "She defies you, laughs at you behind your back." The woman flounced against her chair, sullenly crossing her arms under her breasts.

"When His Majesty tires of her, she won't be laughing anymore, now will she?"

"You could kill her after you marry her and gain the title of duke. Then I could be your duchess. I'd never treat you in such a discourteous way." She leaned forward again to give him a view down the front of her gown.

The young man quaffed his wine, regarding her over the rim of the cup as she used a finger to trace the outline of the tops of her breasts. If he were going to do something like that, it wouldn't be for some whore with a couple of brats. The duchess, for all her faults, was relatively young. Her body, if his guess was correct, had never been ruined by childbirth. He was saved from having to reply by the entrance of her mother.

Nicky watched in amusement as Lady Caroline's hands flew away from her body. "Mama."

"Leave us. Your children have need of you, no doubt," the older woman commanded. She made her own obeisance to the advisor as her daughter stuck her tongue out behind her mother's back and fled. "Your lordship, to what do I owe the pleasure?"

"I have been given to understand by your charming daughter that the foreign woman has been here."

"She had the gall to ask after us before informing us of what the king commanded, and she no longer would have time for our lessons."

"How did they go?" he asked idly.

"Once a day she visited, as commanded, but for no more than an hour. She listened poorly. Half the time, I think she went over business in her head, like some man. I noticed no improvement. She is lacking in womanly graces."

"You should have done a better job of teaching them to her. Tomorrow starts the Harvest Week. I had better not be insulted by your poor educational techniques at our balls by her actions." He let it sink in, enjoyed watching her swallow her rage. "Has she given any clue as to what kind of entertainment she means to provide?"

"No." The countess's eyes were like chips of ice. "I tried to get her to confide in me, but she just laughed saying it was merely a hodgepodge of this and that and no doubt not as grand as anyone else's."

"I hardly expect it to be, now she has been tasked by our king with rebuilding the town."

If the countess's lips get any thinner, they'll disappear entirely, Nicky thought. "A disgrace. I would have thought you would be given command. She even asked my husband for help, and he agreed!"

He waved away her complaints. "Naturally I am guiding her, but I do have the entire kingdom to help run and can't take care of it personally," the advisor lied, knowing her ladyship would spread his lies to her cronies, taking delight in thoughts of what problems they would cause Lady Illyria.

Chapter Twenty-Two

The earl lay beside his wife, staring up into the darkness, as beside him, he knew she did the same. Most of their marriage was spent in silence. The marriage had been arranged, but he did his best to bring honor to the union as he did with all his business dealings.

His mind drifted off to their discussion the previous day.

"I will not have you throwing those women in my face; I understand as a man you have needs . . ."

"Elizabeth, please."

"Let me finish! I will bear your children. I will be your wife and a credit as your countess. But I will not be humiliated by your . . . your paramours. I expect—no, I demand—if you are going to indulge yourself, it is not with women from our own circle. Use the whores if you must, but I do not want to hear any whispers about your indiscretions, or I shall speak with your father on the matter."

"There will be no need. I will keep my 'activities,' as you call them, to the lower classes and out of the gossips' reach." He bowed stiffly to her and left the room. It was not so hard to give her the concession as she had so far been faultless and a proper countess.

"I will not have it, Chadrick. I will not! You promised you would not take lovers from our peers!" Her voice was shrill and full of fury, eyes wild and nostrils distended in rage. "It is bad enough we could not marry either of our daughters to Lord Nicky, but to have you support that woman so much! That tramp of a viscountess who is barely older than our own eldest daughter! The slaves can chatter of nothing else but how she has ensnared you with her wiles. And if they talk, imagine what our peers are saying! You promised!"

"There is nothing between us, I swear. I have kept my word to you."

"I don't believe you; if there were nothing going on, there would not be such gossip!"

His voice and demeanor became icy. "I would not think it of you, listening to what you call 'the conversations of the lower classes.'"

"I would not have to hear it if your decisions with our current king and his advisor had not disgraced us, put us out of royal favor."

"Enough, Elizabeth! I asked for the position! I have already said I have kept my word! What more do you want of me?"

"That you stop going to see her! She is nothing but a whore who got lucky enough to trick a nobleman into marriage. You tell His Majesty you have changed your mind."

"It is not so simple anymore, Elizabeth—"

"I don't care!" she shrilled. "If you have any honor left you will keep your promise to me. Or I . . . I will go to the king and see he puts a stop to it! I will see to it your son knows what kind of man his father really is!" She whirled around into her sitting room, slamming the door and would not speak nor admit him.

His wife's irrational jealousy of the admittedly gorgeous and younger viscountess made him have to tiptoe around his own house. He did not like being cast into the role of an honorless man when he had done nothing to deserve it. His thoughts of present and past unfolded in a jumble.

As he lay there, Sydney knew it was because of his radical views the Lady Illyria would support him. He didn't want unpleasantness in his own household. How could he be taken seriously with known dissent in his personal life?

He rolled over restlessly, his mind a welter. Another memory surged into his consciousness: the day, Alise made him the happiest man in the world.

"Oh, Chadrick, you say the most shocking things. Will your father not disapprove?"

"I am only the middle son, Alise; he cares about nothing but that I do my duty to my family name," he remarked savagely.

"We are lucky the king is so open-minded. They say some of his court want to squash views they feel may lead to treason." She peeked up at him from beneath her lashes. "I would hate to see you in a cell. I do not think it would agree with you."

"I am prepared to defend my ideas, though as an officer of standing with His Majesty's army, I should not speak such things too loudly." He paused, clearing his throat. "Alise, in another year I will have another commission. Would you—could you—consider being the wife of such a man?"

She blinked, and her hand trembled in his. "I thought your father did not approve of us."

"My mother will intervene on our behalf if it is what you desire. I cannot offer you anything as grand as being a marquis' daughter. But I pledge all I have will be dedicated to you and our life together, and any children we may be fit to be blessed with."

She hesitated a moment. "Yes. If our parents will consent to it, I will be happy to be the wife of a man who is only a second son to an earl, and an army man." Alise gave him a sunny, teasing smile.

In the dark and silent bed, he smiled at that happiest of days.

The screams coming from the birthing room reverberated throughout the house. There was the patter of footsteps, calls for more water as the midwife entered. She spared not a glance for the terrified father but followed the elder woman upstairs. It seemed hours passed; he dreaded the times when all became quiet, just as he dreaded the screams. His mother came downstairs at one point, and he rushed to her.

She gave his hand a kindly pat. "Calm yourself, son, have courage. All women endure this to bring life into the world. She is nearing the babe's birth, and it will get worse before it is over."

Tears, silent but huge, welled as he remembered the next moments, days, months.

He sobbed, great, gut-wrenching sobs as he lay prostrate beside the body of his wife and their short-lived son. Chadrick was barely aware of the whispers and careful footsteps of the slaves and his mother. His world had shattered. His beautiful, kind Alise, whom he had only had for three years, and their newborn son. Hands rubbed his back, his mother's voice was kind even as it was tearful.

"Chadrick, come now. She and the babe must be washed and made ready."

"No! No! Alise! Alise! Why? Why?" He clutched at the dead woman even as well-meaning slaves gently but firmly pried him away from the cooling bodies.

Chadrick stood pale and resolute before his father. "I will not!"

"You will do as I say, or I shall disinherit you! Your younger brother is dead, branded a traitor for killing the king. The name of Sydney has been soiled! I wish to the gods it was you—it should have been; yet it is your brother who lies dead!"

"I will not dishonor Alise's memory . . ."

"It is time you got over your grief. A year is too long for a woman who wasn't strong enough to bear a healthy son."

"How dare you speak of the woman I love that way? Disinherit me. It will be a welcome relief if it means I will not have to listen to you soil the memory of a wife who was good and kind."

He stood up from the desk where he'd been, alone, going over his accounts, as his mother entered the room. The woman, heavily covered and veiled, sat in an attitude of utter exhaustion in the room's only comfortable chair. "Please son, I am begging you. For my sake, make amends with your father."

"I'm sorry, Mother, but I cannot. He denigrates everything I hold dear, including the memory of Alise."

"Please, Chadrick, there have been rumors of assassins again."

"Yes, Mother, the army is already alerted."

"They say there is to be a celebration on the birth of a royal son. What better way to add to the festivities than to come back to us and ask your father's forgiveness?"

Rain fell like tears into the open grave. He stood ramrod straight, at attention across from his parents as the body of his eldest brother was laid to rest. As the grave was filled in, his mother crumpled to the ground. The old earl turned away from the display. Her body-slaves comforted her, his eyes met those of his middle son. They burned with hatred and rage. He dismissed the man and walked to his carriage.

"Mother, please, don't cry."

"You are the only son I have left. I can't even acknowledge you still live. I have buried two grown sons already. Please, Chadrick, I beg you, for my sake. Please speak with your father. Please don't let our family end with your father. Please."

"I have no desire to be earl . . ."

"I'm dying, Chadrick," his mother said quietly. "I would rest easier if I knew you and your father had mended the rift between you. That one son of mine at least is earl and continues the family name." She paused for breath. He could see she spoke the truth.

He bowed his head, not wanting the burden of grief and guilt his mother laid upon him.

"I know how immeasurable Alise was to you, but my son, it has been six years. I beg of you, a deathbed request, make amends with your father. Marry whom he chooses and continue the line. In your heart, keep her memory close."

"I cannot love another woman, mother."

"I am not asking you to. Do you think your father loved me when we married? No, it was arranged by our parents. He has treated me well and given me the sons I wanted. It has not been a bad life. It was a business arrangement which worked for the best."

"I cannot live and have children with a woman I cannot love. I do not love any woman enough to marry."

His mother broke down weeping, and left his spartan rooms. He tried to see her during her illness, but his father barred him from the house. She sent word she would not see him unless he made amends. Another year passed, his mother slowly wasting away, and finally he relented.

"Father."

"Have you come to your senses, boy?"

"I despise you and everything you stand for, but for my mother's sake only, I will do what she asks of me." He was pale, exhausted and sick at heart.

The old man grunted, spitting into the fire. "I expect you to sign a contract, and follow to the very letter of it. You will marry whom I choose, and you will plant children within her. Sons, preferably. When I die, if you have not disgraced me or her, and fulfilled the terms of our agreement, you shall inherit the earldom and all my lands and wealth."

Chadrick swallowed his anger and his bile. "Very well. Now may I see mother?"

* * *

Morning came too soon for the earl. He woke alone, washed, dressed, and headed to his office. He ordered breakfast and began to go over the accounts with his steward. He was determined to bury himself in work, ignoring his wife and her chilly silences which had only grown over the years. He despised his cowardice, and the life he was living. He felt himself growing cold, uncaring, turning into his father. Nothing brought joy to him anymore. If only the king would grant his request for divorce; he intended to try asking again.

Sydney realized his steward was looking at him oddly; the man had finished listing the losses they endured at the hands of the bandits. It was only some slaves, some wealth, a portion of his wife's jewels, some animals. He was still rich enough; what went missing would not matter, except for the jewels. His wife would demand he send out their personal guard to hunt the bandits down and get them back. Or barring that, buy her new ones.

"I'm sorry, Raynauld, the affair with the sheriff..." He trailed off.

"It's about time His Majesty learned the whole of it, but is it true? You volunteered to help train and rebuild the office?"

"Yes, much to the displeasure of my lady wife."

His steward hesitated the barest instant. "I imagine she is worried she will lose you. Life will be harder for her and the children."

"Hah! She would welcome my death. She could find the proper husbands for our children without me to embarrass her."

"I think you are too hard on yourself, m'lord. I remember when you were a young man, full of dreams and the courage to go after them. It's a shame what your father did to you, m'lord. Pardon my liberties; he is long dead, and you are still letting him win, letting him bully you."

The earl stared at his desktop as the man's words penetrated; was it true? He thought back to his first wife, knowing she would be ashamed of the man he had become. He wasn't sure he remembered how to be the person he had once been. The person Alise had been proud of.

"Shall I give you the report on your farms, m'lord?"

"They are still producing? The bandits have not raided them?"

"Yes, they are still producing, and no more raids than usual."
Raynauld stood waiting.

Finally, the earl said to his desktop, "Order my horse saddled. I'm going out."

"Very good m'lord. Shall you be wanting any guards today?"

"No, send word when my mount is ready."

* * *

Sydney left the merchant's hall, oddly pleased with himself. He negotiated for new weapons and armor on behalf of the soon-to-be-reformed sheriff's office at reasonable enough prices. He was just remounting his horse when he saw Lord Nicky and Lady Illyria riding toward him. They were surrounded by the advisor's personal guard; neither looked to be pleased with the other.

The advisor ignored him. She acknowledged his greeting with a graceful nod of her head and a smile. He watched them pass, noting her riding costume was the one about which his wife had fulminated: the leather pants and long, full-skirted coat. He wondered if her ladyship had the intelligence and wits to outthink Nicky. The lady had such a strong will he couldn't conceive of her bending to anyone's demands, least of all a man like Nicky.

She would need to be more careful, he thought. Her appointment by the king had no doubt already incurred the young man's wrath and would bring pain and suffering down on her head. Sydney turned his horse toward the slave markets; the men there owed him a few favors. He had an idea on how he could collect.

"Hahahahaaaa!" The slaver sprayed crumbs as he laughed. "No disrespect meant, your lordship, but you're crazy! I know as well as you that His Majesty never gave no such orders."

"That might have been true before, but with this new attack on his person, he is determined to see the sheriff's office set to rights with men loyal to him. Just imagine who might seize power if he were murdered because you refused to fulfill such a little request."

The slaver blanched, whining. "M'lord, fighting men are worth a lot of coin. I would be taking a terrible loss, and well, what with winter coming on and these raids by the bandits..."

"You will have earned His Majesty's thanks and gratitude for doing your kingdom a great service," the earl replied.

"That don't keep a man warm in winter, or put food on his table." The slaver was stubborn now. "No, m'lord. I'm sorry, but I can't help you."

"You will not have a business when the bandits come back and destroy the town. Who will buy your slaves then, when no one has the coin? You will take a loss just trying to move them to another town with buyers. I am not asking for all your fighters, only the six whom I deem best for the job. Two from each of the slavers."

He waited a beat, adding, "I am giving you the chance to make of them a royal gift before they are seized by the king's orders. Which would you prefer?" The earl lied without remorse, knowing it to be for a good cause. He knew the man before him would believe him; Sydney was known to be a man of principle.

The man before him gave in with bad grace. "Very well. Come with me, and we will find your six slaves."

It took what was left of the morning, but he got what he wanted. Saizar looked up in surprise when he came in with the slaves. "My lord?"

"New recruits, willing to sign and swear their lives to obey and uphold the laws of the kingdom upon pain of a prolonged death should they disgrace the badge."

Saizar looked over the men in silence, scrutinizing them. He took each one to the side, questioning him privately, before addressing them as a group. "I am your commander. You will obey my orders and only my orders or I shall hand you over to the head questioner. I will tell you now why you are the only men here: because the last sheriff was corrupt, along with his men. They are now in the dungeons, cursing the day their mothers bore them."

He paused to let that sink in, continuing, "We will train together, eat together, live together. You will treat each citizen of this town with courtesy and respect, no matter their station in life. You will not use your position to force people to pay you, whether money or food or drink, or have sex with you. When you are on duty, you will be sober. You will be on time. You will do all I ask of you."

The men continued to watch him in silence. "When you have passed your training and trial period, you will take your oaths to remain lawmen, thus gaining your full freedom. If you have problems, speak now, and you will be returned to the slavers. At any point should you attempt to deceive me, and it will be your death."

The earl stood off to one side, watching the faces of the men, hoping, and praying he was still a good judge of character. The men eyeballed each other. One spoke up.

"And when we're off duty? Will we be allowed to drink and visit the whores?" The tone was challenging.

"If you pay for it, and do not demand it be given to you. We are under most intense scrutiny from the king and his advisor. They are expecting you to fail; do not give them a reason to doubt you further. We are not here to start fights, nor show we are the best fighters. We are here to enforce the king's peace."

"What kind o' pay are we to be receiving?" the man who had asked about the whores inquired.

"A pittance while you train, more when you take your oath and join fully. A raise, should you merit it, each year thereafter."

There was some grumblings. The men knew they could have made more in the fighting pits, if they lived. Here, they were being promised liberty without almost having to die for it a lot sooner.

"Step forward and sign here or make your mark if you agree to these conditions."

There was more silence, but the man who had asked the questions was the first to come forward; after that, the rest followed. The earl had never been inside the sheriff's barracks. He was surprised at the filth. The army kept much cleaner quarters. By the time each man claimed a bed, Raynauld was at the back with some slaves and food for the new recruits.

The earl managed to conceal his wince at dirty plates, only gave a slight pause at drinking from the equally filthy cups, joining in the new meal. It was eaten in silence, each man eyeballing his new brother, or Saizar, or the earl. When the simple but filling meal was over, the men had their first task.

Saizar set them to cleaning out the dormitory. There was some grumbling before the men slowly got down to the job. The earl stood by the only stair and watched, conversing with the new sheriff in low tones.

"They will rebel, sooner or later."

"I am expecting them to, my lord. After I defeat the first man, the rest will be glad to do what I ask of them."

"You think you will win? What if it isn't just one man, but two or three or all of them?" Sydney inquired.

"I have known men like them before, and lived with them, too. I remember all too well how to handle them." He gave a grim smile. "It is food and drink I worry about. We used to have a cook after a fashion, but it was an old woman and she died. After that, we had to fend for ourselves. I do not wish for these men to do that. I think it would be too onerous to deal with and bring about rebellion sooner, but I have no skill with food."

"Hire someone."

"The former sheriff hid the coins he received each month for our pay and upkeep. I have searched everywhere and cannot find it. I do not even know what kind of budget he was getting. I can find no papers from His Majesty, no charter, nothing. I am loath to go begging after what happened; what if he refuses?"

"I negotiated with the merchants to supply arms and armor at a reasonable price. They will bill you; you in turn will pass it off to the royal treasurer to be paid. The same arrangements can be made with the butcher, and farmers." Sydney was happy to solve these problems.

There was the barest hint of displeasure. "What if they don't get paid? The townspeople will consider me no better than Jake. I shall lose my life and those of these men for something I could have prevented."

"Such documents must be here, hidden behind a loose floorboard or some such thing. You will have to search in what spare time is provided, without the men knowing."

"I do not see a lot of that in my future," Saizar remarked sourly.

"I will train them starting at first light; look then."

The man mulled this over, only breaking his silence to say a few harsh words to break up a blossoming fight. "Your lordship, not to question you, but why are you doing this? Why dirty your hands like a common man, risking the displeasure and scorn of your peers?"

The earl took a breath in, meaning to deny the question, but the answer came out. "I was happiest when I was an army man. I had a wife

I loved, honest respect from the men under me, a place I had earned which was my own. A place my father didn't buy for me and couldn't threaten to take from me. I had freedom. Even though I was bound by rules and regulations, it was still freedom."

"Not the wife you have now?" the other man delicately probed.

Alise. Dear, sweet, gentle Alise. Will you like me better now? "No." His tone let the other man know he shouldn't ask any more questions on the subject.

They stood in silence, watching the new men scrub and clean as the sun sank, the room growing darker. It was near midnight when the earl started for home. The streets were empty, the sunset curfew having cleared them. He encountered one of the palace guards on patrol; though they grumbled, they let him pass. He was almost at the bridge when a dark horse and rider came down, turning toward the forest.

There was no mistaking the horse; he knew horseflesh, and whose mount was whose just from the profile. That was the duchess's mount.

What is she doing out at this hour, cloaked and hooded in such a way? Maybe someone is borrowing her horse? He didn't think it boded well, and doubted that anyone but she was able to ride the stallion. It was also none of his business. He toyed with the idea of stopping at the Silver Thorn until noticing the shut gate.

* * *

The earl snuck out of his mansion just past daybreak, *like a common thief!* His wife had already moved into another bedroom, he noted. The cook had a pot of porridge ready, loaves of bread, hard-boiled eggs, and half a barrel of ale. The meal should make the men happy, he thought as his grooms loaded up a packhorse. The town was just waking up as he came down off the bridge. The new recruits were in the yard dunking their heads in a barrel of icy water.

The food was welcome but met with suspicion.

"I thought we were not to accept bribes, food or drink from others?" the quarrelsome man from yesterday questioned.

Saizar came into the still-filthy eating area in time to hear the reply. "We have no cook as yet. The earl has consented to gift our endeavors, as has Lady Illyria. This is part of a tax the king has ordered the nobles to pay to help get our numbers back up. In addition, the earl was an army man. He will be helping me train you until we can get a new master of arms."

The earl managed to keep his face neutral. He knew the tax section to be a lie, wondering who had thought it up. Something told him her ladyship was behind the latest ploy. He wondered how she was going to get Lord Nicky go along with it as Saizar sat, helping himself to a share of the food and drink. Sydney joined them. It was another mainly silent meal; after finishing, all the men trooped out into the dirt practice yard. Under a crude wooden shed was a pile of mismatched weapons, armor, saddles, bridles and other detritus. The men got to work sorting it out, tidying up before Saizar unlocked the door to the armaments room. He brought out wooden practice shields, swords and quilted jerkins.

The earl dearly wanted to know where it had all come from. He had a bad feeling Lady Illyria had done some raiding herself, or ordered it done.

"Line up, choose a partner. I want to see how you hold a weapon, and how you use it. This side will defend, the other attack. Now!"

Immediately, the yard rang to the clack of wood on wood, the occasional grunt as a blow landed. Sydney walked around the perimeter of the yard, watching the men. Three had some skill, one had none at all, and the other two middling. After a good bout, he called a halt.

"You three, what are your names and where did you learn to fight?"

"I'm Gordy. I was in the army across the sea. We were defeated in battle. My company was taken hostage, marched to the coast, then sold into slavery. We were bound for the fighting pits when pirates sank the ship. I was resold here." A man in his late twenties, with short blond hair, blue eyes, corded with muscles and a few scars.

"I'm Toras. My father was a slave; I was born a slave. My master saw I liked to fight, so he trained me to be one of his guards. He was betrayed, I ran—not very far, it seems, as I am still a slave." He spat upon the ground. The man was built like a bull, thick upper body and neck, massive thighs and legs yet with a particular lightness on his feet all the same.

"I'm Guts. I haven't got any other name. I was a butcher. My town was overrun by bandits and slavers. I was sold, same as the others, to fight in the pits. I managed to survive, but my owner lost all his money.

We were all sold again to slavers who brought us here." He was in his thirties, thinning brown hair and muddy brown eyes.

"You three are good and will get better. Guts and Toras, I want you to work with the two who are middling, help make them better. Gordy, you will work with the one who has no skill, so he may benefit the most from your knowledge," Sydney instructed them before turning to the three remaining men.

"And what are your names?"

"I am Merrit. I was just a simple farmer before my crops failed and I joined the army. I was not with them long before our company was ambushed. Those who could fight were killed, and those of us like me who hadn't real skill yet and managed not to get dead were enslaved and sold." He had long black, wavy hair and dark eyes.

"I'm Cregen, his brother," he pointed to Merrit. "We joined the same army, same company, same story." His hair was short and curly, and he had his brother's eyes.

"I'm Frog. I was just a simple fisherman. Pirates captured me one day, selling me to slavers. They called me Frog 'cause they liked to make me jump and take orders." He was tall, with sandy hair and brown eyes.

"From now on, these will be your sparring partners unless we are learning melees or combinations. Those of you with longer hair, cut it short like Gordy's. Long hair is a liability in a fight. Your opponent can grab it, like this." Sydney grabbed Merrit's hair, yanking his head back, putting his dagger to the man's throat. "You will be dead, just as quickly. Keep it short." He released the now-scowling man, continuing to address them.

"You will keep clean, both your person and your clothing. I want no stink that could warn others you are nearby. Do not give them any advantage which can be prevented. Can anyone ride?"

Gordy was a decent rider, and the farmers after a fashion, but the other three not at all. "We will learn riding, and one other weapon to start: either bows or staves. It is not safe to rely on one weapon only, not when your enemies are bandits."

"Lastly, we will work on our stamina, and our letters."

"What do you mean, our letters? Nothing was said about that." Merrit was still smarting and belligerent over having been used as an example.

"The king and his advisor or other officials will often give you warrants, judgments, writs of arrest to carry out. We will be more effective at our jobs if we all know what they say. It will lessen our chance of being ill-used for personal vendettas." The last part the earl tacked on. He could not say what made him do it.

Historically, the Macinas sheriff's office and its men had been little more than uneducated brutes, concerned with using fists and weapons to keep the peace. The earl made the men line up single file, running around the yard carrying shields and swords. He mentally reminded himself to find logs for the men to carry on their backs, boots and proper clothing. He ran them until they dropped, to see who could last the longest.

To his surprise, it wasn't Gordy, though the former soldier gave a good attempt; it was Frog. Around noon, one of his slaves came in the yard with another packhorse loaded with a hot midday meal, along with a letter for him.

"Put your practice gear back; dunk your heads and wash your hands before eating. After dinner, we will do more."

The men trudged wearily to put their gear back, then to cool off before heading inside to eat. Sydney took the letter, asking as he did, "Are you to wait for a reply?"

"Yes, m'lord," the slave replied.

Chadrick broke the seal, read the brief, furious communication from his wife. She was demanding he return home at once, to quit avoiding her as they had much to discuss. They were due at the baron's hunt on the morrow. He crumpled the note, fighting his rage.

Why would she not understand his endeavor? These men were needed, as was he. They may not like him; they might, in fact, despise him, but all the same, they listened to what he had to say. He turned to the waiting slave.

"You may inform the countess, I am busy. I will be home when my work here is done for the day." A thought crossed his mind. "Before you do, send word to the duchess—er, Lady Illyria—asking if she can see me on a business matter later today."

The slave bowed, barely able to keep the look of pity off his face. It infuriated him further. Even his slaves thought he was ineffectual, did they? The earl turned, entering the still-filthy eating area. He took what food was left, brooding into his ale.

* * *

After lunch, Chadrick set the men to cleaning the downstairs. There was more grumbling.

"To stay clean, you must live in clean areas. We are not beasts, we are men." He didn't mention it let him have a better view of what needed repairs.

The men kept at it—the earl even pitched in, helping take out soiled rushes and building a bonfire to burn them, carting buckets of clean water in and dirty water out. He didn't know how long they worked, but soon he was aware of Saizar beckoning him over.

"Your lordship! I shudder to contemplate what will happen if your peers saw you laboring like a commoner."

"It is honest work, of a kind I had almost forgotten how to do." He wiped his hands clean, asking, "Have you found anything yet?"

"Yes, thank you. The sheriff seemed distrustful. I found hiding spots all over his room."

"It is your room now," Sydney reminded him.

The man gave a wan smile. "And in need of scouring as badly as this one. I wonder if I might continue imposing upon you with the subject of these papers?"

"That bad?"

"I'm afraid so."

"After supper," Sydney replied. Soon the area behind the partition was as clean as it was likely to get. Supper was roasted pike, mashed turnips, brown bread, and ale.

"I am sure you must be tired. It has been a long two days. We will not train tonight," Saizar announced.

"Does this mean we may go outside the barracks?" Merrit asked.

"You may for a few hours; however, we resume training on the morrow. I want no drunk or hungover men; therefore, you will not be receiving coin tonight."

There was some grumbling as the men filed out slowly, and their voices filtered back inside, suddenly excited. Saizar and Sydney rose, entering the small front room. Lady Illyria had just entered, her gold brocade finery and white lace putting the shabby sheriff's office to shame.

"Lord Chadrick, Sheriff, have you time to meet with me?"

"Yes, of course, my lady. This way, if it pleases you." Sydney stood aside to allow her passage.

The new recruits bowed, feasting their eyes as she passed. The door shut off their mutterings.

Saizar spoke, "If you had need of words, my lady, you had only to send for me and I would have attended you."

She waved it away. "I had business in town; it was no hassle to stop on my way back." She turned to Sydney. "I'm afraid your lady wife is in a terrible temper, sir." Her eyes twinkled mischievously.

"She is not satisfied with my offer to help train the men," the earl said.

"Nor with me, truth be told. I made a poor student. Or mayhap the lessons she had to teach are so deadly dull." She looked around a moment, sitting as both men winced. Her dress would be filthy when she stood; dirt still lay upon the furniture.

"Saizar, have you discovered how much the crown pays?"

"That is what I was about to discuss with his lordship." He paused; she had shown to be trustworthy thus far, and he only hoped he could continue to place his faith in her. "It seems Jake was keeping the bulk of the money for himself and two of his closest henchmen." He told them how much the crown provided.

"It is a decent amount. Why do you not look happy?" she asked.

"It seems Jake spent more than he should have, most of it on personal items for himself and various cronies. What he didn't spend, he forced the merchants to give him." He paused, frowning. "Jake couldn't read or write, it seems, and possessed a crude understanding of numbers. It is Geoff, one of the former second-in-commands, who recorded all this. Let me bring in what I have found; you will understand better."

Once the man left, Sydney turned to Lady Illyria. "I trust my lady wife did not take out her displeasure with me on you?"

She gave a smirk which set his belly fluttering. "Do you think I care what she thinks? She can prattle on at me about what a lady does and doesn't do, can and can't wear, as long as she likes. I will not change who and what I am because it won't fit her narrow definition of a true lady's nature." She gave him a searching look.

"I wanted to warn you, she is determined to turn your children and our peers against you for what you do here. The marquis no doubt will go along with it, and some of the women, a few of the lesser nobles who think it will curry favor."

Her words left a bitter taste as of anise in his mouth. He couldn't help but ask, "Why do you tell me?"

"I see a man of principle and honor being mocked and torn down. Being forced to be and act as someone he isn't by a woman who should be giving support. If you are truly happy turning into that person, I am sorry for you. If you aren't, I want to let you know there are still some people in this world who will stand by you and your decision to remain true to yourself."

The earl felt his throat grow tight; her pity, if that's what it was, was not what he really wanted. He nodded once, sharply, and swallowed. "Thank you. If I may, what is the talk I have heard about gifts for the sheriff's office and a new tax? I know of none."

Her smile was naughty. "I think Saizar will be glad for it. Sheriff Jake was not the type of man to spend the crown's coin on expenses for the crown's men."

"I fear for you," he blurted out, laying his hand over hers. "Lord Nicky will not like these developments. New taxes must be approved by him first. He will hear of this if he hasn't already."

"Leave his rages to me; he will let it pass." There was a dark undercurrent to her tone, which gave him pause.

"Is it true, the rumors you were taught swordplay? It wasn't just a story you told us at dinner to amuse?"

"Why? Sydney, are you looking for a sparring partner? I would have thought teaching the new recruits challenge enough." Her lips curved into another of her wicked smiles.

He blushed! What was wrong with him? "I . . . no, of course not! You should not suggest such things."

She gave a shrug, removing her hand from under his. "As you wish. Do you plan on teaching the men to ride? I have horses as well, to go with the other items my slaves brought."

"Surely you didn't buy all this? 'Tis a costly gift."

"Let us say the bandits donated it, and leave it at that." Her eyes gleamed in amusement at some private joke. Her head turned toward the door to the back, as Saizar entered with hands full.

The earl was both glad and irritated with the man. He still had questions to ask of her. Saizar set down the chest, opening the broken hasp. He began to draw out scrolls and sheets of paper until the table was heaped over. "This is all of it; it covers everything: who joined, what they were to be paid, how much was spent and on what."

The two nobles reached for scrolls. Her Ladyship seemed to skim through each one. "He did spend a small fortune, it seems, on women and wine, a fine suit of leather armor, a horse, a very nice sword." She set down a scroll. "But nothing on jewels or ornaments, so they must have been gifts, or bribes. I will send someone to speak with the dungeon master; his sword and armor should be returned here as it is by rights property of this office."

"Allow me; you should not subject yourself to the place." the earl replied.

"It is not a problem. I have already been warned Rablias is a toad of a man with an inflated sense of self-worth," she murmured as she read another scroll.

They read a while more, Saizar pointing out things he thought they should know. Finally, the bulk of the documents had been gone through.

The earl began, "You need to feed the men. They need better equipment. Winter is coming, which means you have need of heat. You need to purchase a slave who can cook, a few to keep the building clean. Men, not women, so the recruits are not tempted to rape them."

"Or you could ask for them as gifts, as part of the new tax," Illyria said. "Remember, there are more than a few nobles and merchants bankrupt by the raiders. They will have to get rid of what they can."

"I do not think they will be pleased to give something over for nothing—not if they can sell," Sydney pointed out.

"They will, especially when they find out by donating to the new sheriff's office, they can get a cash refund from the royal treasury for the market value of the goods."

"But His Majesty," both men spoke at once. "Lord Nicky—"

"Is an advisor only. The final decision does not rest with him but with the king. Leave our monarch to me. It will do him good, providing for his people for a change, and not wasting the royal treasury on harem girls, entertainments, and food." She drew a scroll out of the pouch at her waist, handing it to Saizar.

He unrolled the parchment, reading, letting out a low whistle, looking up at her in awe. "This is . . . is more than I had dared hope for. How did you manage to convince them to do this so swiftly?"

She gave her mysterious smile again. "I have my ways; I can be very persuasive when I want."

Chadrick took the scroll. Everything from household goods, to slaves, to other odds and ends had been pledged. Every noble listed, from the poorest up to the richest, including her. He noted the marquis' name, nearly laughing aloud at what she had managed to winkle out of him.

"I trust this helps?"

"Yes, immensely. Thank you." Saizar bowed deeply.

"Good, I leave the merchants up to you." She stood, as did the men. "The king, it seems, still plans on holding the Harvest Ball festivities, and they start tonight. A week of events. I understand merchants are still pouring in for it. If you will excuse me, I have to finish my plans for my part of the event."

Saizar winced. "There will be many drunken fights, and no lawmen to break it up, save me."

"Oh, the palace guard will be patrolling. I have heard they hate it and are grumbling over it," Illyria replied. "I will leave you to your planning. Will you walk me out, Lord Sydney?"

He bowed to her. "Yes, of course." They left Saizar shaking his head, trying to put the records in some semblance of order.

Outside, he saw an enclosed carriage in the colors of another noble, the coat of arms scratched out and all the slaves which went with it. He saw a driver, a dozen outriders, and three footmen, "What is this?"

"I had more than one reason to visit our fellow nobles. We are a much smaller, and poorer bunch. I bought what I was able to help out, but I'm afraid, instead of being properly grateful, most are resentful."

"The raids do not seem to have touched you. You have garnered many favors and power at court in a short time," Sydney answered, troubled.

She bowed her head. "Understood. I try not to flaunt my wealth, but when all I had was stolen or lost, I must needs replace it; what can one do? Money and jewels were all I managed to save."

"They do not remember, not with the way you have grown and prospered. Most people would not be able to recover as swiftly as you."

"I will try to be more inconspicuous, but I'm afraid I am not much good at it." She gave him a smile. "Goodbye, Sydney. Shall I see you at the baron's hunt this weekend? If not, I do hope you can take time out of training to attend my event. It will be the last before the closing ball."

He helped her up into the carriage, not wanting to let go of her hand, but forcing himself to relinquish it all the same. "I will be there; I will be at as many as I can. My wife will expect it of me, and hopefully it will help our relationship."

"Until then." She signaled to the driver. They rumbled off.

Chadrick watched until the carriage turned out of sight before making his way back inside. He would be damned if he returned home before the festivities started.

Chapter Twenty-Three

The sounds of music drifted down the night street across the bridge. The masked reveler presented his invitation, entering the elegant mansion. Naked slaves held platters of elaborate painted, colorful masks for those who had none. The rooms lit by a small fortune in candles and oil lamps. He knew his wife and children were somewhere in the throng as they had taken the carriage, arriving well before him. He was hoping to avoid them. Slowly he cruised the rooms; there were more people than just the nobles. The earl surmised the marquis had invited the prosperous merchants, a move out of keeping with his nature. He wondered why as he scanned the crowd. The earl knew from past events the marquis would have a space set aside for those wishing to gamble, a buffet, and a room for those wishing to dance. Perfumed colored oil lanterns were strung both inside and outside. Incense smelling of musk, poppies and some unknown scent drifted thickly everywhere. The dancing was held out under the stars and the cool night air.

"It's disgusting the way they flaunt themselves, even after the raid."

"I don't see it's stopped you from attending."

"Free food and drink? A chance to win some money from these pigs? Use 'em while I can, I say."

A couple of men burst into raucous laughter as the earl passed them, heading down the stone terrace steps. The marquis had been demanding a costume masque, and due to the raid, he had gotten it after a fashion. Those townspeople with coins or fabric left went into a frenzy. Any female halfway decent with thread and needle spent the intervening days sewing feverishly for those fortunate enough to score invitations. The result was a jester's motley of fabrics and colors. Since not everyone had enough of coin or fabric, more skin was shown. Bizarre styles, based on the imaginations of the wearer and what cloth they did have to use, dominated, no doubt courtesy to the leading influence of some of Lady Illyria's outfits.

"Did you see what she had on? She looked a whore!"

"She has the body for it. I wish I had half her nerve; the king is loath to leave her side!"

"Please, what good is it if she only ends up as a mistress and not a queen?"

"She will still have many favors granted."

"The king! That woman has all the men, married and single panting after her! It's disgusting!"

"My dear, most of them look half-clothed!"

The women cackled. He noted bare shoulders, arms, legs and stomachs abounding on both men and women. He knew his wife was no doubt hating it. She had dragged out gowns from years past to clothe herself and her daughters in, much to her offspring's dismay. A woman passed by, wearing a sheath woven of reeds and grasses, long ropes of acorns fashioned into a necklace and bracelet. Leaves made up a flat hat and mask. Her partner had thin shingles of wood strung together to form short pants and a sleeveless shirt, with a collar of wooden nails sticking up. He blinked, realizing they were not the exception. If it could be used to create clothing, it had been.

The earl became more intrigued; he knew of only one noblewoman bold and mad enough, who would deliberately start a trend by wearing something to set the town talking. He knew he saw her when a flash of bright, bold red passed by in a new dance pattern. Across the space, he could see his wife's mask bobbing amid a knot of her cronies. No doubt she was busy trying to ruin the reputation of her enemy.

Lady Elizabeth and her friends, in protest, wore heavy velvet and brocade fashioned into shapeless robes. They had wrapped matching material around their heads, over the ears, and under their chins so that no hair showed. Over this, the women draped thin white veils to help hide their faces and wore soft thin white deerskin gloves. Sydney wanted to tell her it was a lost cause whilst her enemy had the king's attentions.

He looked back to the dance area, where people formed two lines, men and women facing one another, arms extended overhead, clapping hands. Females had their right leg extended out to the side, men their left. They shimmied forward four steps with arms at shoulder height, hands pointed outward; then the parallel lines turned so the woman was in front, the man behind. They slid to the left a few paces before the dancers pushed off with their right in a kind of hop, landing, feet together, arms still at shoulder height and hands clasped. Next, the men lifted the women up, half-turning with them, as they came down. The women kept their right arms slightly out to their side, left above their heads in their partner's clasp, and turned in a circle until they faced the men. The dancers then brought their hands overhead and clapped again as the women slid to the opposite side in an X pattern and a new partner. The women whirled left around the men behind them and then around to their right before beginning the whole series of steps again.

It put the woman in red directly in front of him. His eyes widened behind his plain black mask at her outfit. He felt an unexpected stirring in his loins. She wore a three-quarters face mask in the shape of a fierce fiery half peacock/half eagle glittering with jewels, feathers dyed to mimic flames. The feathers at her temples and sides of the mask curved downwards to her shoulders with ropes of rubies intertwined. Other feathers curved back from the brow to halfway behind her head. Her hair had been bundled into an elaborate knot at the back of her head, with tendrils dangling loose below. Somehow her dresser had colored strands of the hair red.

The rest of her garment couldn't quite be called a gown, at least not a proper one. A single strap about the neck held the brief top up along with ropes of rubies, topazes and amber beads around the tops of her surprisingly well defined arms. What looked like fiery feathers scantily covered her breasts. A small swatch of sheer fabric began under the right breast to angle across her body, around the left side and back, attaching to the right hip. From there, it turned into more feathers riding scandalously low, held in place by a peacock eye emblem and gold chains wrapping around her slender waist, leaving toned stomach muscles bare. The opaque portion of the skirt extended only a hand span past the joining of her thighs, from there, it became sheer veils of jeweled fabric, which made her legs appear wreathed in flames. To complete the shocking ensemble, she wore jeweled chained sandals. She had lacquered her fingernails and toenails to match.

The skin behind the generous eye-holes of the mask was painted to blend, giving her a fierce yet still exotic look. If this were Lady Illyria, soon to be made duchess, she was ensuring she would be talked about in the weeks to come unless something more shocking happened. When it came time to shimmy, her hips rolled and wiggled in a way never seen before, setting her skirt to flowing, her stomach muscles to flexing. The men whooped appreciatively. She gave Sydney a look as bold as her outfit. He had not participated in dances since the last harvest ball, and he took a moment to recall the steps, before taking the place of another dancer far back enough that when they changed partners she would come to him.

The woman he was with had the accents of a merchant's wife. "Can you believe the nerve of some women? We all heard the marquis say he wanted us to wear costumes to this mask, but no one believed him."

Her outfit reminded him of an owl, and her size as a fluffy example of the bird. He barely managed to lift her off the floor. For all her criticisms, he noticed all the females attempting to emulate the hip-shaking shimmy of the red woman.

The earl caught a glimpse of his wife and her cronies, no doubt glaring out at the dancers as he passed. He was sure she recognized him as his outfit had not changed, only his mask, but he ignored her. After another round, the red lady whirled around to his side. He kept silent, letting his gaze bore into hers, she returning his stare with a knowing one of her own. When she was in front, the lady pressed against him as they slid left. On the lift, Sydney let his hands caress her waist, gripping firmly; she felt like a feather. For one instant, they pressed tight, front to front, before she moved to put space between. Her spicy, musky perfume invaded his senses, and he breathed deep.

His turn with her was fast coming to an end, and he was reluctant to have it end. As she made to move off to another partner, she gave Sydney a naughty wink and a smile. Sydney felt his blood pound. He took in a deep shaky breath as his new partner presented herself. If he didn't cool off, everyone would see how she had affected him. Mercifully, the dance came to an end shortly thereafter. Men and women bowed or curtsied to whomever they ended with. The musicians struck up another tune and people flowed, some leaving the floor, others switching partners or joining the dance.

Sydney left, stopping to greet men or women he thought he knew, chatting with them. It mattered not who they were; the main topic was Lady Illyria and rumors of what she had managed to advise the king to do for the town.

"Aranthus has told me the king intends to reinstate that foreign woman's title at the royal ball for all she is doing for the country."

"Lord Nicky is furious, I hear, but the king threatened to fire him if he spoke one more word against the new tax reliefs."

"I, for one, am glad of them; with winter coming, it will be a struggle just to keep food on the table. My neighbors are still without a dwelling, and though I wish I could help, my own is barely large enough for my own family."

"I foresee a lot of deaths from starvation and cold."

"Baroness Rothsbury has been placed in charge of some public works project, along with her husband and Baron Stavic."

"It must be a new experience, having the ear of a peer in power." Raucous laughter followed the words, the earl joining the group.

"What do you think, good sir?"

"Time will tell, as will the new band of sheriff's men."

"Yes, I heard the most appalling rumor, my lord. Earl Sydney is said to have all but moved into the barracks. Not only training these slaves, but laboring with them like a commoner. Tell me it's not true! It's bad enough we have to suffer slaves in the role the corrupt sheriff and his men once occupied, but to free them, as well? I like it not."

"I am afraid, gentlemen, for the moment, I have taken on the role," Sydney replied gravely.

Shocked exclamations greeted his admission. "But why?"

"Preposterous! If your father were still alive, he would be ashamed."

"As you know, Sir Dalton, my father never approved of anything I did until I married Lady Elizabeth."

"Let us hope she can weather the taint. If I were you, my lord, I wouldn't spend so much time there. Forgive me my boldness, but the town talks, and not in a good way. If I hadn't served with you in the royal army, I would think you lost all honor."

Sydney bowed. "I thank you for your warning and wise counsel. I will take heed. If you will excuse me, I must make my obeisance to our king."

They bowed back. He left them, worming his way through the people in the gardens. Slaves circulated with trays and amphorae of drinks. Armed men stood guard before a long, wide curtain cutting off the garden. The marquis had a raised platform built for the king. His Majesty sat off to one side, sheltered under swaths of colored fabric, attended by many slaves and his chamberlain. Couples or singles passed before, bowing or curtseying before moving off. The earl made an elaborate bow and was called up.

"Sire."

"Ah, Sydney, you don't change. I believe you wore the same outfit to all the former masks. This is supposed to be a time to let go, to be someone else!" he bellowed, drinking deep.

"I doubt he would even remember how to do such a thing, although laboring as a common drudge? Tsk, tsk," the marquis drawled. His eyes glittered maliciously behind his elaborate lion-headed mask. It appeared to be made from the head of a once-living lion.

"He is doing a noble deed; if anyone could retain their honor, and impart it to others, it would be he." Maceanas gently rebuked the man beside him before continuing, "You had best make sure, sir, they do have honor or it's your head I'll be having."

The earl bowed his in acknowledgment. "As my king commands, so shall I obey."

"As I was saying, Sire, I think you will enjoy the entertainment I have managed to arrange."

"I hope it will be soon?"

"Before we unmask."

"Good, I am hoping the temptress in red is Lady Illyria. I cannot think of who else would be so bold." He turned to the Earl. "Let us hope your wife has taught her enough of court manners in the time she has had."

"I am sure no fault lies with the countess."

"Hah! Which suggests the lady is the one to blame for failure? We shall see. Has anyone seen Nicky? I told him to attend me, but he has yet to present himself. Go get him for me, both of you. Tell him to attend me at once or he will be banned from my presence for a week. I have grown tired of his tantrums and disobedience."

Both nobles left the platform, Jenabram saying. "Here I thought you could sink no lower. Living, eating and training not even commoners but slaves. It's a wonder you are not stripped of title for the disgrace of it all."

"You and I have different definitions of what disgrace is, Kendall."

The marquis sniffed, giving his chilly smile. "At least I do not have the threat of a beheading hanging over me. Now where do you suppose our orphan advisor is hiding? Maybe I shall find Lady Illyria instead, and show her what a true noble-born man is capable of."

"I believe she already dislikes you, if rumors are true. Nicky is not a man to take such slights toward his person lightly."

Kendall sneered, "Bah, the pup doesn't know how to use a sword properly." He disappeared in the crowd.

The earl decided to cruise the rooms. He grabbed a cup of some drink, sipping as he prowled. He didn't think he would have another as it had a slightly sour aftertaste, not in keeping with the marquis' standard stuff. The gaming room was filled with men intent on the play before them. Slaves ran to and fro, either refreshing drinks, smokes, or to be fondled as good luck pieces. A smaller room had been set aside for the women to play more ladylike games. The advisor was not to be found in either, nor was he at the crowded buffet.

He appeared out on the terrace, the musicians halting. Slaves begun striking gongs to get the crowd's attention, the presiding fool crying out.

"Silence all, silence all! As king fool, I command you to silence!"

Gradually the noise level fell; any person who had attended the mask in the past knowing the marquis always had something special for his guests. One year it was dwarves jousting and pantomiming mock battles. Another, female slaves who wrestled in pits of various substances. Last year, he gave male and female slaves away in pairs to everyone. It was rumored only his special friends received the ones trained in the arts of love.

"Fine folks, step this way into the gardens for tonight's show! It will amaze you, but will hopefully not leave you speechless." He waggled his extravagant brows and butt to laughter. "And may it inspire you!"

The curtain opened to allow slaves to roll out large, tall wooden platforms, positioning them in the clear space. A murmur rippled through the crowd as they moved closer under brightly colored spots of oil light, slaves directing people to fill the areas between the platforms. The earl let himself be carried along, spotting the red woman. Beside her stood a man who could only be Lord Nicky, his red-gold hair a giveaway. He was more elaborately dressed than usual, having elected to wear a plain gold mask, his gray eyes glittering in lust as he spoke to the red lady. The earl made his way through the press of people to come up beside the young man.

"Your pardon, sir, but His Majesty commands your presence immediately."

"Piss off," came the snarled reply.

"I'm afraid, Lord Nicky, I must insist."

"If I were you, I would hold my tongue and not presume to give me any orders."

Sydney bowed. "His Majesty sent both the marquis and me to find you and deliver his message. He sounded most displeased you had not presented yourself yet. He is threatening to have you banned from his presence for it."

The insane rage leaping into the gray eyes at his words had the earl fighting not to give way. The young man opened his mouth to say something in return when trumpets rang out. The king fool mounted the center platform.

"Hear ye, hear ye! For your viewing pleasure, may I present the sun kingdom slaves of love and beauty." He gave an exaggerated, open-mouthed wink. "Oh yes, and should Lord Nicky, our esteemed advisor, be present, His Majesty says get your hiney over to the royal platform posthaste or he shall send the royal guards!" He hopped in a circle as he bent, wiggling his ass at the assembled guests.

It provoked a nervous titter of laughter as the fool hopped down, the guests waiting for the dancers to take their place.

"My lord, it sounds serious. Were you not just telling me the king is to be obeyed in all things?" The red woman laid her hand on the young man's arm. It almost sounded as if she was mocking them both. "I am sure I will be safe, with our noble knight here to keep watch over me."

He flicked one last glare to the earl, before shoving through the crowd.

Many bells chimed out. The earl moved closer to the woman before him, whose identity he had guessed correctly. Lady Illyria. She gave him an amused sideways glance before shifting, so she was mostly in front of him. The dancers, nine couples, mounted the three platforms, as braziers set up around the garden suddenly billowed with fresh incense. They started off the dance to the bells with graceful, slow movements. The men and women went barefoot, covered in short, white gowns. The press of people made the cool night seem warmer. The feathers of Illyria's headpiece brushed his cheek and head. He could smell the oiled perfume she wore: musk, sandalwood, vanilla. The top of her head was on a level with his chin.

The bells were soon joined by a slow pounding of drums, both patterns growing in complexity. As the dancers bent and stretched, the outlines of something which jingled could be seen underneath. The crowd shifted restlessly, expecting something more. The quiet murmurs grew louder. The drums suddenly stopped, together they gave one great boom of sound.

A ripping noise echoed, pieces of fabric floating to the ground. The guests gave a gasp as the dancers' lithe, muscled bodies were revealed.

The comments ran from shocked, to gleeful, to lustful, and the earl heard Illyria give a laugh of appreciation. He was unsure how to feel. On one hand, the display was lewd and lascivious, intended to excite. On the other, it was meant to offend those who disapproved of such sights. The males wore golden cod pieces made up of coins and jewels, the women two pieces covering breasts and groin.

Suddenly the drums came back in a fierce, throbbing rhythm, punctuated by the clash of bells and cymbals and the seductive piping of flutes. The dancers moved again, still graceful, but in faster, more frantic movements, causing the coins to jingle wildly.

Sydney only hoped his wife and children had left before the entertainment started, or he would never hear the end of it once he got home. In fact, if he stayed whilst they'd gone home, and she got word of it, he may as well move fully into the sheriff's barracks. He risked glancing around; the crowd had fallen silent, watching open-mouthed in shock as the performance unfolded.

Another swell of music, and the dancers were naked and writhing against each other. The crowd gasped again as it became clear what they worshipped. The buzz roiled in shocked disapproval, falling with the king's shout of approval and clapping. The earl's hands came up to grasp Illyria's arms below her jeweled straps. He bent toward her ear.

"This is scandalous; you should not be watching! Let me take you out of here." He was straining to keep his body away from hers.

He should have known the marquis would pull such a stunt. The rumors of what he got up to in some of the whorehouses and private parties of his cronies hinted at much worse.

She half-turned toward him, raising up on her toes to murmur,

"These are royal dancers; this is a religion to them. This is how they worship. Damn that degenerate marquis for making something sacred to them into a cheap show. Go if you must, but I shall remain; they are not whores."

"But . . ." he was shocked at her words.

She laid a finger upon his lips before continuing. "There is nothing shameful in the naked body, or consenting adults doing acts to show their feelings for one another. You dishonor their religion by thinking it is something dirty, tawdry, or sinful."

Her eyes glittered behind her mask as she pressed against him. He could barely breathe. He felt shameful on one hand, aroused on the other. He reminded himself of his vow to his wife even as his erection grew between them. The earl opened his mouth to say something when movement in the crowd caught his eye, bringing his gaze off her sharply.

The marquis didn't just want to entertain and shock; he wanted to degrade everyone. The incense billowed, now sweet and heady. The crowd heaved as men and women groped and ground against each other. They were jostled, nearly toppled.

"No, we can't stay here," the earl said in alarm, feeling his head swim and buzz.

"I wonder where he found the means to drug his guests for a mass orgy."

A billow of the incense floated over their heads, pushed by the breeze. Her nose wrinkling, she hissed in anger, making those nearest to her draw back in alarm. Illyria took the space created to draw the earl after her into the crowd. He stumbled, light-headed, as hands reached out, trying to caress him or stop their transit.

The music pounded furiously, or maybe it was his blood. A trickle of sweat ran down his brow and into one eye. He blinked; she was an avenging flame moving ever onward. The press of people turned away from them or moved to create a path she hustled him through. He almost felt she half-carried him. They gained the stone terrace to have a clearer view. People rutted on any convenient surface, clothes came apart or were shoved to the side, or ripping.

The earl swayed as his head pounded to the beat of the drums. He saw her toss a look over her shoulder toward the royal pavilion. He turned in a half-circle, and saw the king being serviced by a bevy of slave women. There was no sign of the marquis, or Lord Nicky.

"Come," she snapped out, and as a slave presented her with a tray of drinks, she snarled, "Out of the way," causing him to draw back.

"What? I don't—"

He found himself jerked forward and almost fell to his hands and knees. She lifted him up to his feet as if he were a child. The impossibility of it flashed through his mind before fading away, and he obediently followed her swinging hips. Another slave crossed her path; she stopped him.

"You, go to the stables and find the raven slaves. Tell them to bring my carriage to the front quickly!"

"Yes, m'lady," the slave squeaked in terror at the force of her command and bolted off, dropping the tray of drinks he held.

"Come, sir knight, we have to get you out of this air. How much have you had to drink?"

"You are so forceful," he said in wonder, trying to stroke a bare shoulder.

She took his upper arms and forced him to look into her masked face. "How much have you drunk? How long have you been breathing in the fumes?"

He felt disconnected as she shook him, his head snapping back and forward sharply before he tried to crush her to him. "Enough, or I shall be sick!" He stood a moment, blinking. "I . . . I, only one drink, and I am unsure how long. Several hours, at least."

Illyria easily broke his hold and began to guide him once more through the marquis's mansion to the front. Sydney tried to follow in her wake. They encountered another crush of people in the entrance hall, all waiting for their carriages to be brought around. The perfumed oil lamps and incense burned even in this section.

"Damn the man! The poor little marchioness, to be used by whomever without her consent by that asshole." It sounded like she muttered, "We must get out of the stink."

He lazily cast his gaze around, not really concerned. It seemed his body throbbed in time with the drums even this far away. The earl was musing over her words, that worship with the body was sacred, when he felt a tug. He followed her willingly down a darkened side hall, a bright, pulsing star before them. It wasn't long before they crossed a room, out another door, and found themselves farther down the front of the mansion.

"This is yours if you run and guide the raven carriage to us, quickly now."

The earl watched the bright star retreat away from them.

"How many times has he done this, at his parties?"

It took a moment for the question to sink in. "I . . ." He shook his head further to clear it. "To my knowledge, he has never drugged them unwillingly." After a pause, he asked, "Do you still hear those drums?"

She sighed. "A little."

He only saw the outline of her body in the darkness. The fog slowly cleared from his head. By the time her carriage arrived, he had become more or less sober. The foot slaves lowered the steps, opened the door, and helped them both inside. They still wore their masks as they seated themselves.

"Not to my house," he said to her urgently. "She must not see me arrive in your carriage."

"Did you not ride together?" she asked him gently.

"No, we never do. I ride; my horse is still back there. Please, I . . ." Words failed him and he shook his head.

She regarded him solemnly before saying, "You spoke of vows you made. I will not be the reason you break them. I shall take you to the Silver Thorn."

"Surely you know by now our marriage was arranged. We don't love each other." An image of his sweet Alise came to mind and then faded. "We never have." He settled back against the cushions, sighing. "My vow was not to take lovers from among our peers, and for the most part I have not. His Majesty refuses to let us divorce, and unlike the marquis, I will not order her killed. So we muddle along, hating each other a little more each year." Sydney opened his eyes, turning to her. "You would not be destroying anything. There was nothing there to begin with. If you doubt me, ask her. Ask anyone. I shall wait."

Illyria leaned out the window, and gave a few instructions to her slaves. The earl let his lids fall shut, felt the vehicle jerk, rattling over the uneven street. A short time later, he opened his eyes, seeing the dark bulk of buildings before them.

"I don't understand."

"I wanted to hear your story from your own lips. I know the truth, and if you had lied to me, we would not be here. You must be sure this is what you want. No guilt, no regrets."

"I only regret I ever let my father bully me into such a union."

"Then come, and we shall worship together." She exited the carriage.

* * *

The earl wasn't sure what woke him. The room was chilly, and he was alone in the empty featherbed. "Lira?" he called out softly. Sydney tried to rise, surprised to find himself weak as a baby. His head pounded, the room swam, his veins felt on fire. He had a terrible thirst.

He lay a moment, gathering up his strength before managing to roll onto one side. With some effort, he sat up. Squares of lighter darkness ringed the room. He could hear birds chirping and twittering. What had happened to draw her from his side? He managed to reach a bell set by the side of the bed and rang it.

A moment later, a slave stepped through the door, "What hour is it?" the earl inquired.

"The last of the dark before the dawn. Shall you be wanting anything?"

He needed to get home. The earl hoped no one had noticed when he left the party or with whom. His wife would go on a path of vengeance for the insult done to her person. Sydney prayed the slaves here could keep their mouths shut.

"Water to wash with, a bite to eat and some wine to drink."

The slave bowed, hurrying off to do as bid. Sydney struggled out of the swaying bed, wondering how he was going to get his horse back. He sat down to his brief repast after cleaning and reclothing himself, when he felt a swirl of chilling air at his back. He turned to see her striding across the room still in her costume from the night before; only now she and it were splattered with dark streaks as if she had bathed in blood.

"I hope things are all right?" he asked, breath catching.

"They are now," was all she said, sitting across from him. "Your mount is being brought around. If you leave quickly, you can make it back home before full dawn."

Sydney felt oddly hurt by the brusque, matter-of-fact tone she used. He bowed his neck, stiffly continuing to eat.

She arched a brow. "You said you vowed not to sleep with a peer. Am I wrong in thinking you prefer she would rather not find out?"

"No, of course not. You are right." He was perturbed all the same, scared his tone gave him away. "She will be hurt, vengeful, and will take the brunt of it out on you."

"Naturally," she remarked dryly.

He finished his meal and stood, as did she. She walked him downstairs—not one slave in sight.

Before she opened the door, he turned to her, saying, "I must see you again."

"There is another ball tonight. I will see you then, and we can slip away. Now go; it is becoming light at an alarming rate." She stood on tiptoe and gave him a deep, fierce kiss, before breaking it off to open the door.

He had no choice but to leave, the sky already turning pale. Domiano stood, holding his horse's head. He mounted up and when he turned back toward the door, found it already shut. Sydney shook his head, already feeling the loss of her. He spurred his mount into a gallop up the hill to his home.

Chapter Twenty-Four

"**I**s that her? The duchess?"

"No, not that sour-faced old fart. It can't be!"

"Oh! I think that might be her!"

"Where?"

"Over there, with the handsome man in green and black."

"No wonder His Majesty fawns over her."

"The earl is rumored to be her lover."

The speakers cackled like hens, their voices rising briefly over the general mishmash of sound before subsiding into the buzz.

Saizar frowned, glaring at the speakers over my head. "It seems your notoriety extends to all corners of the kingdom. Why do you let them speak so ill of you?"

I couldn't help the amused smile curling my lips up. "What would you have me do? Everyone gossips. If I were to act like I cared, people may think there was some truth to the matter."

"It is not right they think you a loose woman with no morals." He was offended for me.

I shrugged. "What they think is of no concern to me. They have small, petty minds if that is all they can talk about. I am surprised you care."

He appeared uncomfortable, "I . . .you have no one to protect you, or your honor. What if talk becomes more?"

"I am capable of protecting myself." My answer was a bit snappish. I noticed when he realized he had made me mad. "Let us speak of more pleasant things. How goes the training? You have been at it for what? A week now?"

"Yes, Your Grace. It will take a lot of effort and time before they are ready to patrol by themselves. I have been taking a different man with me each night, and showing them what will be required of them."

"I am glad to hear of it, and I hope the men are up to the task."

"They seem to be." He hesitated before continuing, "The earl has been training them, so I may help patrol during the day, and sleep enough to be alert during the night."

"I do hope you and your men are not running yourselves ragged. It would be a shame to have such a promising start ruined by a bout of ill health."

"It is why I have given them today and tonight off, so we may all recover." His eyes tracked over the palace gardens, looking for his men.

A steady stream of people flowed in and out of the palace and gardens. At my suggestion, the king ordered the hastily drawn-up sketches and maps of the new town mounted, displaying them in a nearby, easily accessible room. He also found some slaves to build miniature mock-ups of different parts of the designs, which rested in the center of the room and could be viewed from all angles. A few guards were posted, so nothing became maliciously damaged. The grand ball was packed with people as this was the first time even the lowest born was allowed to attend.

The week's festivities would end tonight with this revelry. Tomorrow, work would begin in earnest on rebuilding the town. It was doubtful how much could be done, with winter fast approaching. The king had commanded any slave or freeborn who could play an instrument to present themselves tonight. The result was a motley assortment on a platform at the middle of the gardens. Every brazier had been hauled outside to illuminate the night. Torches burned at the edges of the space, as much to mark the limits of the grounds as to help provide light. Tables and chairs had been hastily built by the slaves, but even then, over half the guests must still stand when they wished to eat. To call this area a garden was laughable at best. An obelisk-shaped stone fountain rose in the middle, dirt paths crossed in ordered lines through the dry grass. The beds were outlined with scraggly bushes, and what flowers remained appeared half-dead.

We continued our slow walk around the perimeter. I knew the people also gossiped about Lord Nicky and our power struggle over the king. I could hear a babble of voices in different languages as visiting merchants and tradespeople also took part of the festivities. They brought many needed wares, but it still wasn't enough. We were drawing abreast of a group of young ladies. I saw Lady Sally in the middle of the group. She was doing her best to be the leader of her friends. They all curtsied to Saizar and me, cooing over my dress, congratulating me on my reinstated title, before we were able to continue on our way.

The marquis's masquerade was not the only dance for which the people must scramble to create new outfits. It seemed the raid had woken them up from their complacency. Some of the daring had taken to trying new styles. Women were showing more bare shoulders, arms, and bosoms. I was in a green gown. What passed for a bodice met in a twist of four straps, two between my breasts and two on the outside that met in a twist near my collarbone. One strap went around my neck, the other two around my shoulders, attaching near the waist so that my whole back was bare to my butt. The material of the bra-like top flowed in a shimmering waterfall of green, and formed the rest of the long skirt which just brushed the tops of my gold-chased shoes. I wore my hair up in a half-knot secured with diamond, emerald and pearl hairpins. I also wore a tiara, given me by the king to befit my reinstated status.

Some few noble and common folk attending did not approve of the new styles, responding in a diametrically opposed manner by fashioning what clothes remained to them into shapeless sacks, veiling their heads and necks, wearing long gloves while in public. I shall give you three guesses as to who instigated this latest choice, although I'm sure you shall only need one.

We continued our stroll, such as it was. I was stopped every few feet by people I had either appointed to committees, or those who wished for my patronage and favor. It wasn't long before a palace slave found us, requesting my presence elsewhere. I left Saizar and followed the slave back inside. His Majesty stood still while his dressers made last-minute adjustments to his ermine-trimmed cloak. I curtsied, finding my arm taken by Lord Nicky.

His face was a thundercloud as he hissed at me in an undertone, "You were told not to wander off."

"I am not a dog, to obey your every command. We should not be having this discussion again." I gave a pointed glance at my arm. He reluctantly released me.

"We will have whatever I want until you learn your place!" He snarled back, a little louder than he intended as we heard some snickers behind us.

I had tried to enter the king's dreams, manipulating them so he would do what I wanted, but it didn't go well. Since the attack, the feelings of dread and wrongness hanging about the town seemed to increase.

Retreating, I joined the court awaiting attendance on the king. We lined up before His Majesty, according to importance. Two of the senior harem ladies, Melisel and Jennet, stood behind Lord Nicky and me. By title, he should be announced earlier, but he had thrown a fit pointing out being the advisor gave him extra leverage. Our view was blocked by the Jenabrams. I had caught a glimpse of the countess as I came in; she glared at me in hatred.

We listened in silence as the trumpeters blew a tucket, and the babble outside died down, Aranthus announcing the most important nobles making up the inner court. Those of lesser status went first, with the highest ranking peer, me, to be announced before the king stepped forth.

Each noble stepped out in turn, making a double line before the guards. As Lord Nicky was announced, boos, hisses, and a smattering of perfunctory applause greeted him. I saw the ugly look on his face as he tried spotting who didn't like him. As my reinstated title was announced, the crowd roared long and loud. I was surprised; all the thoughts I had been overhearing were not kind toward me. Out of the corner of my eye, I could see Lord Nicky was about to burst with rage over my supplanting him in the king's eyes.

I just couldn't help myself, standing alone on the top step longer than the others. I gave my most bewitching smile, bringing my clasped hands up toward my heart and making a bow from the waist as I brought my hands forward, opening them up to thank the people. The gesture caused another roar of approval. Nicky's glare promised ugly things to come. I gave a regal wave, stepping down toward him as the cheering continued. The advisor reached out grabbing my arm in an ugly, pinching grip.

"You bitch!" he hissed at me, making no attempt to smile at the people.

"Careful, Lord Nicky," I murmured as I walked forward to take my place in the waiting line. "If the townspeople take offense, public opinion may sway the king against you permanently."

The grip didn't let up one iota as he led me to my spot before taking his. He continued glaring at me as the cheering slowly died down. His Majesty was announced. The assembly cheered again, but there was a marked difference in it. I was the most popular one tonight, it seemed. The king had not failed to take note of it. He waved his harem ladies behind him as he stopped in front of me, holding out his hand. I took it in my own, letting him pull me toward him as we stately made our way toward the covered platform set up for the king and the inner court. The townspeople cheered loudly again, gaining in volume as I smiled at them and nodded, making as much eye contact as possible.

"They love you, Duchess, more than me, it seems," he said to me, a tinge of jealousy in the sound.

"Nonsense, Sire. They are cheering for you," I replied.

"There is no need for you to flatter me the way the others do; I can hear with my own ears," he rebuked me.

"I am sorry, Sire. It is not my intention to steal any love away from you," I answered.

He patted my hand. "Nicky and the countess complain about your behavior, but it seems they don't know how to get the masses to support them."

"I have often heard it said, Majesty, that it is better to be feared than loved, for those who fear will hesitate to take advantage."

He merely grunted as we ascended the platform steps, and walked along the curving table toward his seat in the middle. The king stepped up behind his chair. I dropped back and to the side to stand beside Lord Nicky. The king greeted his subjects with a speech meant to welcome and engender enthusiasm for a new town and the start of a new era. After the proper amount and length of cheering, he signaled for all present to continue with the celebrations. The musicians struck up a tune as Maceanas turned, commanding his harem ladies to sit at a place behind him. I was beckoned forward and seated on his right, while Nicky was shuffled to his left. The rest of the order remained more or less the same. As we sat, slaves began to bring us food.

"Lovely, lovely. This has turned out better than I expected. My scribes are informing me there is significant support from the populace for our new town. I must commend you, Duchess, you are a rare jewel, and have done more for my kingdom since arriving than any who were born here. I shall have to give you something special to mark the occasion."

Nicky hissed in annoyance, "She should be thankful for your gratitude and the use of her title and nothing more. The royal treasury cannot support gifts of favor, not with the disaster befallen us. Besides, nothing has been done yet, and until it has, a gift is premature."

Farther down the table, I heard Lady Elizabeth haranguing Sidney over lost chances.

"I would not look to be compensated for serving my king, Majesty," Jenabram drawled spitefully beside me. "The mere act itself would be honor enough." He snapped for a slave to refill his cup.

There was, to some degree, envy and jealousy from my peers. The king chose to ignore the marquis's sycophancy. Before us, the revelers energetically twirled about through a large dance area. I thought I saw the countess's daughters dip and sway past at one point as I tried to engage the marchioness in conversation. Her replies were hesitant and timid, with many glances toward her husband, seeking reassurance she was doing what he wished of her. He ignored her, continuing to drink steadily and bicker with Nicky, both of whom were trying to insert themselves into the king's conversation with Sydney. Lady Elizabeth sat, stiff of back, her face set in a rictus compounded of unhappiness, boredom, and disapproval. She took frequent small sips from the cup before her while keeping her eyes on a point halfway up the palace wall across the garden when she wasn't shooting hateful glances my way or making snippy remarks aimed at me.

Aranthus stayed behind us, directing the slaves on bringing us plates of food from the long serving tables. I faked eating as always while a lively reel played.

"Tell me, dear duchess, did you enjoy my ball?" The marquis's eyes glittered in anger. "I did not see you at the unmasking."

"Yes, I did."

My reply gave him pause for a moment. "You should have stayed. I would have loved to share a private performance with you." His eyes raked down my front and back up knowingly.

"I have heard rumors of what you enjoy. Play your games with the other little dogs and you will live longer," I answered softly with power. "Few can meet my price."

His lip curled up as his eyes found the exposed tops of my breasts. "I pray for the day the advisor finally pries your claws from the king," he replied. The bravado was gone, and an undercurrent of fear ran through his words.

I merely smiled at him. He refused to look at me, instead turning back to the king as I spotted Nicky glaring at us—for what, I could not fathom. The marquis didn't recall my late visit to him the night of his ball, the blood and havoc I had created which he scrambled to cover up the next morning, not remembering how it had happened and actually growing afraid for a day or two.

The banquet continued, an endless array of dishes. When winter came, and people began dying from starvation, the memory of this night would come back to them. Pages came and went, asking the king if this or that person could approach and speak with him. He was in a good mood and nodded assent. The music continued. I wanted to join in and dance. I excused myself, only to find Lady Anne at my side.

"If it pleases you, Duchess, I will accompany you to the privy." Her eyes meet mine pleadingly.

"Of course," I answered with an internal sigh, even though it was not my destination.

We descended the platform, I leading the way, shielding her frail body from the jostling of the crowd. I waited for her, deciding who might make a good meal while chatting with the other ladies who waited their turn. Another tune was playing when she finished. I saw the longing look she gave the dancers and the small sigh of envy.

"Come, let us join in." I said, as it was the type of dance not requiring a dedicated partner.

"Oh, I . . . I shouldn't." She cast a frightened glance back toward the dais.

"Nonsense, we will have fun," I urged her. "He is too busy drinking to care, and we don't even need a partner."

She hesitated, then shook her head in the negative. "I . . . I can't," she gasped out and fled.

I sighed, as Baron Stavic came up to me and bowed. "May I have the honor of congratulating you on regaining the use of your title, Duchess? Might I also have the pleasure of your company for this dance?"

I consented, giving him my hand, and we joined the dancing throng.

We were greeted with smiles as I joined in the outer circle of women. The men faced us in their own circle. There was much jollity as we flowed through the steps, swapping sides, dancing with a new person every few turns of the circles. It was more a peasant dance than a court dance, but it didn't matter tonight. We flowed into a more stately number as Stavic tried making conversation.

"I did appreciate your contribution to our festivities, Duchess. It was . . . different," he said, hastening to add, "but in a good way, unlike what the marquis provided. I . . . I do hope you managed to leave before the entertainment. I heard things got out of hand." *I would hate to think she had taken part in such a degenerate scene.*

"I was there," I replied, "and I saw part of what he deemed 'entertainment.' I started to feel sick from all the incense and had to leave. Why? What happened? I have heard so many wild rumors. Please don't tell me there really was an orgy!"

He lost his footing, fumbling for a moment before replying, "My dear duchess! You should not know about such things, much less admit to it!"

I nearly rolled my eyes, instead replying. "My dear baron, you know I have traveled the world. I saw many things that would make a sheltered woman faint. My mother did not believe in keeping any of her children ignorant from what she called 'the realities of life,'" I lied.

He goggled. "But . . . but you are . . . I mean . . ." He couldn't go on. The dance pattern forced us to part, and when we came back together, Stavic moved onto another topic. "I wanted to thank you for the opportunity you give me with the rebuilding committee. Quite a few of the merchants and tradespeople who came here for the festival express an interest in staying."

"I am glad, though the way things are looking, we will require farmers or those who can import food."

"I'm not sure why; the snow will be falling soon, and they can't plant."

"True, but after winter comes spring, and we will need sustenance. Can those people help us?"

"I-I don't know. Do you really think we are in danger of shortages? The advisor says we are not."

"He is no doubt trying to stave off a panic, so I trust you will not repeat this with any but the Rothburys. There will be starvation this winter. Please keep this in mind, and be on the lookout for those who can help us avoid or at least lessen it."

The baron goggled at me again while he made assurances it would be his top priority. He looked entirely too pleased with the idea he knew something very few did. I hope it didn't go to his head. As the dance came to an end, another man stepped up and bowed to us both as Baron Stavic wandered off to find the Rothburys.

"If I may, Duchess?" The earl stood before me, hands clasped behind his back.

"Of course," I answered as we began to dance.

His eyes burned into mine, saying what he couldn't out loud as we chatted. "I am sorry for my wife's attitude toward you, Duchess. I fear she doesn't consider you a good influence on the marchioness. She is upset Lady Anne seems to prefer you over her, especially since they have been friends for years."

"Lady Anne is hurting, and has been abused for far too long. She needs someone who will be gentle and understanding and help her find her sense of self-worth again. We both know your wife hasn't the patience for those she views as weak, such as her ladyship."

"Still, I am sorry all the same." He paused. "You have more compassion than most." He lowered his voice to whisper. "It is part of why I love you. I need to be with you."

He hissed in frustration as we separated in a movement and met back up. "She has already grown suspicious with the amount of time I am gone and will not believe I stay at the sheriff's barracks. She believes the whispers. I don't understand how it got out."

"Chadrick, think. Do you wish for more problems to be heaped upon your head if we are discovered here and the rumors made truth? You have warned me before she will not take it lightly."

He hesitated a moment. "I don't care anymore. There is a room inside." Swiftly he described it to me. "Meet me there later?"

"I shall await you anon." I smiled at him as we partnered up with other dancers.

* * *

It was much later in the night when I left off dancing to wander through the crowd of people, stopping to converse. I noticed Susafan and Mary Elana whirl past in one of the dances. The young girl appeared to be enjoying herself, despite her continuing despair over her circumstances. I had fed deeply earlier, but my hunger was returning slowly, something it usually did not do, making me slightly worried. I would have to feed again. As I was trying to decide upon whom, I was accosted by my seamstress. I was exchanging pleasantries with Emilee, much to her never-ending delight, when the marquis stumbled against me, saying,

"This is a royal ball, not your shop to accost a noble and bore her to death with your petty needs for payment."

I saw the woman's face pale at those words. "I was under the impression this is a ball for everyone, noble or not. I see no reason to be rude to the woman who has been so diligent and so accommodating in getting a wardrobe together for me," I retorted.

He merely sneered, "If you love them so much, why don't you give up your title and join them? Lord Nicky has remarked upon your need to chat at length with the help. Do you really want to have her come to his attentions in such a way?"

I turned to Jenabram, anger in my eyes. "It is not up to you, or Lord Nicky, to choose whom I will speak with. Do not ever presume to threaten those I treat with again."

His hand shot out, trying to wrap around my upper arm but missed as he leaned close and breathed wine fumes on me. "I want a dance, and I aim to have one. You think you're so much better than us. You're just some foreign, insolent whore who managed to trick the king."

I kept my smile on my face, though it turned feral. "If I were you, I would forget about dancing and go back to your drinking."

The anger leaping into his eyes only made me want to laugh as he scowled. "I will have my dance," he insisted, grabbing a goblet of wine off a tray heading to the royal table. "I have seen you dance with any who presume to ask you, noble or not." He tossed the contents back letting the empty goblet fall to the ground. "You will dance with the peasants but not me?"

"I find your behavior distasteful; remove yourself from my presence immediately."

"Dance with me." He insisted trying to reach for me again.

I neatly avoided him. The marquis stumbled away from me, his drunkenness working in his disfavor.

I slipped into the crowd as those around us exclaimed aloud at the small ruckus. I was almost on the other side of the garden when Eron found me.

"Your Grace, has it come to your attention Colin and Mica haven't been heard from since before the raid?" he drily asked.

I cast my glance about the gardens, noting the level of drunkenness was rising. "Has it been that long, then?"

He nodded, concern in his eyes. "Mica's obsession would never let all the chances of seeing Nicky's dupe pass by. I stopped by the house you rented for them, or what was left of it, after the raid. The remaining slave said they had received a note and called for their horses and some food. They never came back. I'm wondering . . ." He hesitated, then plunged on. "I'm wondering if Nicky learned they are looking for him and laid some sort of trap. I think it's time we grabbed the dupe."

I was about to answer when the marquis stumbled toward us, anger in every line of his bearing. "So, you refuse to dance with me but not with a freed slave?" he spat. "You should have been hanged."

"You are drunk, and an insult to us all," I replied while saying to Eron, "Your concern is duly noted, I will take care of the matter should the opportunity arise. Enjoy the celebration, steward." I made to leave.

"Lord Nicky should know of this."

A quick flash of irritation had crossed Eron's face before it hardened into one of disgust. "Her Grace is more capable than the advisor."

The marquis clenched a fist as he swung wildly. We were attracting quite a group of watchers. Their shouts let us know they were enjoying the antics of the nobility as the inebriated marquis lost his footing and crashed backwards into a group of dancers.

Most of them went sprawling to the ground. Jenabram sat splay-legged, a look of startlement on his face quickly changing to anger.

"How dare you push me!" he accused the men picking themselves and their partners off the ground.

"Ain't none of us pushed you, you fell and pushed us," one of the men replied angrily.

"Peasant dog!" Kendell replied, the rest lost to his slurring as he tried standing.

I was all for letting him get pummeled; he was soused enough he might not remember who attacked him. Eron tried to defuse the situation as Jenabram spewed insults at everyone. The other men who had been pushed were not as drunk. They realized by our rich velvets, silks, and brocades we held a higher station. I could sense it would not be to our favor, not in the middle of peasants.

"I'm sorry, gentlemen; if you will permit me to apologize for the insults made to you on behalf of his lordship." I was graciousness itself. "I would not want to ruin anyone's pleasure over easily rectified slights."

Behind me, the marquis clapped hands on my shoulders trying to shove me out of the way. "Don' need no damn woman apologizing for me, 'specially to these peasants."

The sober men glanced at each other, the women with them whispering behind their hands. I stomped hard on Kendall's foot.

The drunk before me didn't want to let the matter go easily. "You damn . . . damn nobles," he slurred. "Think . . . think you can just push us around and treat us no better'n slaves."

"It is to the detriment of my peers so many of them do, for which I again apologize," I said respectfully.

The drunk opened his mouth to say more, and stood there in an attitude of befuddlement while he tried to make sense out of my words. Jenabram made a rude noise behind me which I ignored.

"If you will pardon us, we shall leave you to your merriment."

The men hesitated. I spoke in a low tone just for them, "Please don't insist any further. What you would get in immediate satisfaction would quickly pale before future indignities upon your group."

I watched comprehension come over the men and women. Muttering, they pulled their companions back into the throng of dancers. Jenabram had remained oddly silent during the last exchange. I glanced toward the marquis to see why. His head drooped downwards. Eron, in a tightly controlled fury, might have gotten involved in a brawl when the earl and Saizar suddenly appeared.

"Your Grace, my lords and gentlefolk." He bowed.

"Sheriff, you can help us. The marquis has indulged a fair amount and needs a quiet place to recover in while his carriage is brought round."

He eyed us all, a sour look upon his face. "As you command, Your Grace. My lord, with your permission, I shall help escort you inside."

Jenabram mumbled something incomprehensible. Saizar took the man's left arm and slung it around his shoulders, preparing to walk the man inside the palace.

"If I may impose a moment more on you, Duchess?" Sydney said with a bow, "I had a thought of some import on a topic you mentioned earlier. May I walk with you around the garden and discuss it? I fear it cannot wait until the morrow."

"Very well. If you will excuse us?" I said to Eron. He scowled but walked away.

We left, unobtrusively making our way inside the palace. He had enough control to pull us down a side hall before he kissed me. His mouth moved with a ferocity and intent letting me know how unstable his emotions were. It took some effort on my part to keep his tongue from scraping against my fangs. His mouth trailed the side of my jaw, to my neck, and toward my breasts as he pressed us close.

The hallway was not as dark as it could be, and we were very close to the main hall. He was desperate indeed. "Lira, Lira, I couldn't stand it. Watching him assault you and touch you. I wanted to tear him off you and smash in his smirking face."

I stroked down his head, neck, and back. "He is no one, Chadrick."

He groaned, almost a sob. "He can still try and harm us with his jealous tongue."

"Let us not mention him, not now." I said. It would not take much power to cloud his mind. I could feed at least a little.

A drunken, raucous voice interrupted us. "You whore! Nob . . . nobility be damned! Where's my daughter, the whore! I know she's here. She's comin' back home to her family."

We turned to see Tom, owner of the Bloody Knuckles, with a few of his henchmen, swaying before us, blocking off the hallway.

The earl tried stepping in front of me. "Watch how you address a lady." He got no further as the group attacked.

Tom's henchmen concentrated on Sydney while the tavern owner swung at my jaw. I caught his fist easily in one hand and squeezed, crushing his bones. The man screamed in pain, dropping to his knees. Blood dripped from between my hand, still holding onto what was left of his.

"Duchess, run!" Chadrick yelled, ending on a grunt of pain.

I felt the air swirl behind me and let go of Tom, turning to block a henchman who was preparing to bring a club down onto my head. In that second, I saw behind him the earl on the ground being kicked and stomped by the other two men. I smiled, showing fang, watching the man's face register the fact he was not the hunter anymore. He never had a chance to scream. I wrenched his club out of his hands. Moving in a blur, I stepped behind him and bashed the back of his head in while he was still trying to overcome his fear. The other two men were so intent on the earl they didn't notice their friend had fallen.

A few steps brought me closer; using my speed and strength I brought the club down on their heads. Bone crunched, flying along with blood and brain. The dress was a total loss. The earl was groaning, semi-conscious on the floor, as I dropped the club and turned back to Tom. He was trying to stand and run.

My attack had only taken seconds. I moved swiftly, grabbing him about the neck and lifting him several inches off the floor. "Tom, Tom, Tom. I warned you not to be greedy," I purred.

He kept trying to pry my hand off his throat with the one remaining to him. He used the arm of his injured member to slam down on my outstretched arm while kicking me as I throttled him. His move would have worked on a mortal, but as I wasn't, I merely found it an irritant. He was trying to speak, but only grunts came out. I let him drop as I moved faster than he could comprehend, coming up behind him. I used one arm to pin him to me, the other to clamp tight over his mouth. I had found my drink after all.

* * *

The earl shuddered in pain. "Duchess, what? Are you? I'm sorry I . . ." He swayed, looking in horror at my ruined gown. "We must tell His Majesty about this. The effrontery and brazenness of those lowlifes. You shouldn't have had to fight them all on your own . . ." He gestured to the gore covering my front and side. *I am disgraced; how can she love a man who cannot even protect her?*

"It is mere cloth, easily replaced. Are you sure you are well enough to walk? It was quite a blow you took to your skull."

Chadrick put a hand out, bracing against the wall. "Yes, I will be." He forced himself to take steps forward while I walked beside him to lend support when needed. We had just turned into the central passageway. Personal guards in an all-too-familiar uniform stood before a door. Lord Nicky stepped out of the room and spotted us.

It would have been comical to say who was more startled, the earl or the advisor. They both froze as I continued on as if nothing were the matter even, as Nicky's eyes flared brighter in rage. The earl started shambling again. I could see the advisor's hands clench in fists by his side. He noticed my gore-encrusted gown and the state of the earl. The anger turned to shocked puzzlement. Behind him, someone tried to exit the room.

The young woman stopped short at the sight of us, letting out a squeak as she tried ducking back inside. The guards looked to the advisor for orders as I arched a brow, trying and failing to contain my mirth. "Lord Nicky."

"What the hell is this?" he demanded of the earl, stepping to block our path.

"Sally!" the earl blurted, eyes swinging to the advisor's.

"Yes, what is it?" I couldn't help myself as I noticed the girl tugging her dress in place, her face coloring red in a mixture of embarrassment and defiance.

Sydney chastised his youngest daughter. "Sally, what do you mean by being alone behind closed doors with a man?"

"I can do whatever I want!" Sally shrilled out to her parent. "I'm not married." She yelled at her father and I. "Why are you bleeding and bruised? Why is she all covered in . . . ewwww!"

"You stupid bitch! Shut your mouth and go away!" Nicky hissed at her.

I could feel the earl stiffen in outrage beside me. "Take a care how you address my daughter, Lord Nicky."

The advisor's gray eyes became colder. "You will keep your distance from me and not presume to give me orders, do you hear me? Or I'll have you tossed in the dungeon where you'll soon wish you had never crossed me. Do I make myself clear?"

I could see Sydney pale; for a moment I expected him to crumble. I stepped closer to the young man saying in a low voice, "There is no need to threaten a man we know is perhaps the only noble with no ulterior motives."

Lord Nicky's face twisted up in rage. "You dare to tell me what I can and can't do?"

"I am pointing out what a mistake it would be to punish him for no reason. We all know what an honorable man the earl is." I let my gaze go past him and to the girl. "Why let this get any uglier than it already is?"

Sally screamed and stamped her foot at her father. "Why should she be able to talk and keep company alone with a man? Why should she have all the males courting her and fighting over her? I'm noble! I'm a virgin! I'm not promised to anyone!"

Only two out of the three were true, I thought as this farce unfolded. "He loves me! He said he did! I even proved to him what a good wife I would be! He said I would be his wife!" She turned on Nicky who was regarding her with a mixture of disgust and contempt.

"Tell them! We're to be married!" She clutched at his arm. "You nasty old woman! Why would he want you when he has me! I don't oppose him the way you do!"

"Sally! Apologize at once! We will discuss your behavior when we get home," the earl gritted out to his daughter, trying not to sag against the wall.

Lord Nicky's slap resounded down the hall. "You stupid slut! I told you to go away! Why would I want a little girl who can't even follow orders?"

She stumbled away several paces, clutching her face as tears welled up, gaping at him in open-mouthed stupidity as his words sunk in. With a roar of rage, the earl charged the advisor.

Lord Nicky backpedaled, letting his guards step forward to stop

Sydney.

Lady Sally screamed, "But I love you! You promised me! I did too follow your instructions! Even the nasty ones! Why don't you love me?"

Chadrick struggled in the grip of the guards. One asked, "What do you want us to do with him, and their tale of attackers?"

"Get them out of my sight!" Lord Nicky snarled with clenched fists. "Or I'll have you both tossed in the dungeon! You, for attempting to attack the king's advisor, and you, for being so stupid!"

The girl was sobbing and crying as her father yelled, "How dare you dishonor my daughter?"

Nicky sneered, "You should be thankful I even consented to honor the cow with my attentions. Take him to the king and let him spout his tale. You, go down the hall and see what there is." The advisor dismissed Sydney as he stalked closer to me. "As for you Duchess . . ."

I could see Chadrick struggling with the guards as they forced him along toward the doors. Sally was crying and screaming at her father as a figure hesitated at the entrance, moving aside to let the guards with their burdens pass.

"You will not presume to tell me what to do, not when your own position is so perilous." He flicked a glance at the gory front of my gown. "Clearly you have been involved in something which has a body somewhere. Murder is punishable by death."

I was tired of dealing with three assholes in one night, and my temper slipped. "Perilous how? Self-defense is not a crime. His Majesty knows I am a loyal subject. Am I not in charge of rebuilding the town?"

He was so angry he couldn't speak, trembling with the force of holding his temper back. "You will obey me and my orders the same as if they came from the king!"

"I am not property, and I will not be treated as such. I have told you before, I will be treated with respect. The same as you demand."

A shudder passed over the advisor, as with a wordless scream of rage, he punched the wall. It was stone. I heard bones break from the force he used. He turned back to me, cradling his injured hand and breathing heavily.

"I am the most powerful man in this kingdom! I can have you stripped of wealth and title and tossed in the dungeon to rot! I can order you tortured should I wish it, and no one will help you. Yet you stand there telling me lies?"

I had the weirdest sensation it wasn't a young man of nineteen or twenty who stood before me, but a wounded child of about eleven or twelve. I chose my words with care. "Why should I lie about something easily found out?"

His face crumpled up in a mixture of hurt and anger, wincing at what had to be a stab of pain from his injured hand. "I won't be made a mockery!"

"I wouldn't dream of it. Maybe you would feel better if you were to escort me to the king so I may tell my side of the tale?"

He was set to reply when footsteps sounded behind us. Eron approached after he shut the door to the garden behind the young man's guards. The advisor's face was scary with rage as he spotted the man.

The former slave bowed to us both, his face neutral. "Your pardon, my lord, Your Grace. The king sent me to deliver the message you are both needed in his royal presence at once."

"How dare you interrupt a private conversation? I know you; somehow, I know I do." He took a step closer to the other man.

Eron regarded him a moment, and said, "I don't believe so; I've only been in this country a little while. I have lived elsewhere."

Nicky scrutinized him more closely before sneering and dismissing the man. He addressed me again. "Come, we will get back where we belong, with the king." A smirk writhed across his face. "And we will finish our discussion there."

The man held out his arm for me. The arm with the injured hand. The hand that was no longer injured.

He saw where my glance landed; an evil leer crossed his face. "I told you before, it would be a mistake to make an enemy of me, Duchess. There is much that goes on in this kingdom which you have no notion of. It would be better to beg my forgiveness, and ask for my friendship. Don't be stupid enough to reject me."

He didn't care if I knew something wasn't right with him. I didn't know how to kill him, or even what he really was. Eron and his former employers still didn't realize the kid they looked for and the young man before me were somehow one and the same. I didn't know how to convince them of it without awkward questions arising. I was wondering why the other man stood still; this was the perfect opportunity to over-power and kidnap the young man. I noticed my steward was distracted by something behind me.

"Lord Nicky, Duchess Illyria," a voice growled out, and we both turned to see who was behind us.

One of the men was covered head to toe in an enveloping cloak and hood with a mask, only leaving his pale, watery blue eyes free. He carried an intricately carved staff with a chunk of crystal on the end as he approached us. Behind him lurked another person similarly cloaked and hooded.

"You're a little late for the costume party; it was several days ago. Is this Revenge of the Nerds? Spend a little too much time playing Dungeons and Dragons?" I inquired, catching the hateful look from the man holding the staff.

"What is the meaning of this?" Nicky snarled at them. "I told you not to come, DiJinn, or you!"

I would not have known one of the men was Nicky's slave as he began to laugh and laugh, a guttural sound. The other man looked at me, raising the staff in both hands starting to chant what sounded like nonsense. I got a sudden, urgent sense of danger just as Eron grabbed me from behind and tried moving me back toward the garden door.

"Duchess, get out of here! It's an ambush!"

Nicky was screaming at the men, "You dare to betray me! I'll see you both dead!" He ripped a hidden dagger from his sleeve, lunging toward the chanting man.

Eron was tugging me back toward the closed door, turning to open it. The first man yelled a last guttural sound, slamming the staff down on the ground. The crystal on top flared bright as the sun. I staggered back, bringing my free hand up to shield my closing eyes as I turned my head downward. I was temporarily blinded.

I heard Nicky babbling as something went *fzzzoooommmm!* Heat rocketed past my face as I stumbled backwards and crashed into Eron. It felt like the air pressure lowered drastically and swiftly, until even I had a hard time moving, but I knew it was just an illusion. The man yelled another guttural sound.

"What the fuck!?" Eron yelled nearby, trying to keep us both upright as I was still blind from the light.

The boom echoed, rumbled in the small space before I was deafened as well. I felt Eron, and I lifted up from the power of whatever the man had set free. My body felt like it was floating and dissolving. I had lost all control of my limbs along with the feel of my body. All I saw was a field of white.

Connect with me online:

http://slfiguhr.com/
Twitter: https://twitter.com/SLFiguhr
Facebook: http://facebook.com/SLFiguhr.author

Please continue reading for a sneak peek at Book 2.

Sneak Peek
Book 2: The Reaping

The bar was dimly lit; Eron sat at a small table, toying with a glass of whiskey, listening to the jazz band currently playing. He was contemplating getting good and drunk, though with his fast metabolism it was nearly impossible. The waitress stopped by, asked if he wanted another, which he declined. He could see his friend onstage squinting at him and shaking his head.

After a few more songs, the band took a break, and his friend came over, chatting people up, shaking hands. Well, not really his friend—he was more of a friend of Mica's, though the man was good company. The waitress appeared again and Steve ordered water, with a bottle of beer.

"She likes you. Why don't you ask her out?" Steve spoke in his raspy voice as he lit a cigarette.

Eron shrugged, continued playing with his glass. What was the use? Everyone he loved died eventually.

"Come on!" Steve replied in aggrieved tones. "She's nice, she's *single*. Not like that other one."

Eron lifted his head briefly to glare at the man. "Is that what you think? That I'm mooning over some . . . some unattainable woman?"

Steve took a sip of his water, then the beer. "Well it sure looks like it! I mean, what do you really know about her? Hell, she doesn't seem to always be on the up and up, if you know what I mean."

"Mica tell you that?" Eron asked.

"Look, for someone so old who's supposed to be all wise an' shit, you certainly can pick 'em can't you?" Steve asked in disgust. "Donnie's just a street kid what don't always know better. He gets sucked in too much by shiny, pretty things, easy money."

"He'll learn, Steve; time will give him experience."

He missed the look of disgust tossed his way before his friend took another gulp of beer and acknowledged a patron. "If he makes it that far. I don't like that woman, and you know why? 'Cause she's fake; there's something not right about her. My guys? They can't find any real mention of her. It's like she never existed."

"Steve, there are lots of people you don't have full information on."

"Speaking from experience?" his friend razzed him as he finished the last of his beer. "Look, all I'm saying is, Missy is interested; what would it hurt to ask her out on one date? You might find you have more in common than you think."

Steve left his empty on the table, and taking the water with him, joined his bandmates back onstage as they started into the last half of their set. Eron continued scowling at his drink. Movement nearby had him looking up. Missy was picking the empty up; she leaned over a bit to look him in the face.

"You still okay? Ready for another?"

"I'm fine, thanks" It came out a little sharper than he'd intended.

She compressed her lips, nodded once sharply. "Okay," and turned to the table next to him.

"She likes you." The silky voice near his ear startled him so he jerked and spilled what was left of his drink on the table top. He caught a whiff of some expensive, seductive perfume.

Eron looked to his side, but the speaker had already moved around and sat across from him. He looked over at her, taking in a sharp breath and smoothing his face out so nothing showed, while inside he felt happier. "Not you, too." He mopped up the liquid with the useless paper coaster and his coat sleeve.

He watched as she settled back into the chair, her black camelhair coat falling open to reveal a cream cashmere sweater, tasteful gold link jewelry and belt chain snug around her slim waist. He could just see the top of her skirt, a red and black tartan. She wasn't dressed much different from the other patrons, but the cut and material always made her seem better turned out.

"She is cute. Would you like me to make you reservations at L'Home Blu?"

He lifted his head to glare at her. "I don't need help asking a girl out, especially from you."

Her eyebrow winged up, "What about asking out a woman?" She turned her head to evaluate the waitress. "She is older than a mere girl."

Eron, forgetting he had spilled the last of the whiskey, went to drink another mouthful.

"You do not look happy, ma chérie, is it really so bad? You are alive, no one is trying to kill you, and a pretty woman is interested in you. What more do you want?" She laid her hand over the back of his.

Eron could only stare stupidly at it. She must have fed at some point, for it was warm and not her normal icy cold. The silken feel of her skin against his sent frissons of pleasure through him. *As if she cares; if I were to tell her, I would only be giving her power over me.* He abruptly yanked his hand out from under hers and clutched his glass with both hands.

He noticed it took a while before Missy came back over. "What can I get you?" Her tone had a decidedly hostile note.

"Espresso." Illyria looked at Eron as Missy turned her back to her in dismissal and went to answer another table.

"I'll have another, thanks," Eron called after her, not sure if she heard him. "Why are you here? I didn't think you liked jazz."

"I don't. I find it snooze-inducing."

Eron spread his hands, "So, again, what are you doing here?"

"Waiting."

He looked at her, expecting her to elaborate but she didn't, merely turned her head to watch the band onstage. Missy came back with her espresso, and another whiskey for him. Illyria held up a Euro toward the waitress, not really paying attention. Eron noticed how Missy took it in two finger tips, with a slight sneer for the other woman before walking off. He glanced briefly toward the stage, saw Steve was now scowling at him and giving "what the hell?" looks.

"Is that not your friend on the sax?" Illyria asked. "He is unhappy with you."

Eron hunched his shoulders. "Yeah, he is. Besides, he's really more Mica's friend." *Why the hell is everyone so concerned with my love life all of a sudden?* He noticed she wrapped her hands around the tiny cup but didn't drink any of it.

"I thought you couldn't eat or drink?"

Illyria was now watching the people in the bar, and he idly wondered if she was mentally tallying up which ones could be considered food, and which ones to leave alone. "We do not. But the warmth," her voice sunk a note with longing, "we crave it." She gave a small shudder, her eyes closing briefly and reopening, and her tone taking on a brisker note. "We are in a bar; it is what people do when they are in one, is it not? Order a drink?"

He did not answer, did not know what to say.

She turned back to him, her eyes drifting past his head and he watched as they lit up with happiness. *Why won't they do that for me?* he thought churlishly and felt another presence behind him.

In a moment the man was bending over and they brushed their lips together before he sat down in the chair facing the bar, with his back to the band. Steve's eyes narrowed again at Eron, he cut them to the man and gave a chin jerk. Eron ignored him. He had a scowl on his face. He wanted to sit in peace and think, and now he felt like a fifth wheel. Missy came over again with change, and another espresso was ordered. The drink came back quickly, and Phillip gave his most charming smile to her. Eron watched as she blushed, nearly dropped the money he gave her, and fled, her cheeks crimson.

"Please tell me you two don't intend to spend all night here."

"Don't worry, we have a dinner date later," she laughed.

As the words sank in, he gave a little grimace and downed half the contents of his glass and watched as the male leaned in to whisper in Illyria's ear. He could have stepped from the pages of a men's magazine. He had on charcoal gray slacks, sharply creased, a snowy white, immaculately pressed button-down shirt complete with studs at collar and cuff. When he moved, there was glimpses of his subtly patterned red vest and from the sleeve of his coat peeked an expensive men's watch. The male vamp must have cut his hair, because it didn't fall in its customary waves to his shoulder, but was a mess of curls precisely styled to look like it hadn't been. He also wore a long black cashmere coat and there was the faint scent of some expensive and subtle cologne. Eron was aware the two of them received admiring looks from both sexes. It made him feel scroungy, sitting as he was in his comfortable jeans, slightly worn sweater, peacoat, and beat-up boots.

Missy made another appearance, checking to make sure they were all right. Eron noticed she could barely tear her eyes from Phillip's face, and even though he had not given her any encouragement, it still rankled. After she had left, he risked a glance to the stage. Steve was ignoring him, concentrating on the music.

"I believe that is he now," Phillip remarked.

Eron didn't want to know, but it was like a train wreck: he couldn't help but look. All he saw was a large man in a sharp Armani business suit with two men who screamed "personal protection" at his back. The man made his way to the bar, and by the look on the faces of the waitstaff, was not wanted.

"But that's . . ." He trailed off and looked back at the two vamps.

"Every rumor about him is true," Illyria breathed hungrily, "as is the one he is slippery, and cannot be tied directly to anything."

"He will make a lovely feast. Shall I? Or would you like the honors?" Phillip looked at her.

"You, I got the last one," she replied. "Besides, I like to watch you work." She trailed a glossy red nail down his coat sleeve.

He gave his devastating smile, emerald green eyes lightening with promises of things to come. "As you wish." He stood and seemed to slip through the crowd like butter. In no time at all, Phillip had engaged the man in conversation, and soon Illyria was rising.

"You should ask her out, Eron; she might even be willing to spend the night." The vamp squeezed his shoulder gently and bent her head near his ear to whisper, "You need something to put you in a better mood," and was soon leaving the bar with the other men.

Eron scowled as rage surged inside; he wanted to hurl his glass against the wall. He downed the last of his whiskey instead, wondering how they planned to keep the man's demise out of the papers.

Missy came over, collected the now-cold cups of espresso, his empty. "Another one?"

"Yeah, sure, thanks." He was back to staring at the table top.

When she brought his refill back, she tried to engage him in conversation. "Your friends didn't stay long."

Eron looked up at her briefly. "They only stopped in for a bit, to say hello. This . . . this isn't really their thing."

She smiled at him, a sweet smile that was a little rueful as she admitted, "They did look a little too boardroom for here, like they should have been at some function making millions."

He had to admit she had a nice laugh. It brought a smile to his face, lightened his mood a bit, so they managed to chat some before she had to go back to work. It was a while before Eron realized Steve's set was over, and the band had put away their instruments. The bar was a lot emptier when Steve came over with a beer in each hand and sat down.

"God, what a night." He took a long pull. "Saw that woman come in, and that man. You nearly blew it with Missy, pal; you still might have." Steve gave Eron a look of disgust. "Look, you wanna be alone the rest of your life, chasing after screwy women—"

"There's nothing screwy with those two," Eron hotly replied. *At least not in the sense you mean.*

Steve shook his head again, taking another long pull, finishing off the bottle. "Whatever." He lit another smoke, blowing out a stream, jabbed the end toward his friend. "And another thing, they looked like a couple. What the hell you doing running after her if she's in a relationship? What kind of man are you? I thought you were better than that." He motioned for Missy and held up the empty, turning back to Eron's scowling face.

"Steve, I swear you're as bad as some old woman."

"Look pal, you may be older than me by several thousand years, only you look 30, so lemme tell ya something I've learned and you haven't. Or maybe you've forgotten," he added after taking another pull of beer and another hit. "Guys looking like that one don't generally like poaching on their territory when they're still actively with the woman. And that's another thing—why would you want a woman like her anyway if you know she cheats?"

"Steve, your attitude is positively puritan. Some people are in open relationships."

"Hey, it's called having morals," He shook his head and took another slug and hit. "All's I know, she screams danger, and the business man she her friend were with? Not the kind of people you hang around with voluntarily, if you get my drift. But hey," he lifted a hand and let it fall. "It ain't none of my business."

Missy came over with two more bottles and a full whiskey. "Last call, guys. Here ya go." Eron was all set to refuse the drink when she said, "On the house."

Steve looked at him, a smirky grin pulling up one side of his face as he took another pull of beer. "I'm telling you, ask her out." He ignored the glare Eron gave him and said, "Hey, Missy, my friend's a little shy here. Would you be interested in going out with him sometime?"

"I curse you, and those not of my kind that stand here, perpetrators of crimes against our people. I curse you!"

The short phrase echoed and echoed inside Eron's head. "I curse you! I curse you! I curse you!" He was dissolving into a sea of burning whiteness as the blonde woman's curse thundered through his being. "Missy. That was her name." Eron had not realized he spoke aloud until it wasn't bar light he was seeing, but torches. He was lying on a cold stone floor. Behind him, a door shuddered as people outside tried to break it open. "What the hell?" He couldn't think, couldn't remember what he was doing here.

How long has it been? It was a great effort, but he sat up, a fading ache at the back of his head reminding him of the blow which had taken him out. He had been at the Harvest Ball, the young man who looked like a grown-up version of Nicky had staged a coup, and some weirdo with a staff had set off some firework or something which burned bright as the sun.

He realized a veil had just been torn from his eyes. Stray memories he didn't even realize had been locked away for centuries crashed down on him with an intensity, leaving him momentarily crippled with emotion. *What else am I not remembering because of her? I think Steve was right; I've been chasing shadows.*

Just thinking of the long-dead man, the innocent woman, made his blood boil in anger and frustration. It was almost as great as his anger at Illyria. *We were cursed. She got us all cursed.*

Why now? Why was it broken now? What or who had caused it to break? Was it from those two men and their strange bomb? One thing Eron had learned in his very long life: the older he got, the faster he healed from wounds. Eron sat up, dislodging Illyria's body at the same time.

He only had time to gasp out, "Oh shit!" before her eyes flew open, she sank her fangs in his neck and there was nothing he could do as he fell back against the shuddering wood door to the garden.

Available for Purchase Here...

the US: http://www.amazon.com/dp/B00I5WXA66

the UK: http://www.amazon.co.uk/gp/product/B00I5WXA66

Thank you for reading

Send me feedback: If you have questions about the series, want to point out errors and typos, want to know how to become one of my beta readers or just embarrass me with totally undeserved adulation, I urge you to send me an email at

info@slfiguhr.com

I love to hear from readers and try to answer every email.

Follow my blog: The least amount of effort involved, the blog is at: http://slfiguhr.com/blog-2/

Click on the follow blog via email button, so you'll get an email notice whenever I update my blog.

Share your Opinion: If you enjoy the Immortalibus Bella series, please let others know, either by Twitter, Facebook, WordPress, blogger, or your social media of choice and recommend to your friends.

   Write reviews: Most of the sites where you can buy ebooks or paperback copies have a way for you to post a review, so you can share with other readers whether a book or story merits their attention. The importance of reviews should not be underestimated. With 350,000 new books published, it's difficult for writers to get exposure for their novels.

   in the US: http://www.amazon.com/dp/B00HQOSZ64

   in the UK: http://www.amazon.co.uk/gp//B00HQOSZ64

www.ingramcontent.com/pod-product-compliance
Lightning Source LLC
Chambersburg PA
CBHW061308170626
46817CB00001B/101